BABY-SITTERS
LITTLE SISTER®

KAREN'S HAIRCUT

**DON'T MISS THE OTHER BABY-SITTERS
LITTLE SISTER GRAPHIC NOVELS!**

KAREN'S WITCH

KAREN'S ROLLER SKATES

KAREN'S WORST DAY

KAREN'S KITTYCAT CLUB

KAREN'S SCHOOL PICTURE

KAREN'S BIRTHDAY

ANN M. MARTIN

BABY-SITTERS LITTLE SISTER®

POISE
How to build a UNIQUE STYLE
FOLKS

KAREN'S HAIRCUT

A GRAPHIC NOVEL BY

KATY FARINA

WITH COLOR BY BRADEN LAMB

graphix
An Imprint of
SCHOLASTIC

This book is in honor of the
birth of Maxwell Joseph Lieb
A. M. M.

For everyone who is finding themselves
K. F.

Text copyright © 2023 by Ann M. Martin
Art copyright © 2023 by Katy Farina

All rights reserved. Published by Graphix, an imprint of
Scholastic Inc., *Publishers since 1920.* SCHOLASTIC, GRAPHIX,
BABY-SITTERS LITTLE SISTER, and associated logos are trademarks
and/or registered trademarks of Scholastic Inc.

The publisher does not have any control over and does not assume any
responsibility for author or third-party websites or their content.

No part of this publication may be reproduced, stored in a retrieval system,
or transmitted in any form or by any means, electronic, mechanical, photocopying,
recording, or otherwise, without written permission of the publisher. For information
regarding permission, write to Scholastic Inc., Attention: Permissions
Department, 557 Broadway, New York, NY 10012.

This book is a work of fiction. Names, characters, places, and
incidents are either the product of the author's imagination or are used
fictitiously, and any resemblance to actual persons, living or dead, business
establishments, events, or locales is entirely coincidental.

Library of Congress Control Number: 2022939618

ISBN 978-1-338-76264-8 (hardcover)
ISBN 978-1-338-76262-4 (paperback)

10 9 8 7 6 5 4 3 2 1   23 24 25 26 27

Printed in China   62
First edition, July 2023

Edited by Cassandra Pelham Fulton
Book design by Shivana Sookdeo
Creative Director: Phil Falco
Publisher: David Saylor

CHAPTER 1

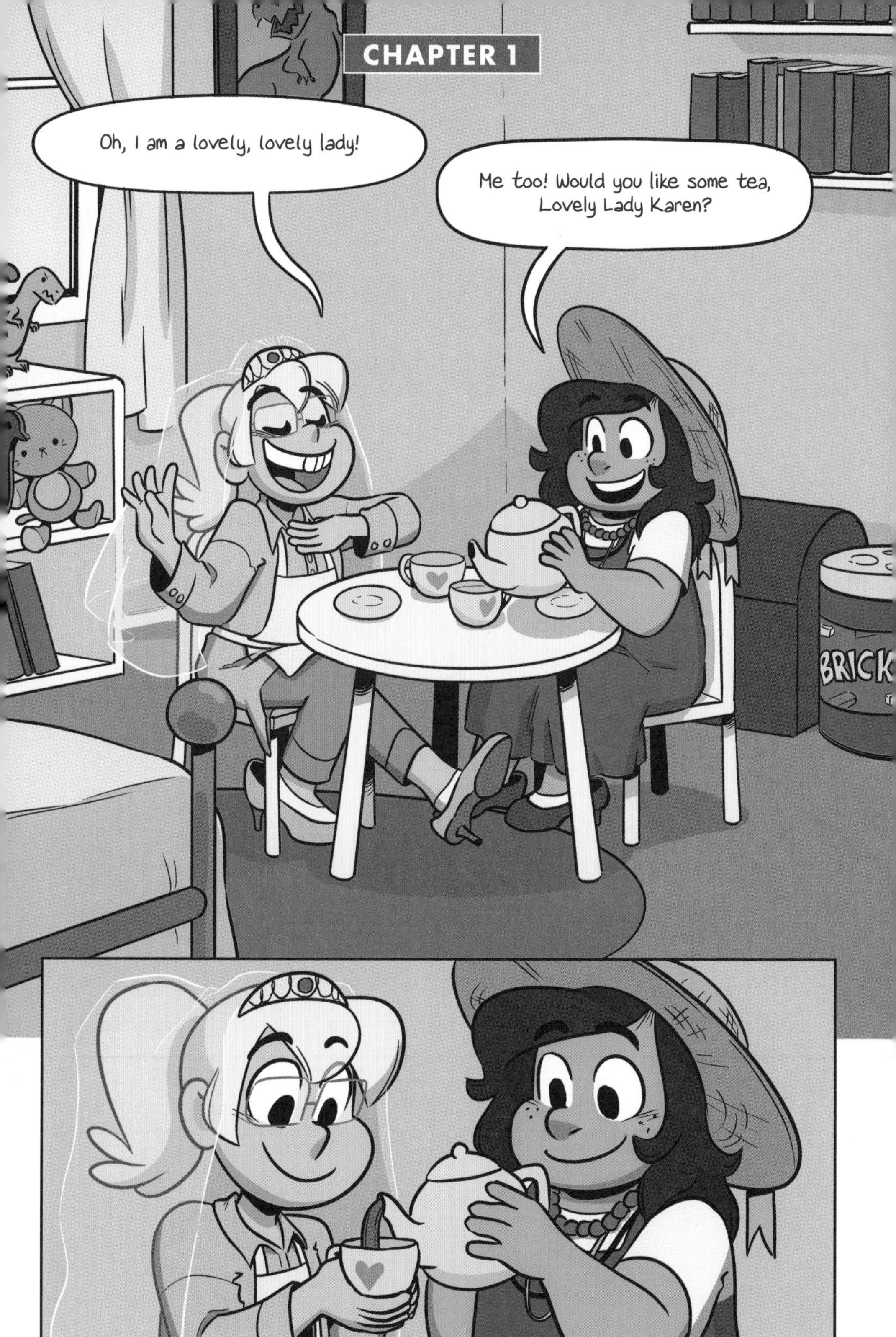
Oh, I am a lovely, lovely lady!
Me too! Would you like some tea, Lovely Lady Karen?
BRICK

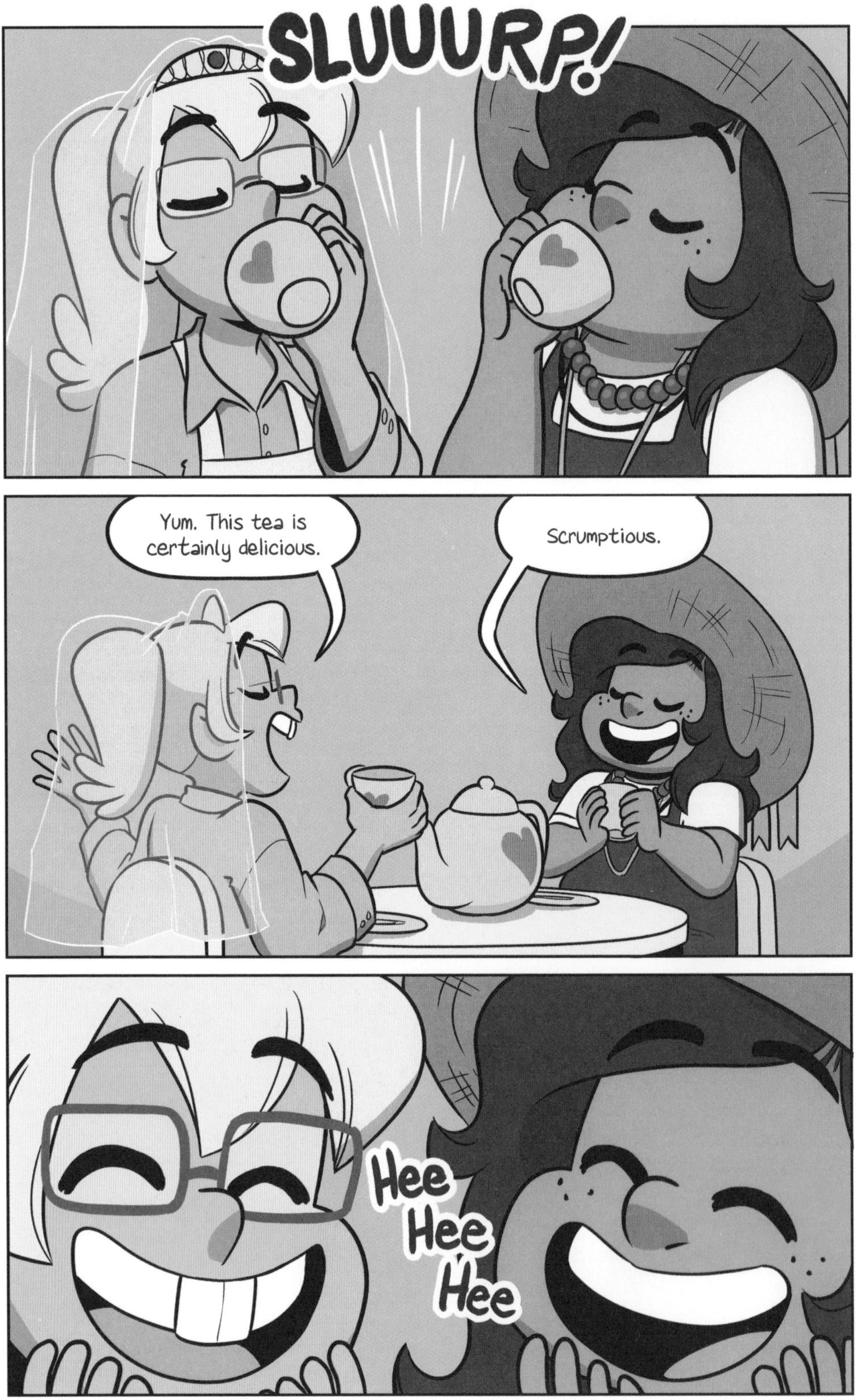
SLUUURP!
Yum. This tea is certainly delicious.
Scrumptious.
Hee Hee Hee

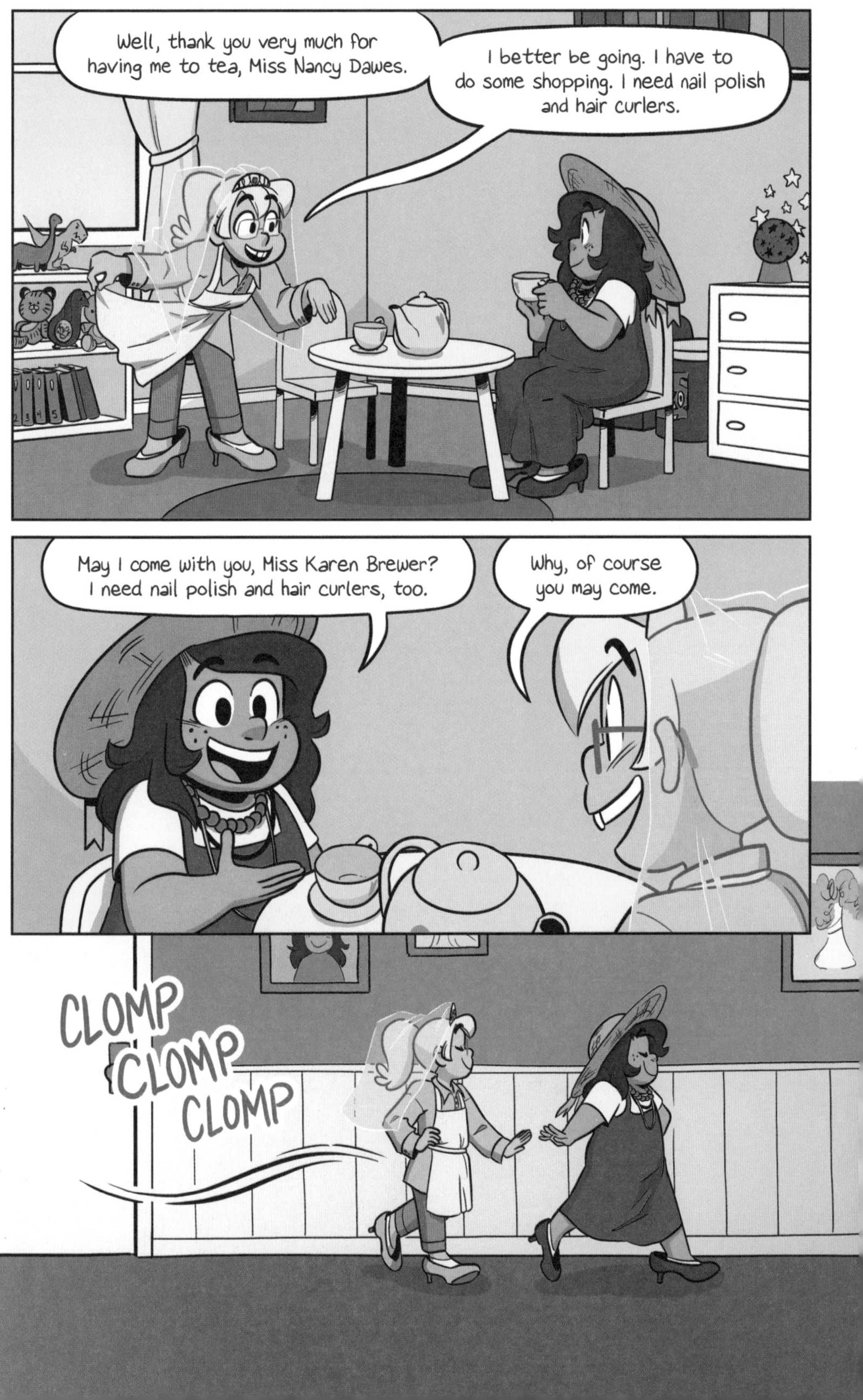
Well, thank you very much for having me to tea, Miss Nancy Dawes.
I better be going. I have to do some shopping. I need nail polish and hair curlers.
May I come with you, Miss Karen Brewer? I need nail polish and hair curlers, too.
Why, of course you may come.
CLOMP CLOMP CLOMP

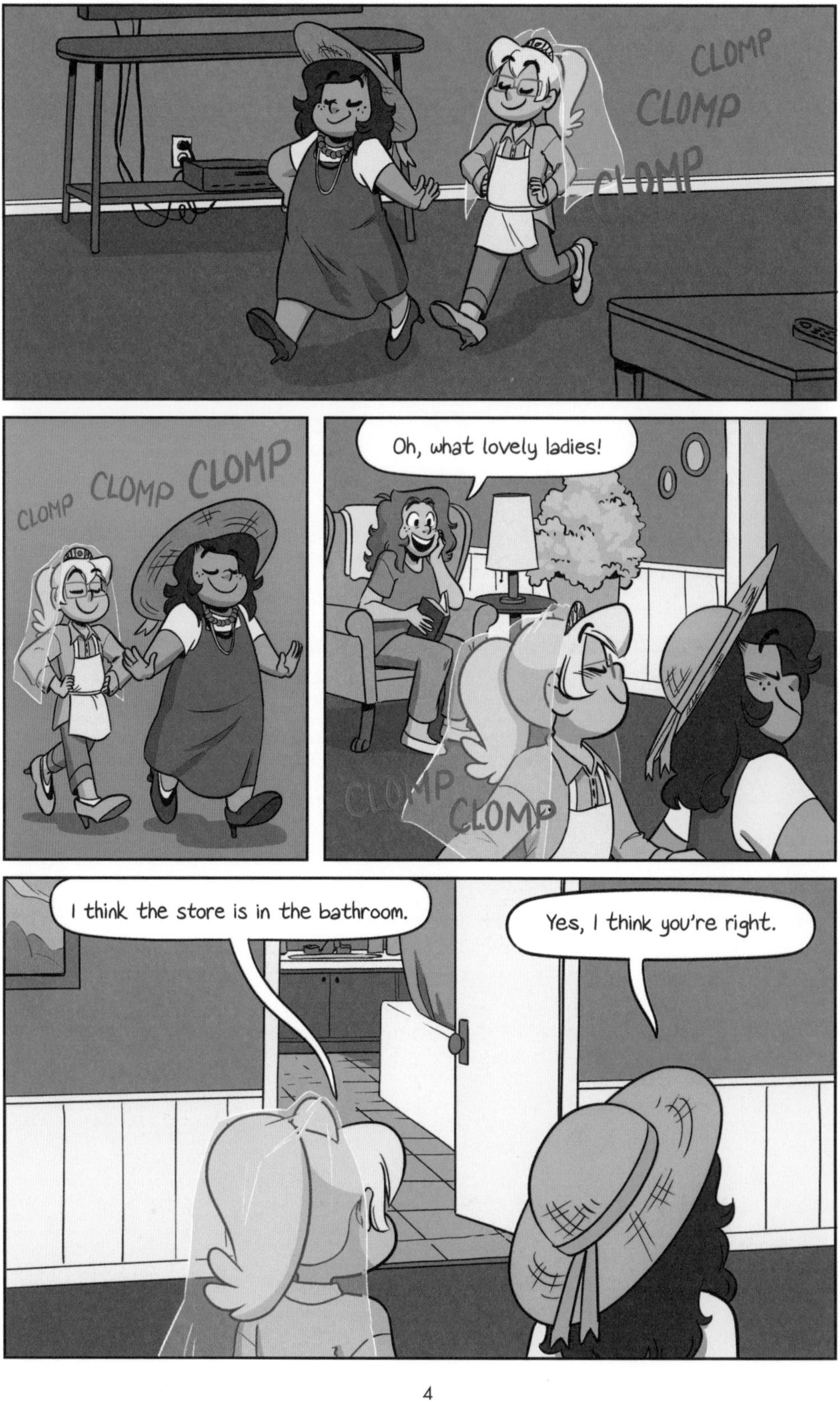
CLOMP
CLOMP
CLOMP
CLOMP
CLOMP
CLOMP
Oh, what lovely ladies!
CLOMP
CLOMP
I think the store is in the bathroom.
Yes, I think you're right.

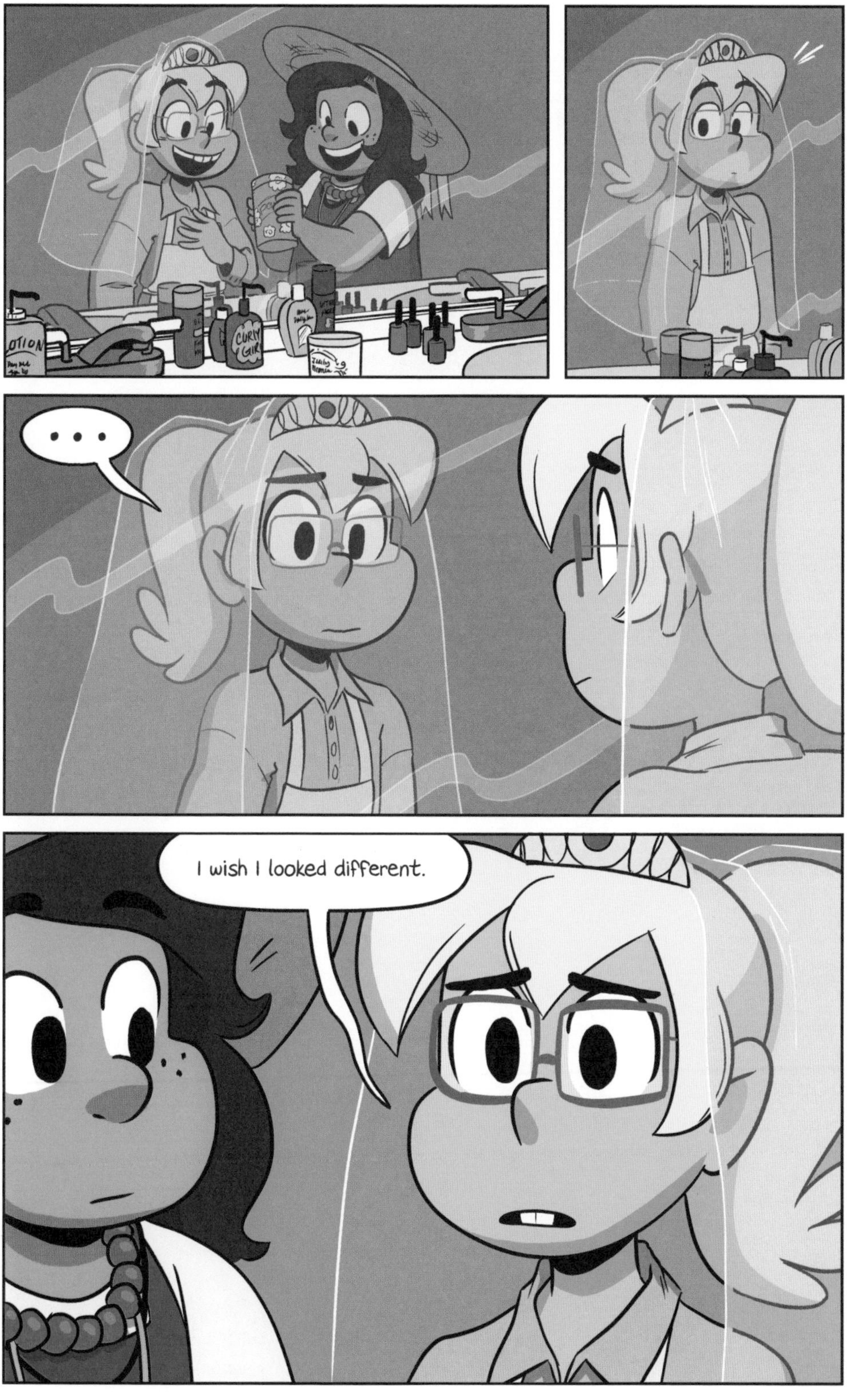
...
I wish I looked different.

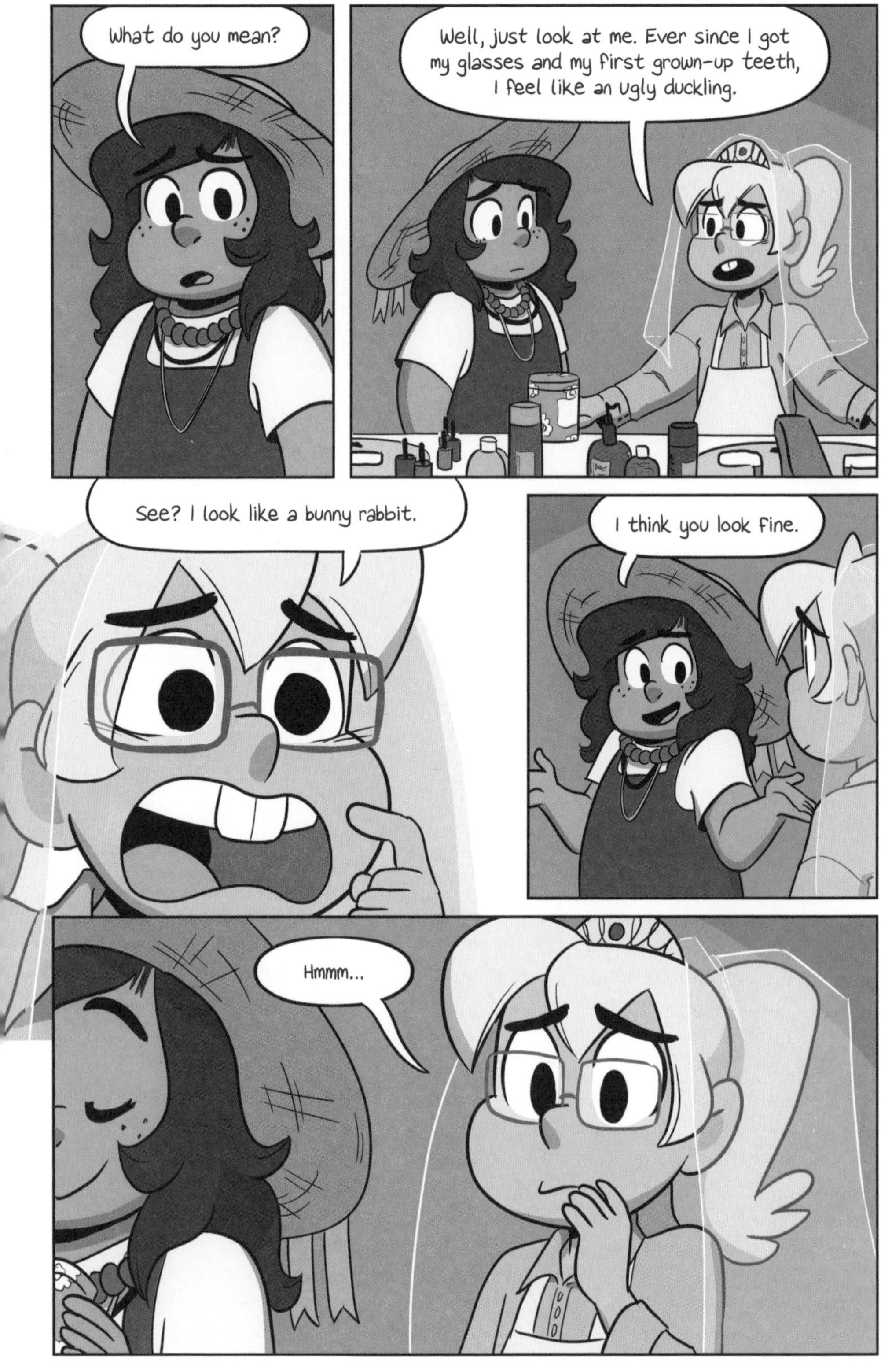
What do you mean?
Well, just look at me. Ever since I got my glasses and my first grown-up teeth, I feel like an ugly duckling.
See? I look like a bunny rabbit.
I think you look fine.
Hmmm...

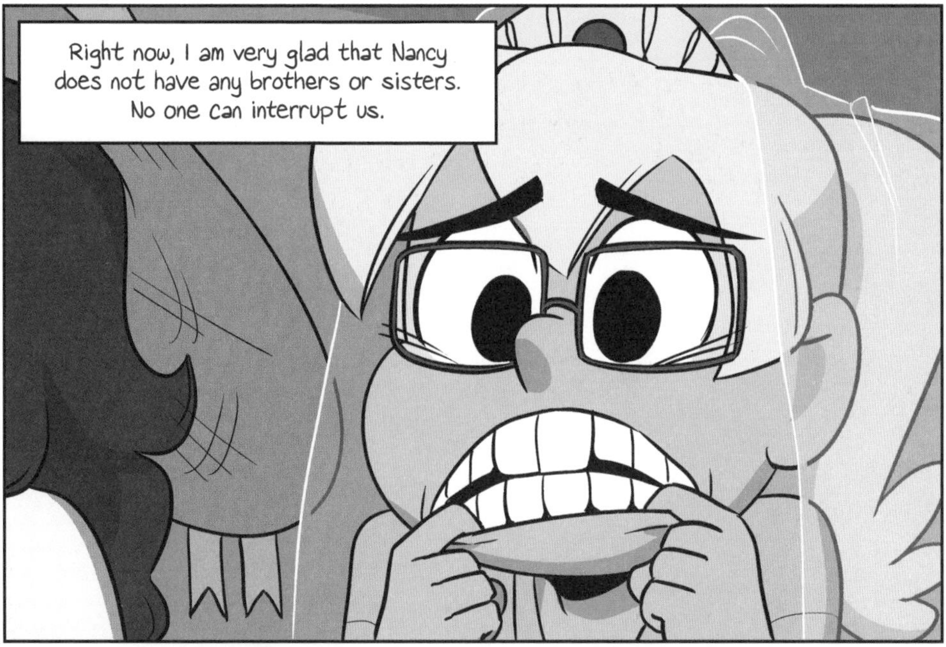
Right now, I am very glad that Nancy does not have any brothers or sisters. No one can interrupt us.

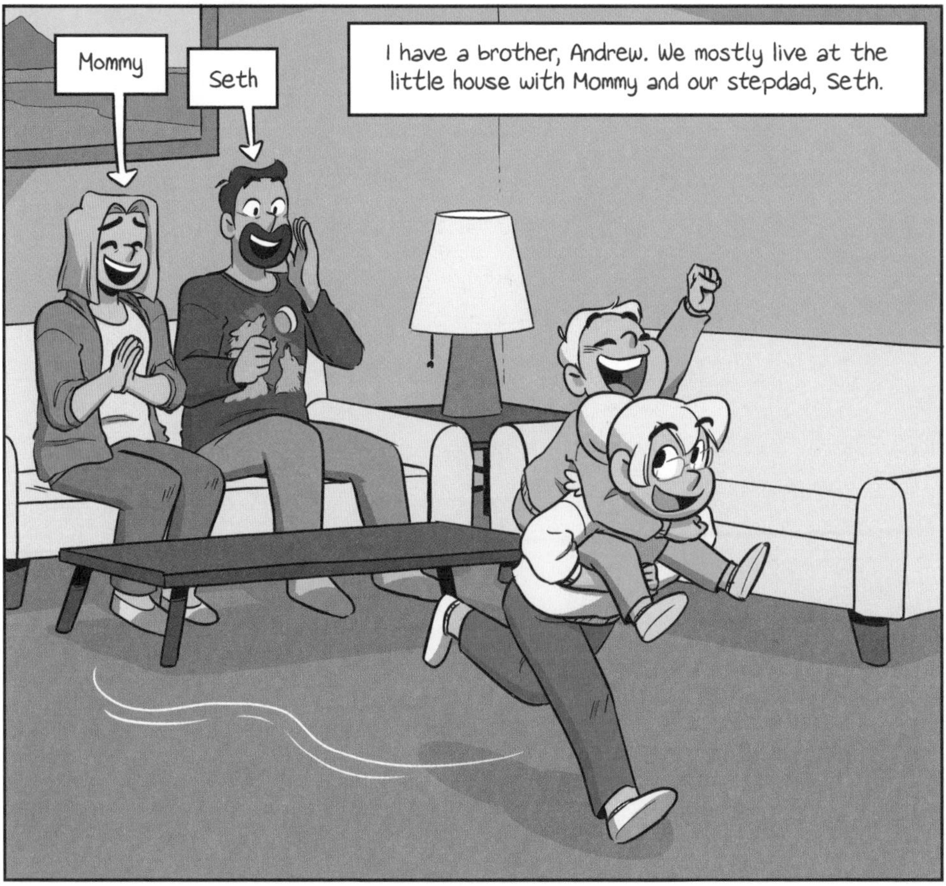
Mommy
Seth
I have a brother, Andrew. We mostly live at the little house with Mommy and our stepdad, Seth.

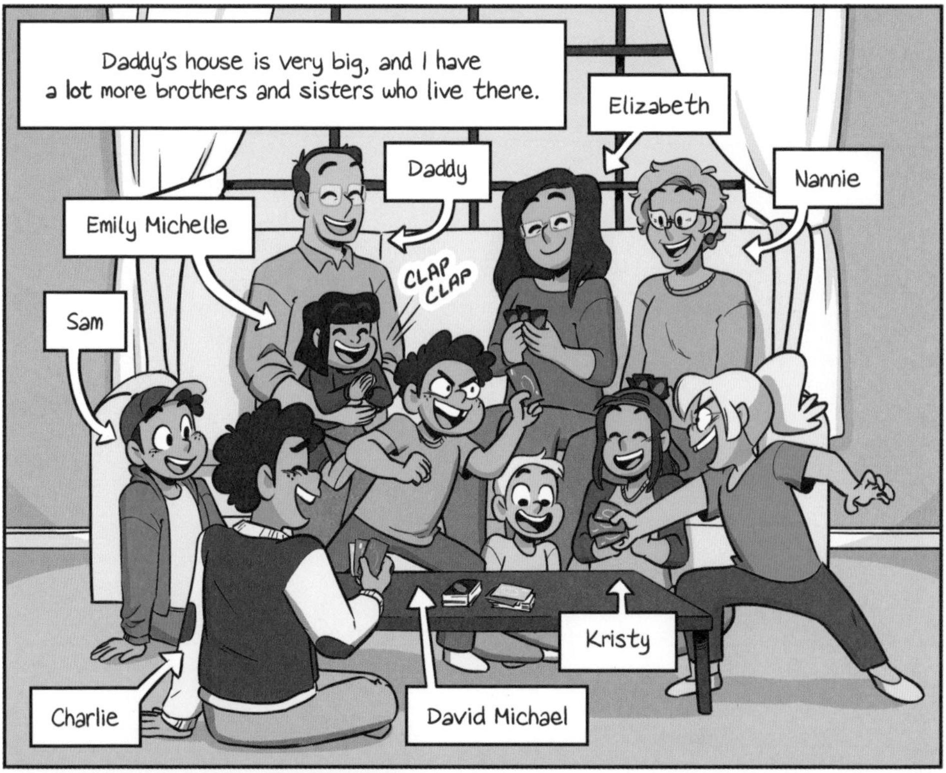
Daddy's house is very big, and I have a lot more brothers and sisters who live there.
Elizabeth
Daddy
Nannie
Emily Michelle
CLAP CLAP
Sam
Kristy
Charlie
David Michael

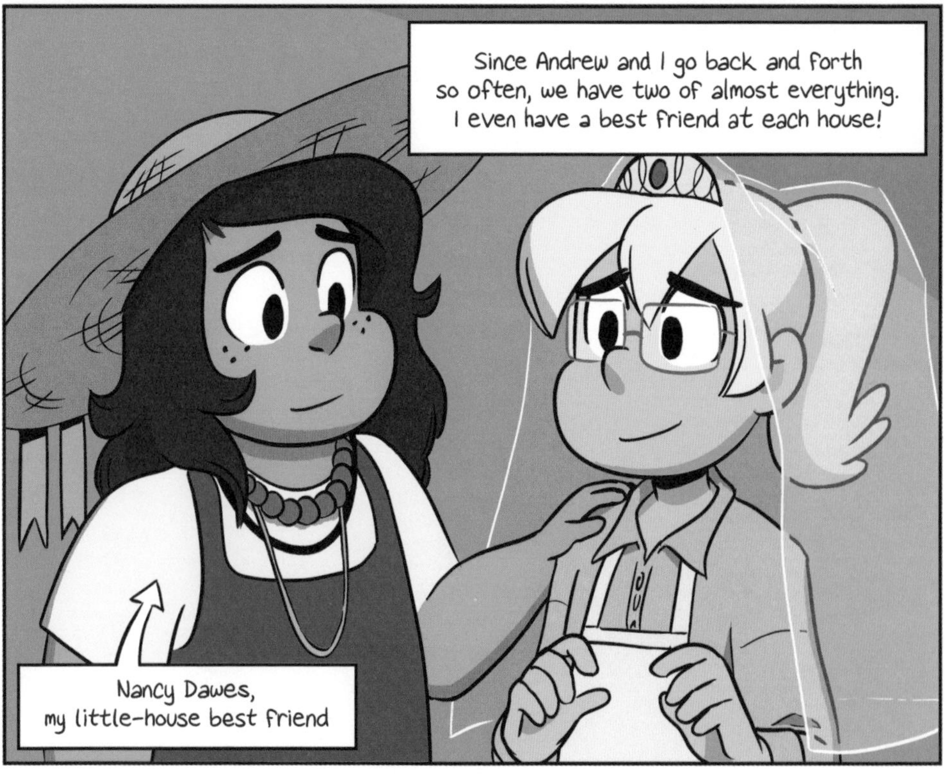
Since Andrew and I go back and forth so often, we have two of almost everything. I even have a best friend at each house!
Nancy Dawes, my little-house best friend

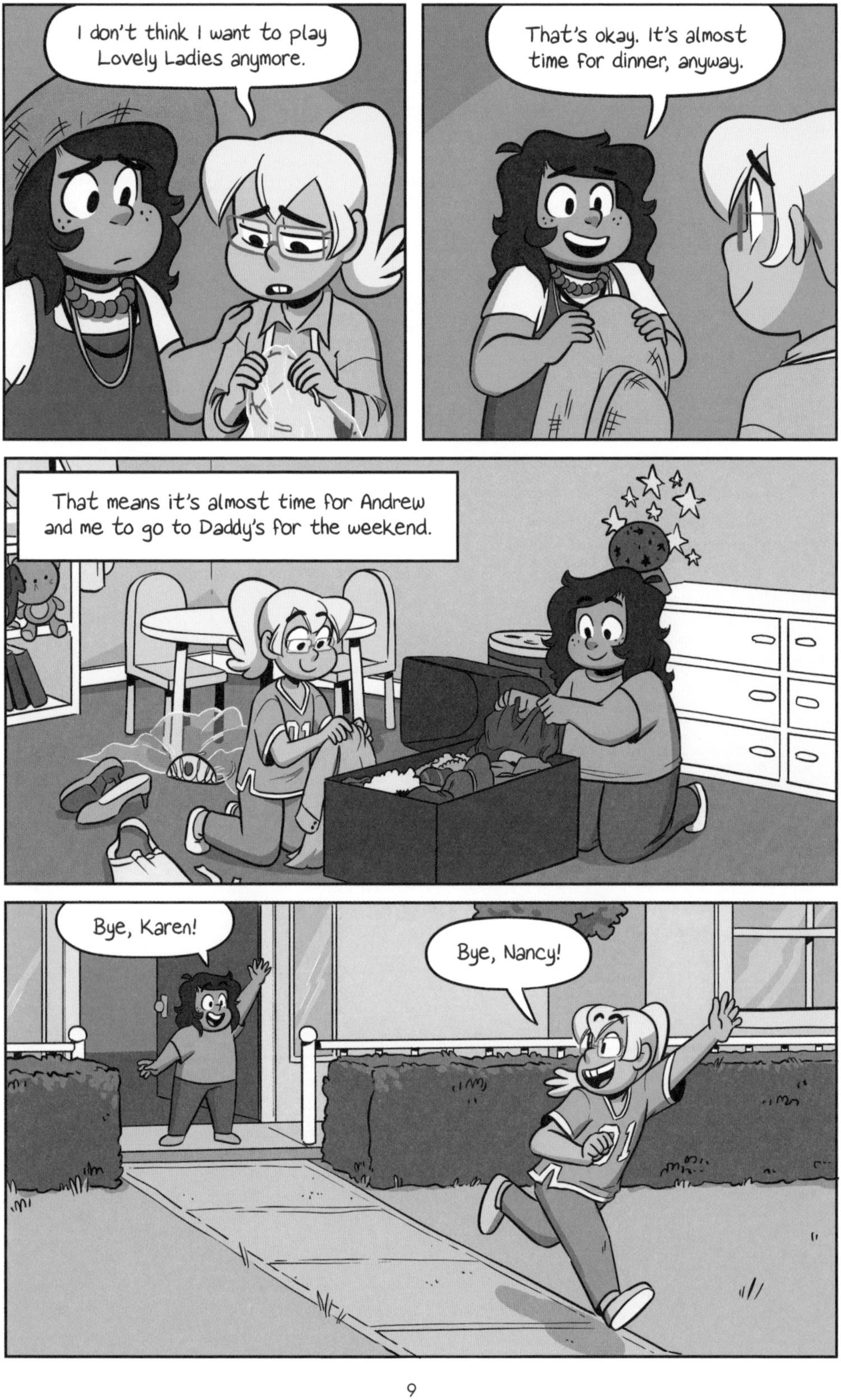
I don't think I want to play Lovely Ladies anymore.
That's okay. It's almost time for dinner, anyway.
That means it's almost time for Andrew and me to go to Daddy's for the weekend.
Bye, Karen!
Bye, Nancy!

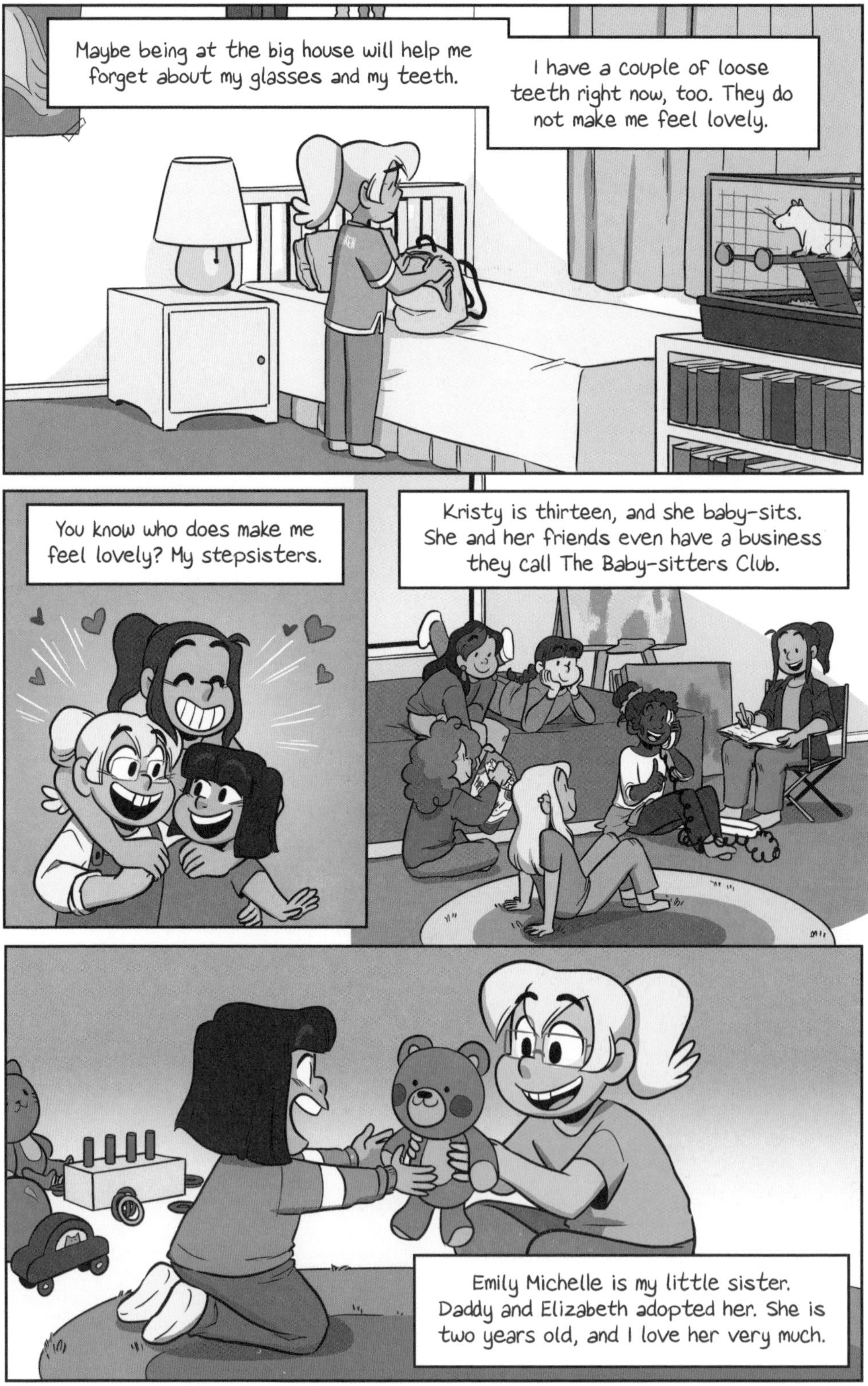
Maybe being at the big house will help me forget about my glasses and my teeth.
I have a couple of loose teeth right now, too. They do not make me feel lovely.
You know who does make me feel lovely? My stepsisters.
Kristy is thirteen, and she baby-sits. She and her friends even have a business they call The Baby-sitters Club.
Emily Michelle is my little sister. Daddy and Elizabeth adopted her. She is two years old, and I love her very much.

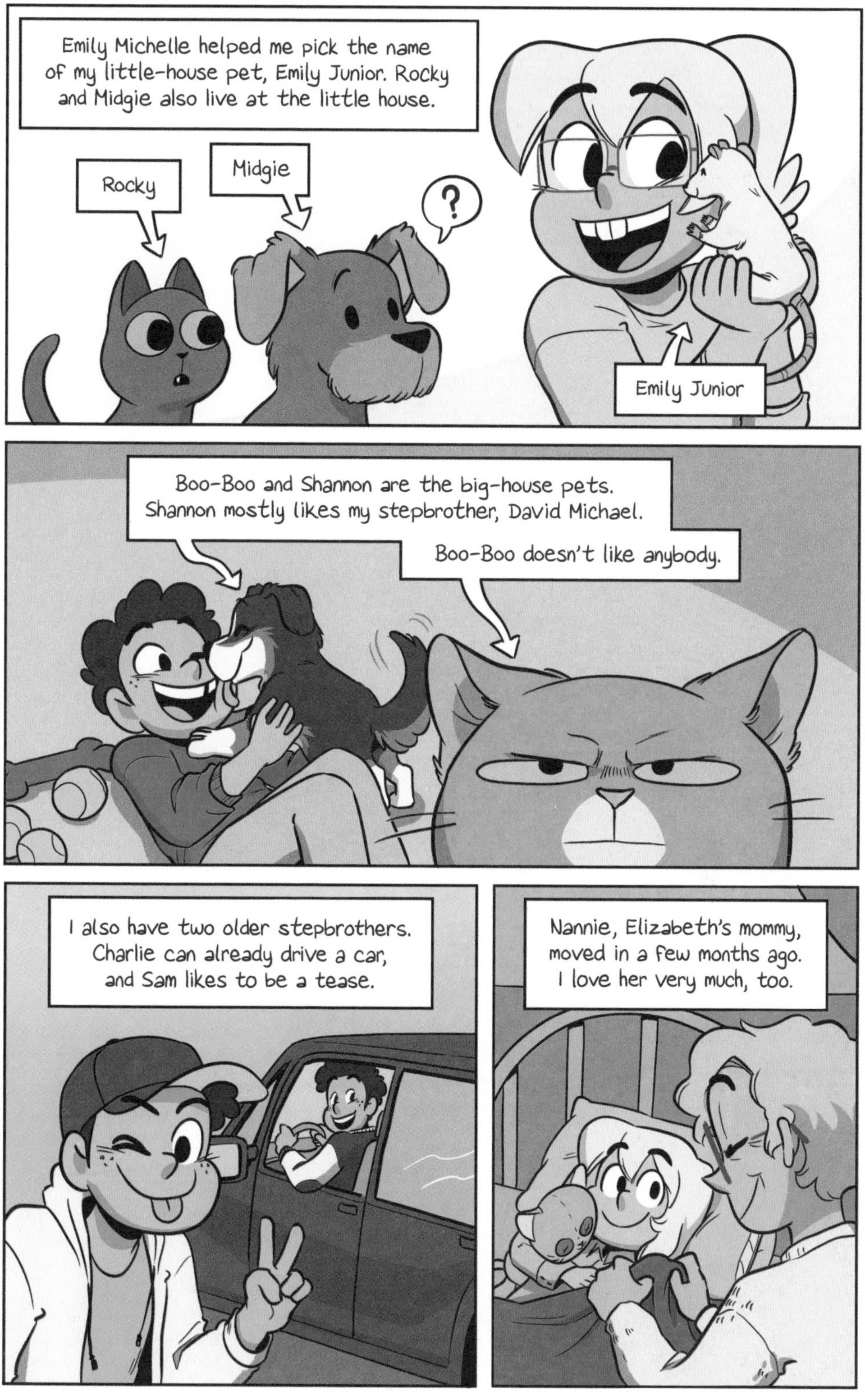

Emily Michelle helped me pick the name of my little-house pet, Emily Junior. Rocky and Midgie also live at the little house.
Rocky
Midgie
?
Emily Junior
Boo-Boo and Shannon are the big-house pets. Shannon mostly likes my stepbrother, David Michael.
Boo-Boo doesn't like anybody.
I also have two older stepbrothers. Charlie can already drive a car, and Sam likes to be a tease.
Nannie, Elizabeth's mommy, moved in a few months ago. I love her very much, too.

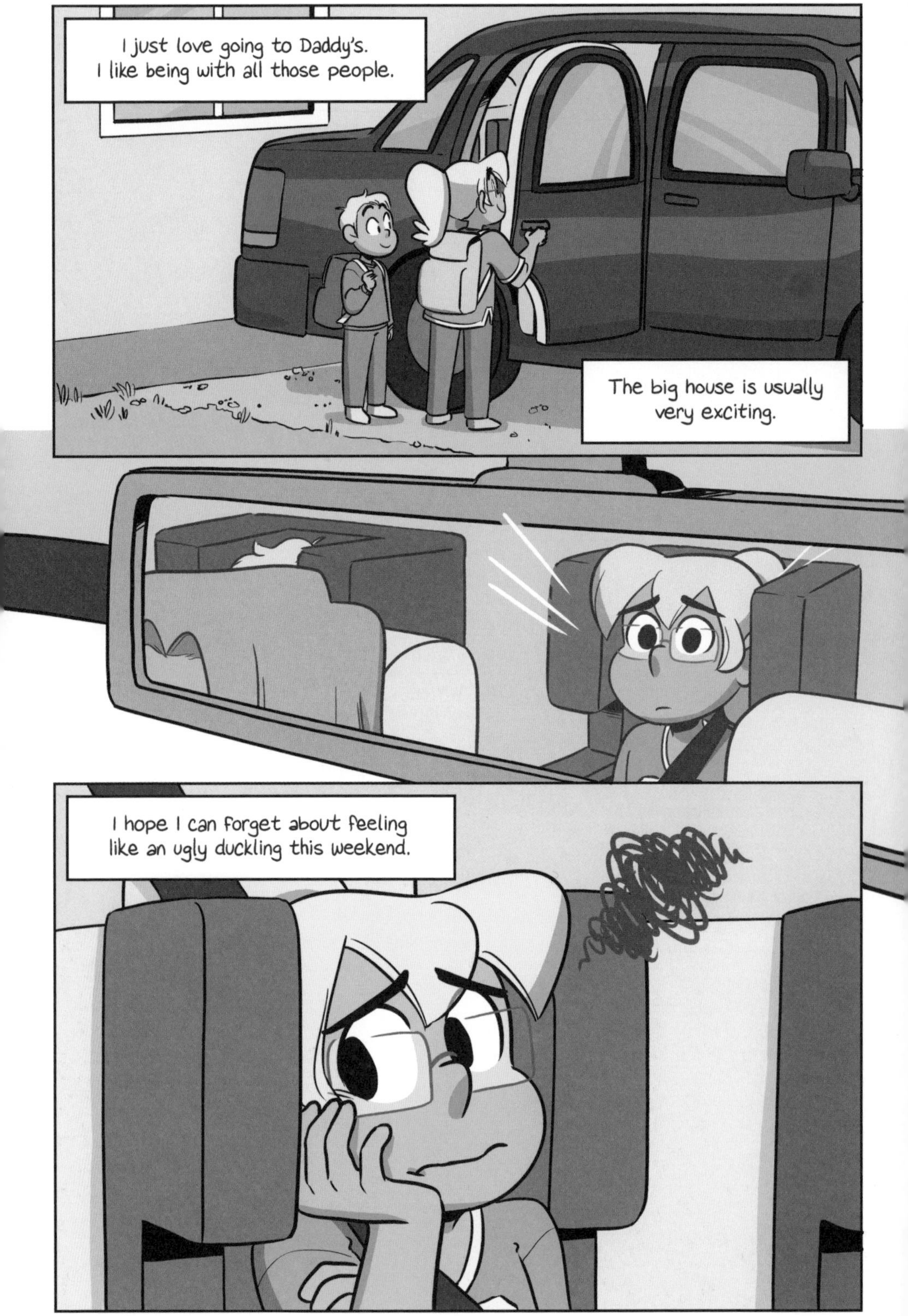
I just love going to Daddy's.
I like being with all those people.
The big house is usually
very exciting.
I hope I can forget about feeling
like an ugly duckling this weekend.

CHAPTER 2

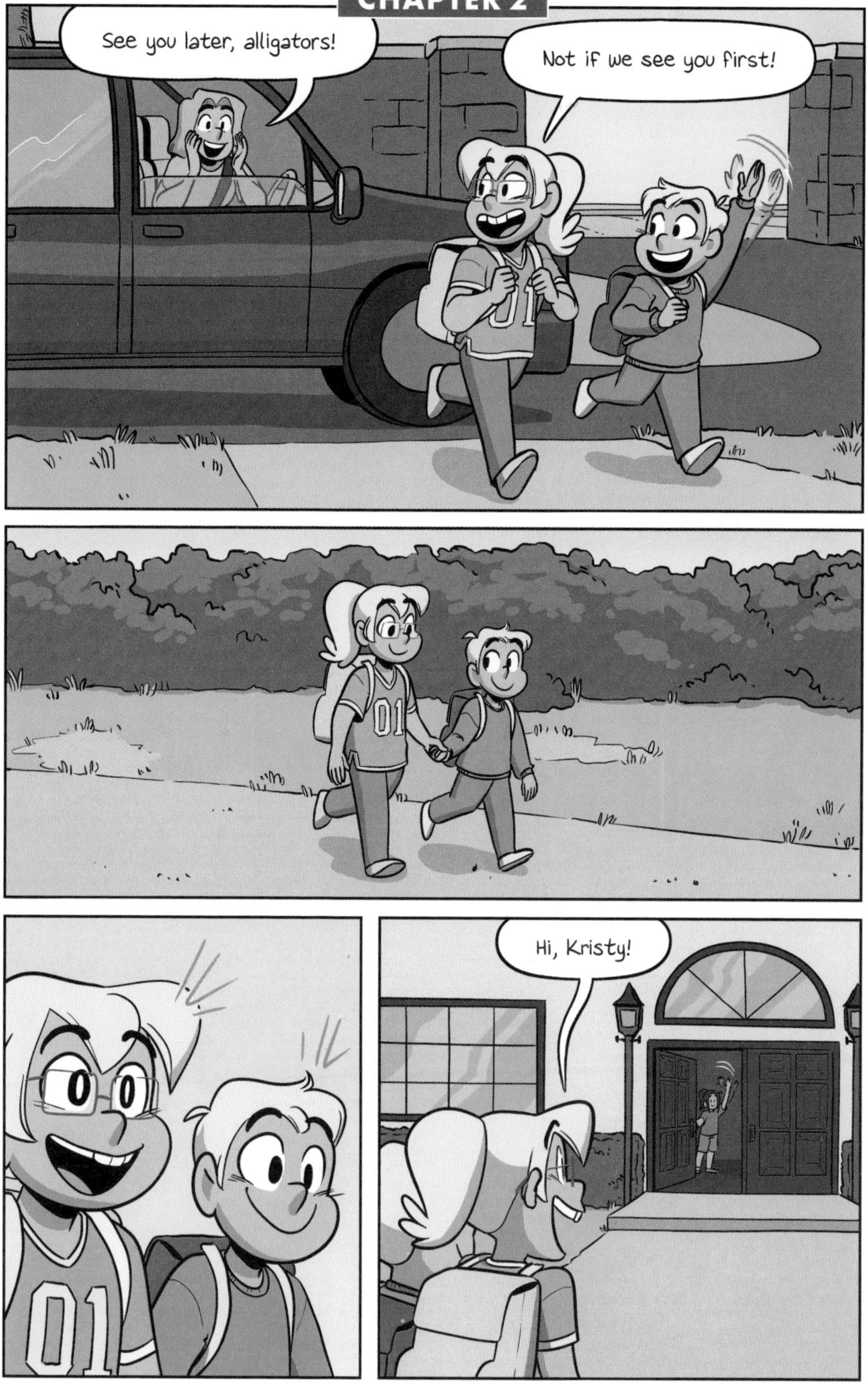
See you later, alligators!
Not if we see you first!
Hi, Kristy!

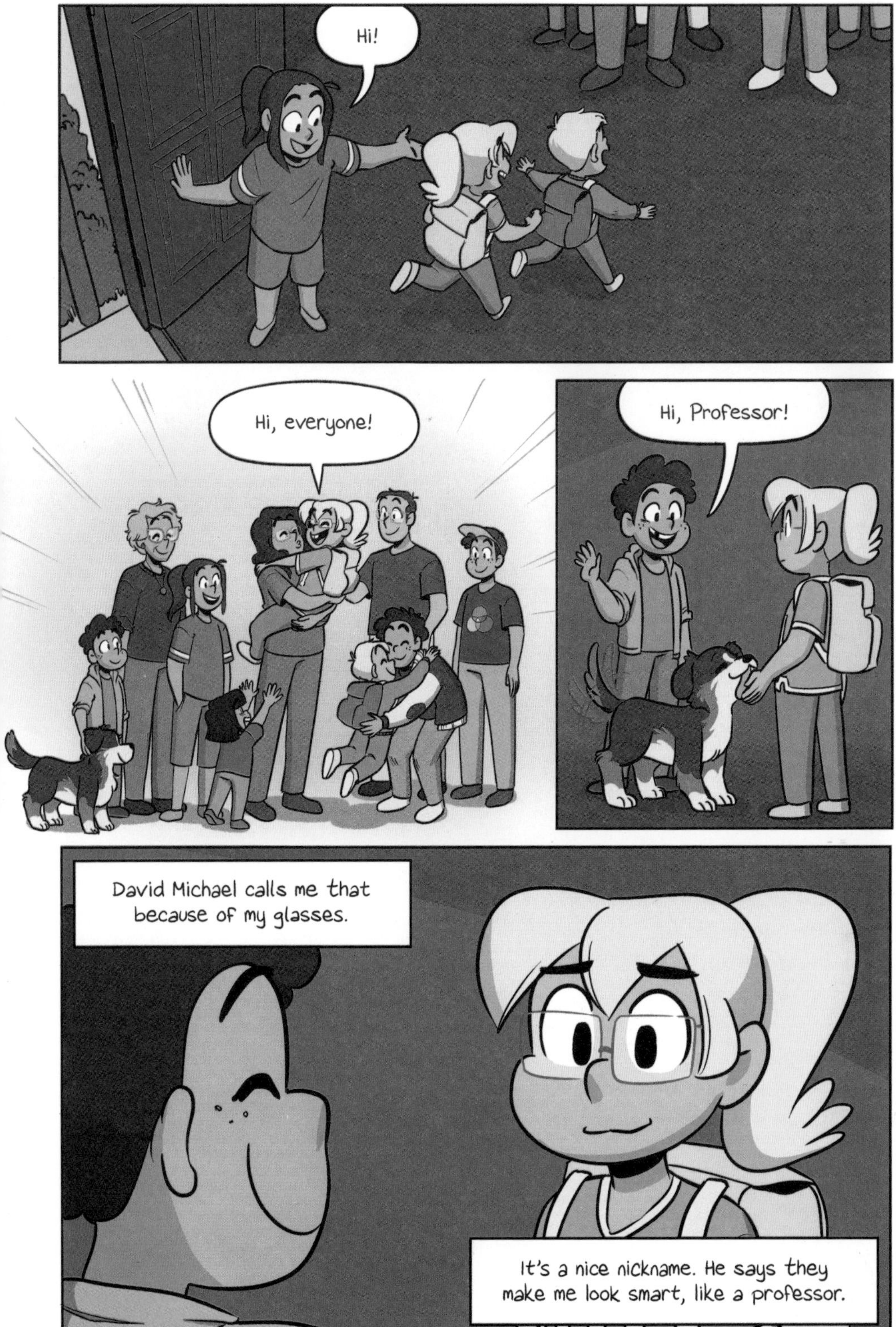
Hi!
Hi, everyone!
Hi, Professor!
David Michael calls me that because of my glasses.
It's a nice nickname. He says they make me look smart, like a professor.

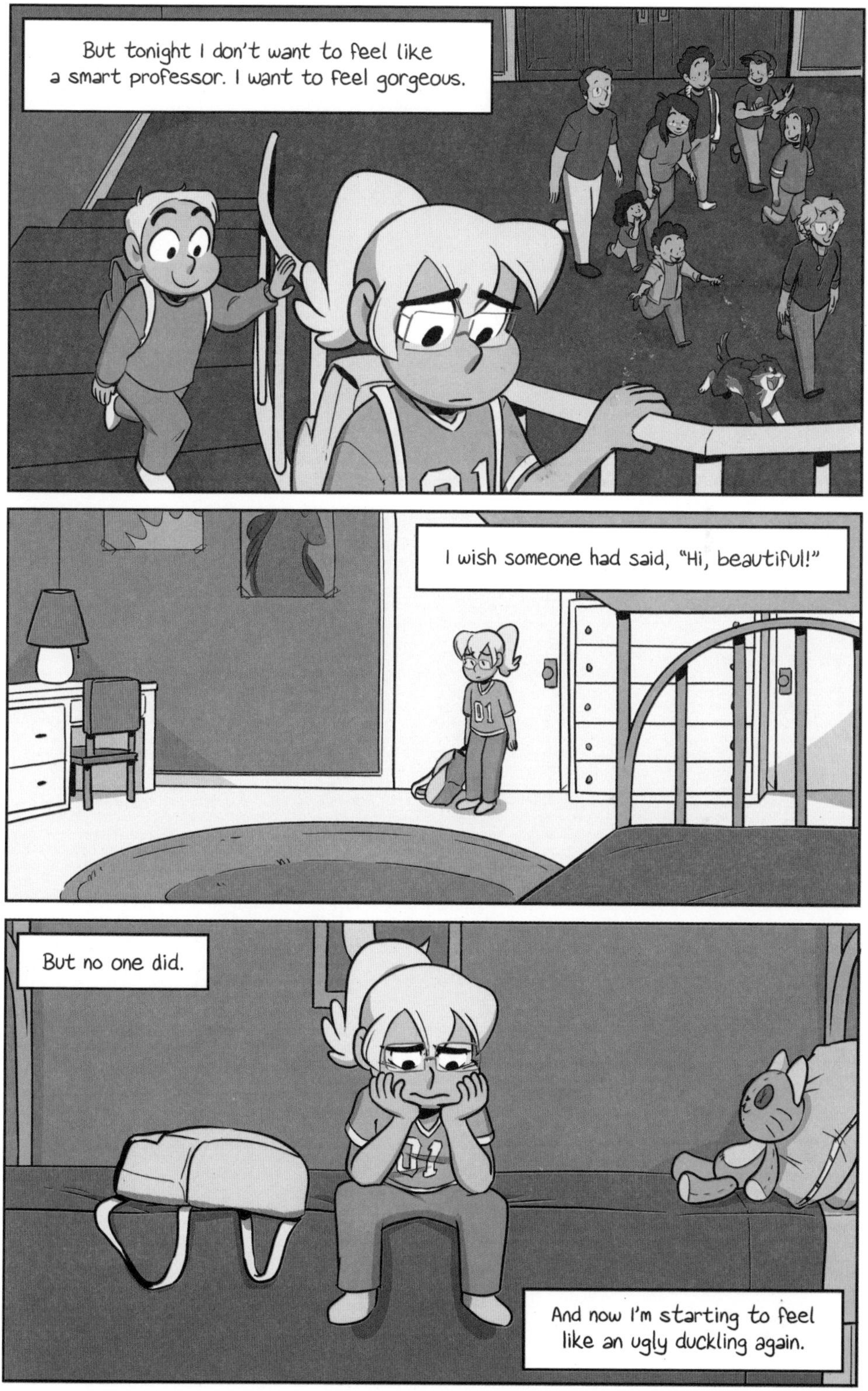
But tonight I don't want to feel like a smart professor. I want to feel gorgeous.
I wish someone had said, "Hi, beautiful!"
But no one did.
And now I'm starting to feel like an ugly duckling again.

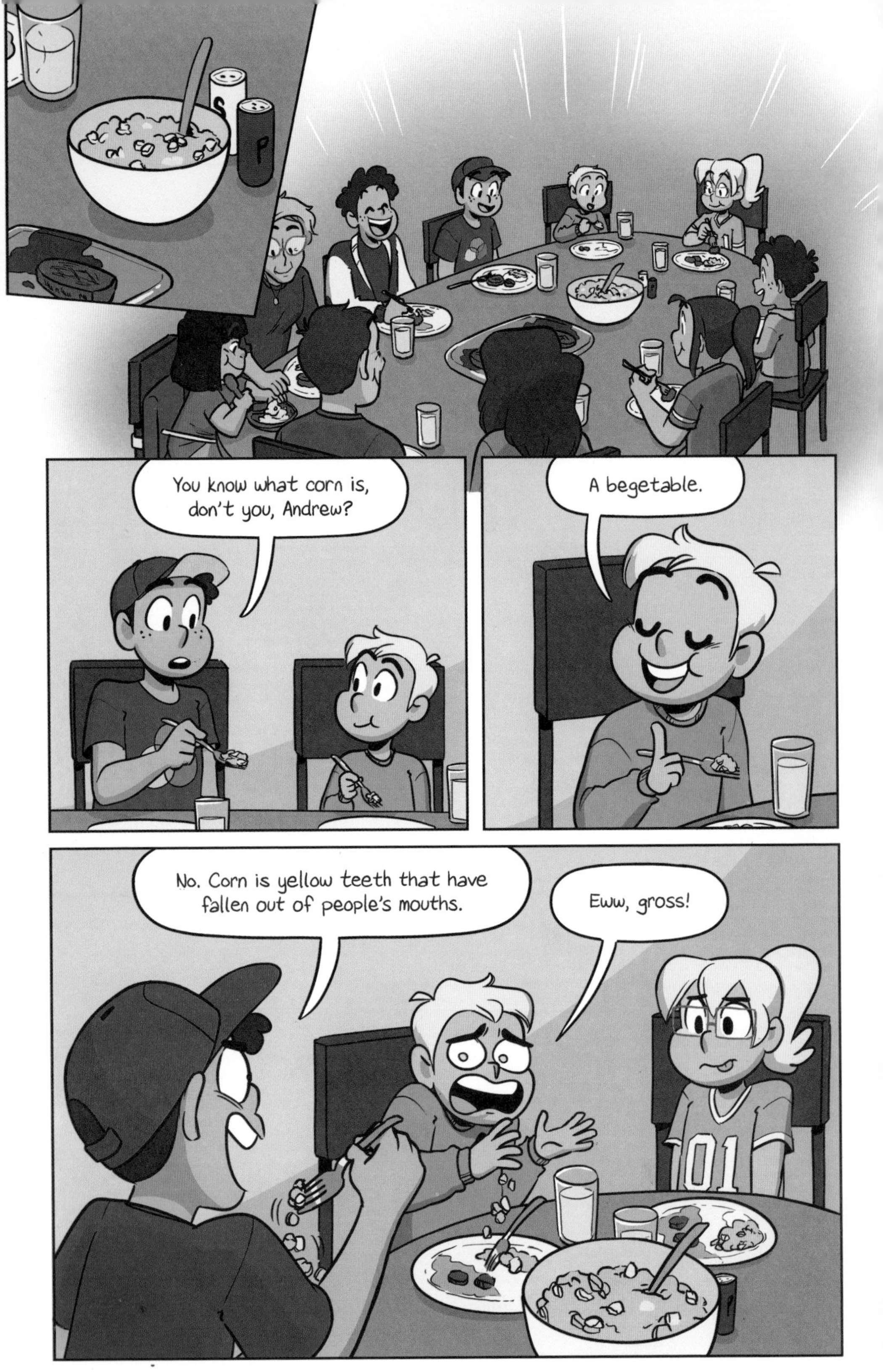
You know what corn is, don't you, Andrew?
A begetable.
No. Corn is yellow teeth that have fallen out of people's mouths.
Eww, gross!

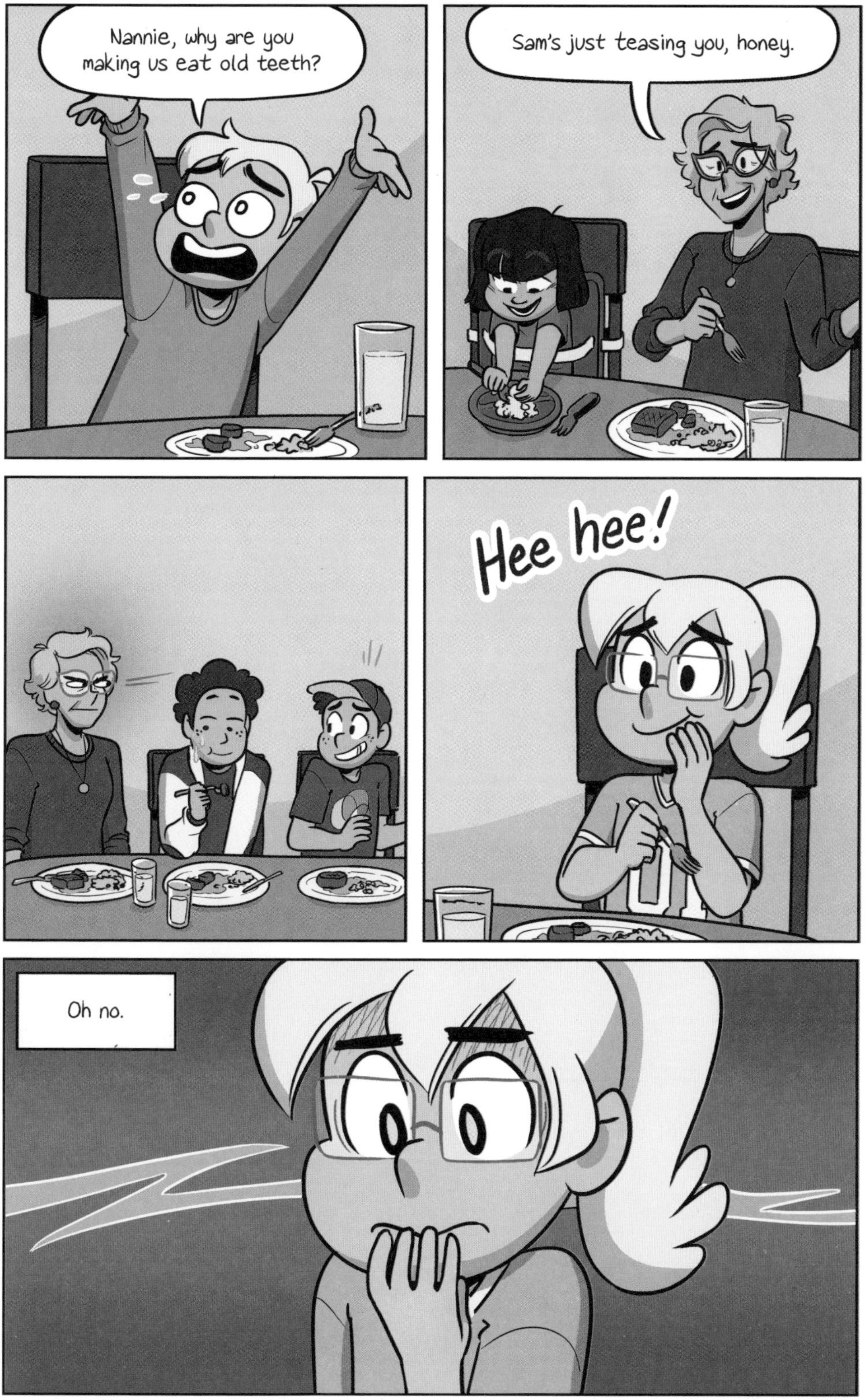
Nannie, why are you making us eat old teeth?
Sam's just teasing you, honey.
Hee hee!
Oh no.

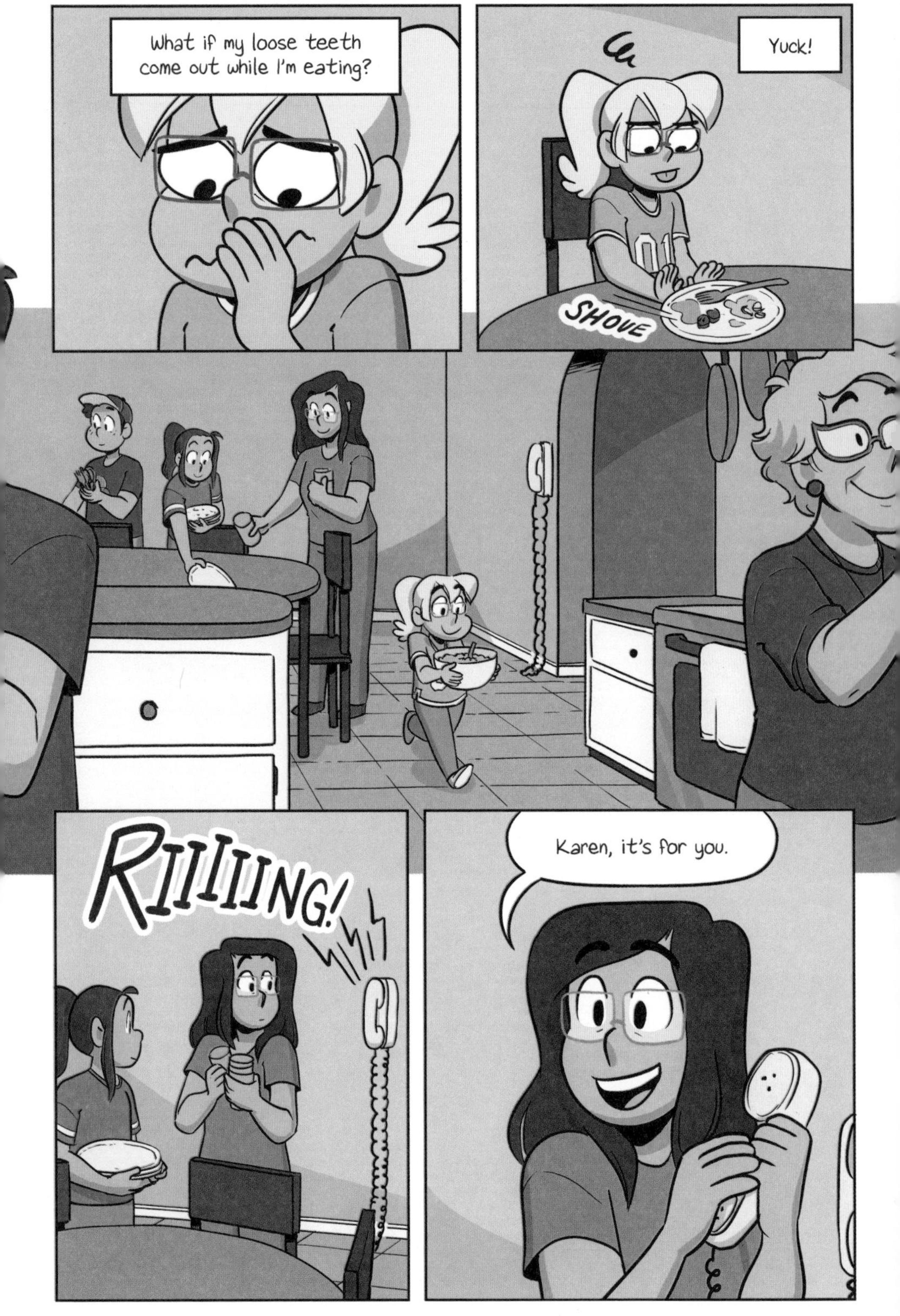
What if my loose teeth come out while I'm eating?
Yuck!
SHOVE
RIIIING!
Karen, it's for you.

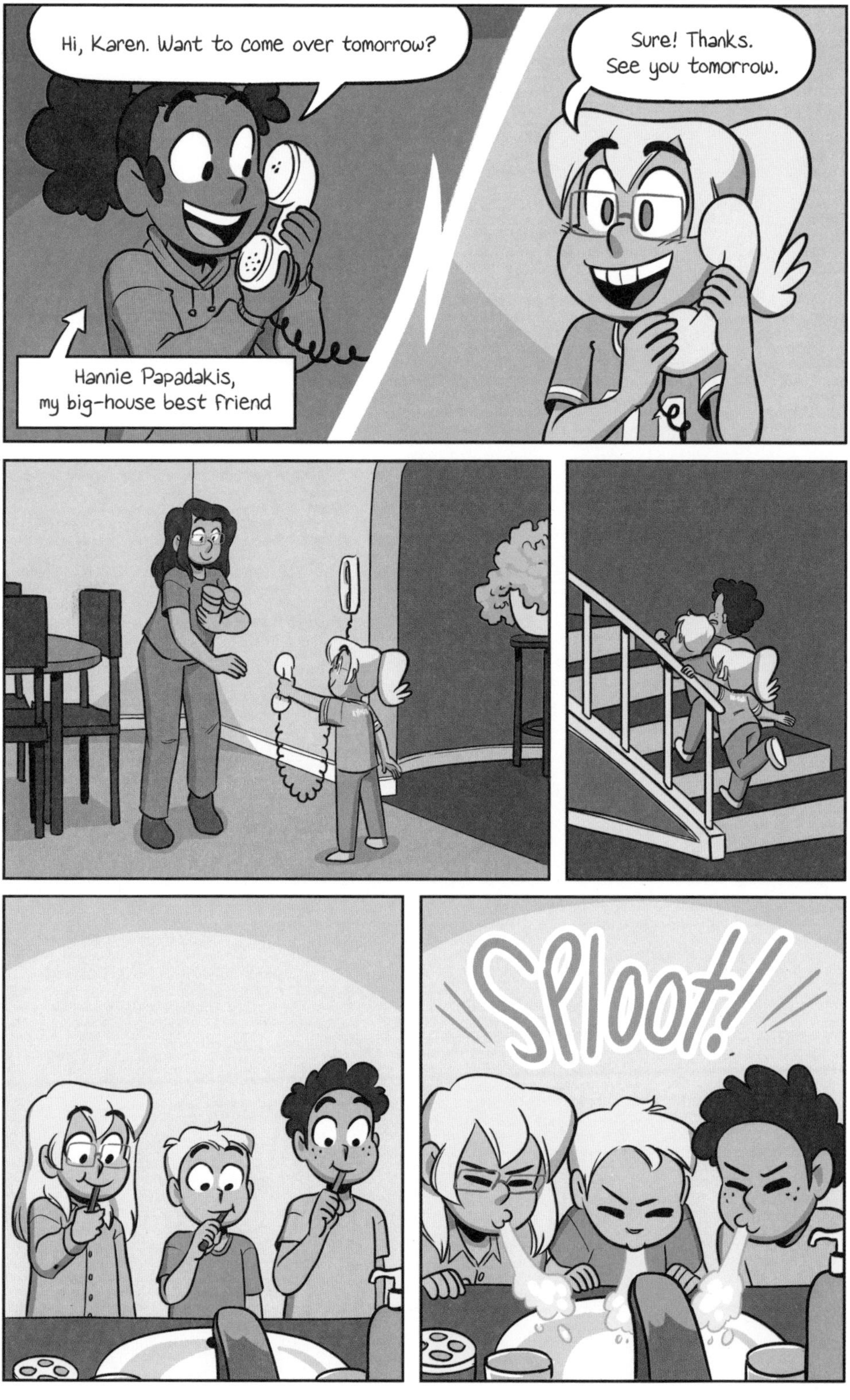
Hi, Karen. Want to come over tomorrow?
Sure! Thanks. See you tomorrow.
Hannie Papadakis, my big-house best friend
SPLOOT!

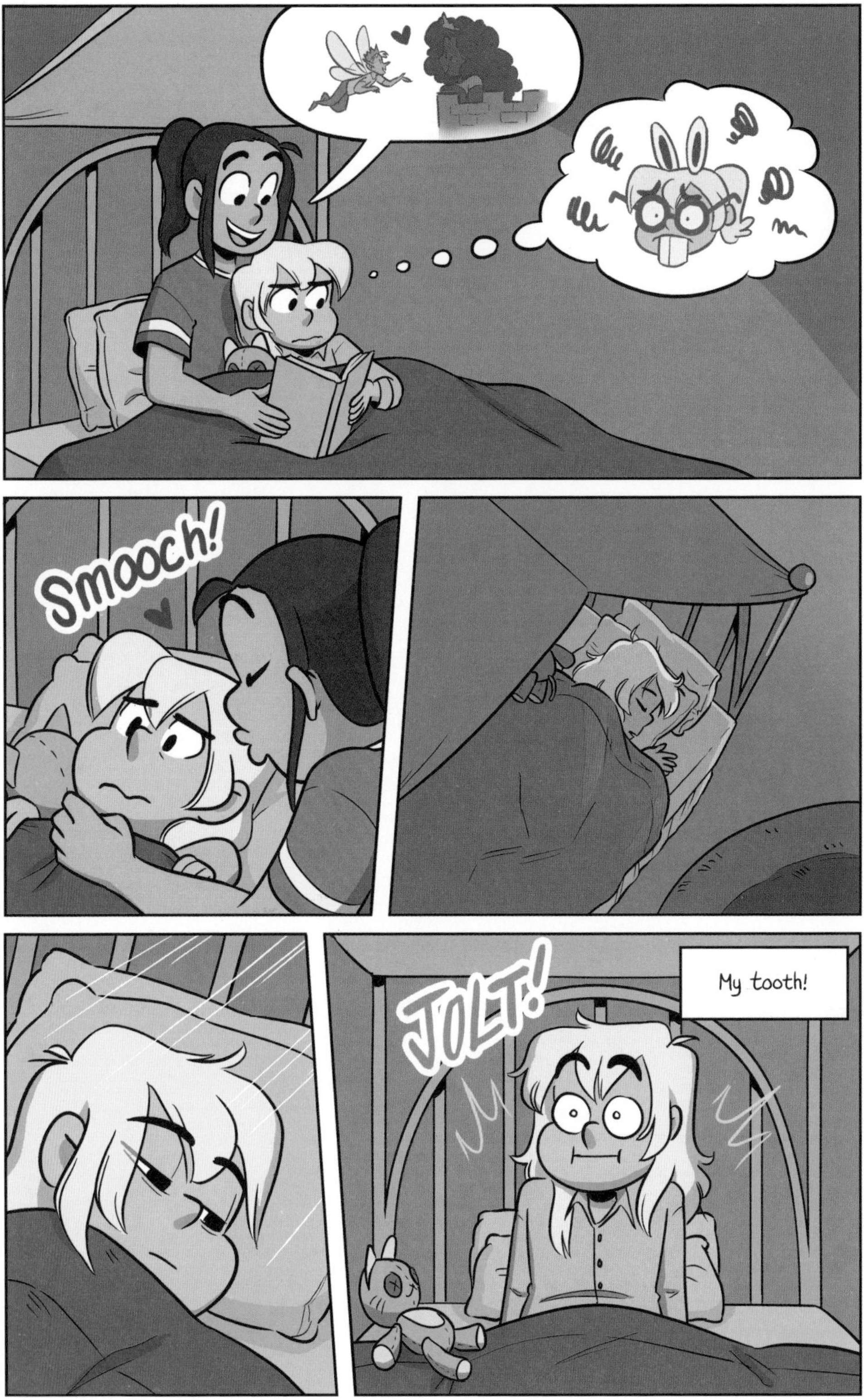
Smooch!
JOLT!
My tooth!

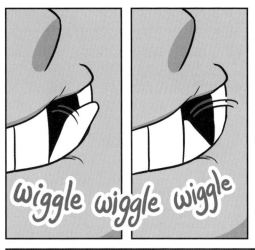

One of them is almost ready to come out.

Wiggle wiggle wiggle

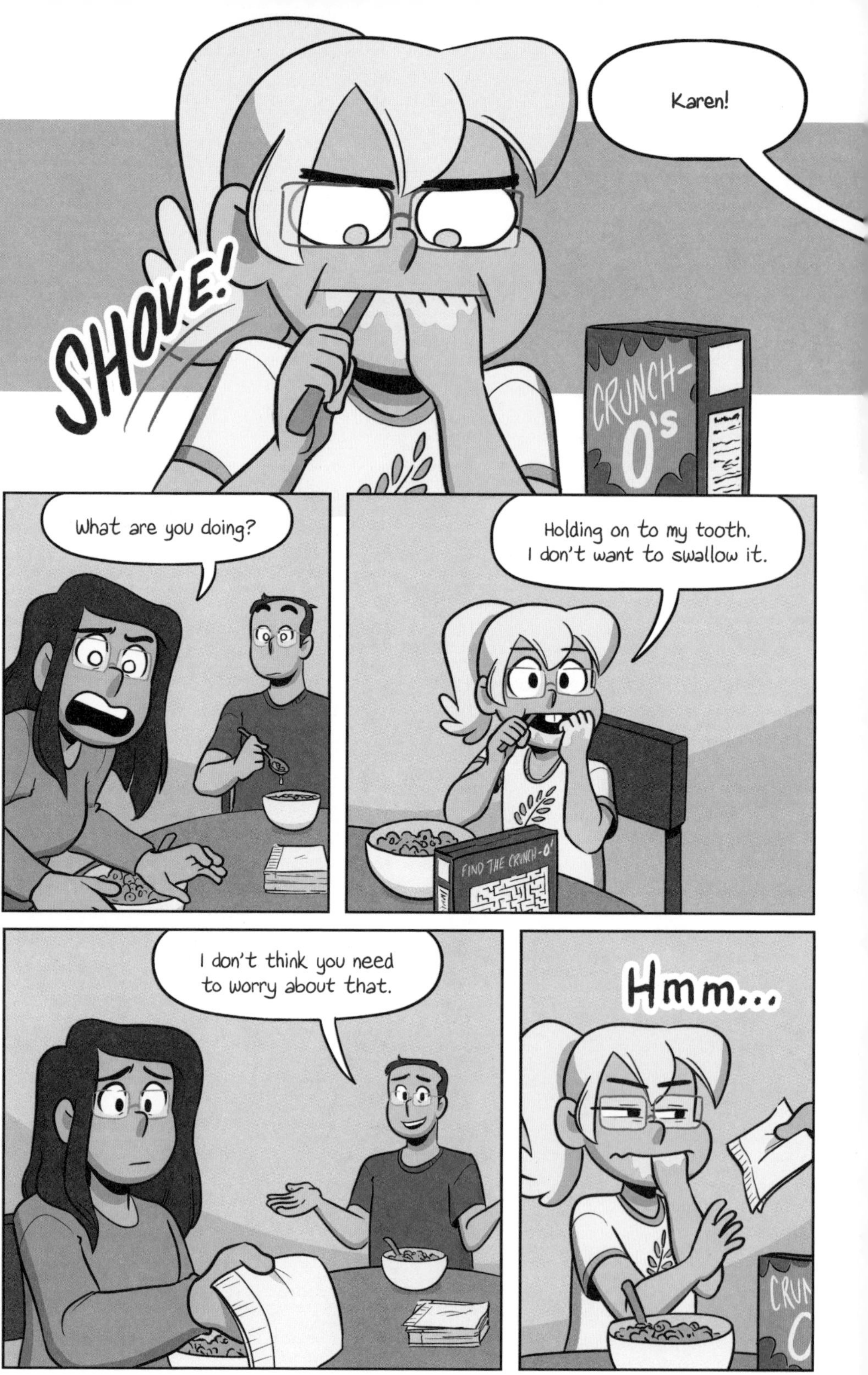
SHOVE!
Karen!
What are you doing?
Holding on to my tooth. I don't want to swallow it.
FIND THE CRUNCH-O'
I don't think you need to worry about that.
Hmm...

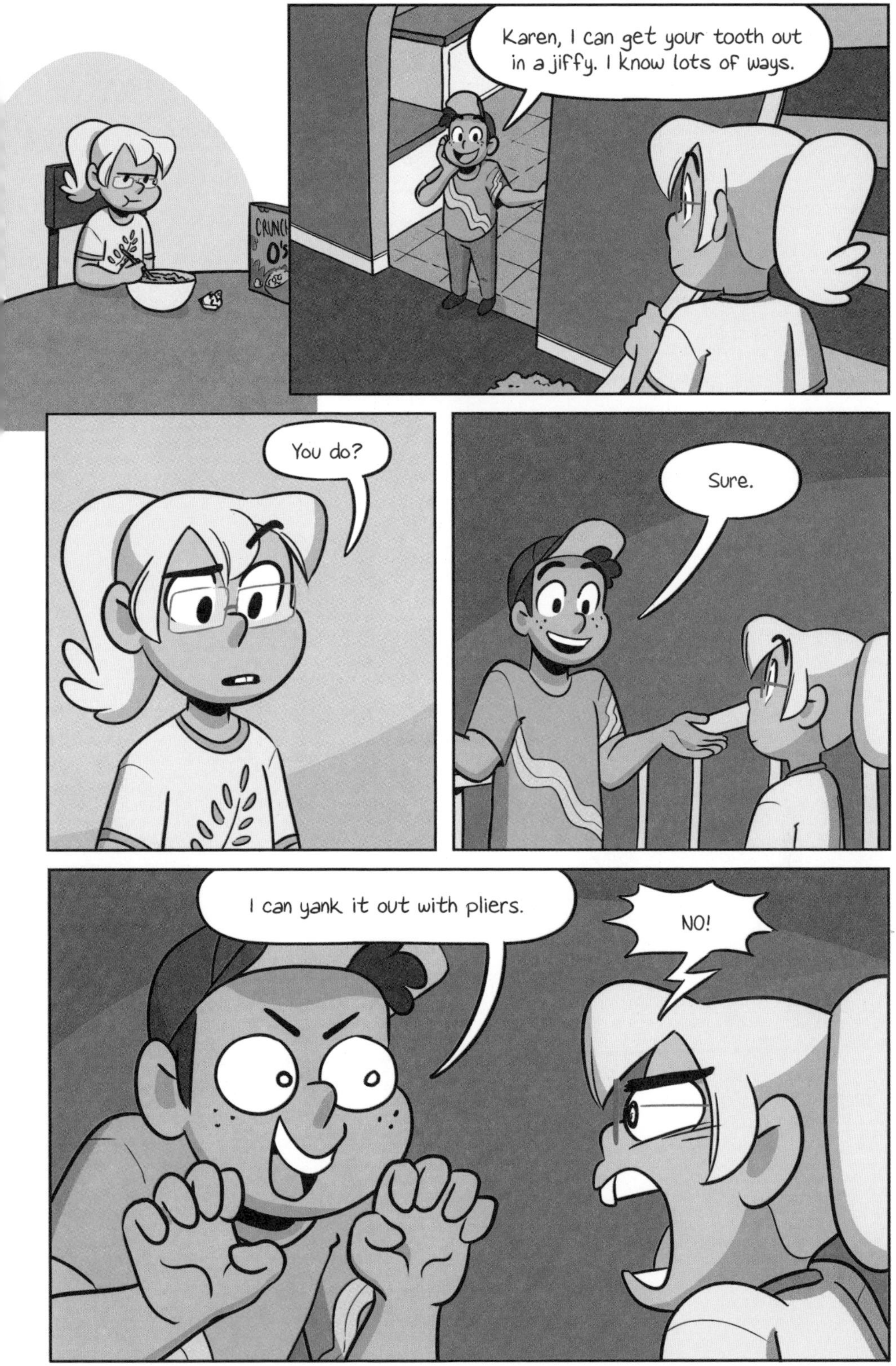
CRUNCH O's
Karen, I can get your tooth out in a jiffy. I know lots of ways.
You do?
Sure.
I can yank it out with pliers.
NO!

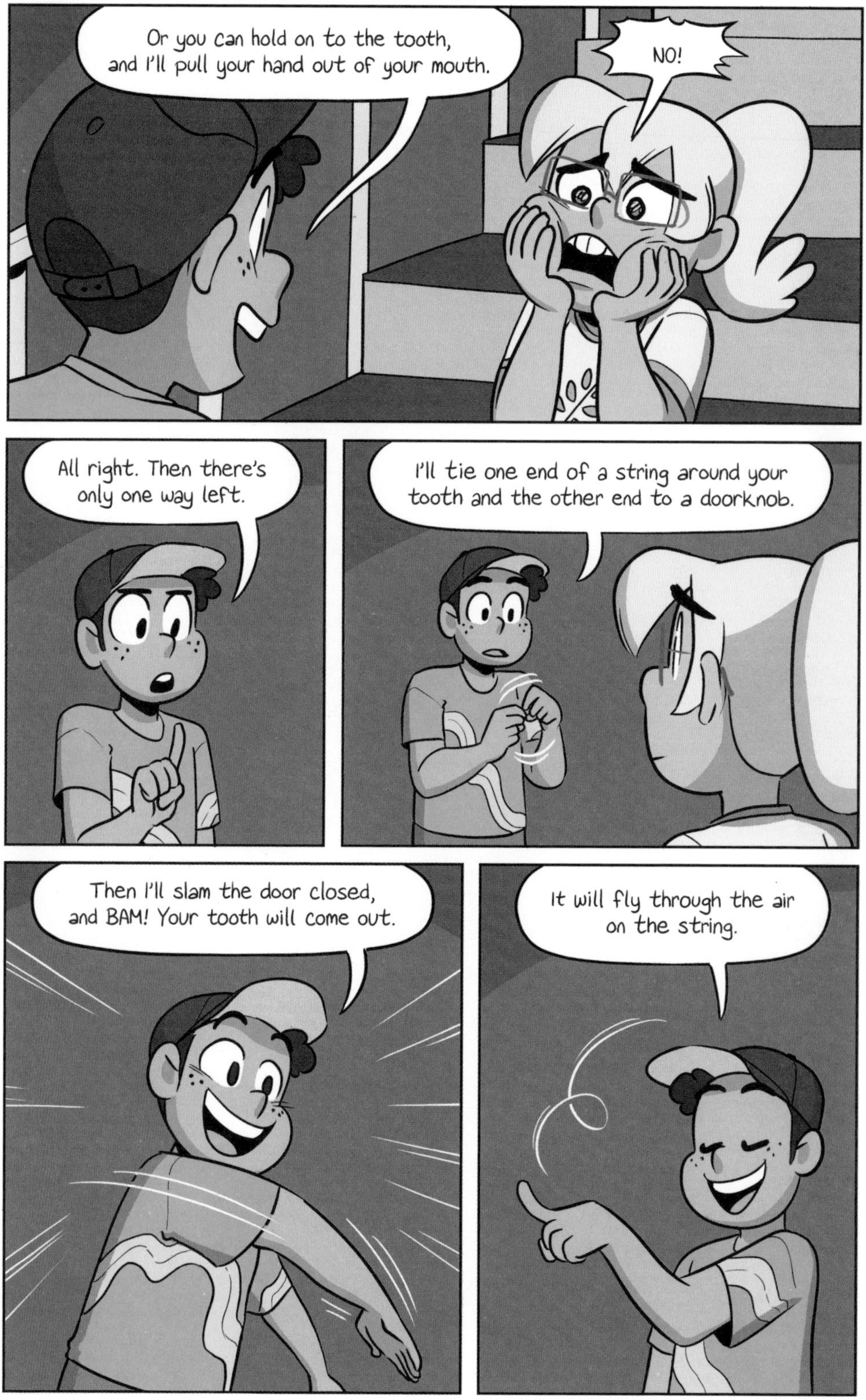
Or you can hold on to the tooth, and I'll pull your hand out of your mouth.
NO!
All right. Then there's only one way left.
I'll tie one end of a string around your tooth and the other end to a doorknob.
Then I'll slam the door closed, and BAM! Your tooth will come out.
It will fly through the air on the string.

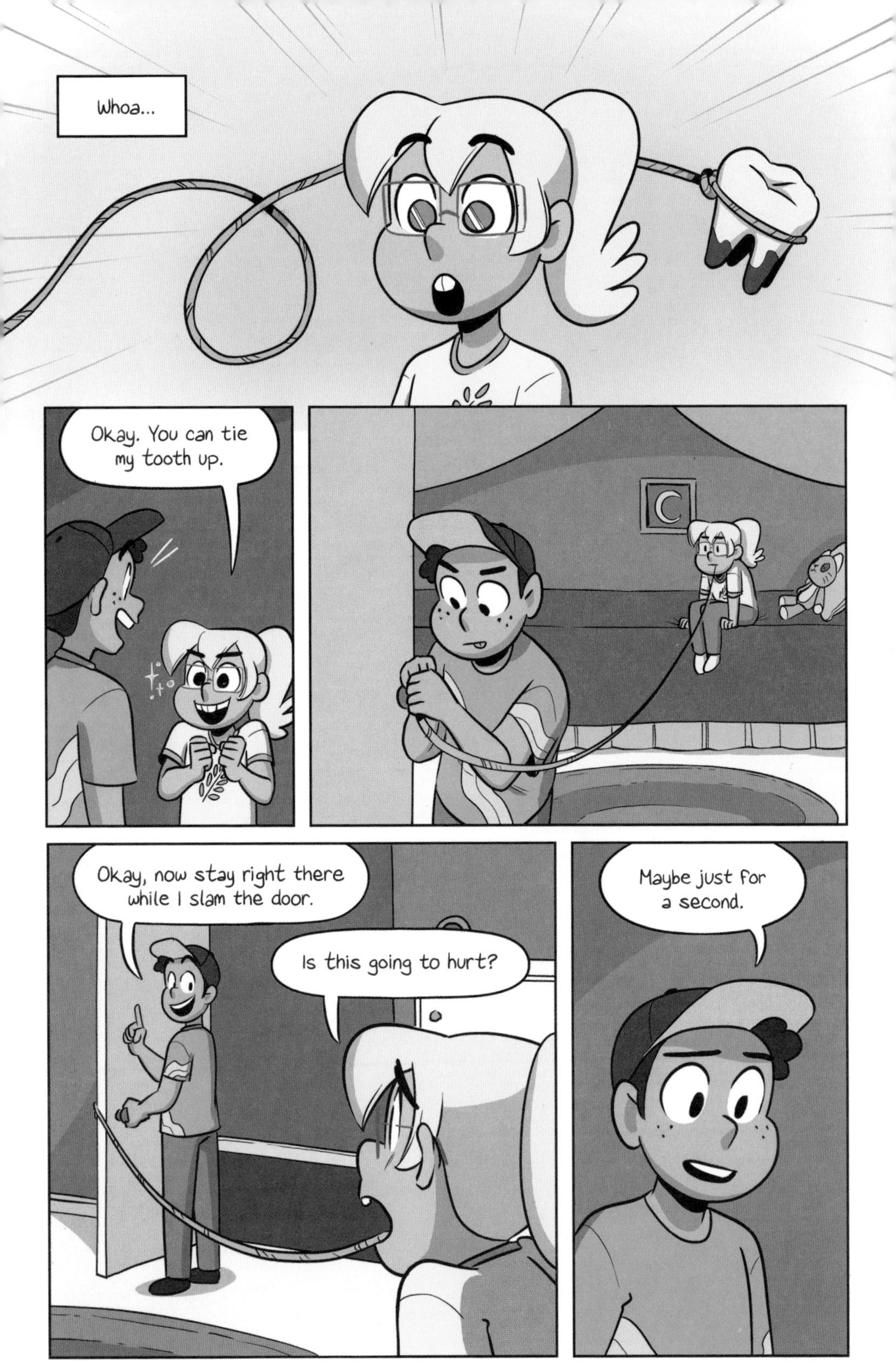
Whoa...
Okay. You can tie my tooth up.
Okay, now stay right there while I slam the door.
Is this going to hurt?
Maybe just for a second.

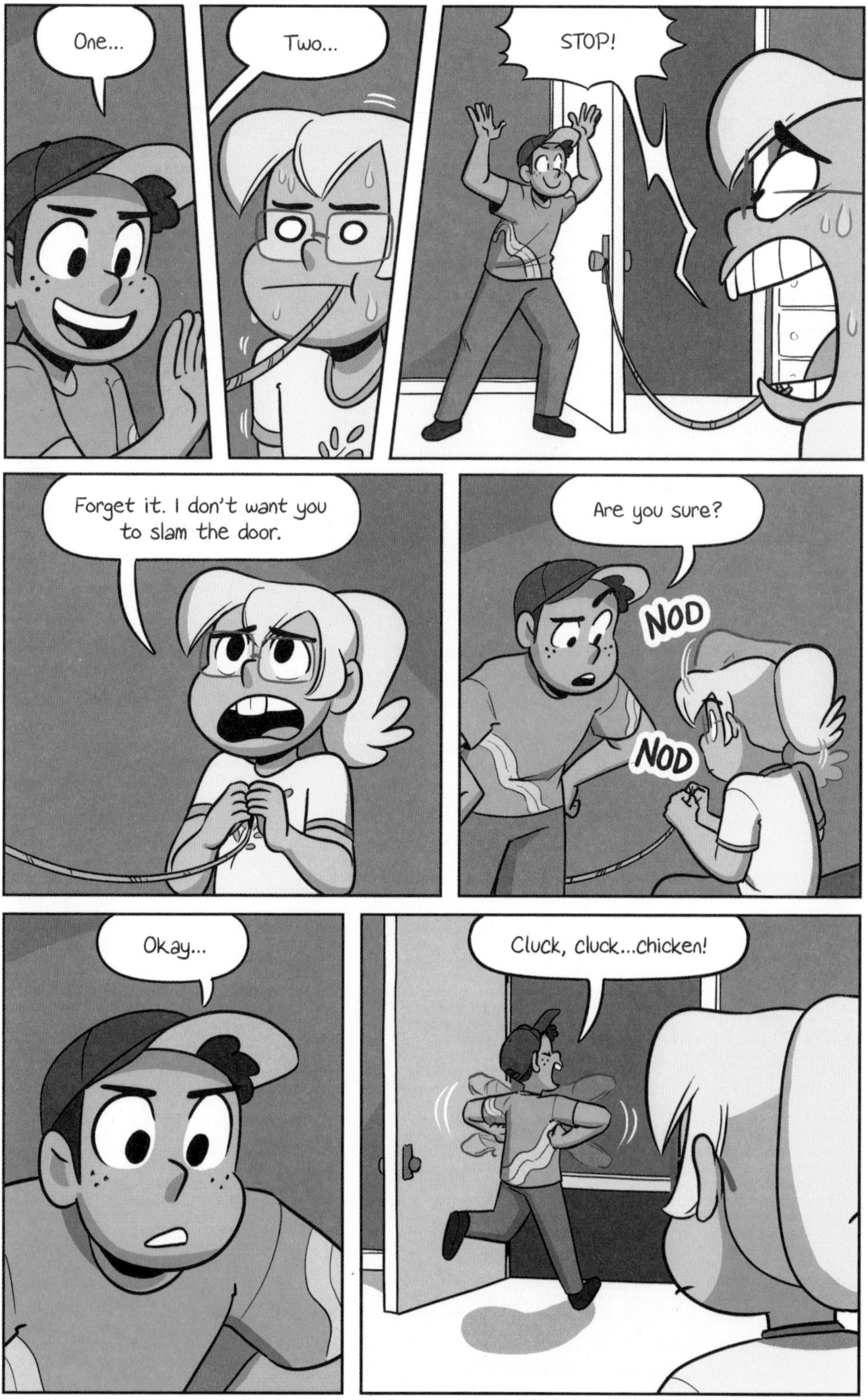
One...
Two...
STOP!
Forget it. I don't want you to slam the door.
Are you sure?
NOD
NOD
Okay...
Cluck, cluck...chicken!

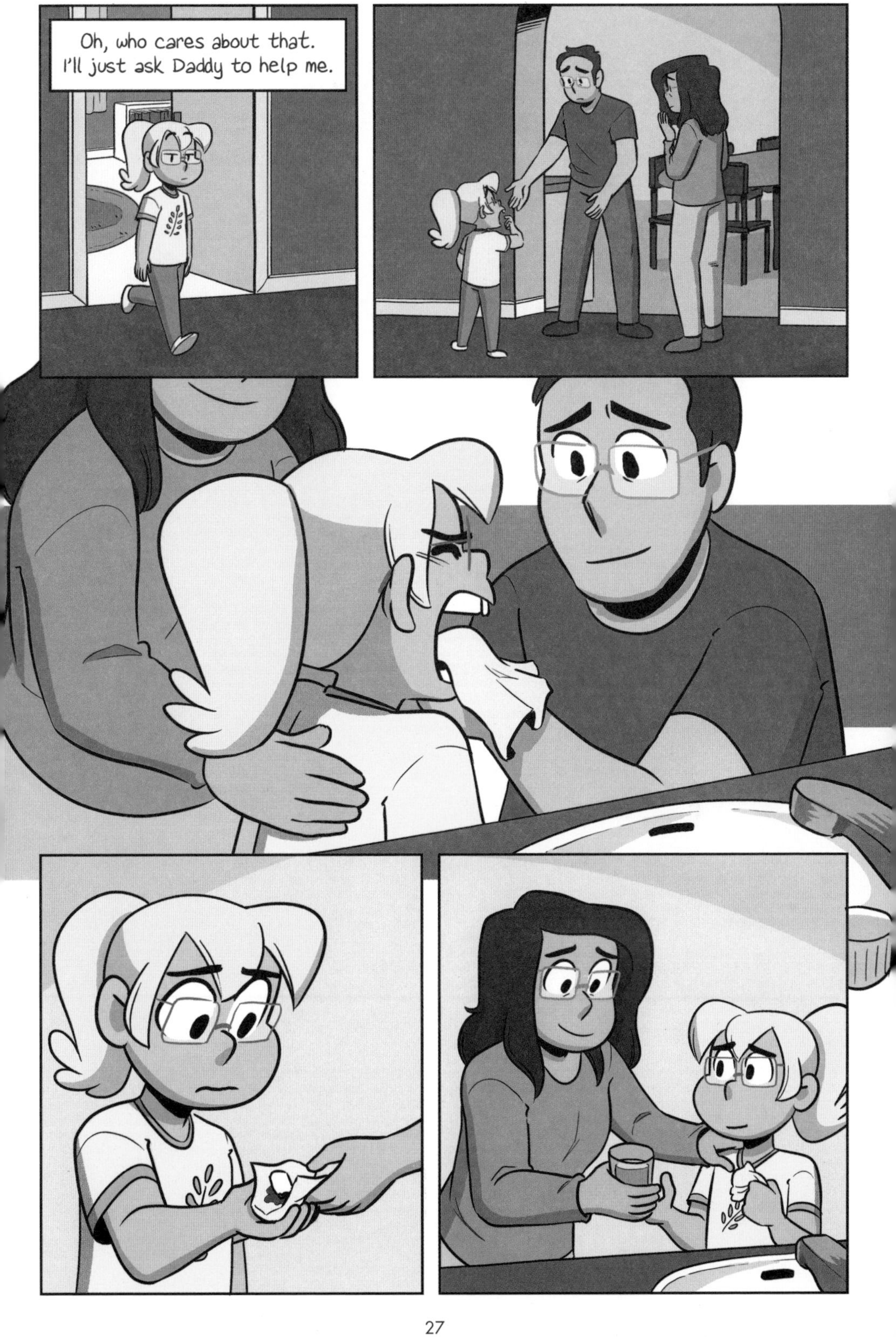
Oh, who cares about that.
I'll just ask Daddy to help me.

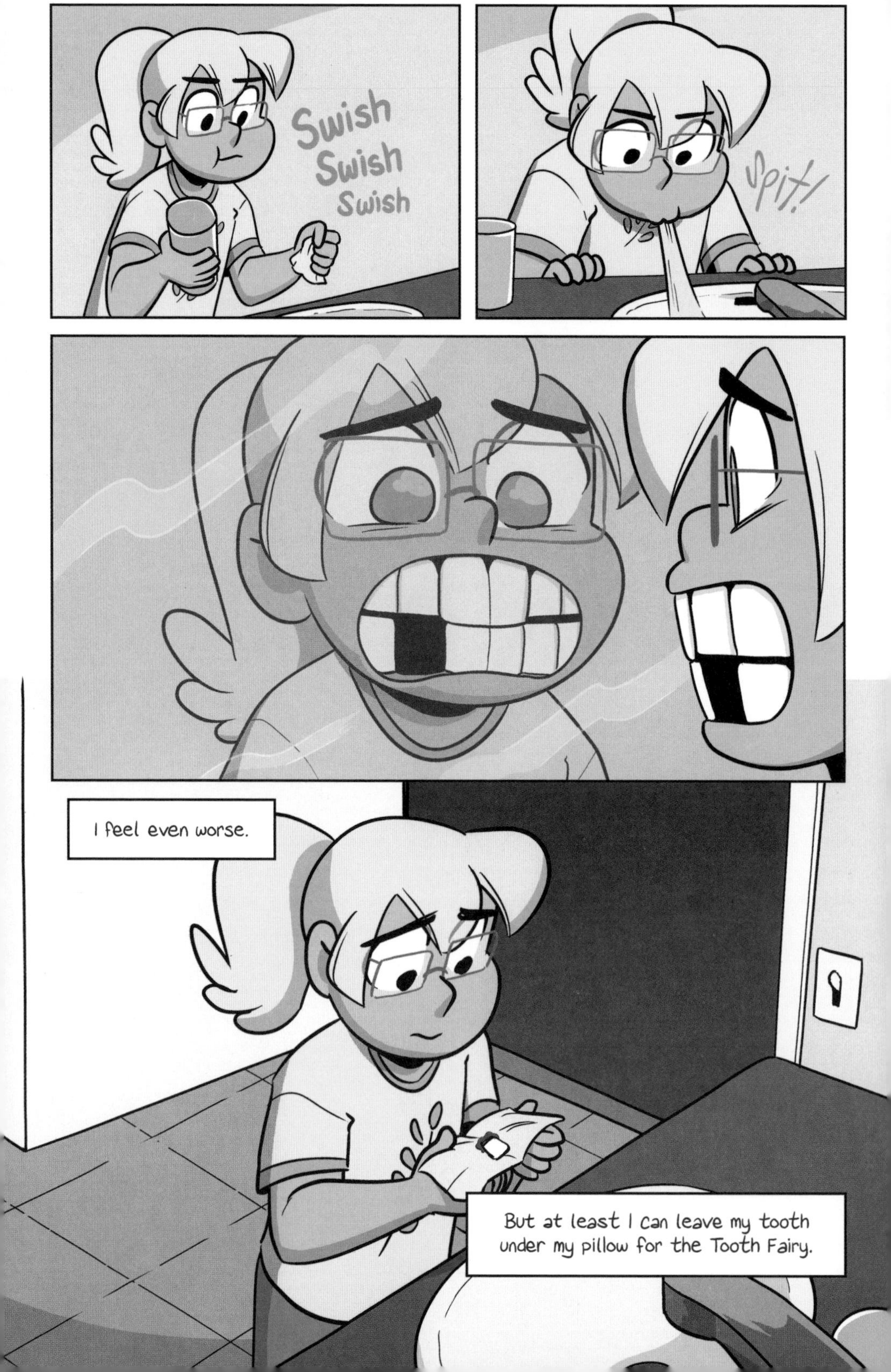
Swish
Swish
Swish
Spit!
I feel even worse.
But at least I can leave my tooth under my pillow for the Tooth Fairy.

CHAPTER 3

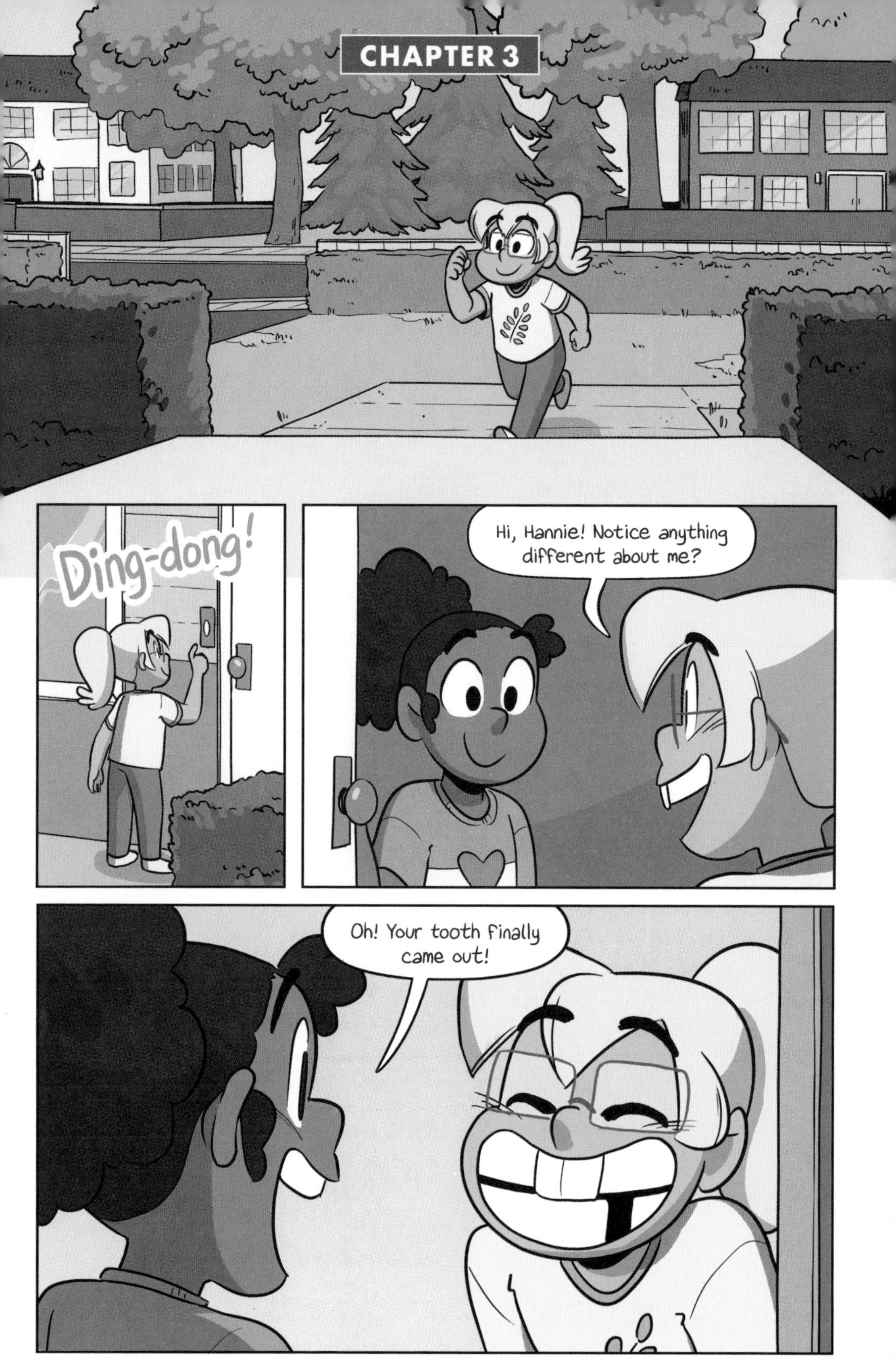

Ding-dong!
Hi, Hannie! Notice anything different about me?
Oh! Your tooth finally came out!

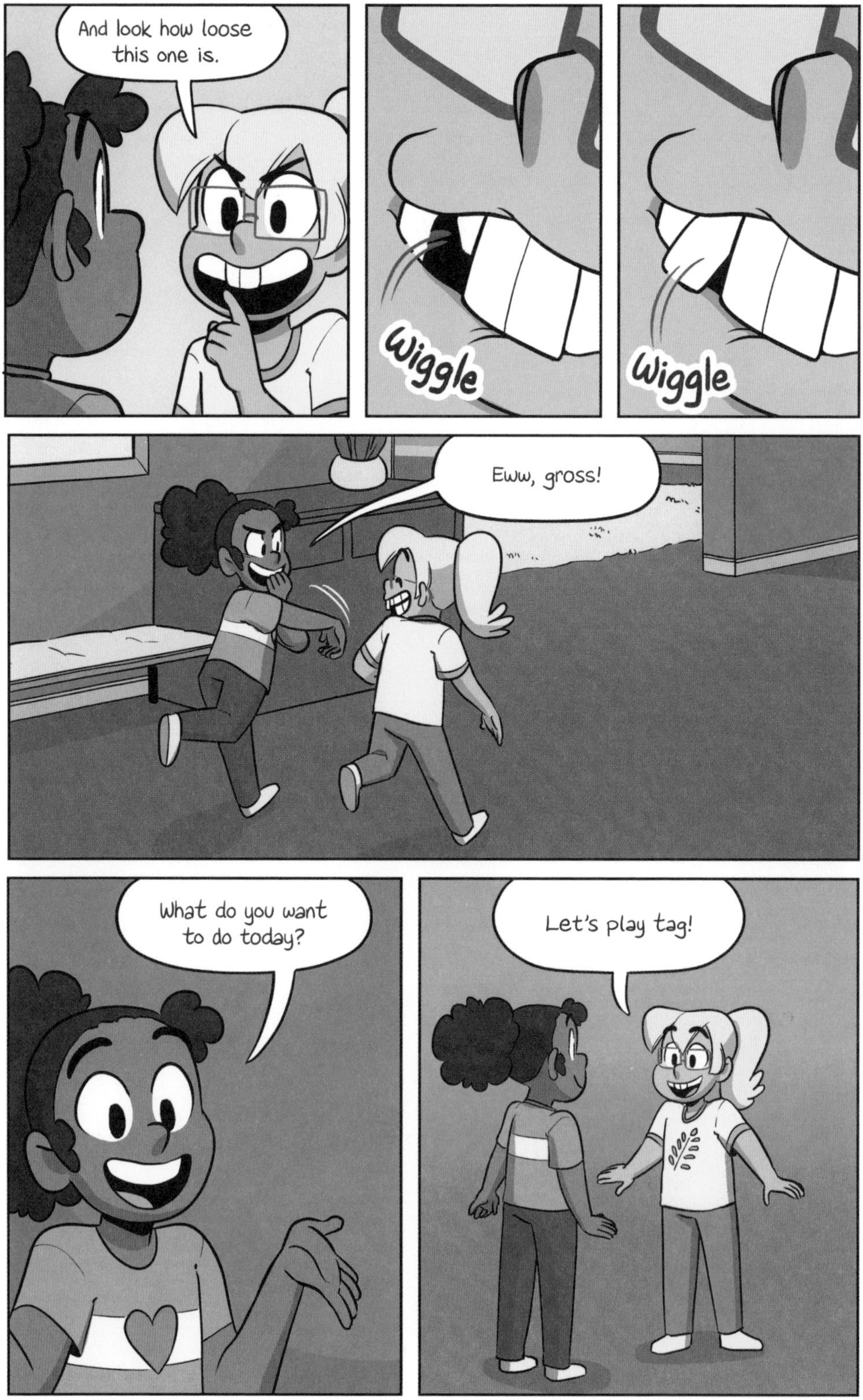
And look how loose this one is.
Wiggle
Wiggle
Eww, gross!
What do you want to do today?
Let's play tag!

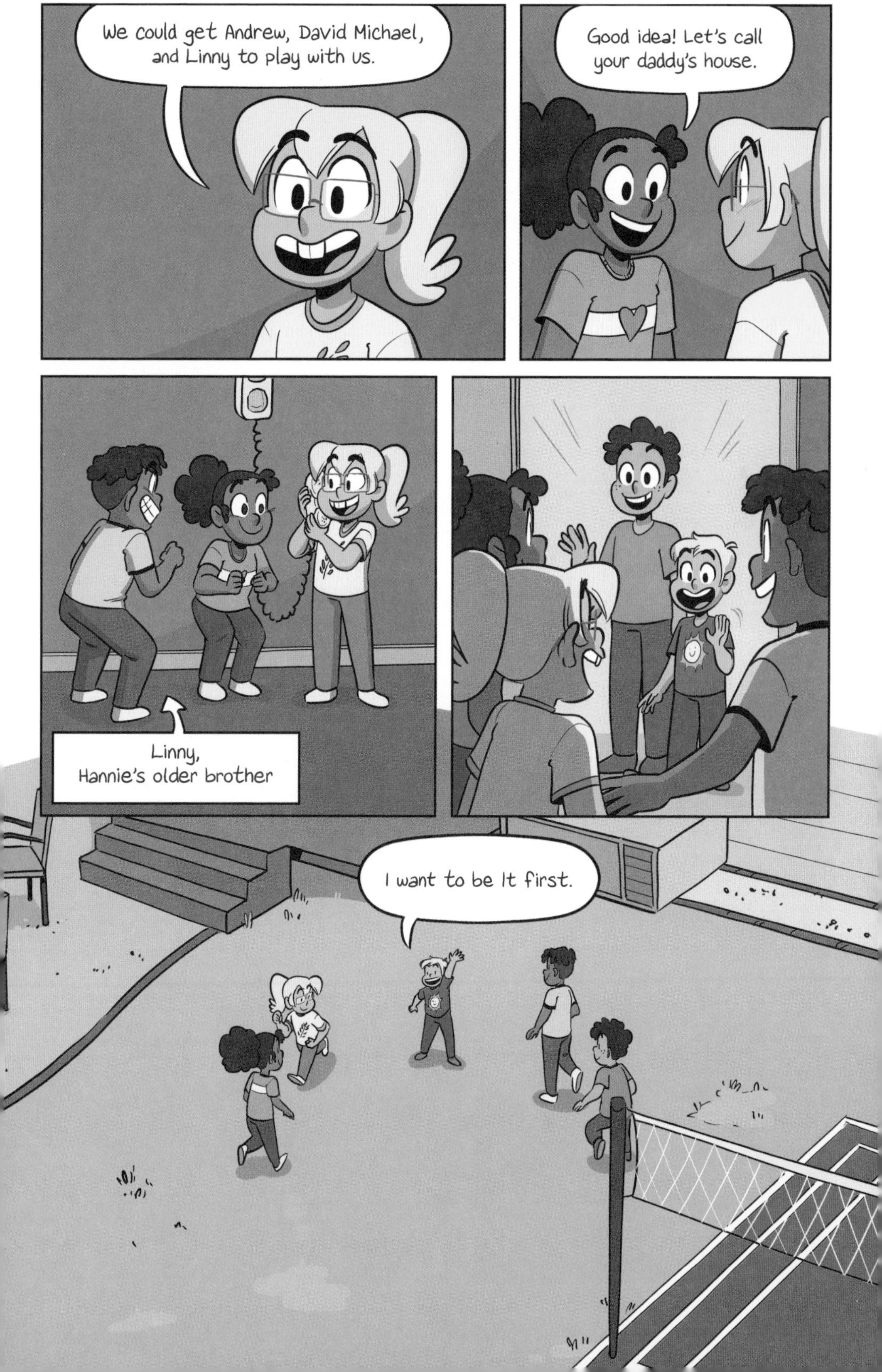
We could get Andrew, David Michael, and Linny to play with us.
Good idea! Let's call your daddy's house.
Linny, Hannie's older brother
I want to be It first.

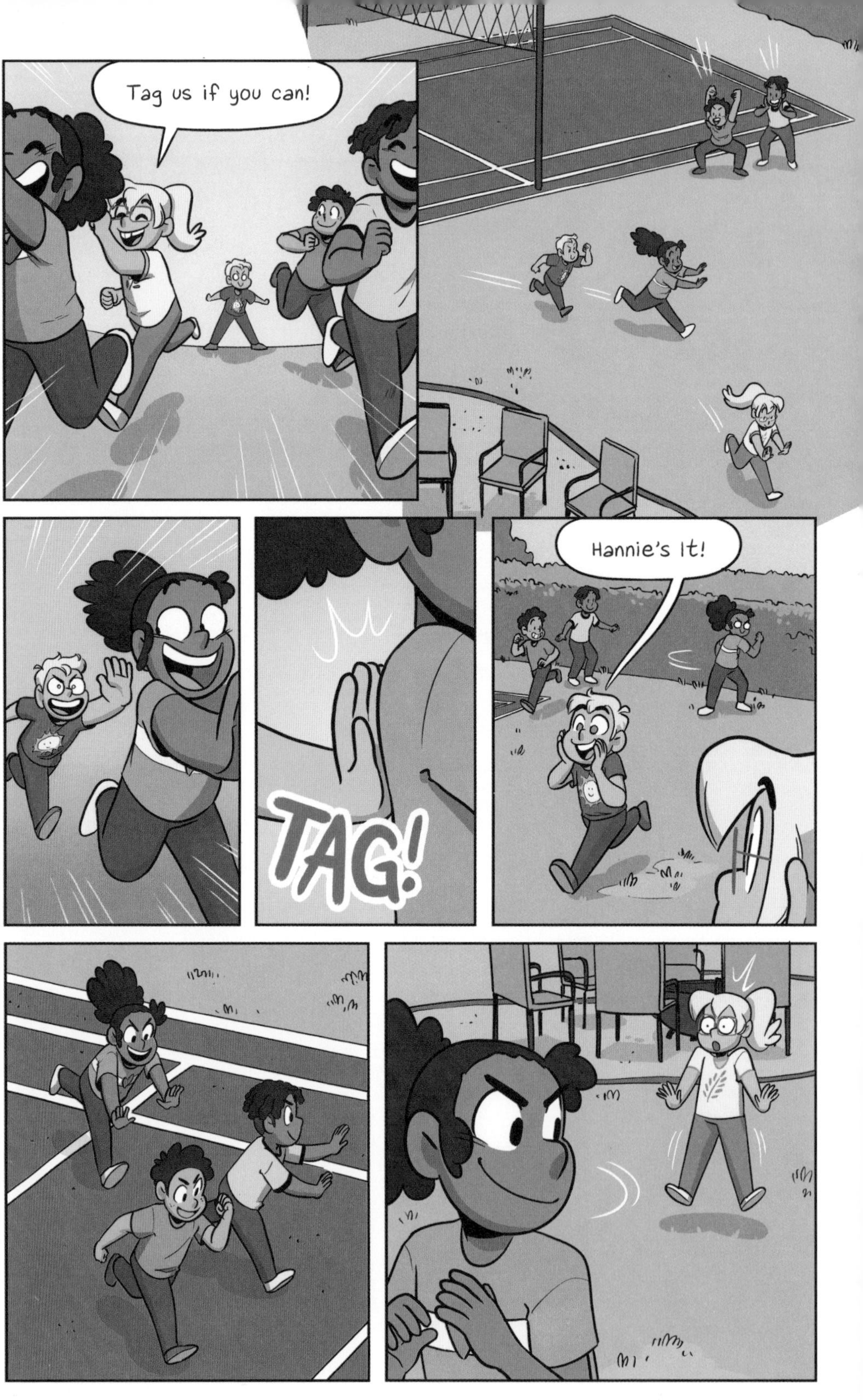
Tag us if you can!
TAG!
Hannie's It!

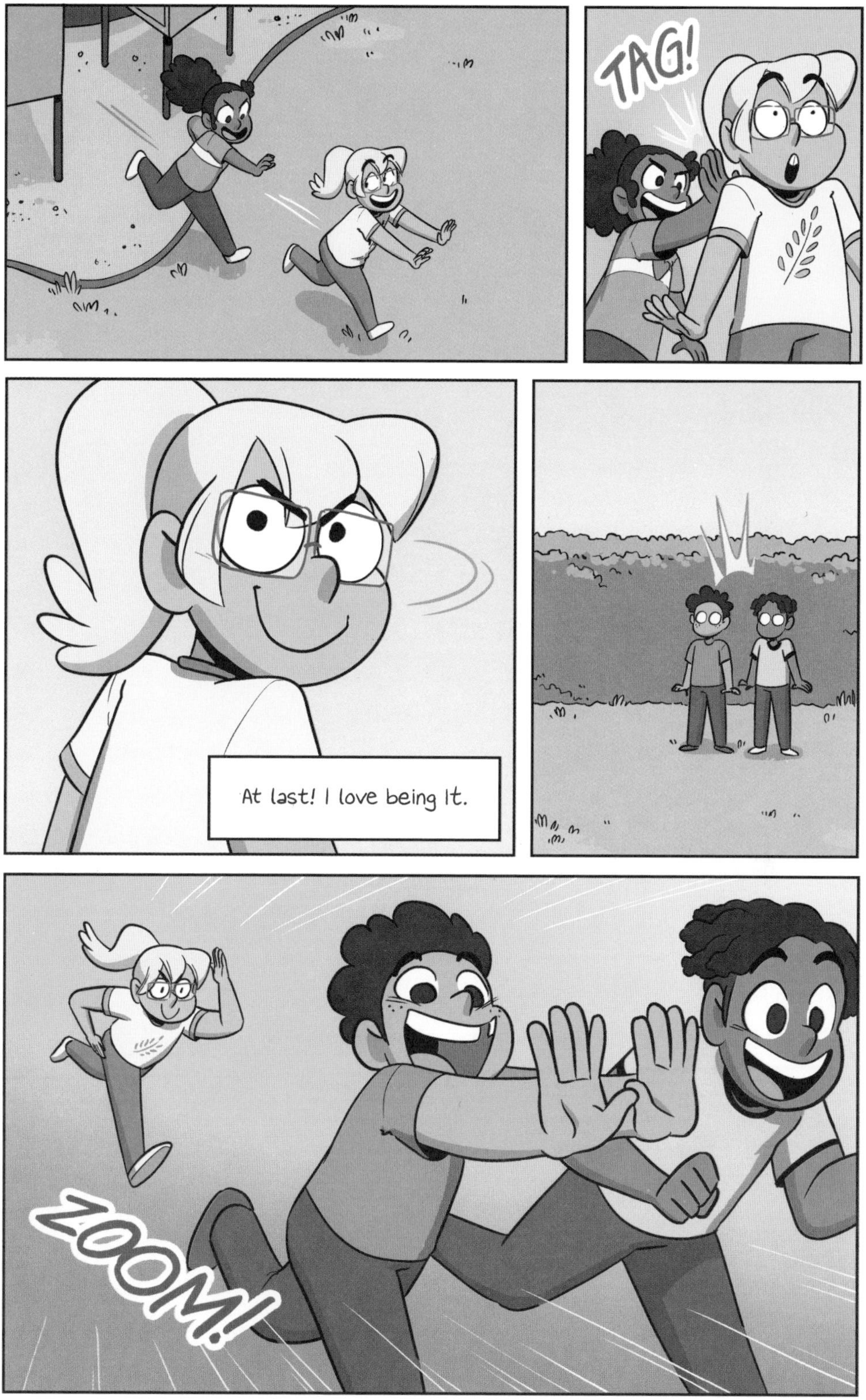
TAG!
At last! I love being It.
ZOOM!

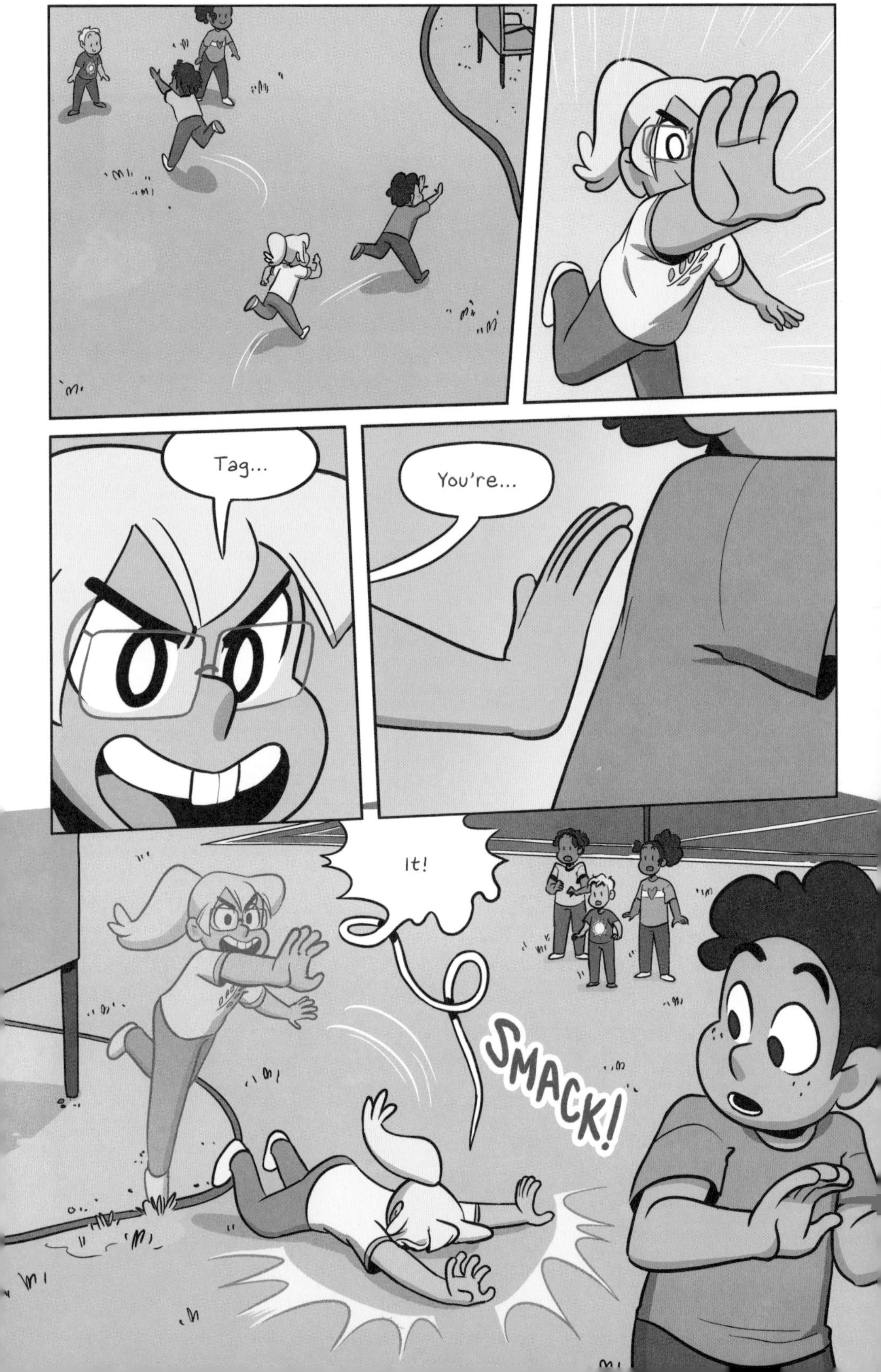

Tag...
You're...
It!
SMACK!

Rattle
Rattle

Uh-oh...

What's wrong?

I lost the other tooth.

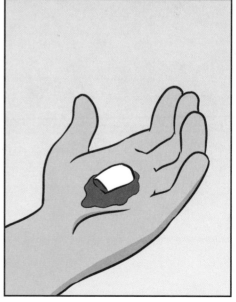

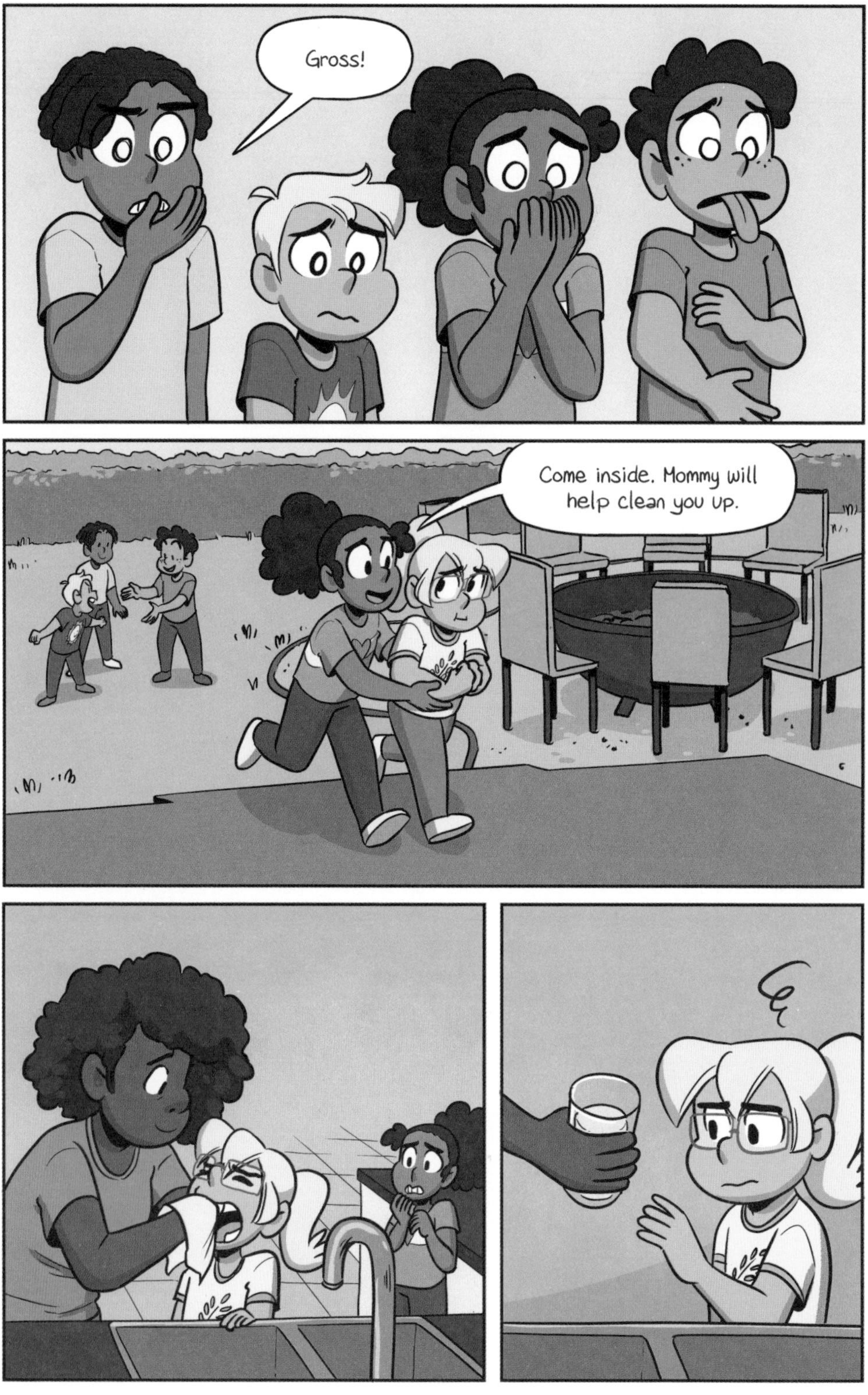
Gross!
Come inside. Mommy will help clean you up.

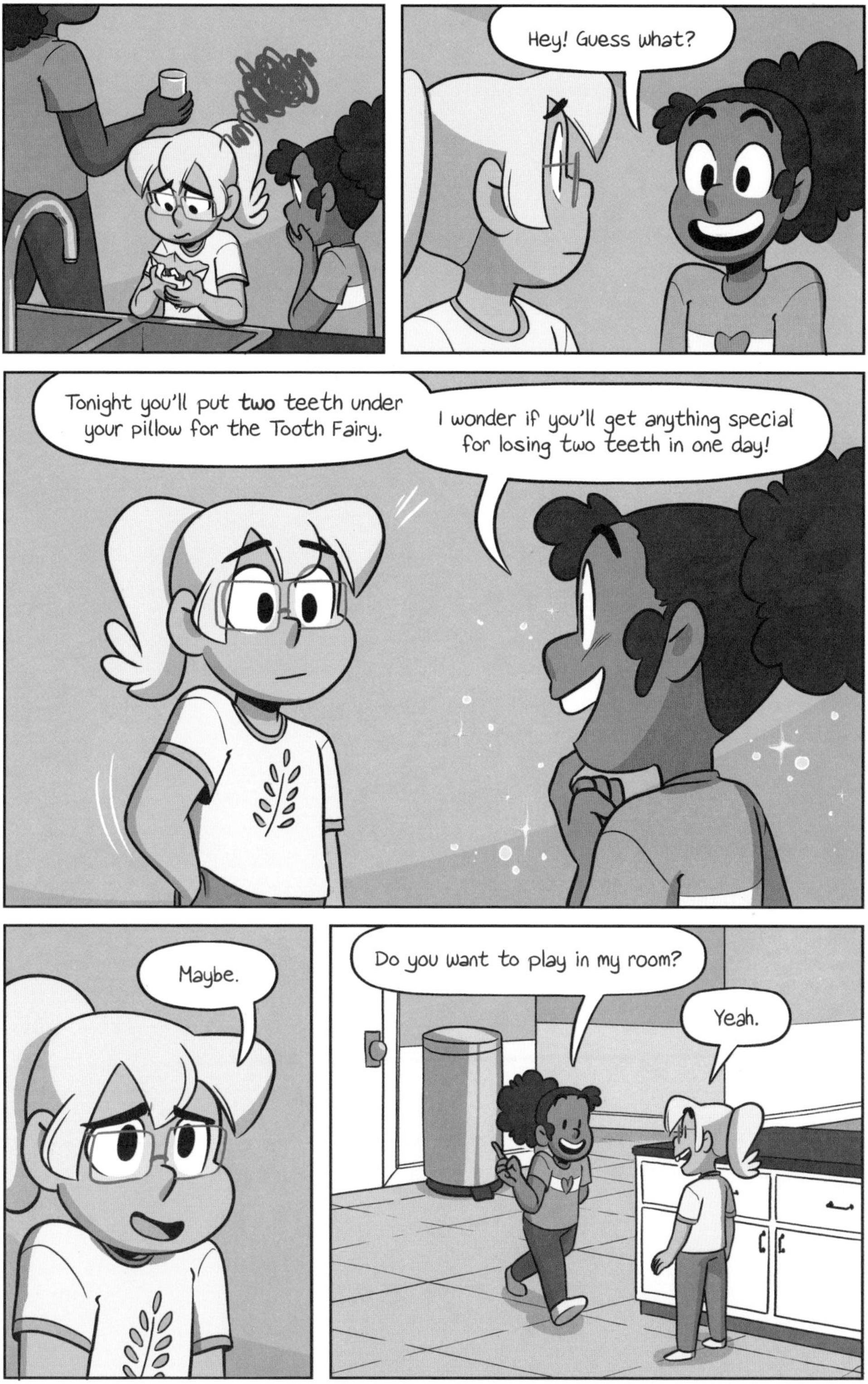
Hey! Guess what?
Tonight you'll put **two** teeth under your pillow for the Tooth Fairy.
I wonder if you'll get anything special for losing two teeth in one day!
Maybe.
Do you want to play in my room?
Yeah.

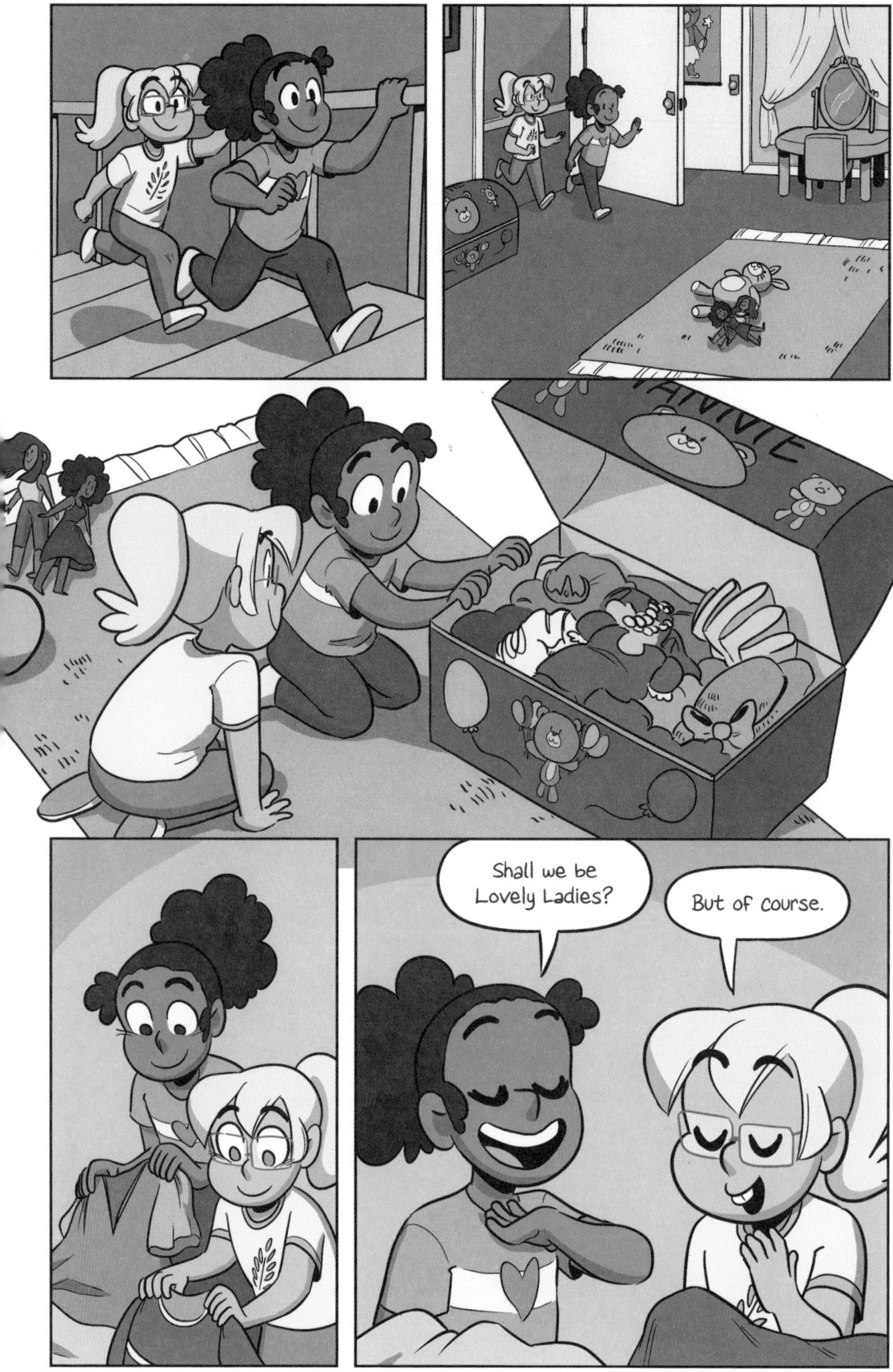
Shall we be Lovely Ladies?
But of course.

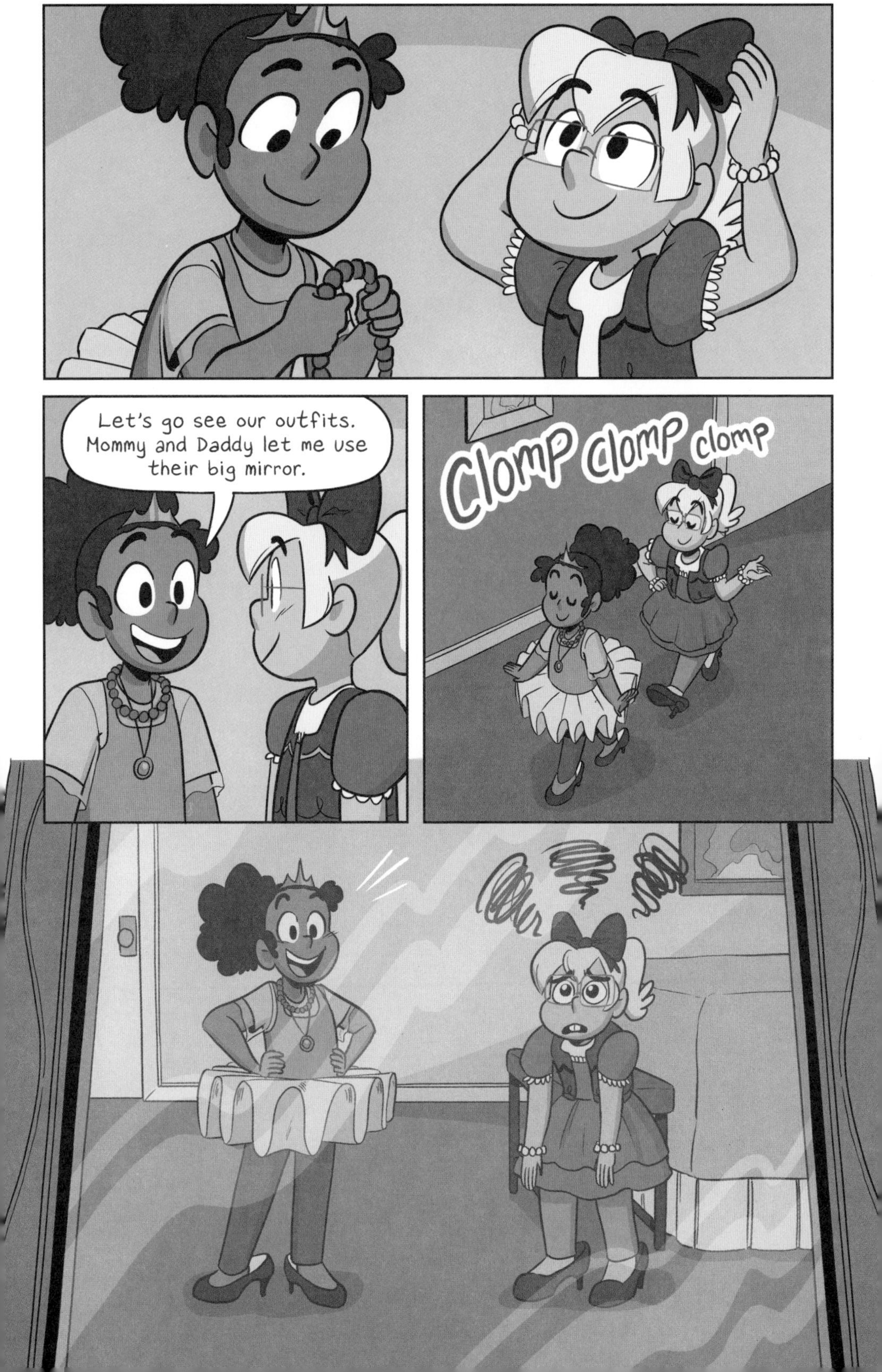
Let's go see our outfits. Mommy and Daddy let me use their big mirror.
Clomp clomp clomp

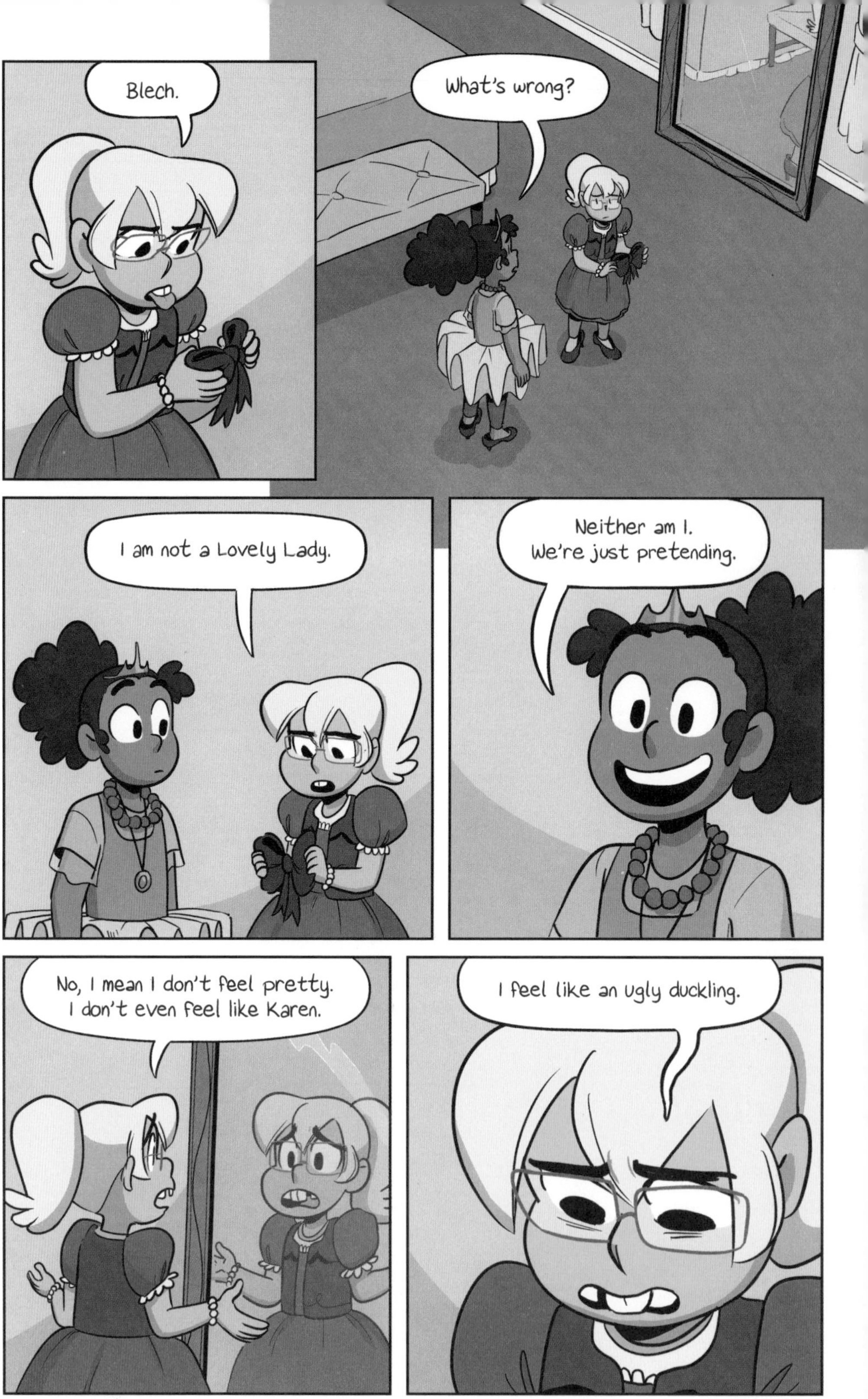
Blech.
What's wrong?
I am not a Lovely Lady.
Neither am I. We're just pretending.
No, I mean I don't feel pretty. I don't even feel like Karen.
I feel like an ugly duckling.

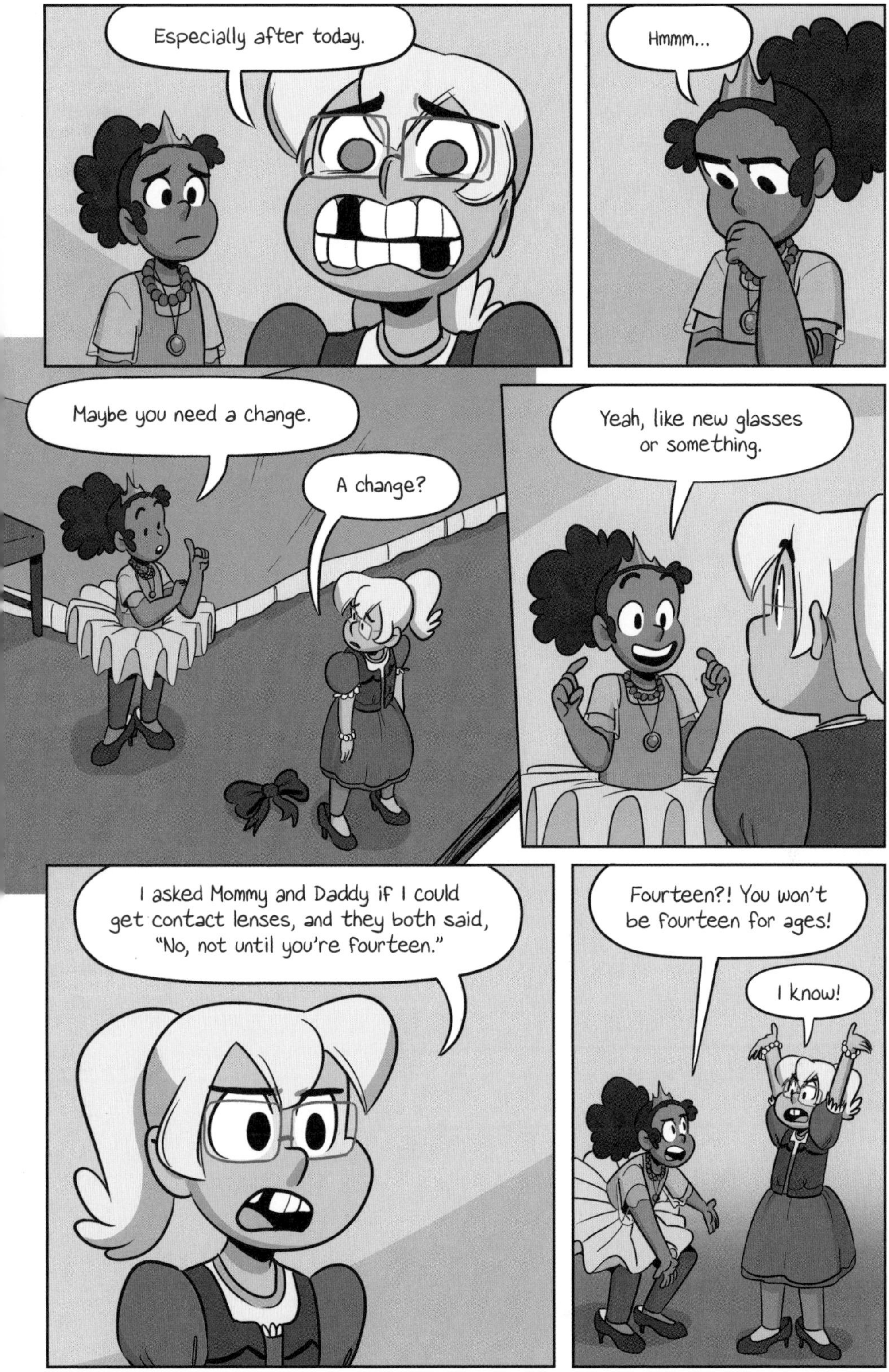
Especially after today.
Hmmm...
Maybe you need a change.
A change?
Yeah, like new glasses or something.
I asked Mommy and Daddy if I could get contact lenses, and they both said, "No, not until you're fourteen."
Fourteen?! You won't be fourteen for ages!
I know!

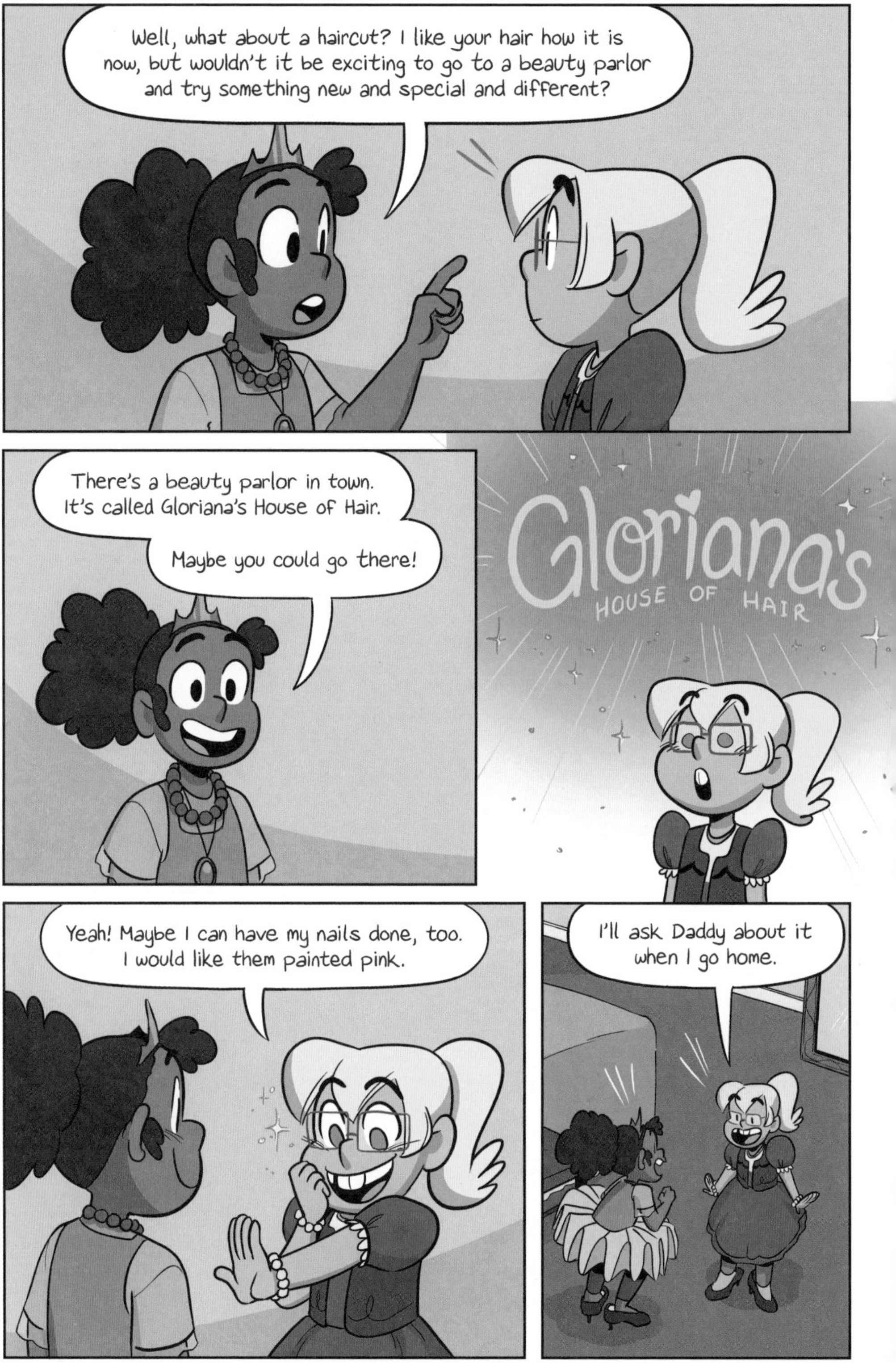
Well, what about a haircut? I like your hair how it is now, but wouldn't it be exciting to go to a beauty parlor and try something new and special and different?
There's a beauty parlor in town. It's called Gloriana's House of Hair.
Maybe you could go there!
Gloriana's
HOUSE OF HAIR
Yeah! Maybe I can have my nails done, too. I would like them painted pink.
I'll ask Daddy about it when I go home.

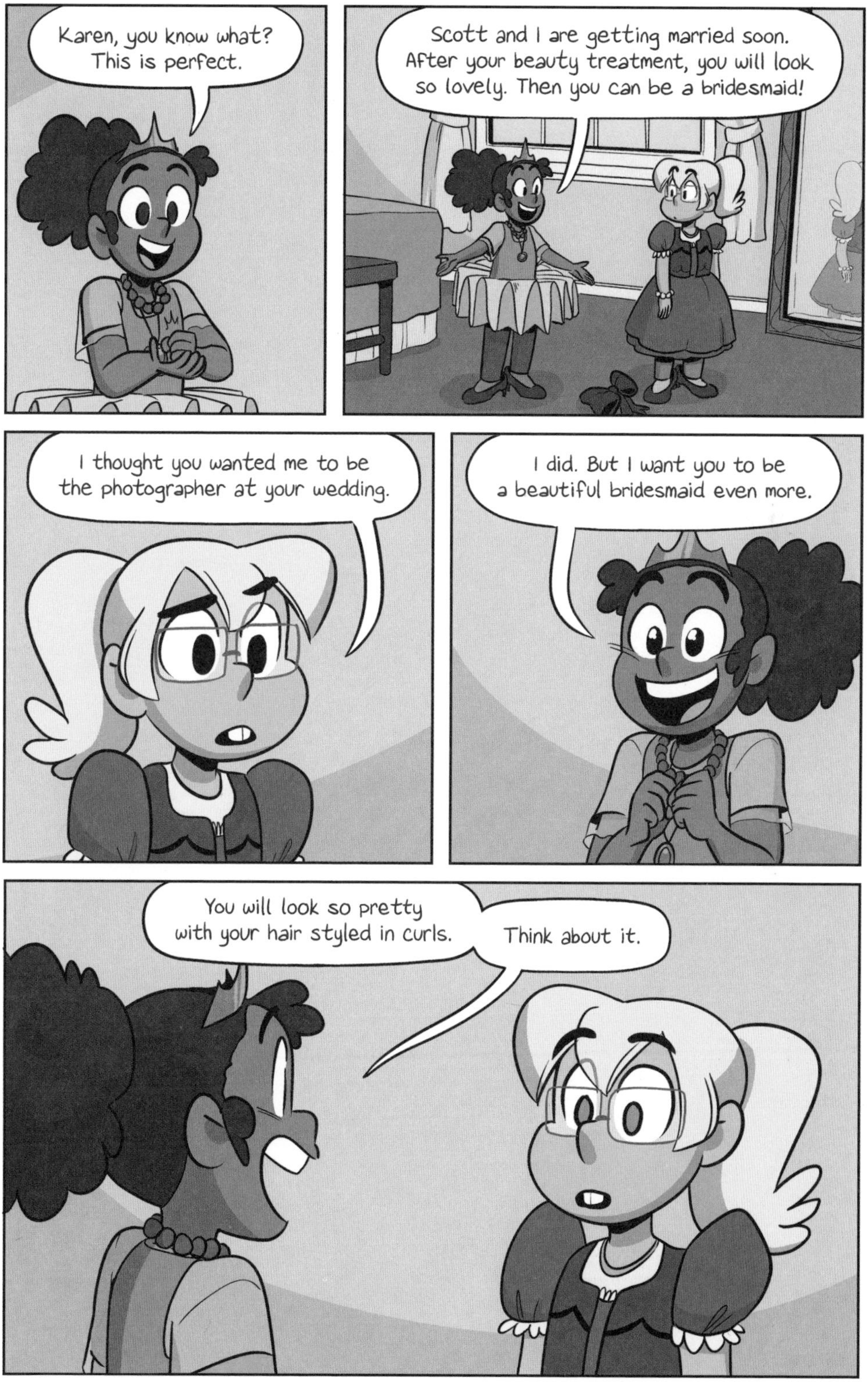
Karen, you know what? This is perfect.
Scott and I are getting married soon. After your beauty treatment, you will look so lovely. Then you can be a bridesmaid!
I thought you wanted me to be the photographer at your wedding.
I did. But I want you to be a beautiful bridesmaid even more.
You will look so pretty with your hair styled in curls.
Think about it.

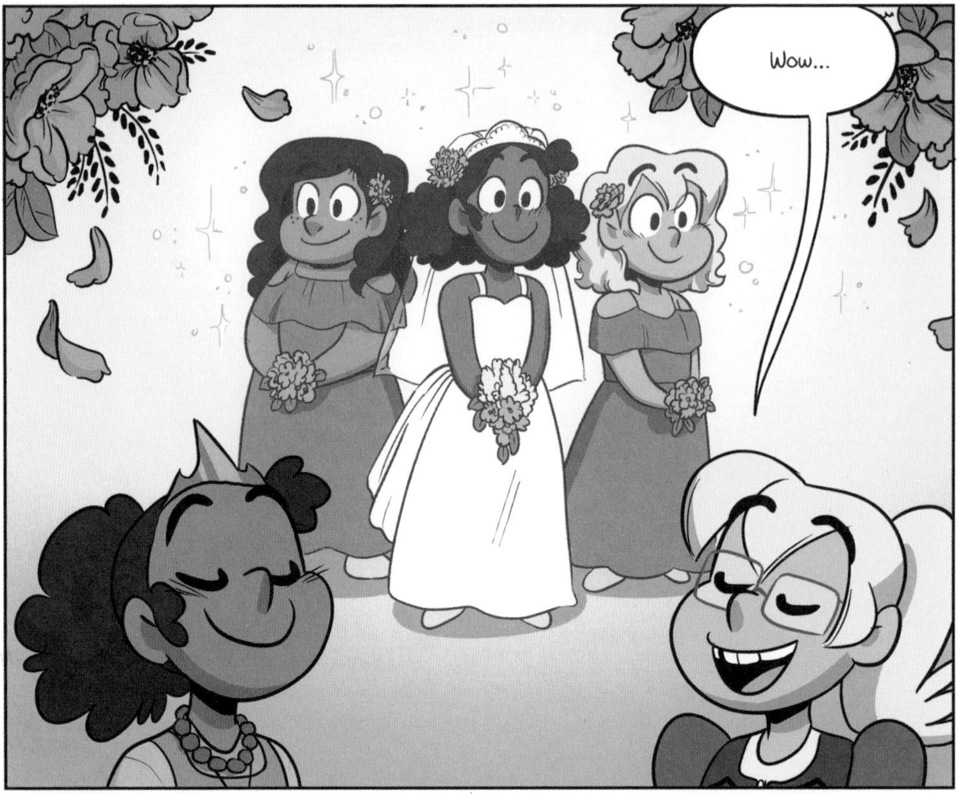
Wow...

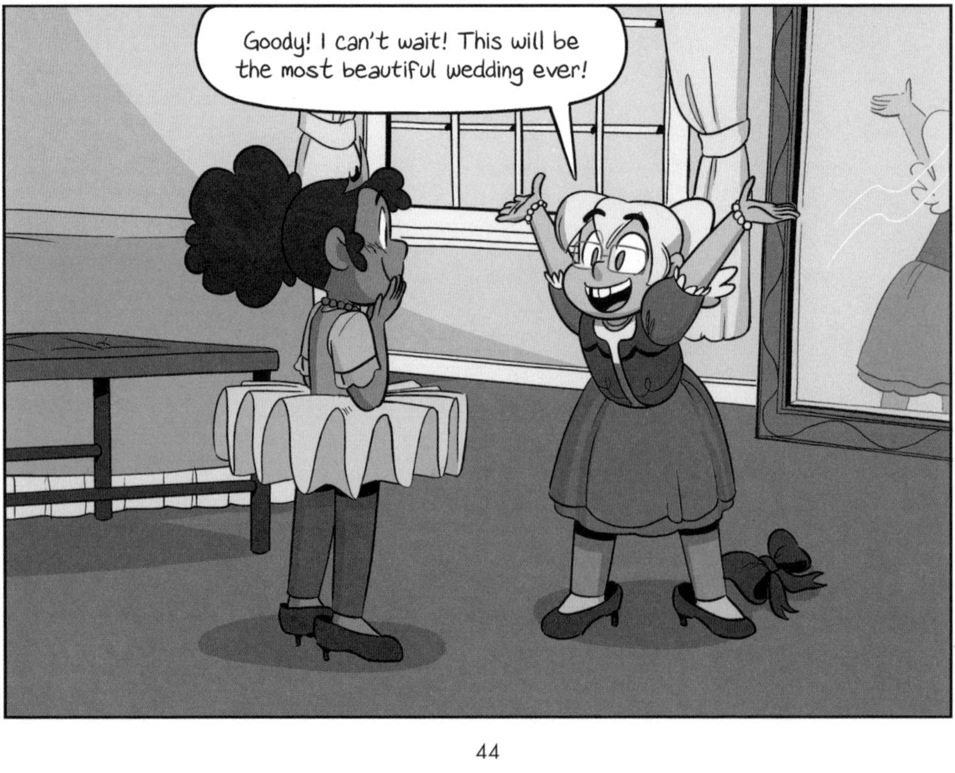
Goody! I can't wait! This will be the most beautiful wedding ever!

CHAPTER 4

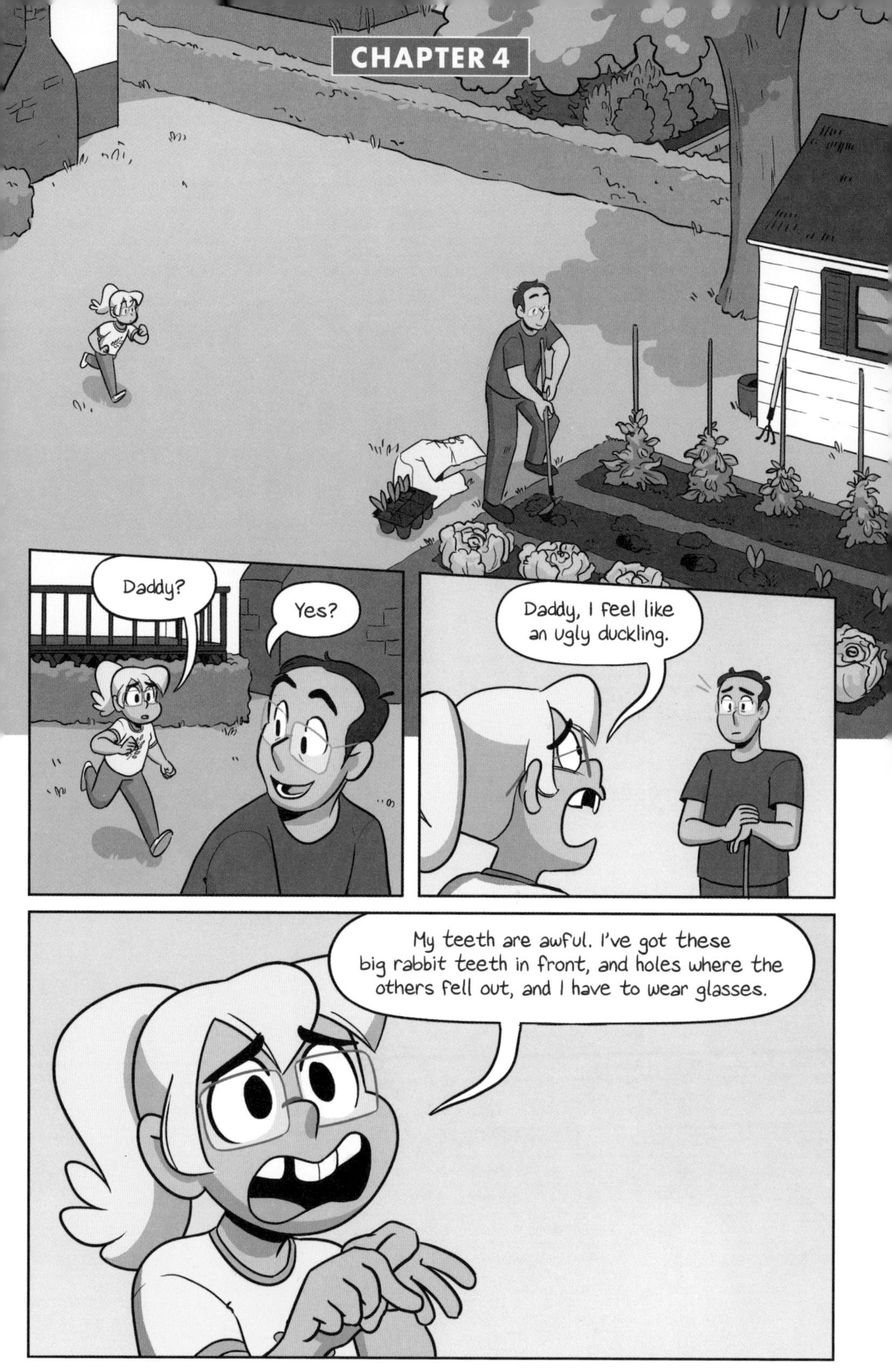

Daddy?
Yes?
Daddy, I feel like an ugly duckling.
My teeth are awful. I've got these big rabbit teeth in front, and holes where the others fell out, and I have to wear glasses.

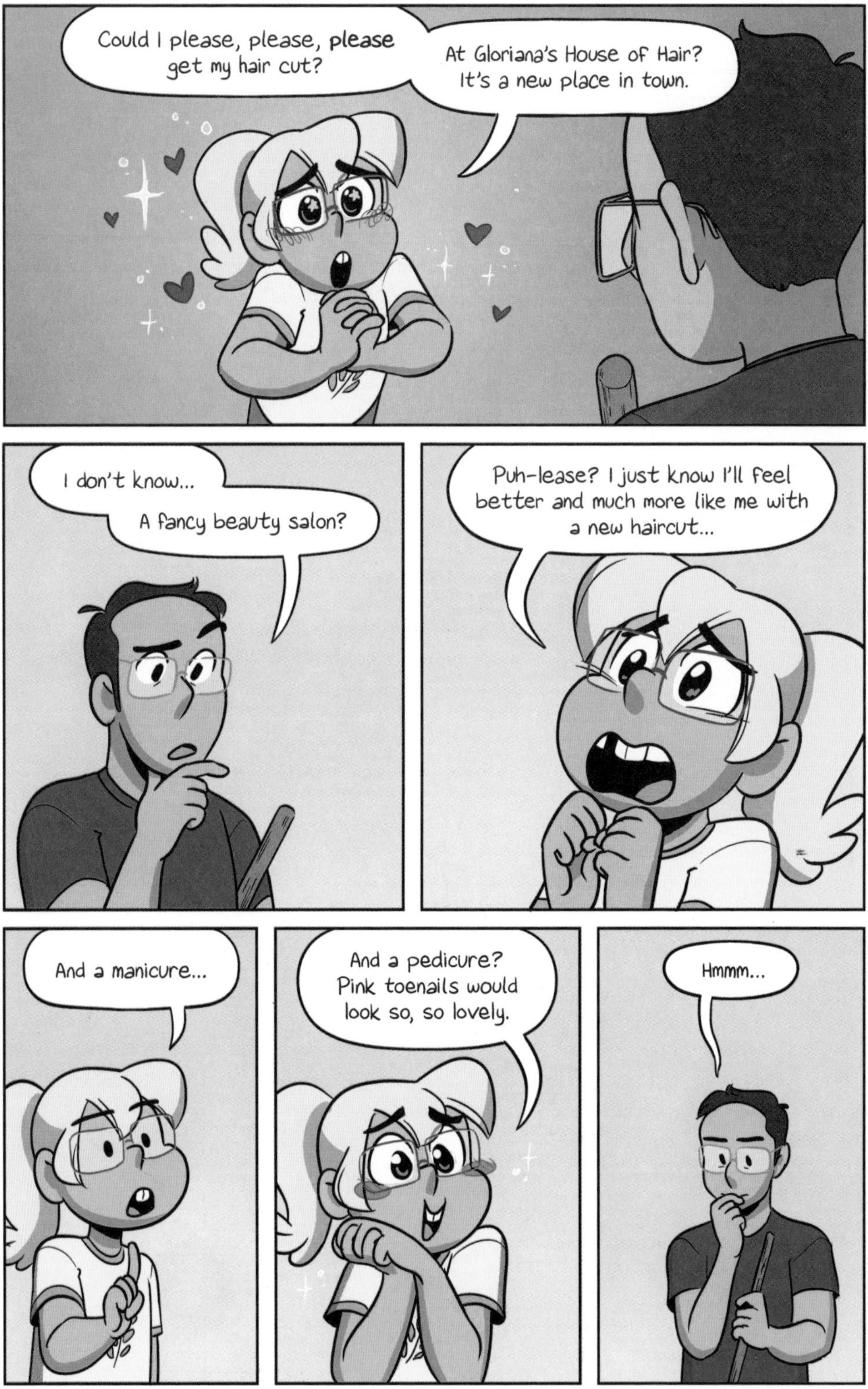
Could I please, please, **please** get my hair cut?
At Gloriana's House of Hair? It's a new place in town.
I don't know...
A fancy beauty salon?
Puh-lease? I just know I'll feel better and much more like me with a new haircut...
And a manicure...
And a pedicure? Pink toenails would look so, so lovely.
Hmmm...

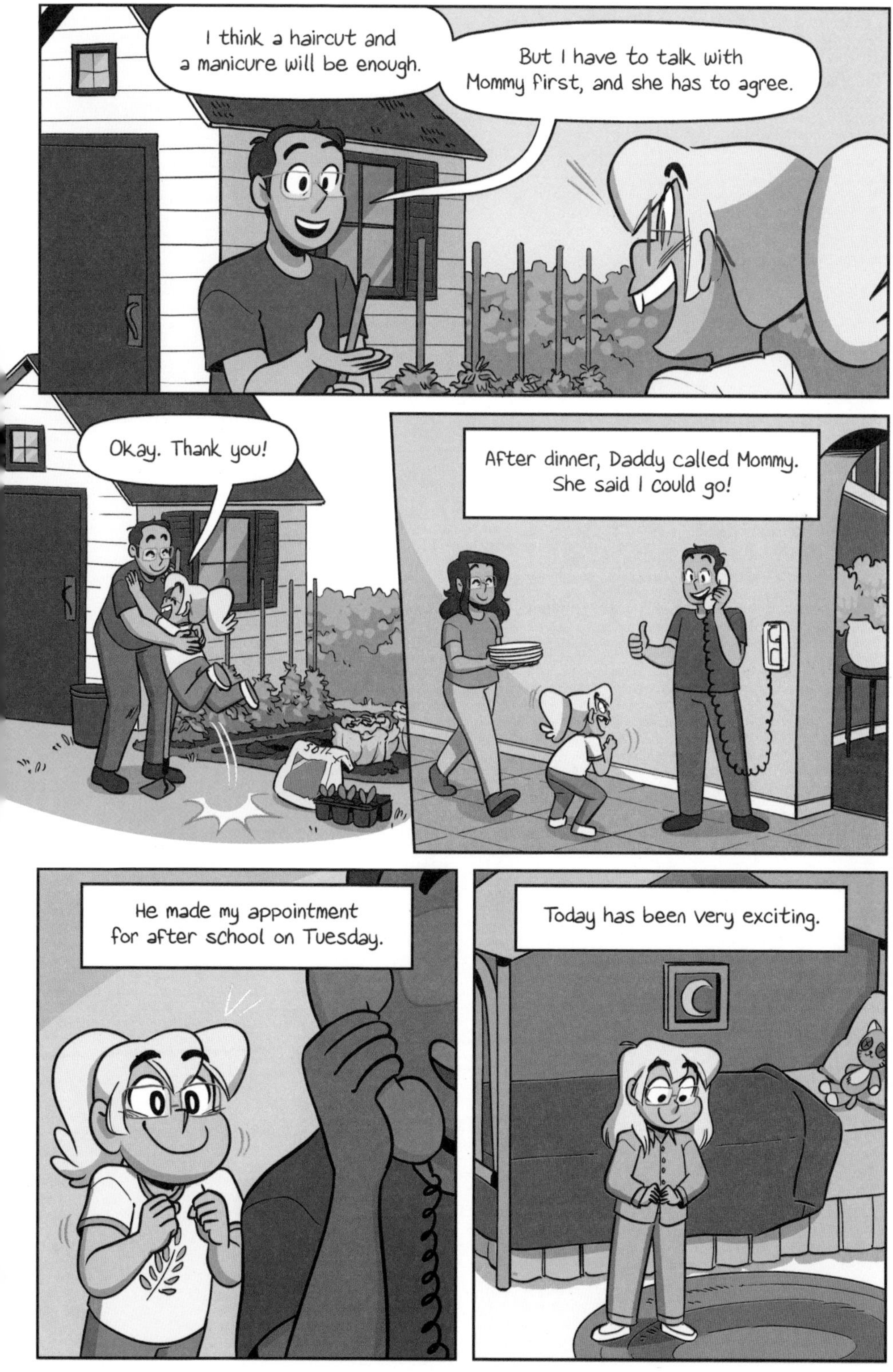
I think a haircut and a manicure will be enough.
But I have to talk with Mommy first, and she has to agree.
Okay. Thank you!
SOIL
After dinner, Daddy called Mommy. She said I could go!
He made my appointment for after school on Tuesday.
Today has been very exciting.

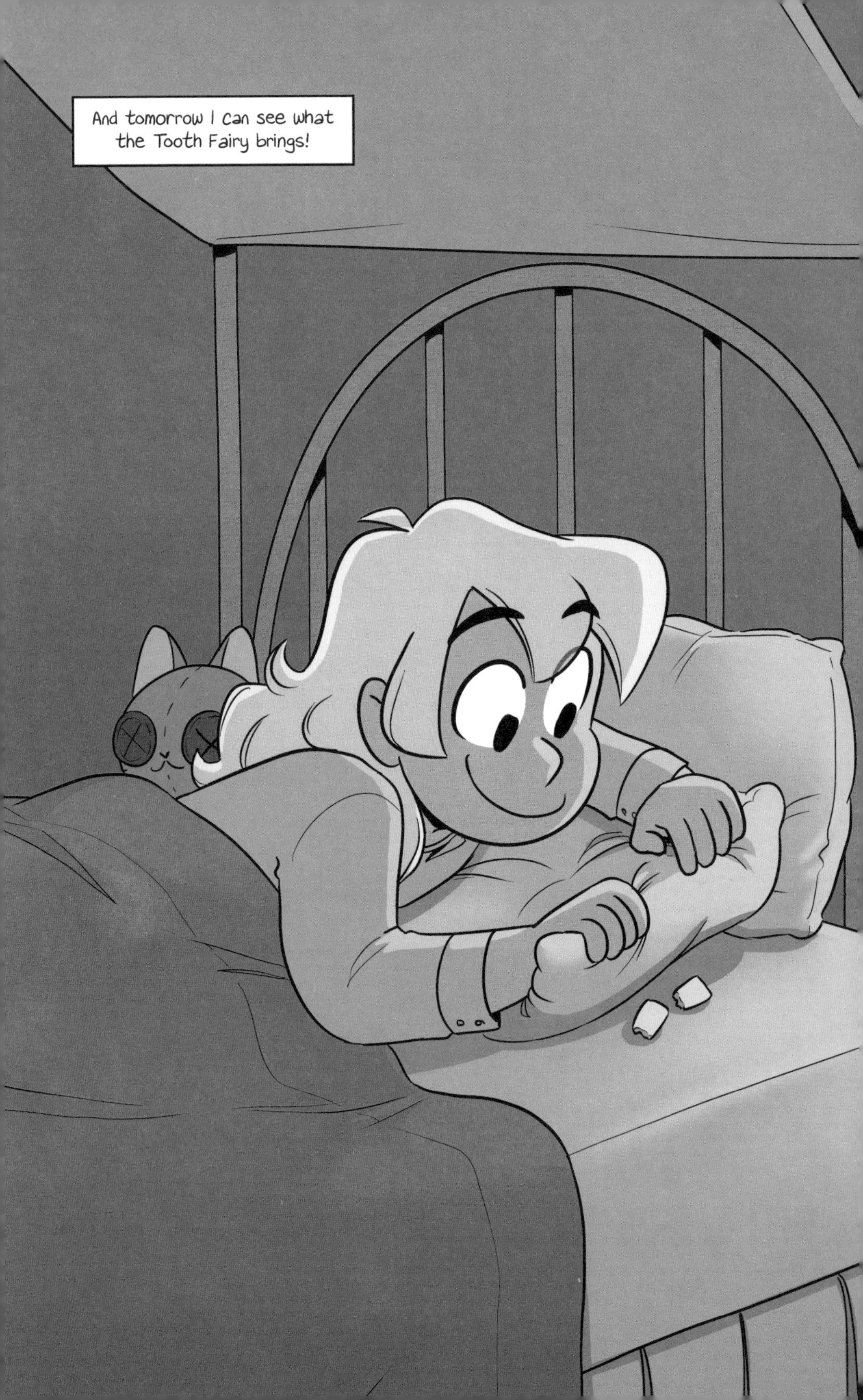
And tomorrow I can see what the Tooth Fairy brings!

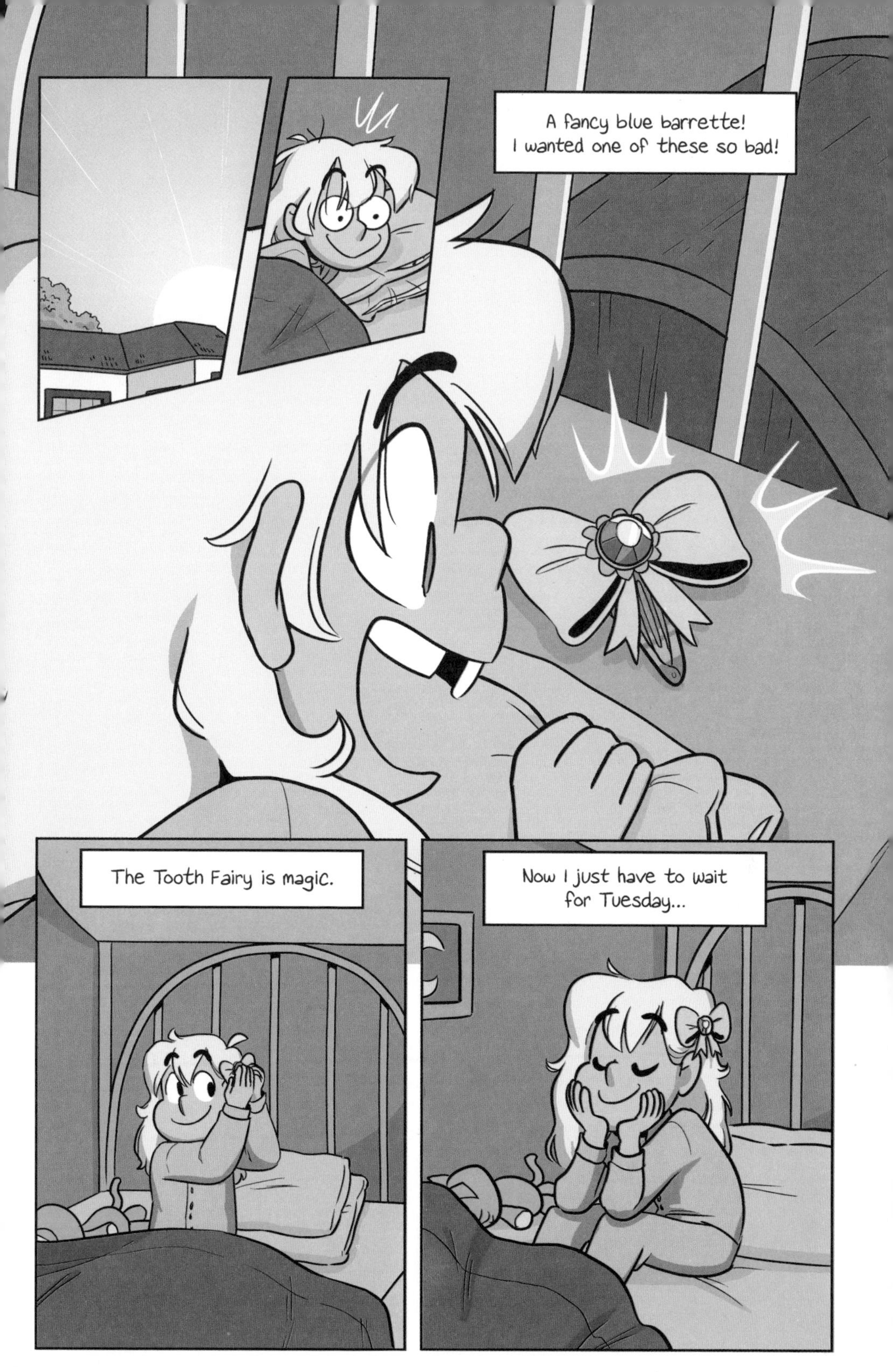
A fancy blue barrette!
I wanted one of these so bad!
The Tooth Fairy is magic.
Now I just have to wait
for Tuesday...

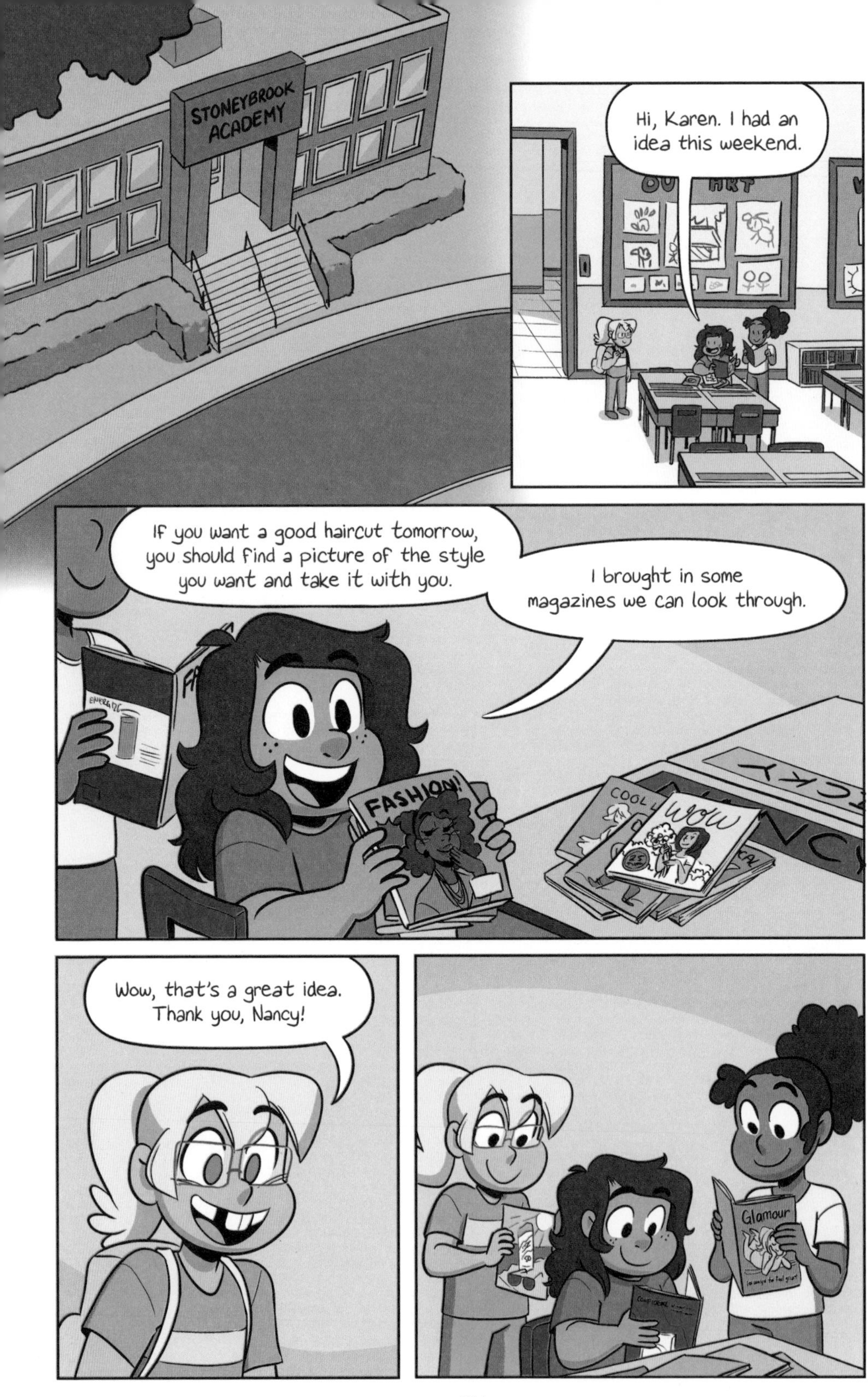
STONEYBROOK ACADEMY
Hi, Karen. I had an idea this weekend.
If you want a good haircut tomorrow, you should find a picture of the style you want and take it with you.
I brought in some magazines we can look through.
FASHION!
COOL
WOW
Wow, that's a great idea. Thank you, Nancy!
Glamour

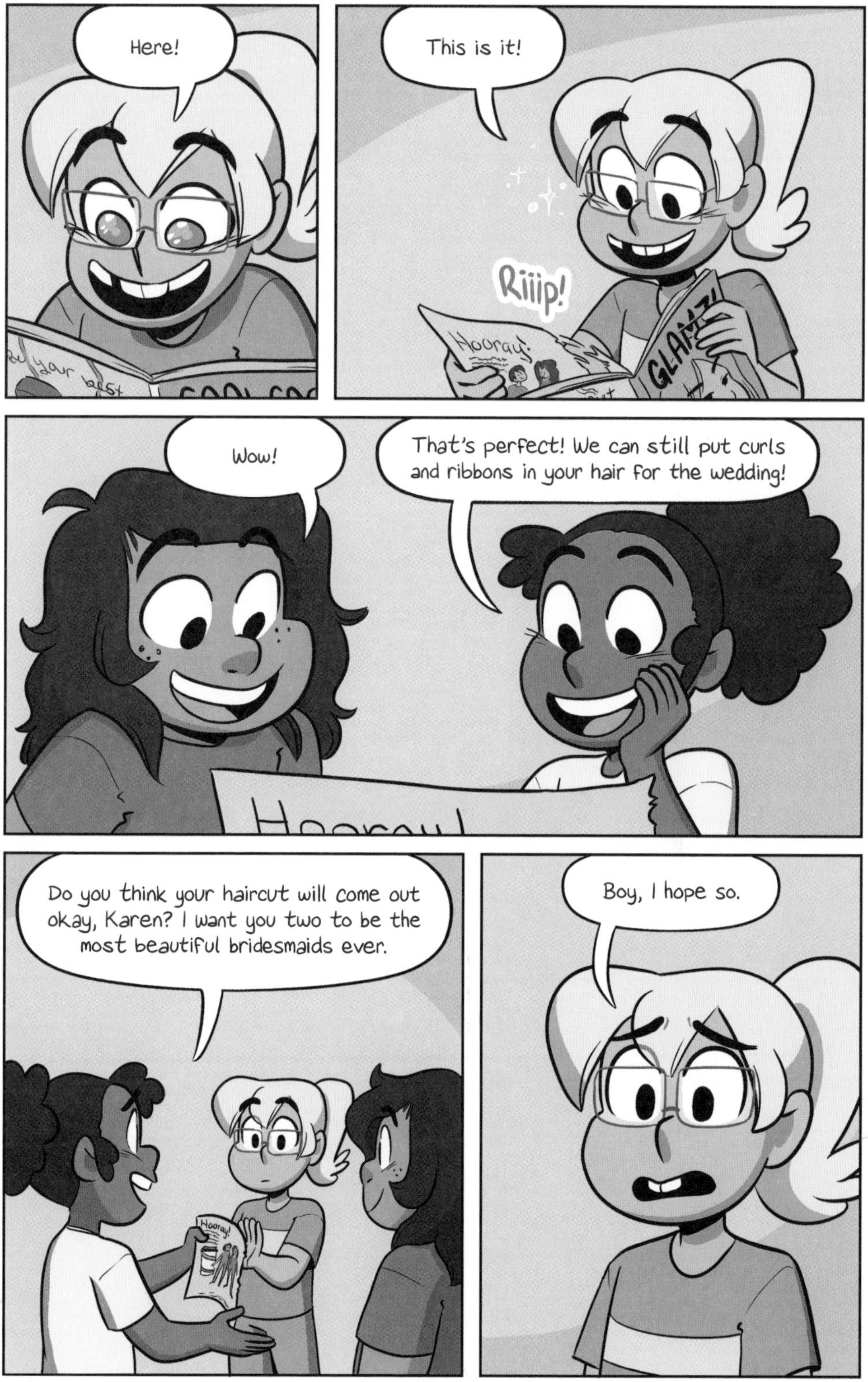
Here!
This is it!
Riiip!
Hooray!
Wow!
That's perfect! We can still put curls and ribbons in your hair for the wedding!
Do you think your haircut will come out okay, Karen? I want you two to be the most beautiful bridesmaids ever.
Boy, I hope so.

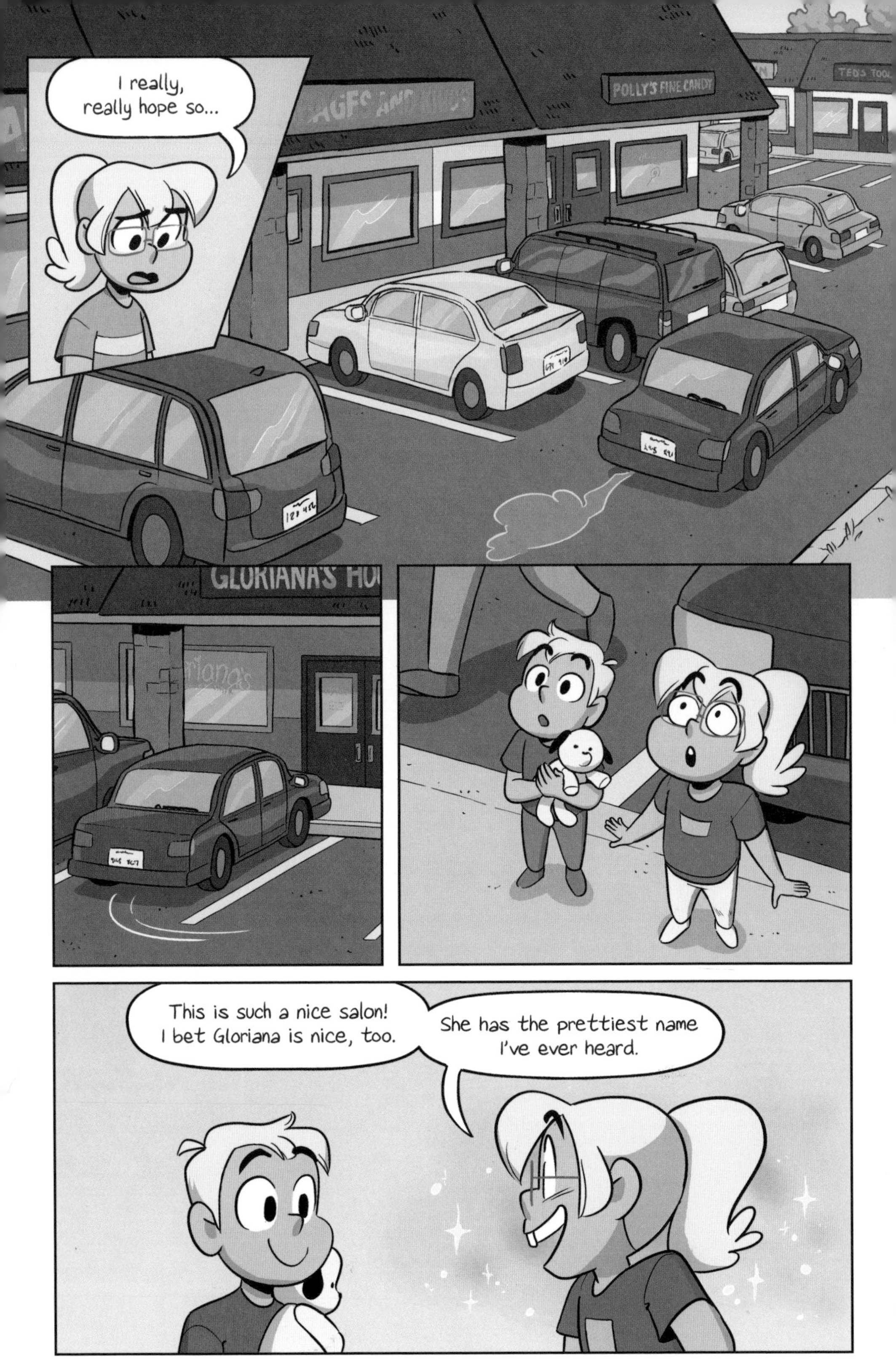
I really,
really hope so...
POLLY'S FINE CANDY
TED'S TOOL
GLORIANA'S HO
This is such a nice salon!
I bet Gloriana is nice, too.
She has the prettiest name
I've ever heard.

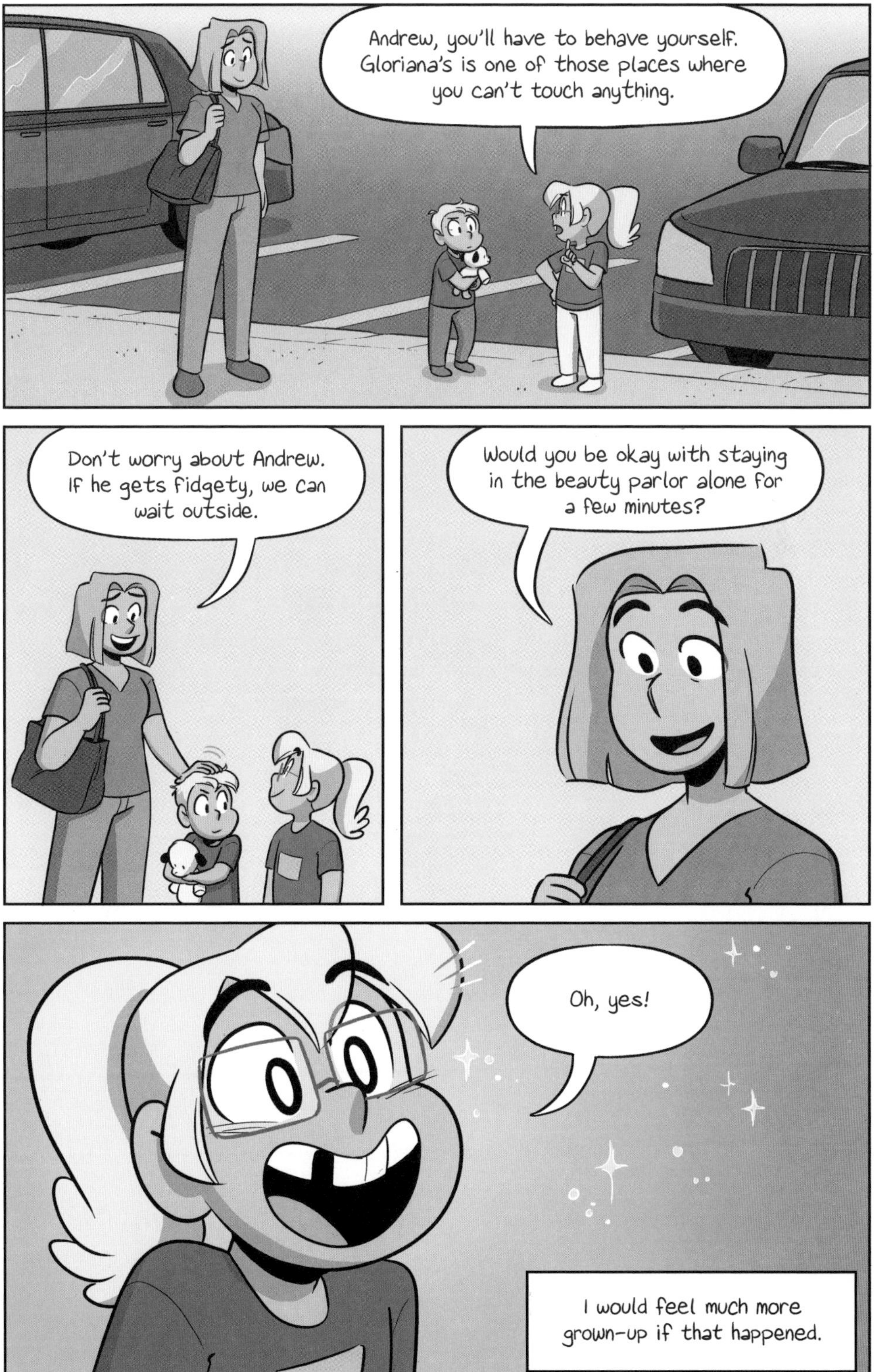
Andrew, you'll have to behave yourself. Gloriana's is one of those places where you can't touch anything.
Don't worry about Andrew. If he gets fidgety, we can wait outside.
Would you be okay with staying in the beauty parlor alone for a few minutes?
Oh, yes!
I would feel much more grown-up if that happened.

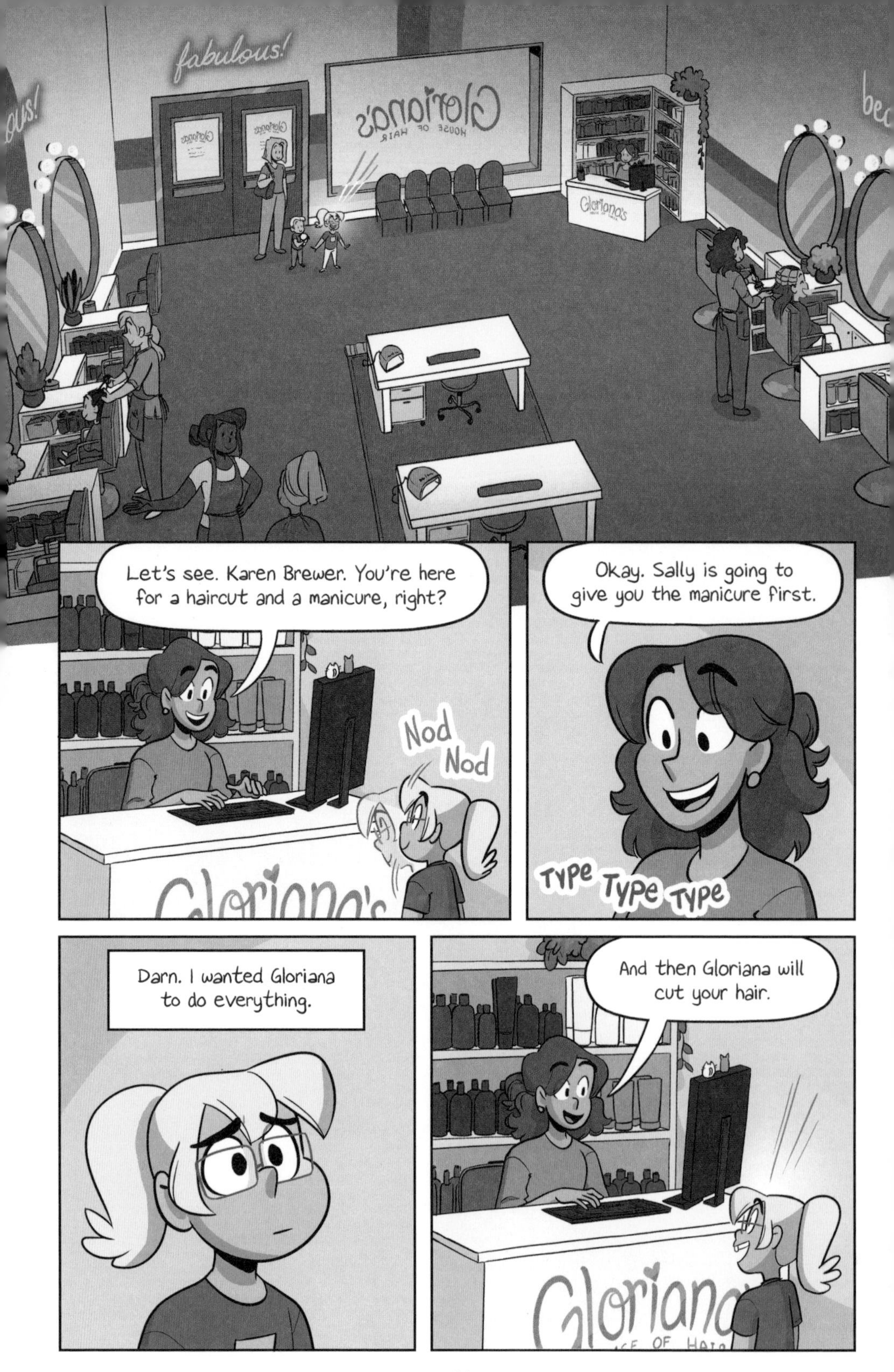
fabulous!
Gloriana's
HOUSE OF HAIR
Let's see. Karen Brewer. You're here for a haircut and a manicure, right?
Nod Nod
Okay. Sally is going to give you the manicure first.
TYPE TYPE TYPE
Darn. I wanted Gloriana to do everything.
And then Gloriana will cut your hair.

Goody!

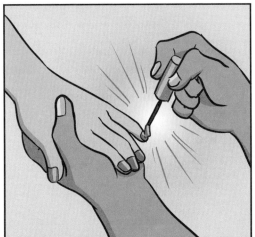

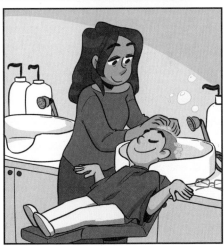

Hello, I'm Gloriana. Are you ready for your haircut?

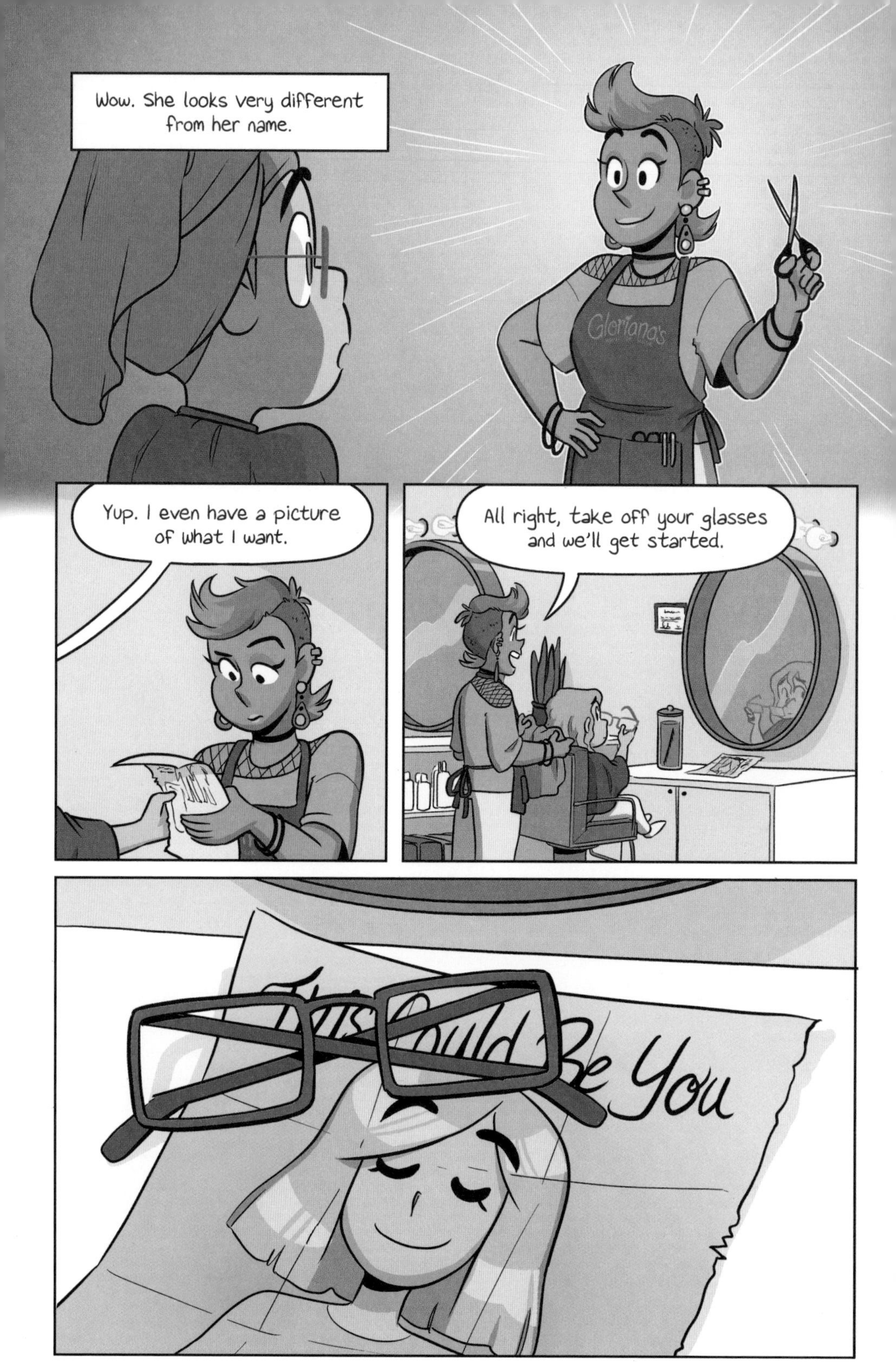

Wow. She looks very different from her name.
Gloriana's
Yup. I even have a picture of what I want.
All right, take off your glasses and we'll get started.
Be You

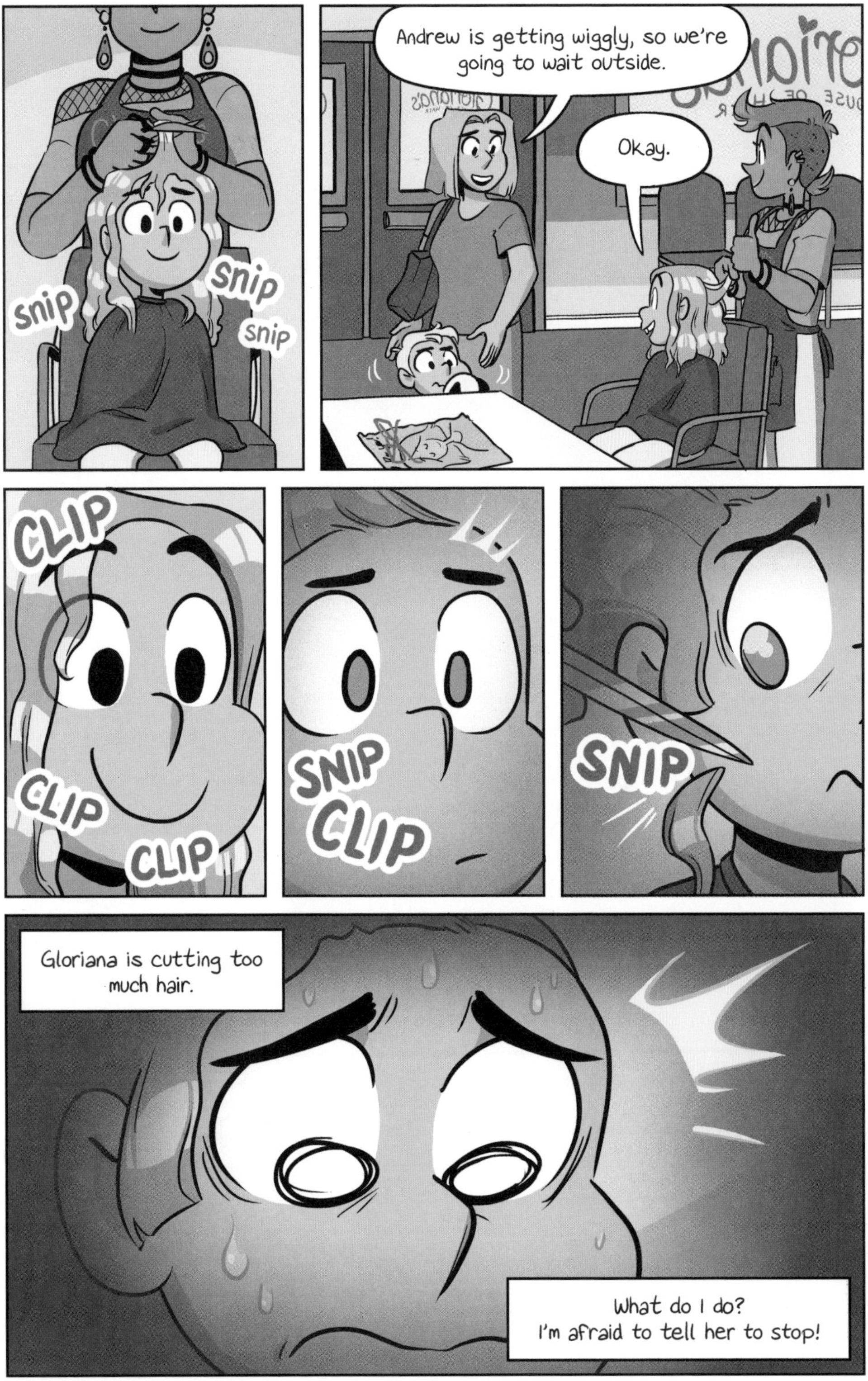
snip
snip
snip
Andrew is getting wiggly, so we're going to wait outside.
Okay.
CLIP
CLIP
CLIP
SNIP
CLIP
SNIP
Gloriana is cutting too much hair.
What do I do?
I'm afraid to tell her to stop!

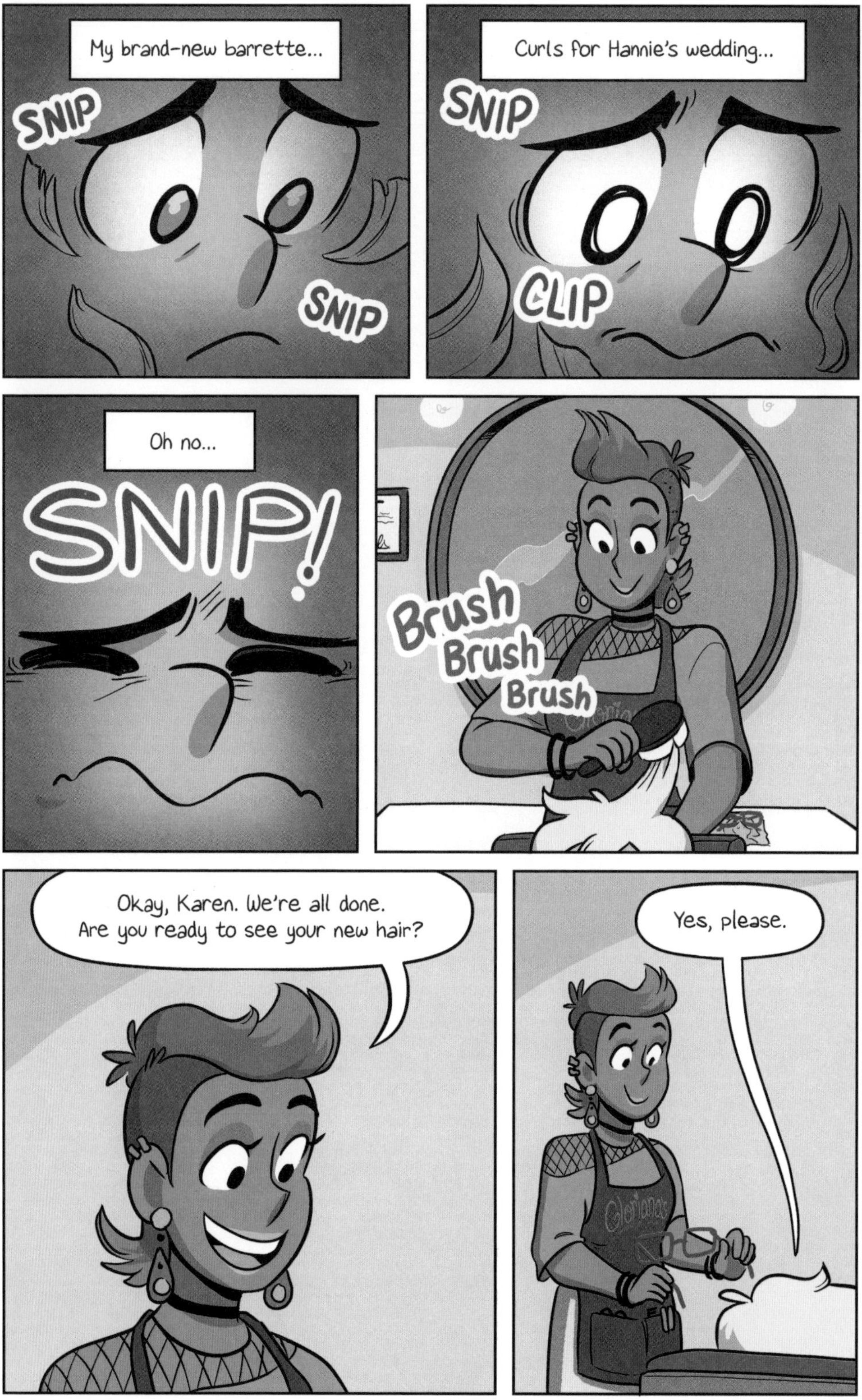
My brand-new barrette...
SNIP
SNIP
Curls for Hannie's wedding...
SNIP
CLIP
Oh no...
SNIP!
Brush
Brush
Brush
Okay, Karen. We're all done.
Are you ready to see your new hair?
Yes, please.

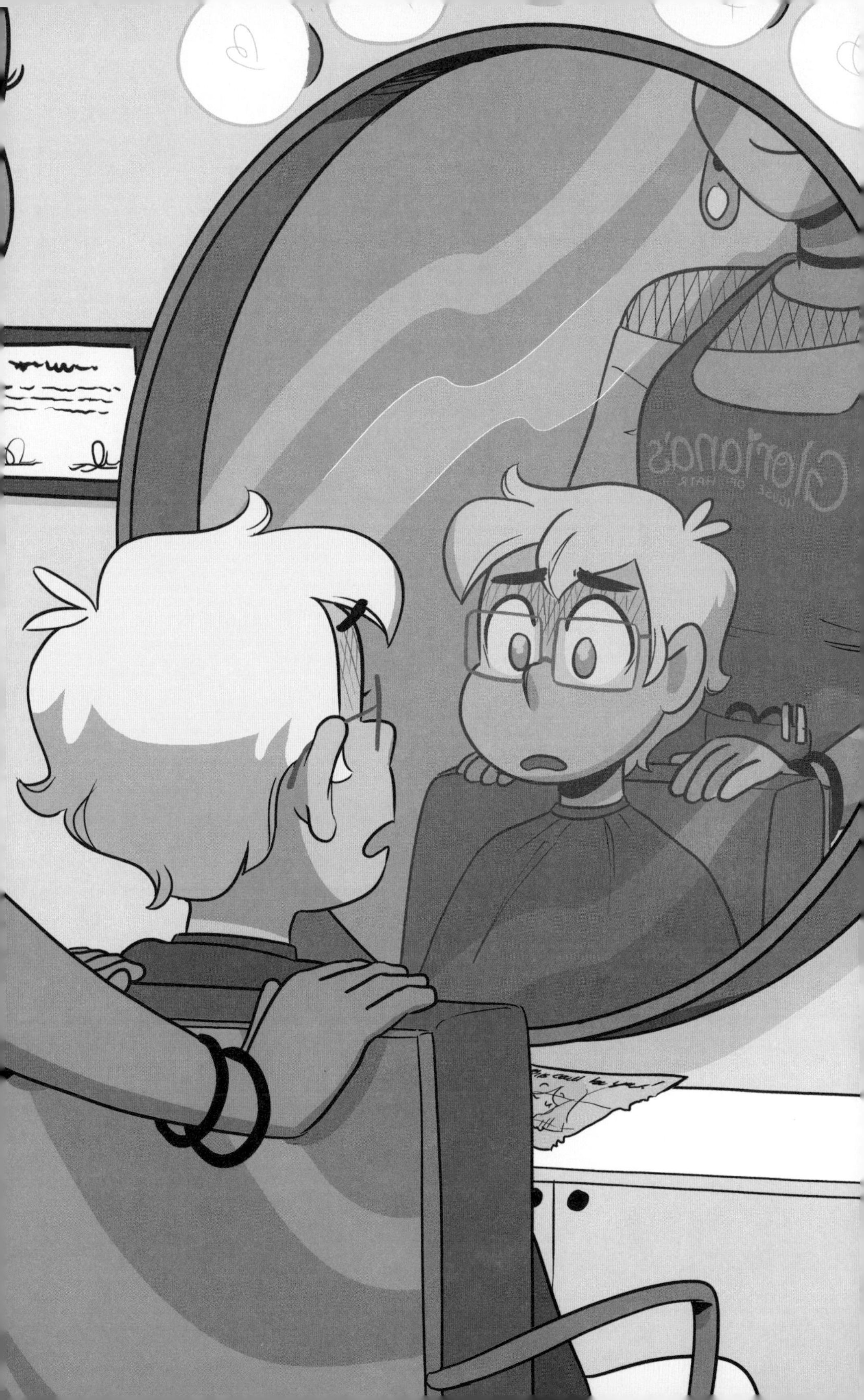

CHAPTER 5

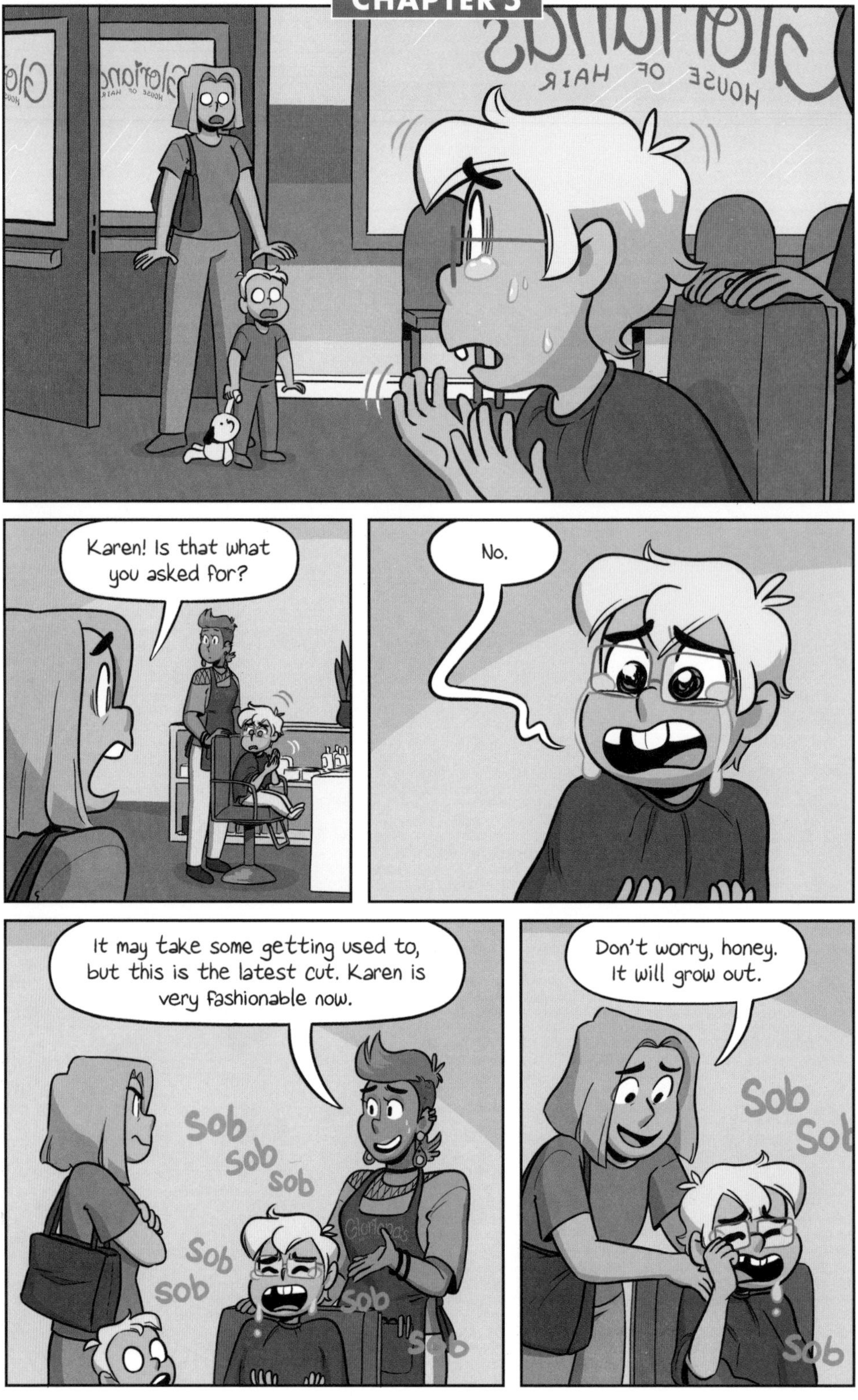
Karen! Is that what you asked for?
No.
It may take some getting used to, but this is the latest cut. Karen is very fashionable now.
sob sob sob
sob sob
Don't worry, honey. It will grow out.
Sob

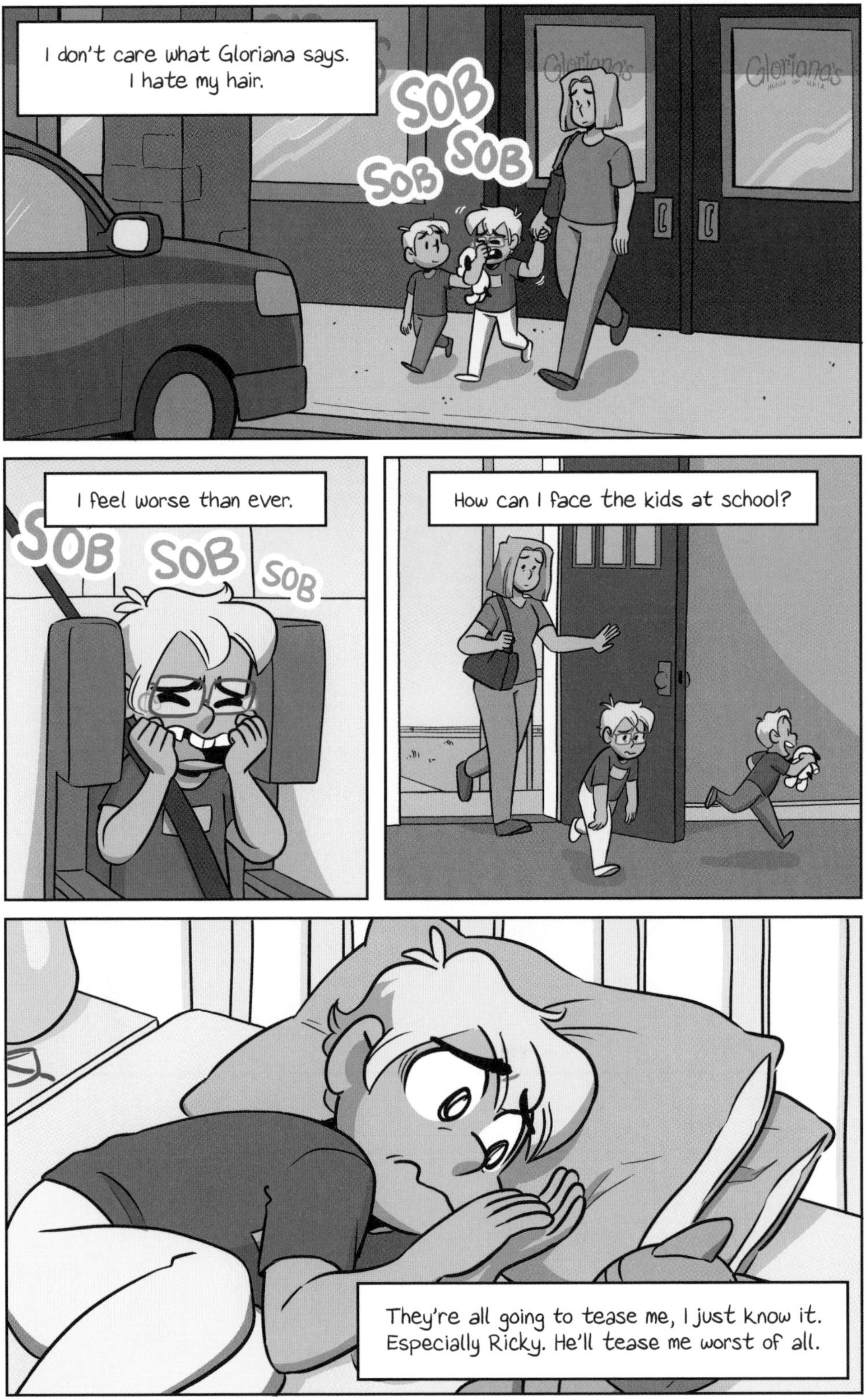
I don't care what Gloriana says.
I hate my hair.
Gloriana's
Gloriana's
SOB
SOB
SOB
I feel worse than ever.
SOB
SOB
SOB
How can I face the kids at school?
They're all going to tease me, I just know it.
Especially Ricky. He'll tease me worst of all.

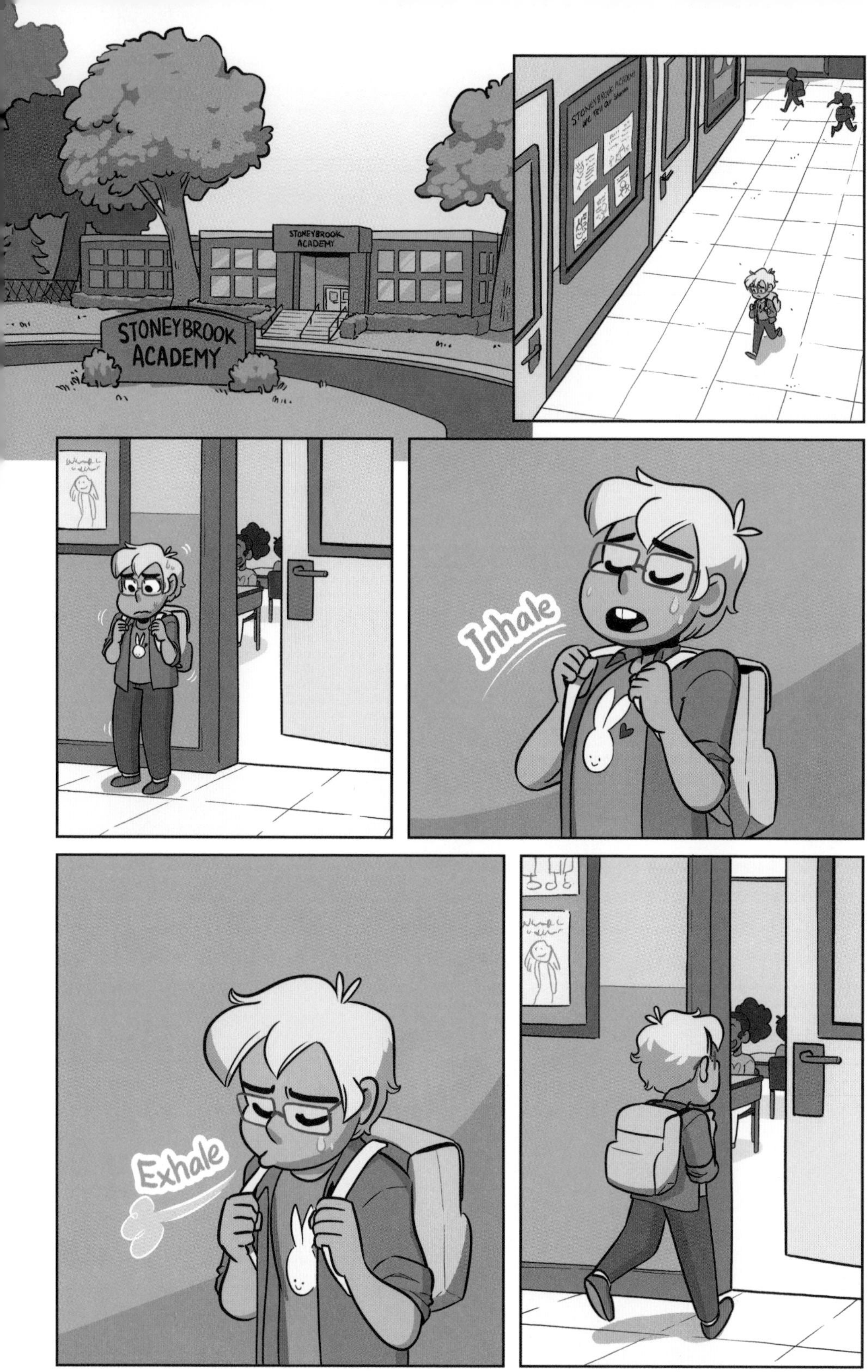
STONEYBROOK ACADEMY
STONEYBROOK ACADEMY
Inhale
Exhale

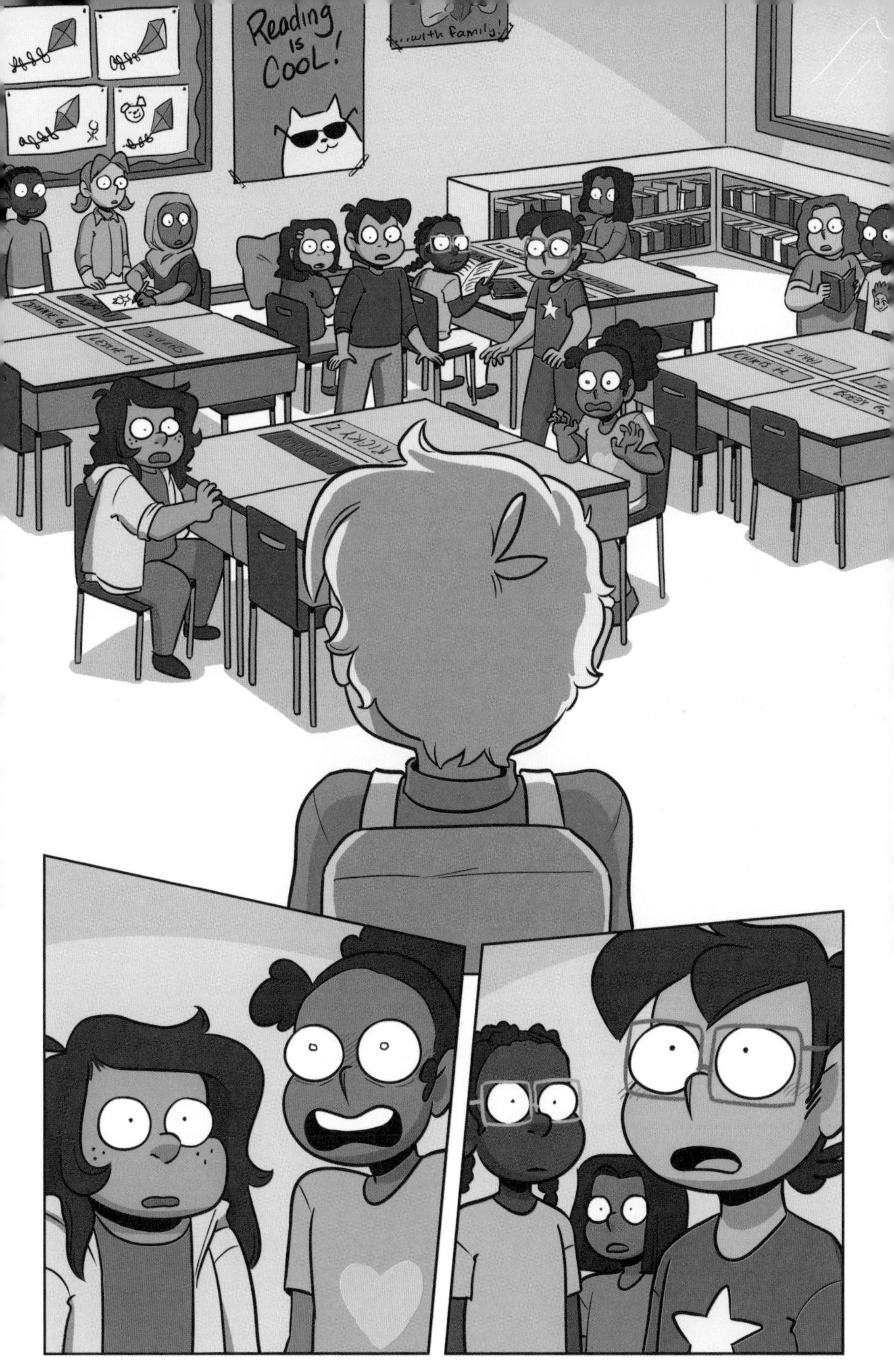
...with family!
Reading is Cool!
CHRIS H.

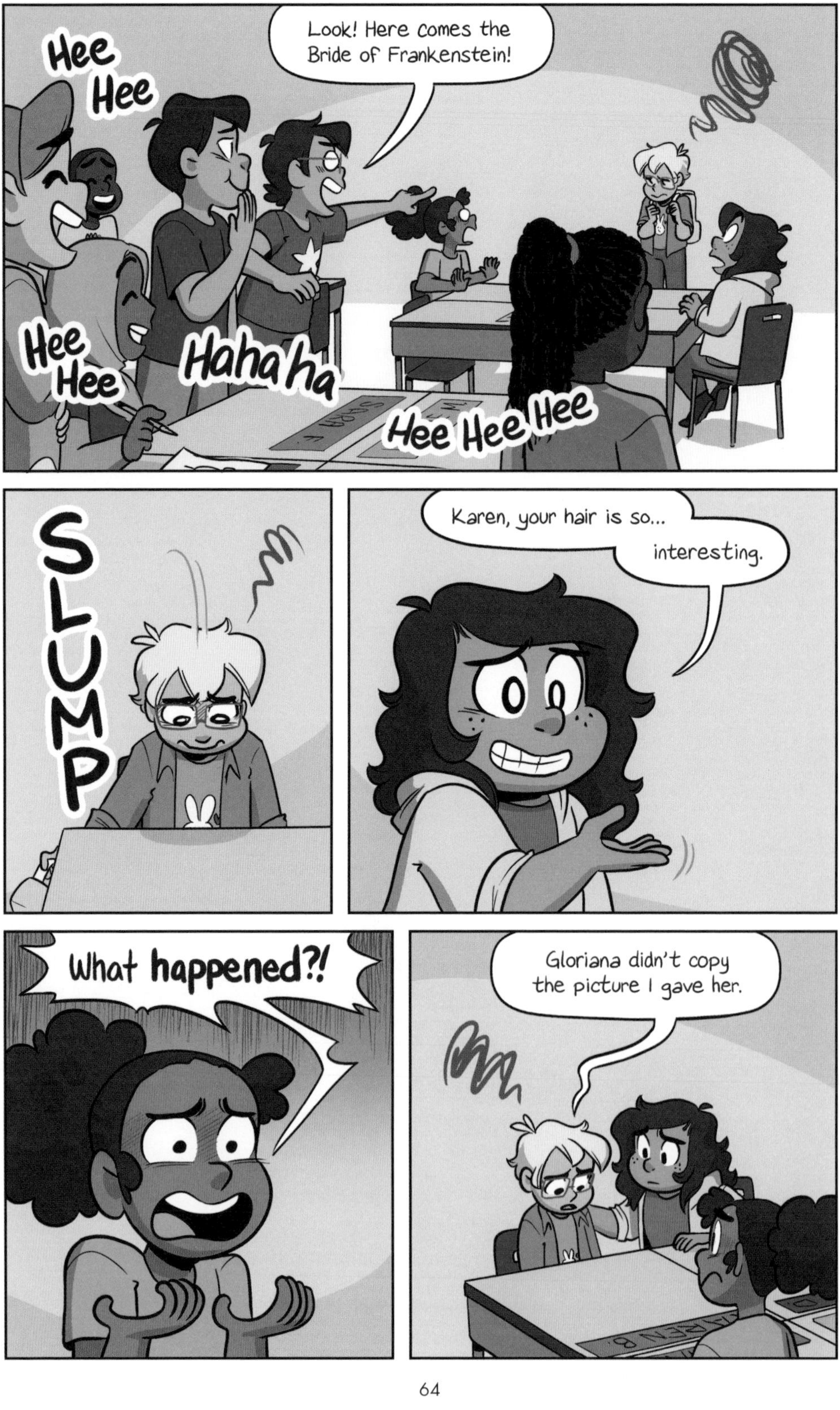
Hee Hee
Look! Here comes the Bride of Frankenstein!
Hee Hee
Hahaha
Hee Hee Hee
SLUMP
Karen, your hair is so...
interesting.
What happened?!
Gloriana didn't copy the picture I gave her.

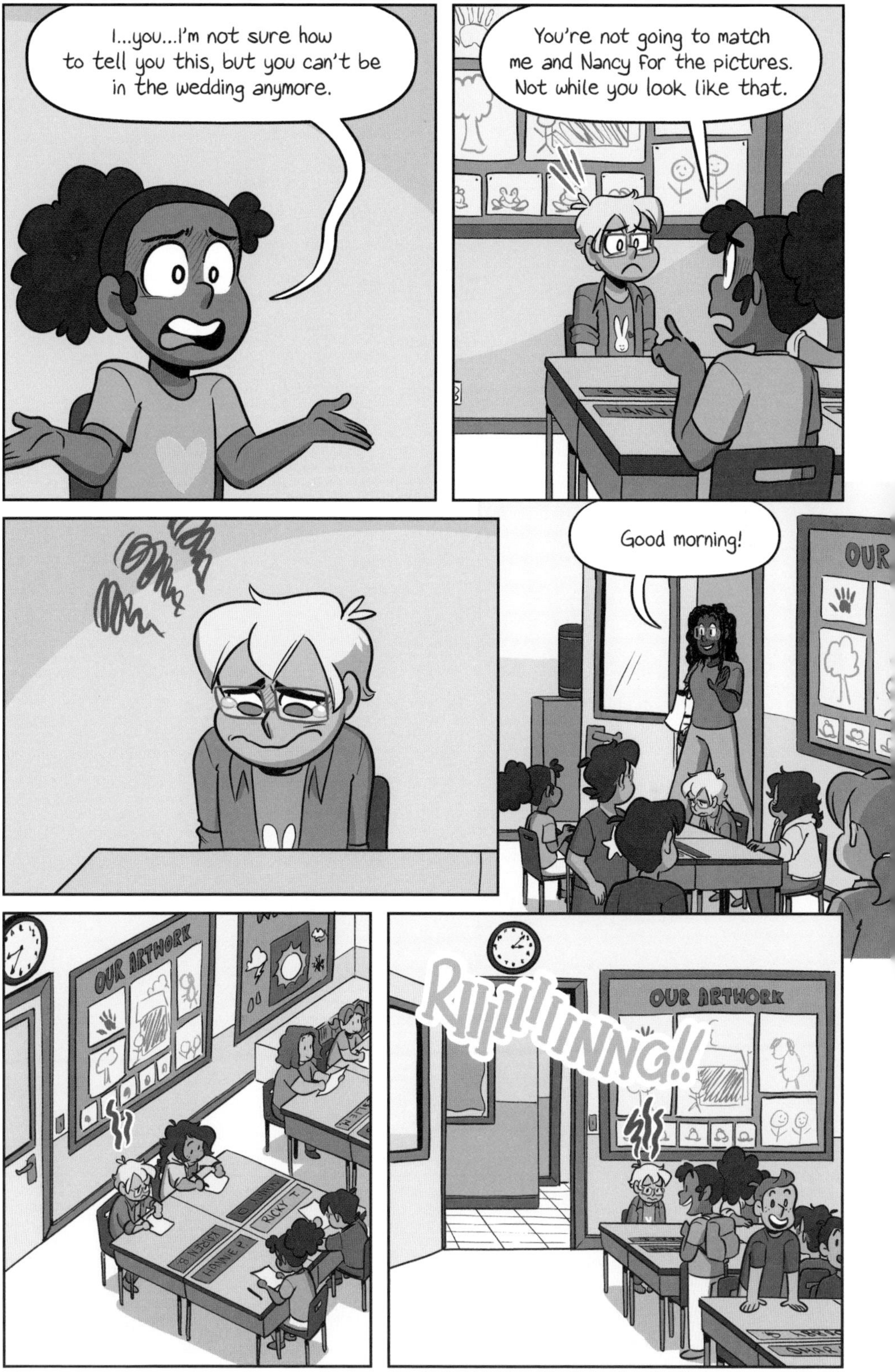
I...you...I'm not sure how to tell you this, but you can't be in the wedding anymore.
You're not going to match me and Nancy for the pictures. Not while you look like that.
Good morning!
OUR ARTWORK
RIIIIIIINNG!!
OUR ARTWORK

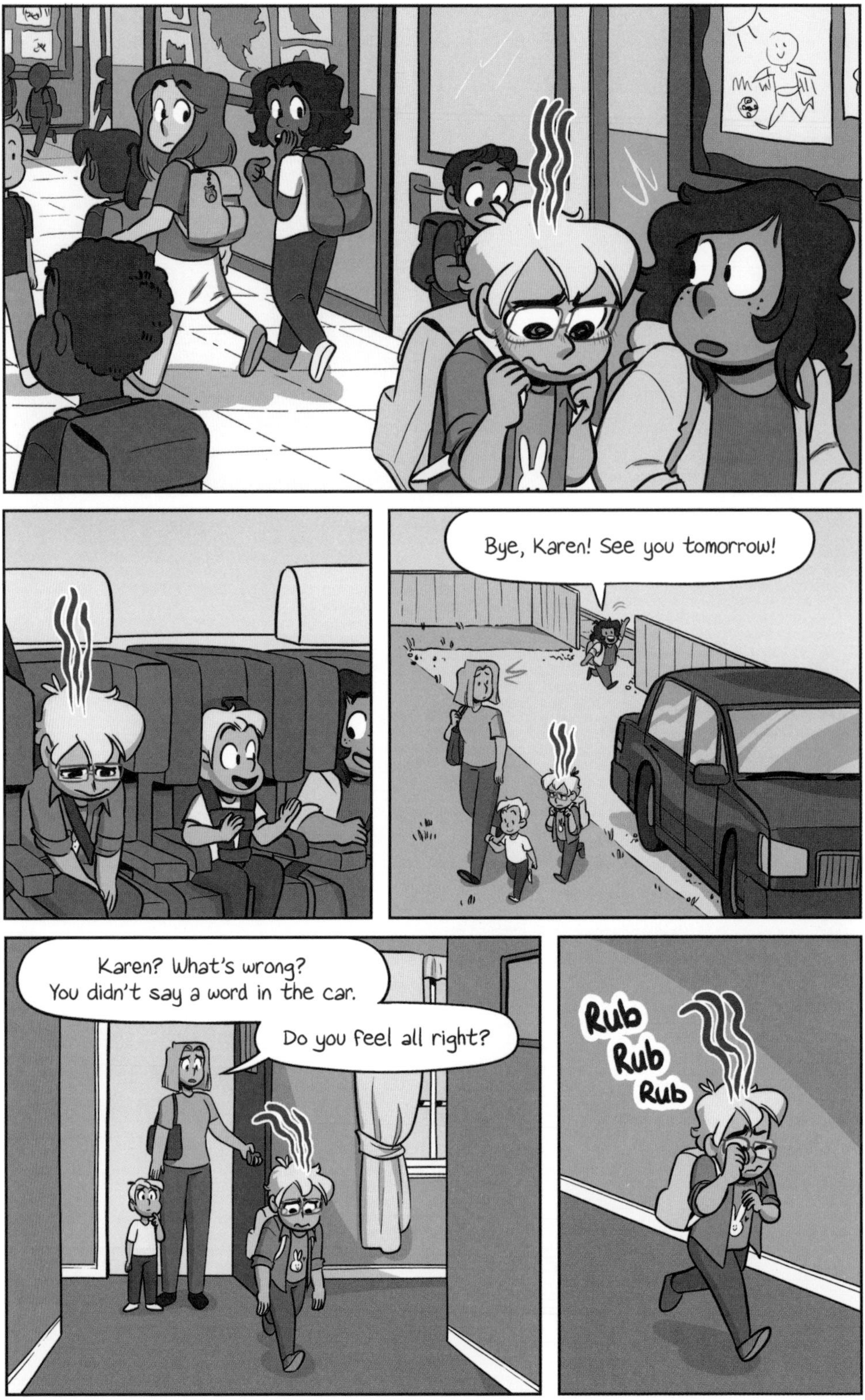
Bye, Karen! See you tomorrow!
Karen? What's wrong? You didn't say a word in the car.
Do you feel all right?
Rub
Rub
Rub

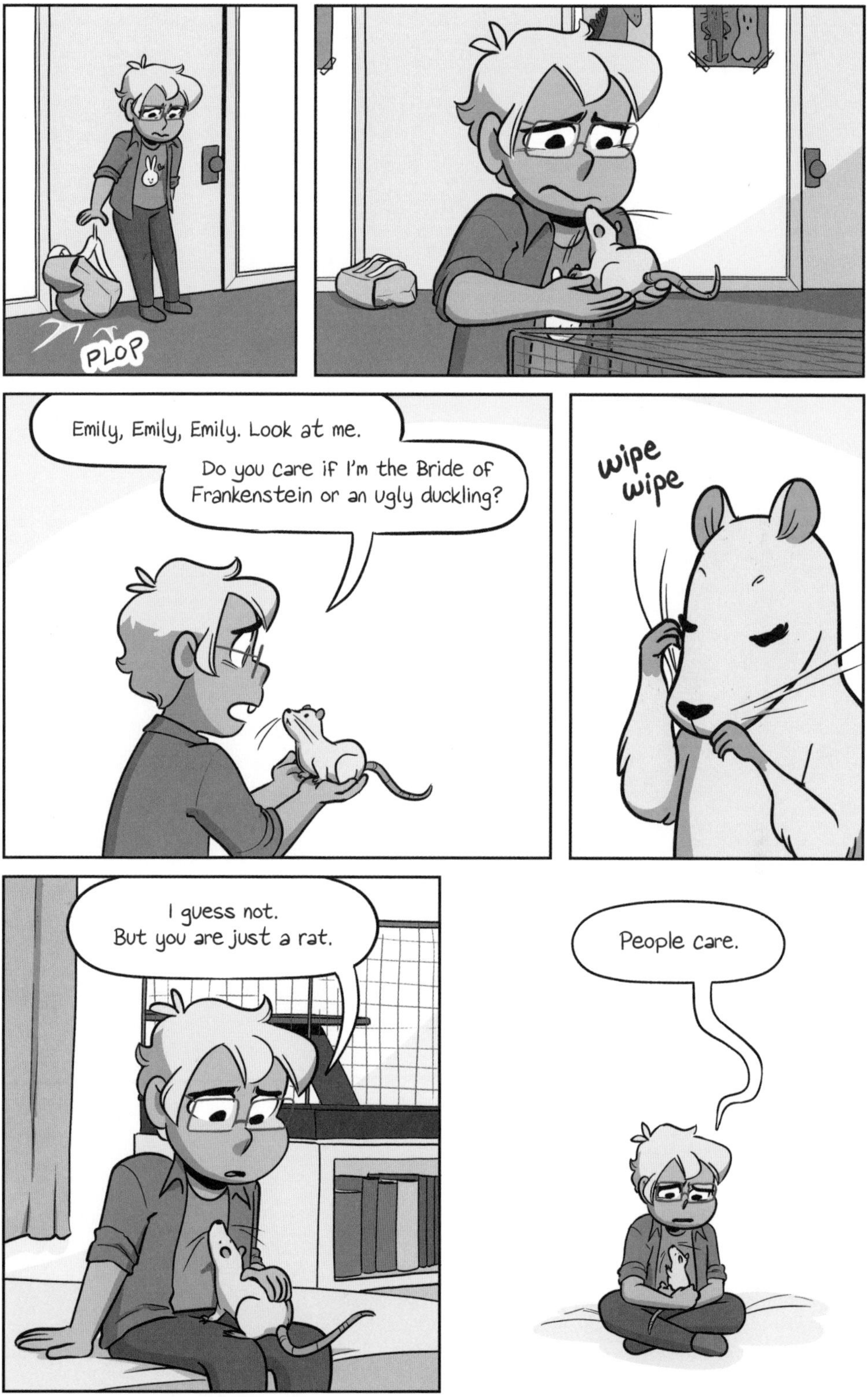
PLOP
Emily, Emily, Emily. Look at me.
Do you care if I'm the Bride of Frankenstein or an ugly duckling?
wipe wipe
I guess not. But you are just a rat.
People care.

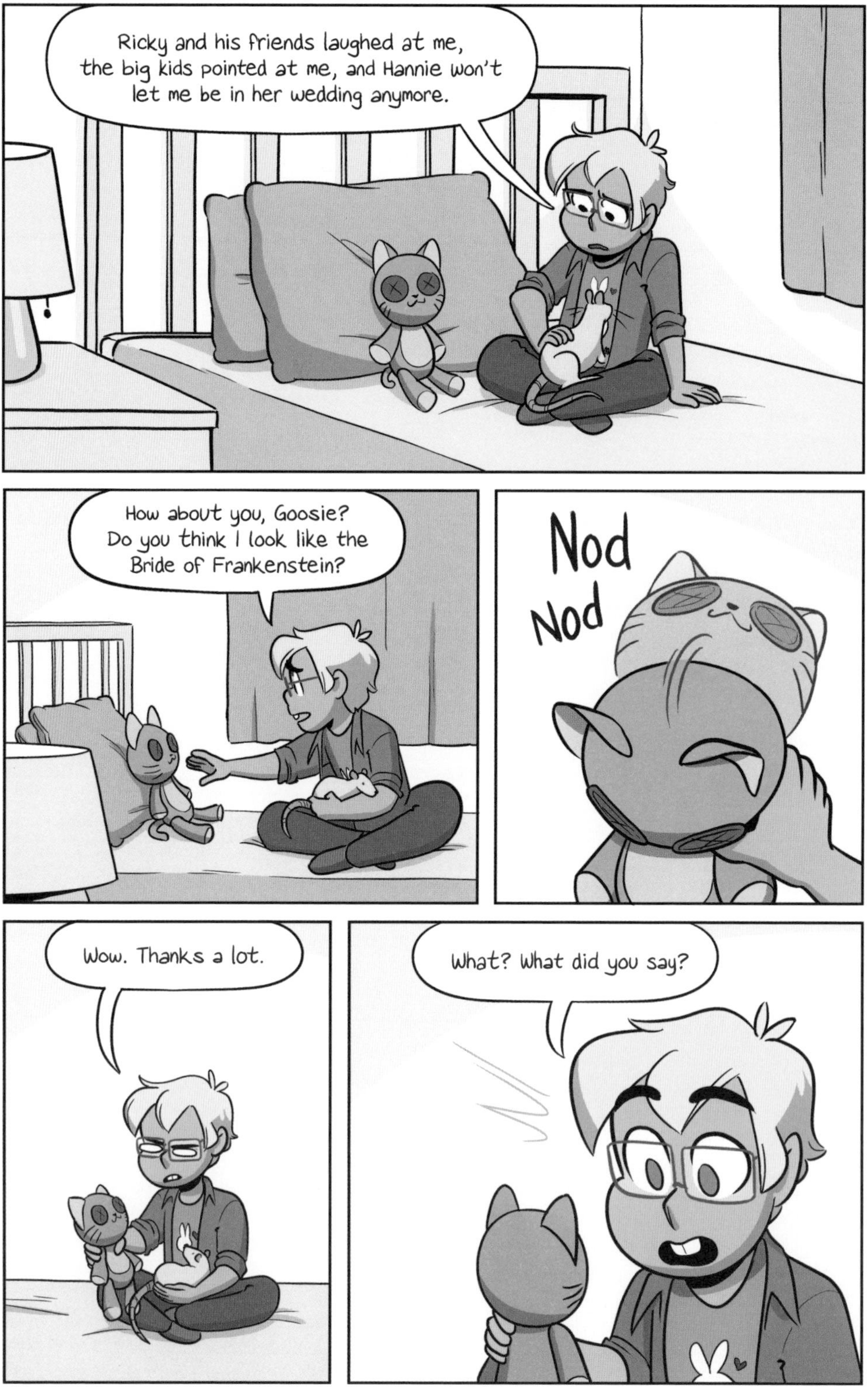
Ricky and his friends laughed at me, the big kids pointed at me, and Hannie won't let me be in her wedding anymore.
How about you, Goosie? Do you think I look like the Bride of Frankenstein?
Nod
Nod
Wow. Thanks a lot.
What? What did you say?

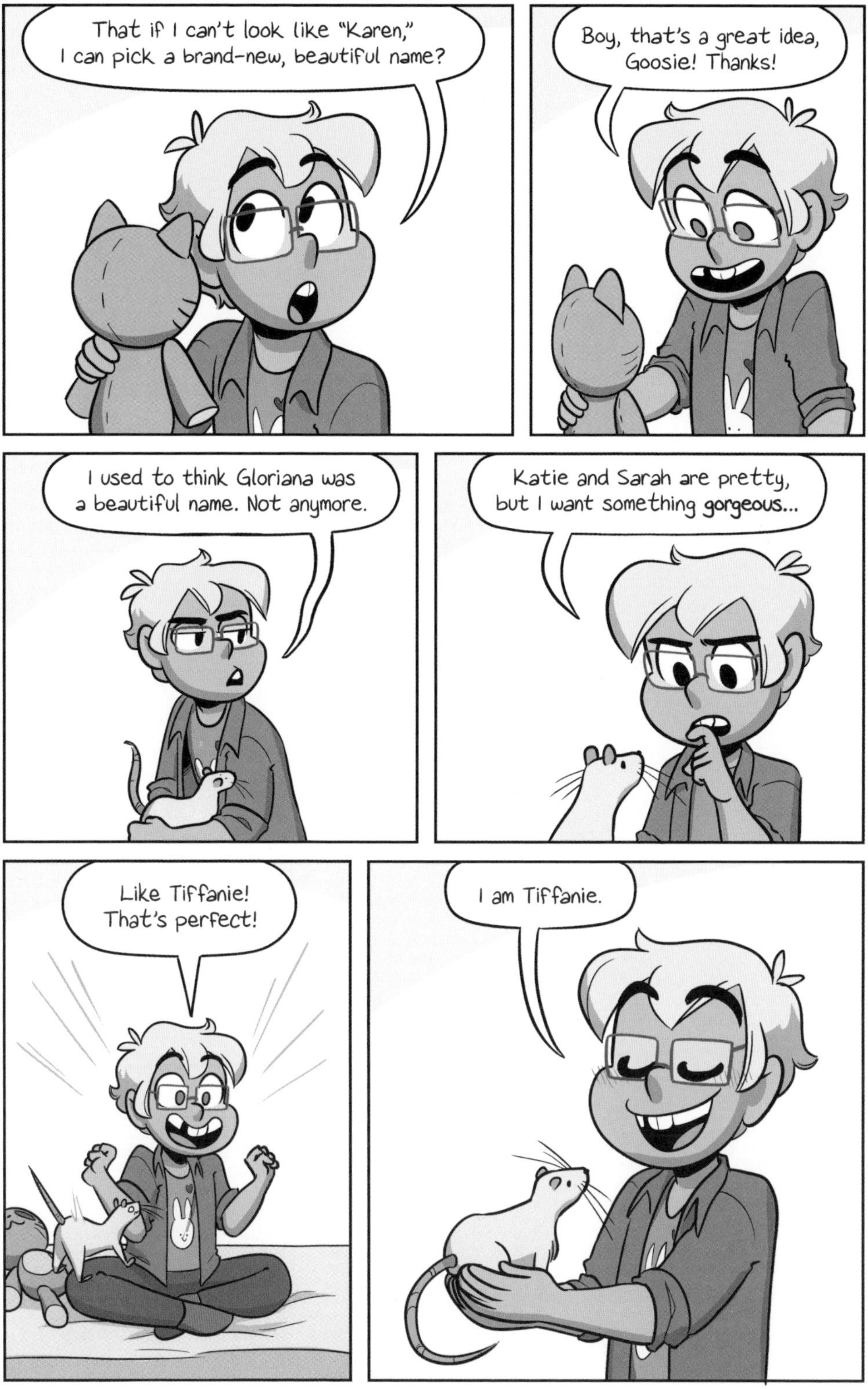
That if I can't look like "Karen," I can pick a brand-new, beautiful name?
Boy, that's a great idea, Goosie! Thanks!
I used to think Gloriana was a beautiful name. Not anymore.
Katie and Sarah are pretty, but I want something **gorgeous...**
Like Tiffanie! That's perfect!
I am Tiffanie.

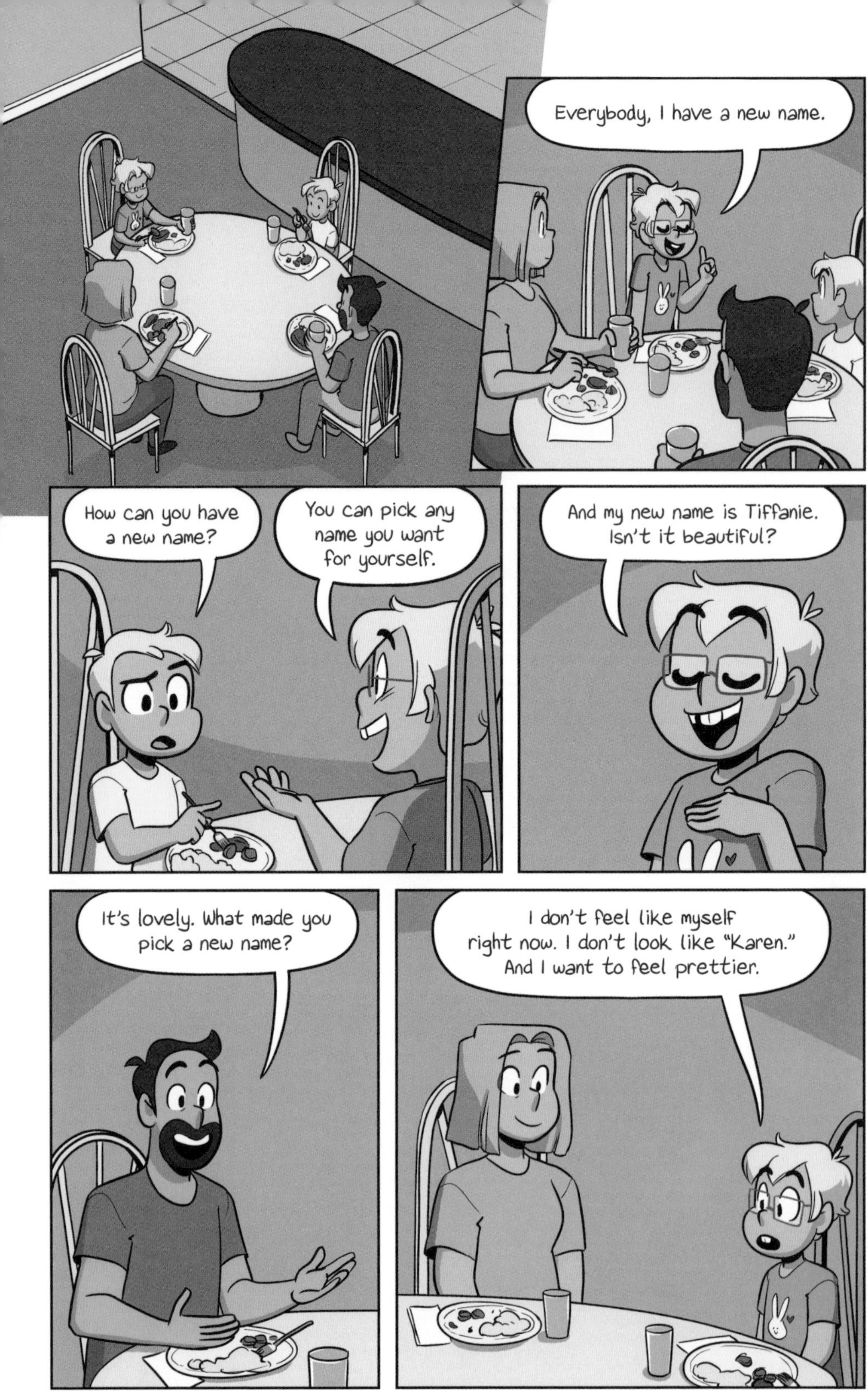
Everybody, I have a new name.
How can you have a new name?
You can pick any name you want for yourself.
And my new name is Tiffanie. Isn't it beautiful?
It's lovely. What made you pick a new name?
I don't feel like myself right now. I don't look like "Karen." And I want to feel prettier.

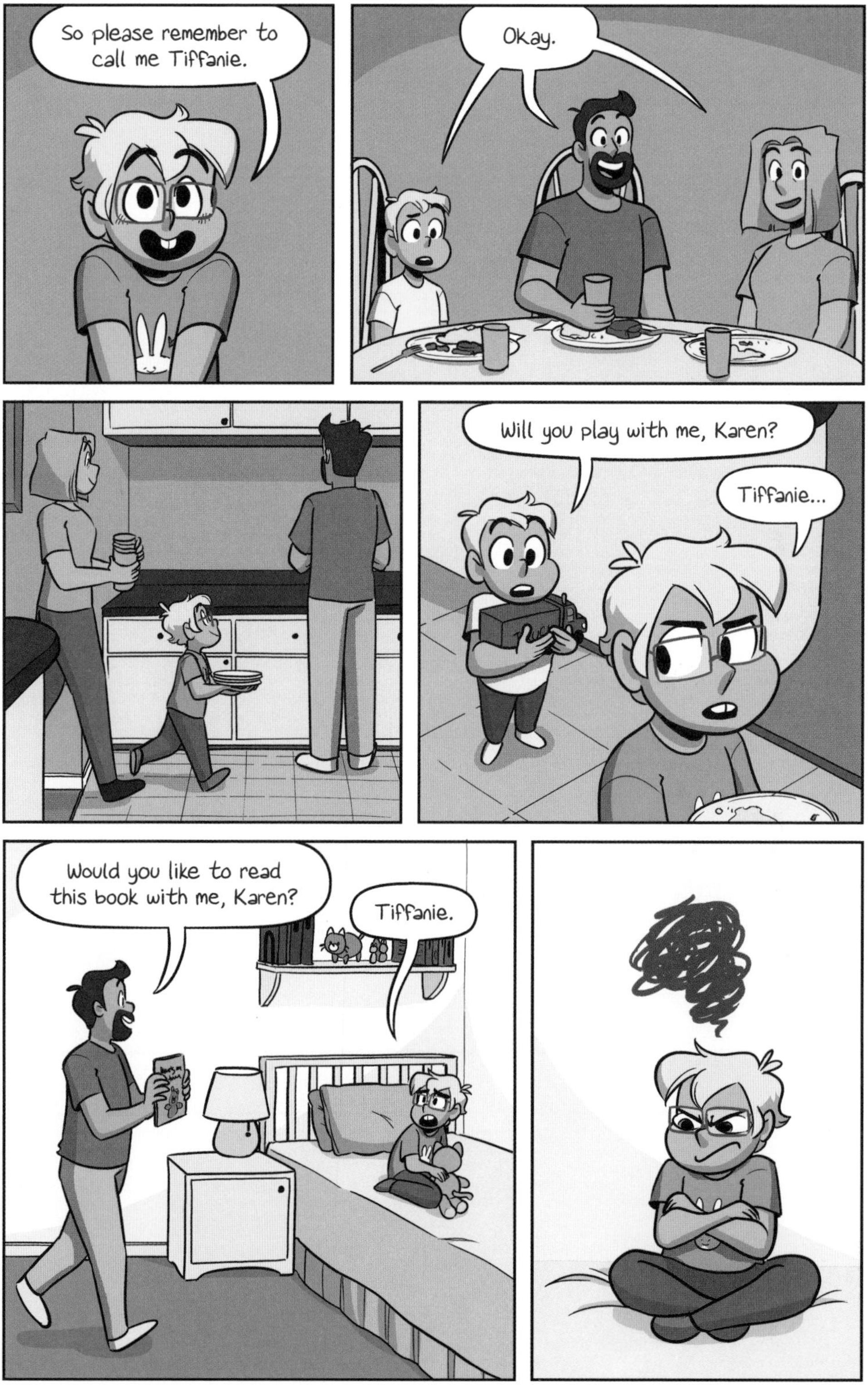
So please remember to call me Tiffanie.
Okay.
Will you play with me, Karen?
Tiffanie...
Would you like to read this book with me, Karen?
Tiffanie.

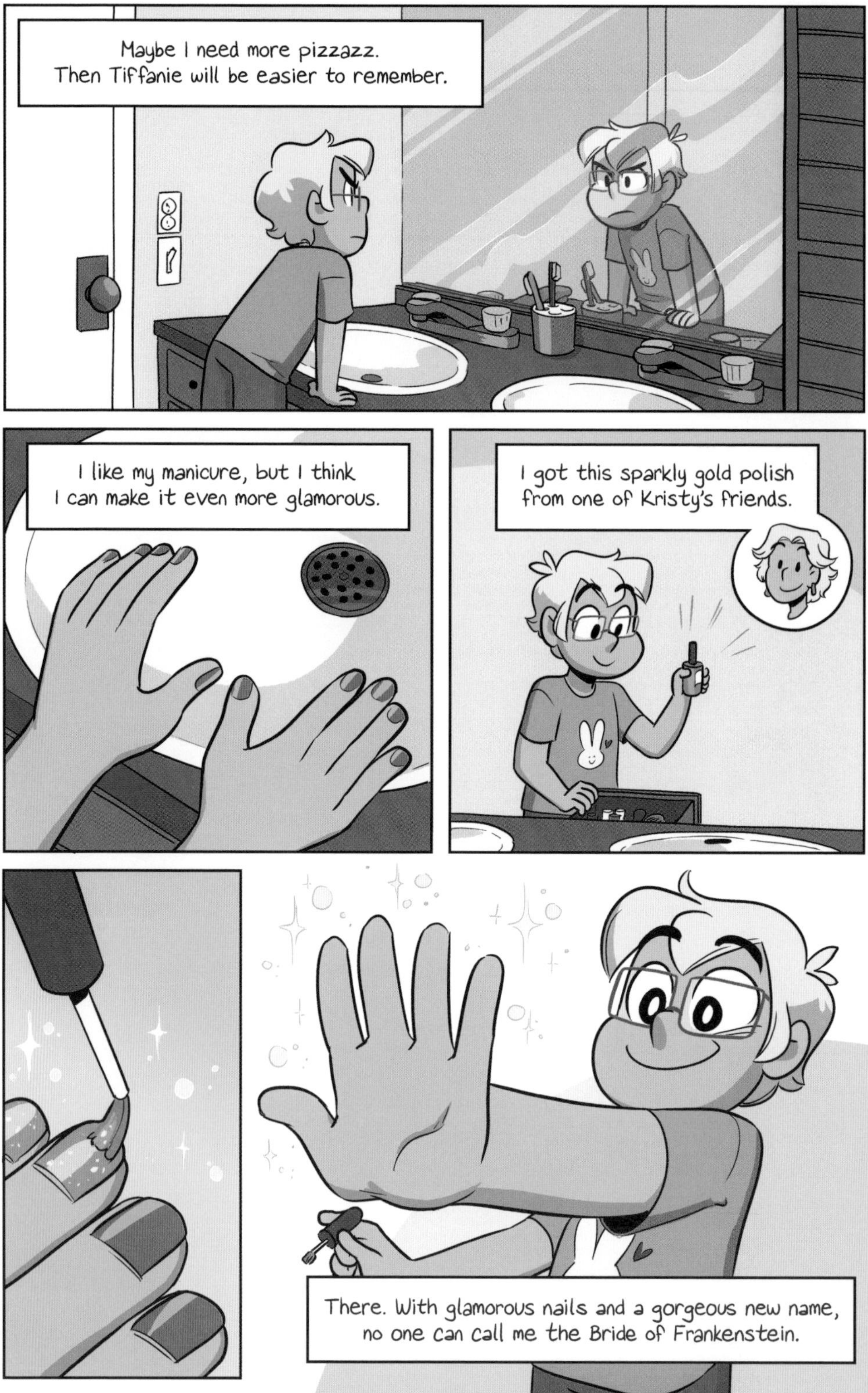
Maybe I need more pizzazz.
Then Tiffanie will be easier to remember.
I like my manicure, but I think I can make it even more glamorous.
I got this sparkly gold polish from one of Kristy's friends.
There. With glamorous nails and a gorgeous new name, no one can call me the Bride of Frankenstein.

CHAPTER 6

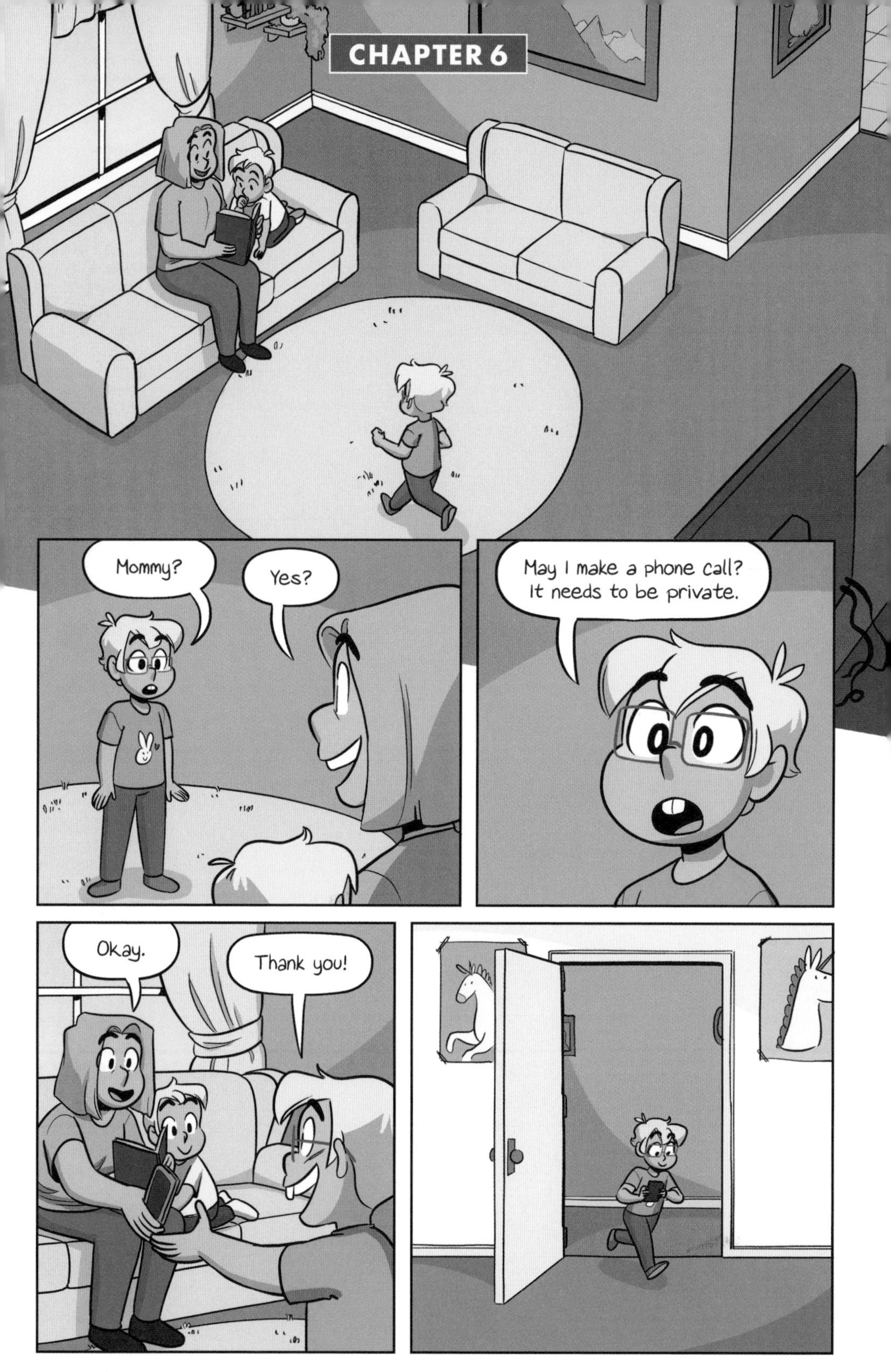
Mommy?
Yes?
May I make a phone call? It needs to be private.
Okay.
Thank you!

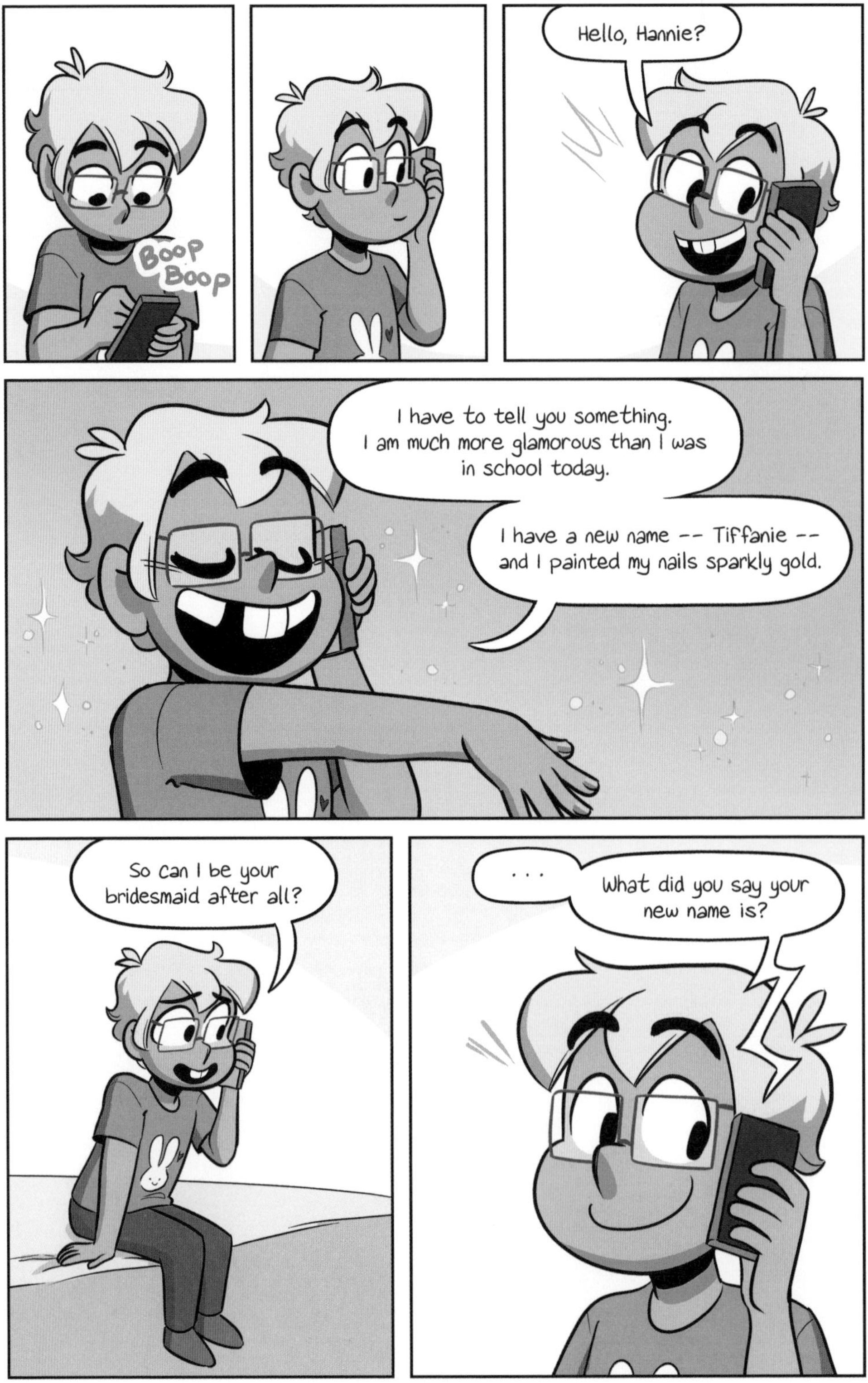

BOOP BOOP
Hello, Hannie?
I have to tell you something. I am much more glamorous than I was in school today.
I have a new name -- Tiffanie -- and I painted my nails sparkly gold.
So can I be your bridesmaid after all?
. . .
What did you say your new name is?

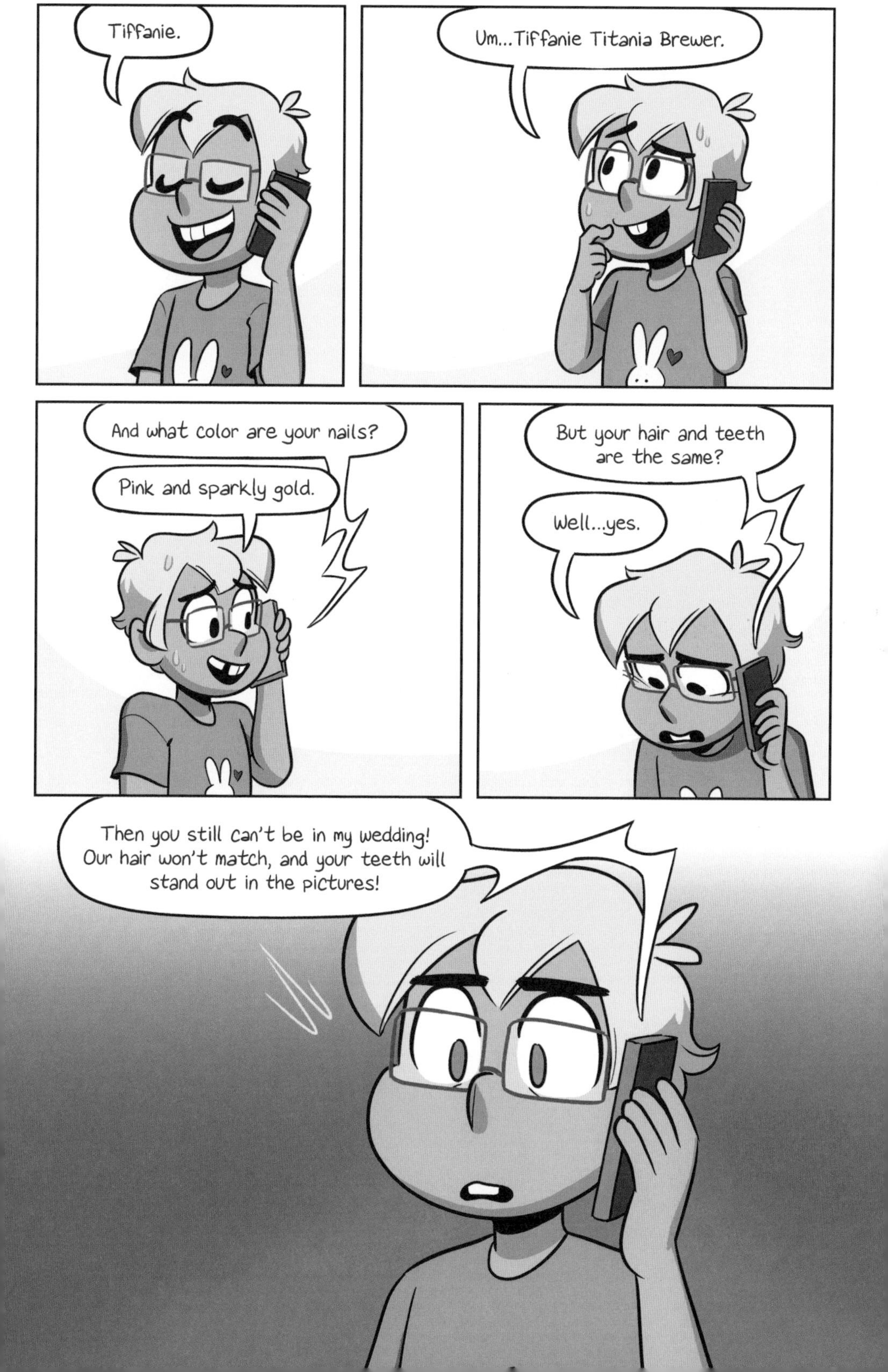
Tiffanie.
Um...Tiffanie Titania Brewer.
And what color are your nails?
Pink and sparkly gold.
But your hair and teeth are the same?
Well...yes.
Then you still can't be in my wedding! Our hair won't match, and your teeth will stand out in the pictures!

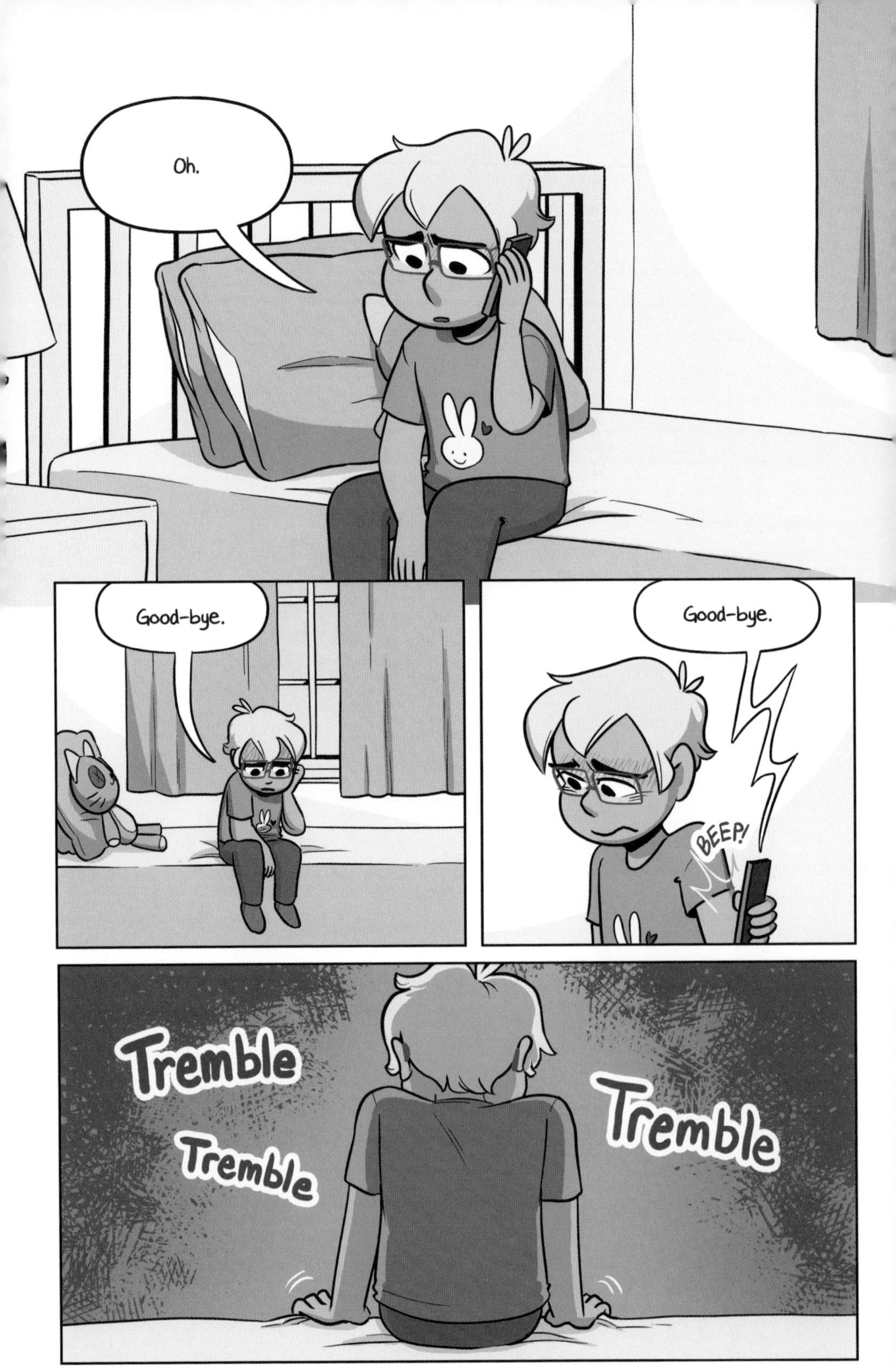
Oh.
Good-bye.
Good-bye.
BEEP!
Tremble
Tremble
Tremble

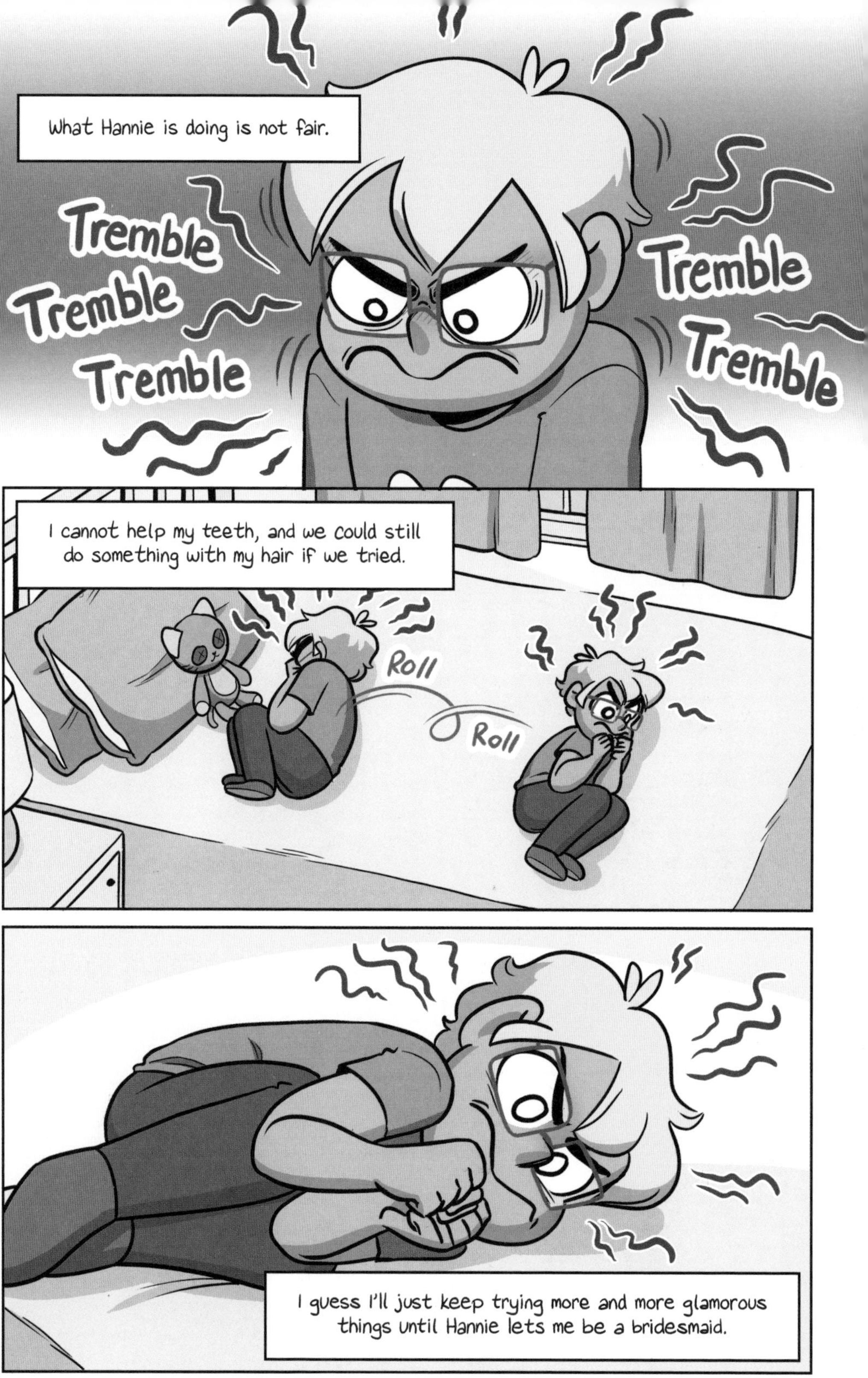
What Hannie is doing is not fair.
Tremble
Tremble
Tremble
Tremble
Tremble
I cannot help my teeth, and we could still do something with my hair if we tried.
Roll
Roll
I guess I'll just keep trying more and more glamorous things until Hannie lets me be a bridesmaid.

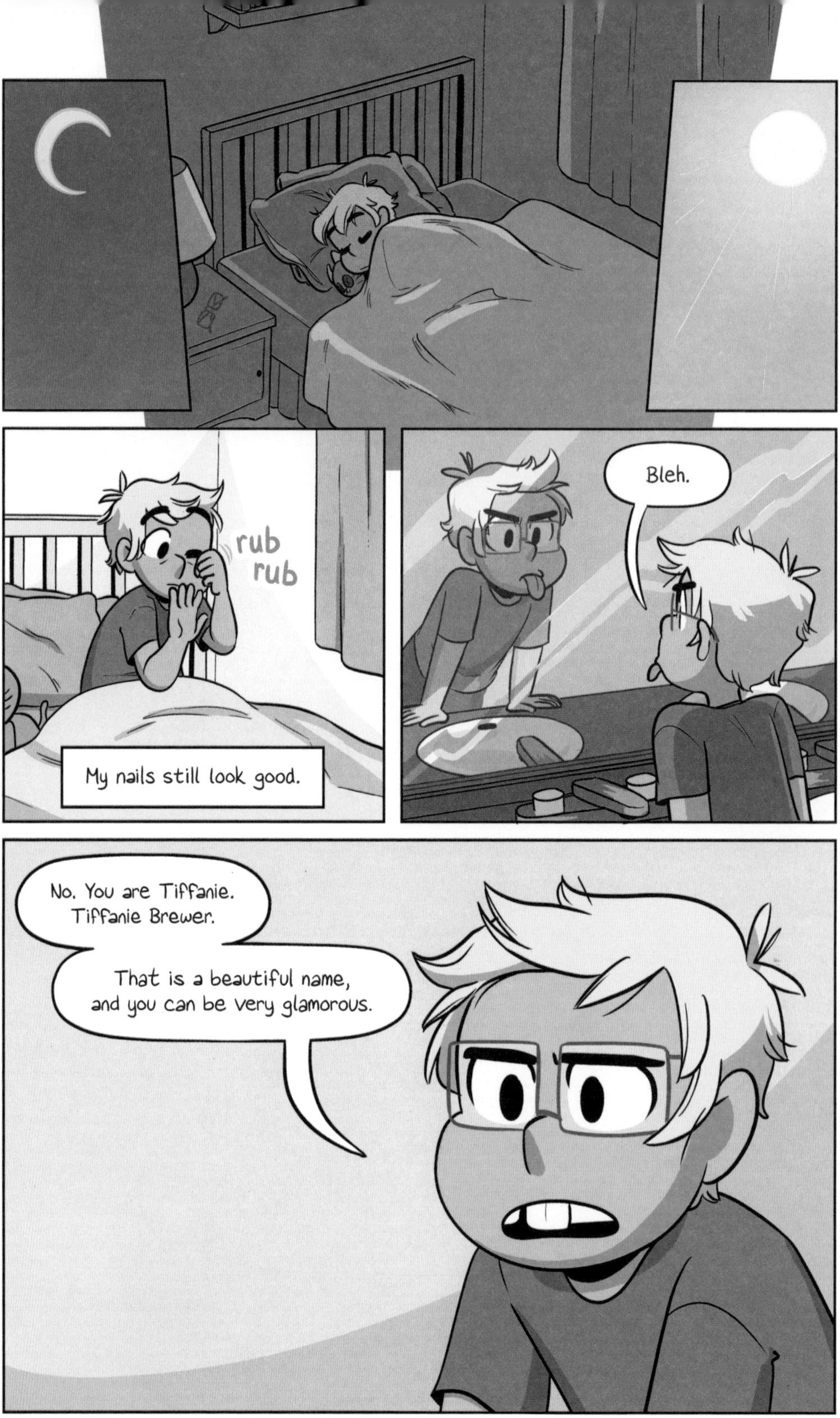
rub
rub
My nails still look good.
Bleh.
No. You are Tiffanie.
Tiffanie Brewer.
That is a beautiful name,
and you can be very glamorous.

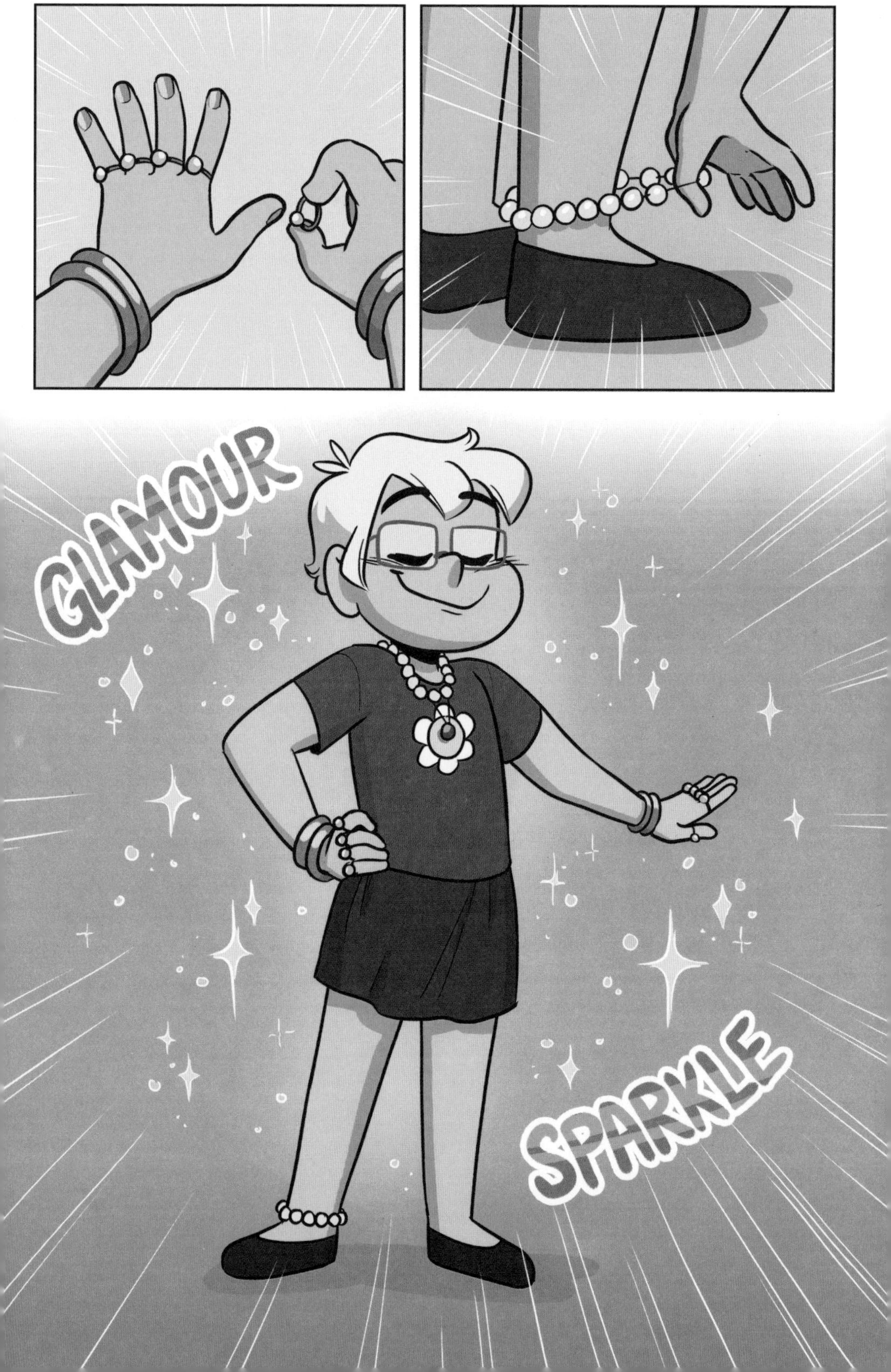
GLAMOUR
SPARKLE

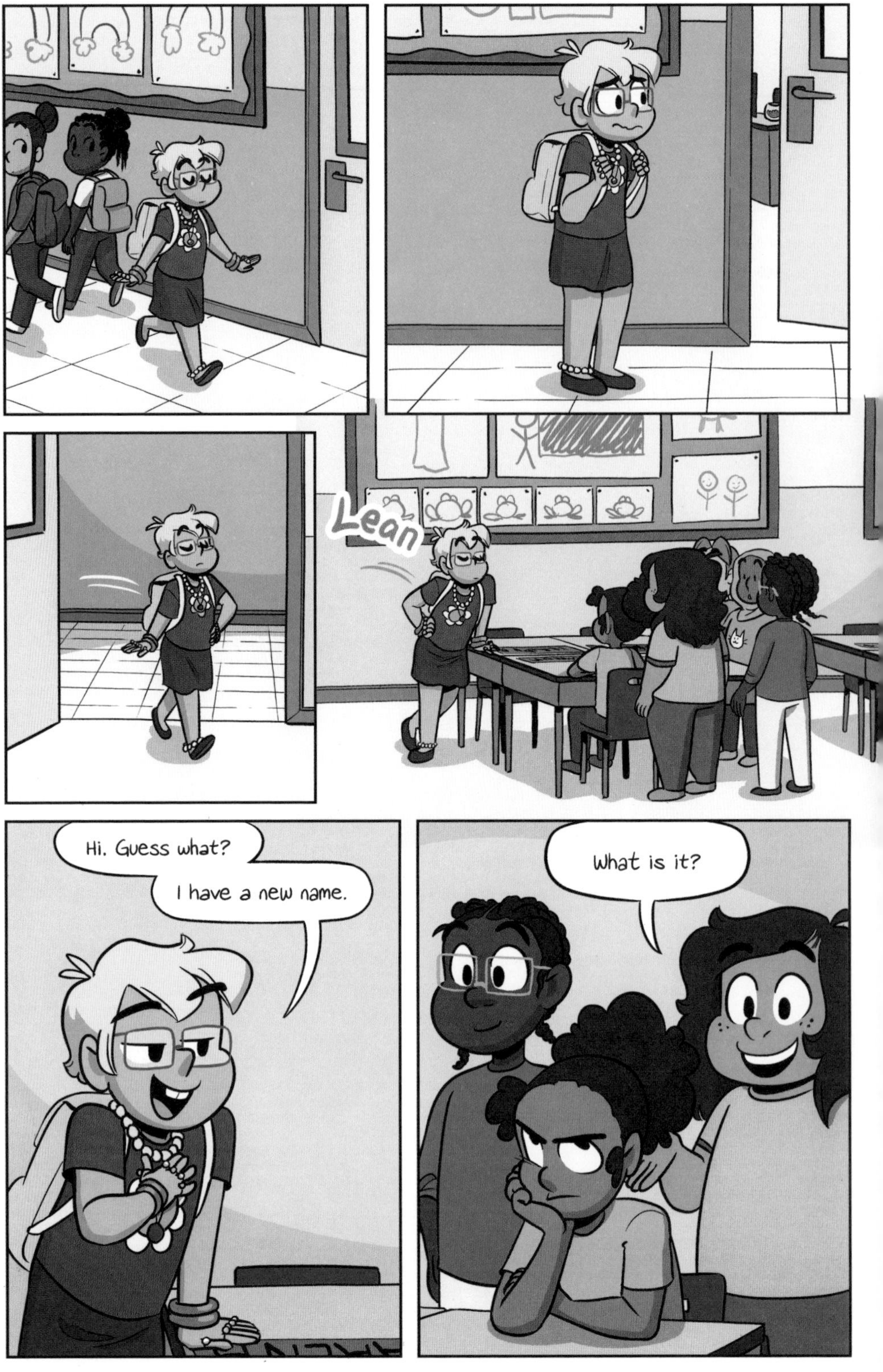
Lean
Hi. Guess what?
I have a new name.
What is it?

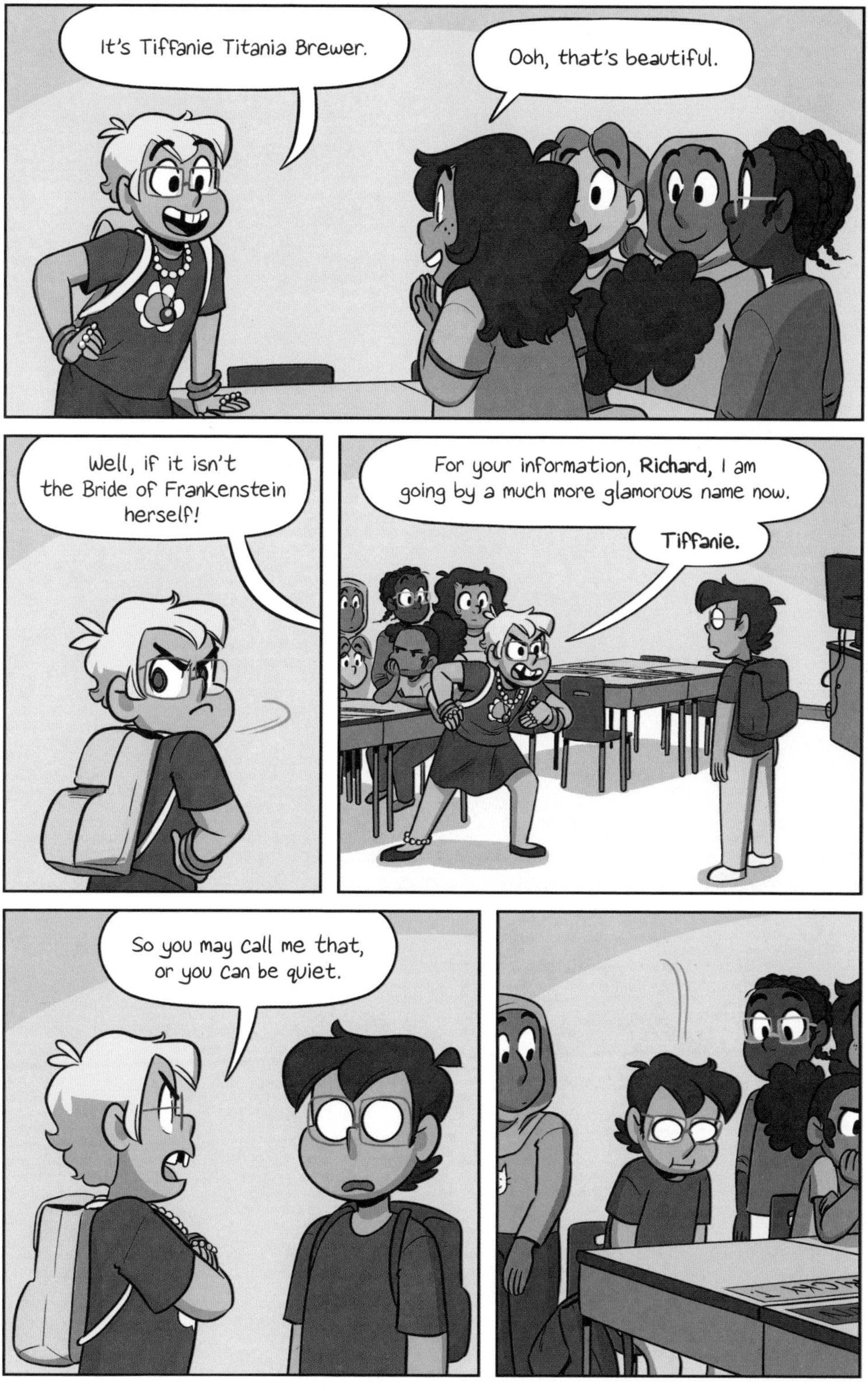
It's Tiffanie Titania Brewer.
Ooh, that's beautiful.
Well, if it isn't the Bride of Frankenstein herself!
For your information, **Richard**, I am going by a much more glamorous name now.
Tiffanie.
So you may call me that, or you can be quiet.

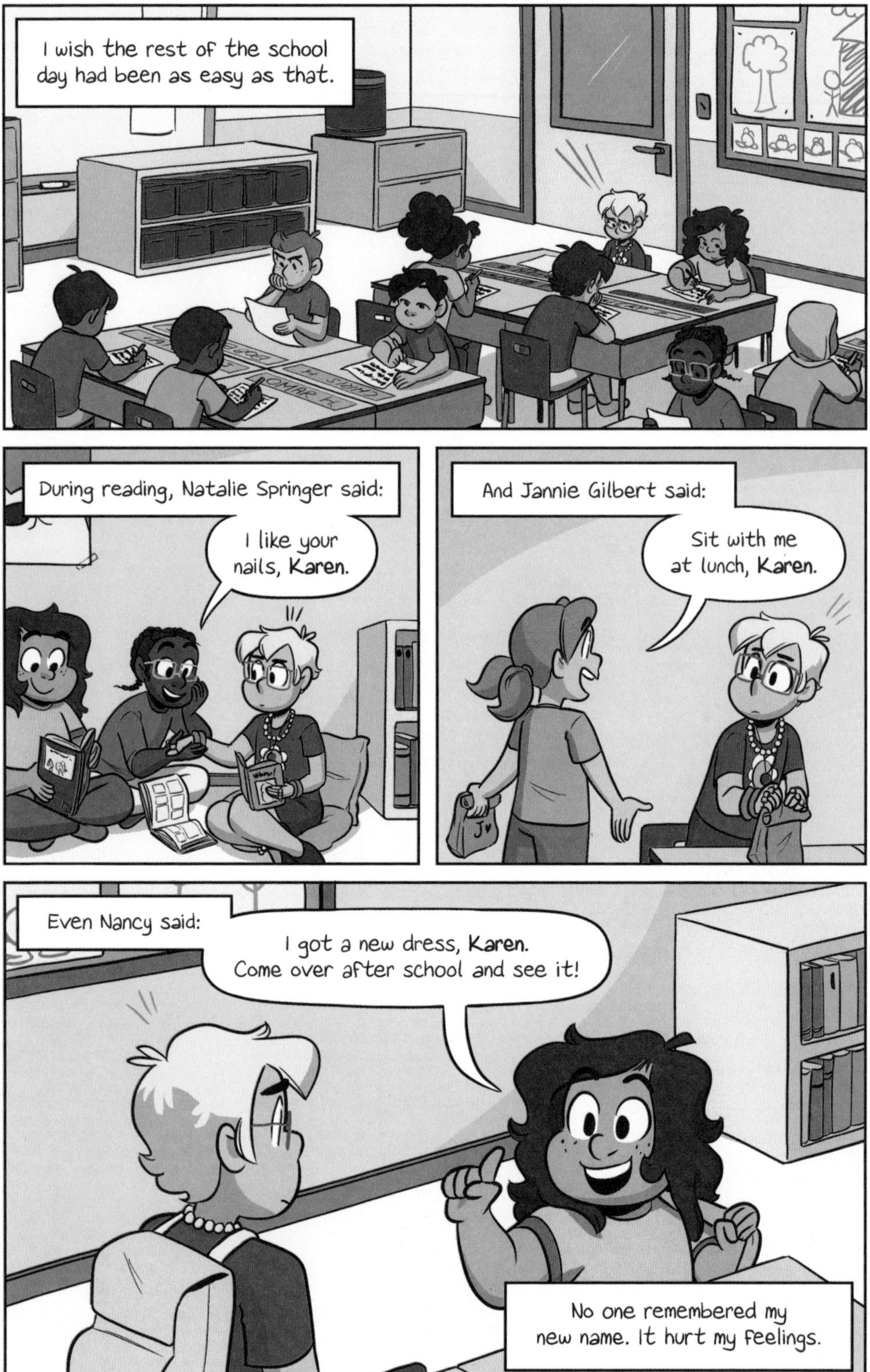
I wish the rest of the school day had been as easy as that.
During reading, Natalie Springer said:
I like your nails, Karen.
And Jannie Gilbert said:
Sit with me at lunch, Karen.
Even Nancy said:
I got a new dress, Karen. Come over after school and see it!
No one remembered my new name. It hurt my feelings.

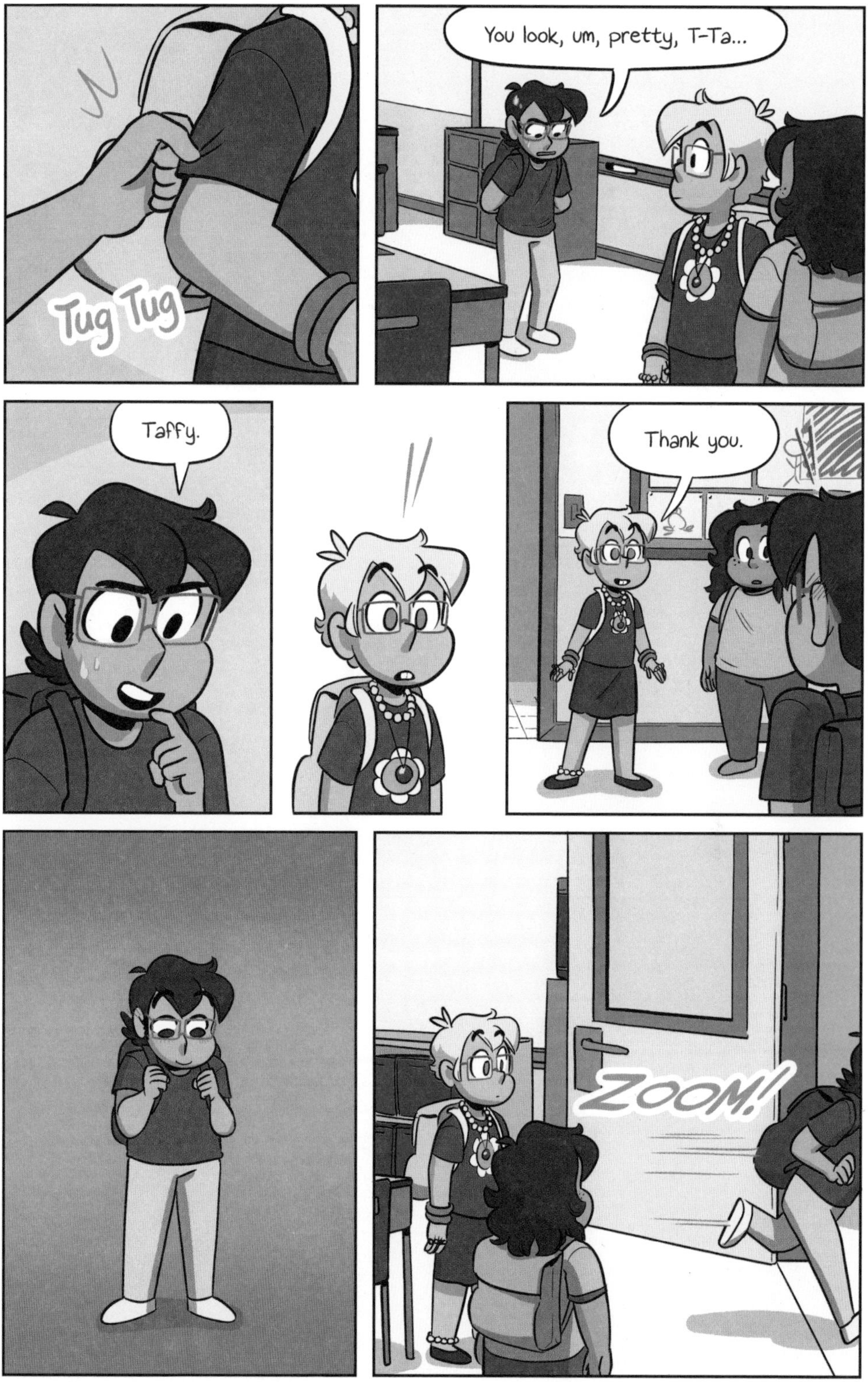
Tug Tug
You look, um, pretty, T-Ta...
Taffy.
Thank you.
ZOOM!

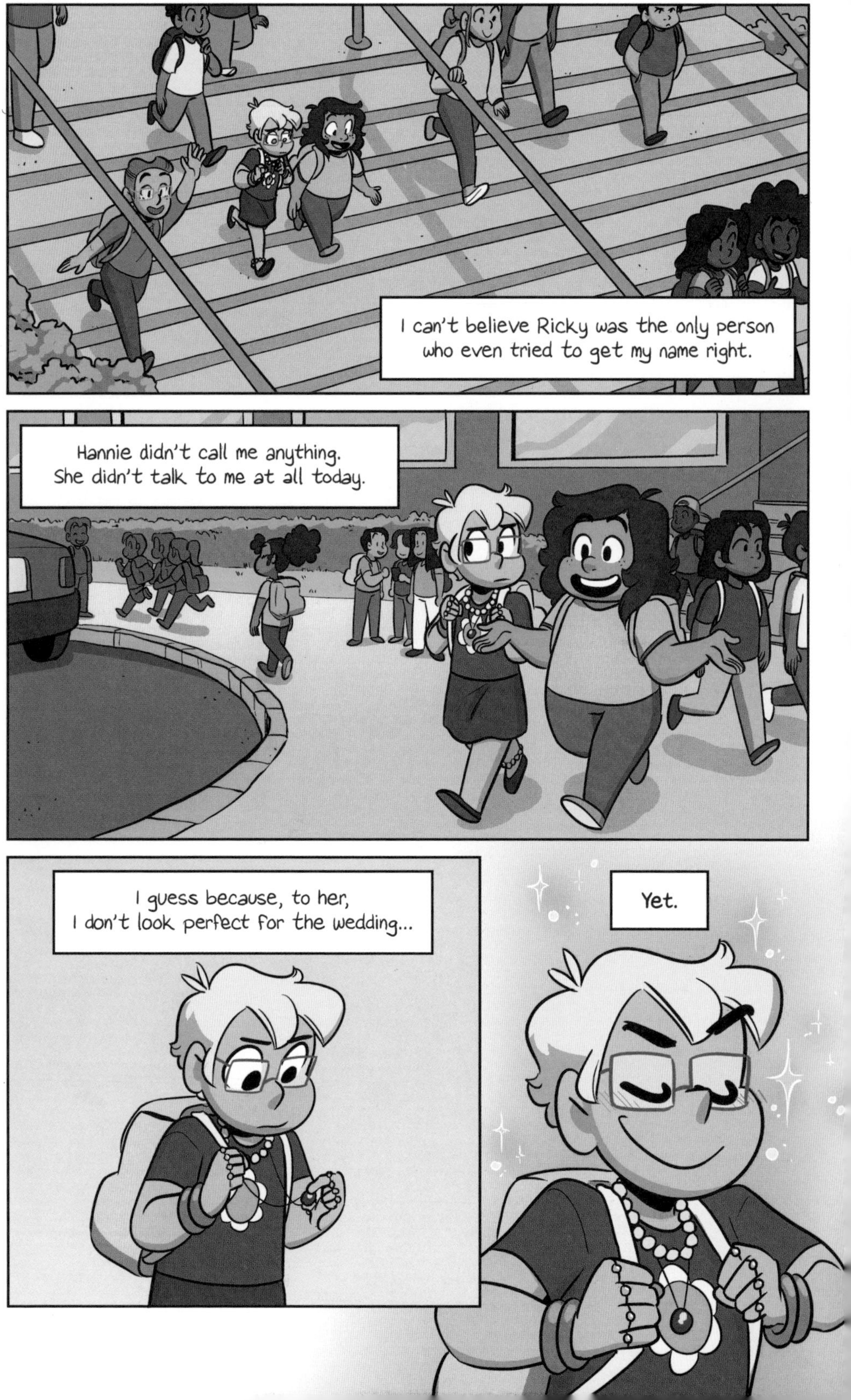
I can't believe Ricky was the only person who even tried to get my name right.
Hannie didn't call me anything. She didn't talk to me at all today.
I guess because, to her, I don't look perfect for the wedding...
Yet.

CHAPTER 7

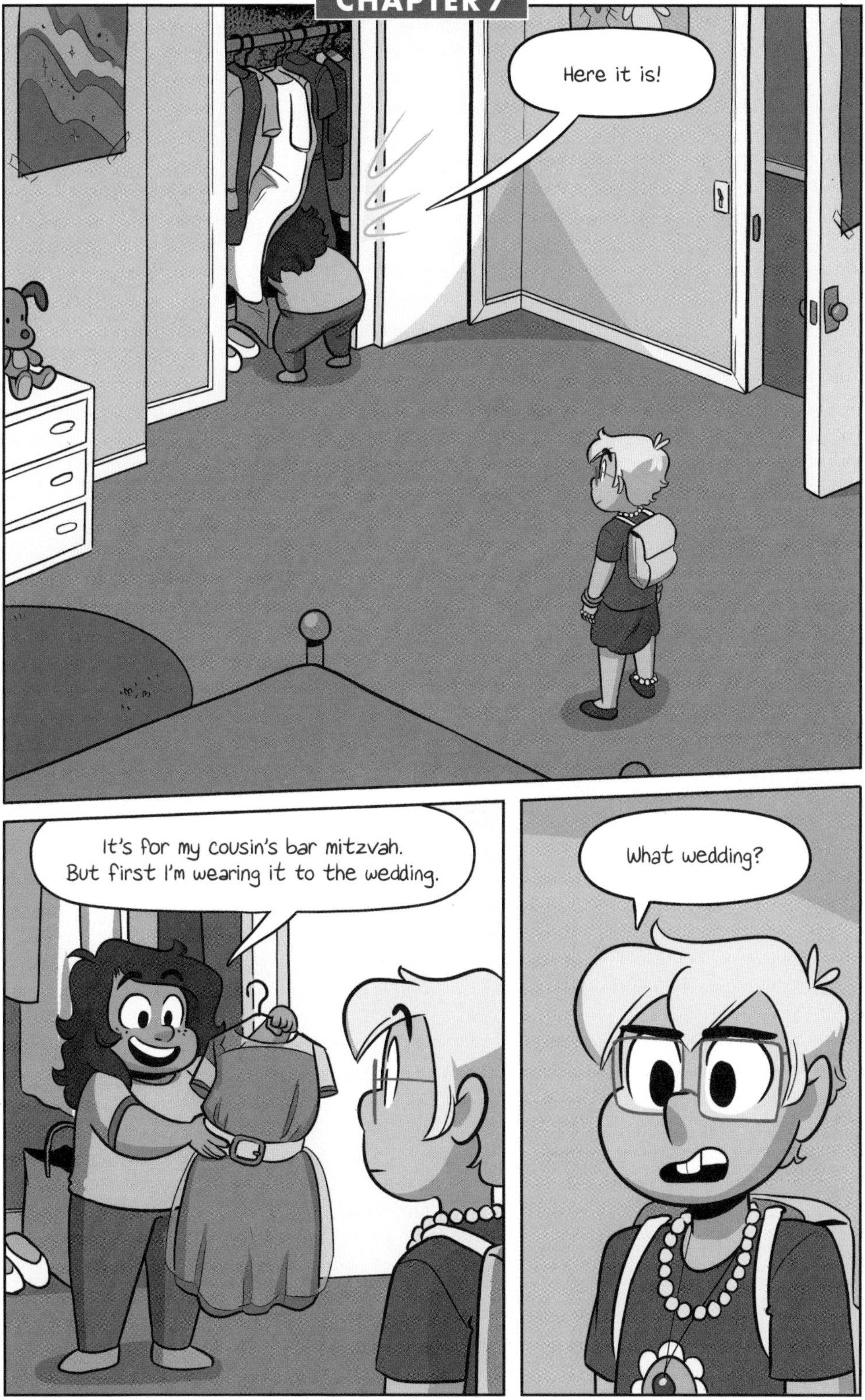
Here it is!
It's for my cousin's bar mitzvah. But first I'm wearing it to the wedding.
What wedding?

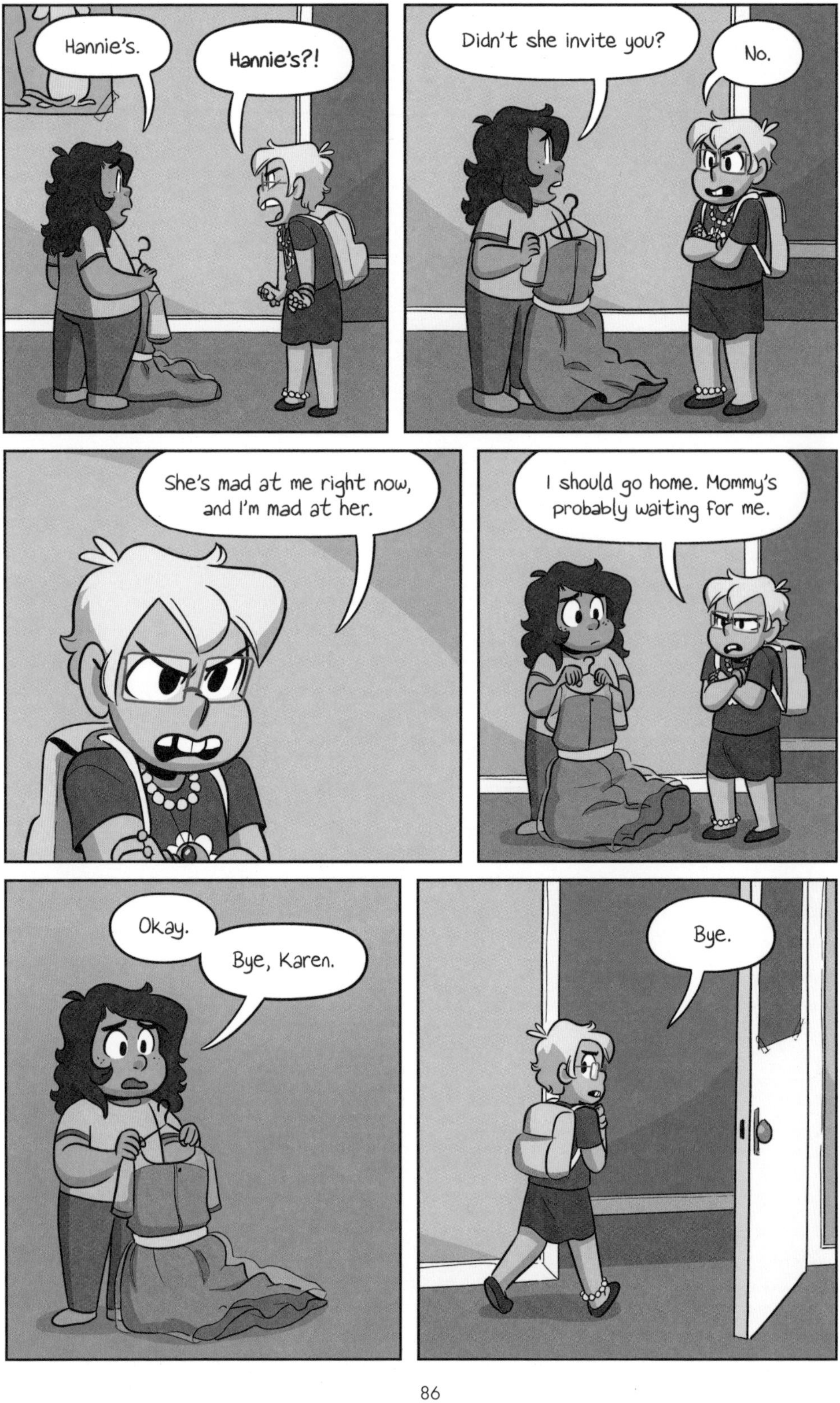
Hannie's.
Hannie's?!
Didn't she invite you?
No.
She's mad at me right now, and I'm mad at her.
I should go home. Mommy's probably waiting for me.
Okay.
Bye, Karen.
Bye.

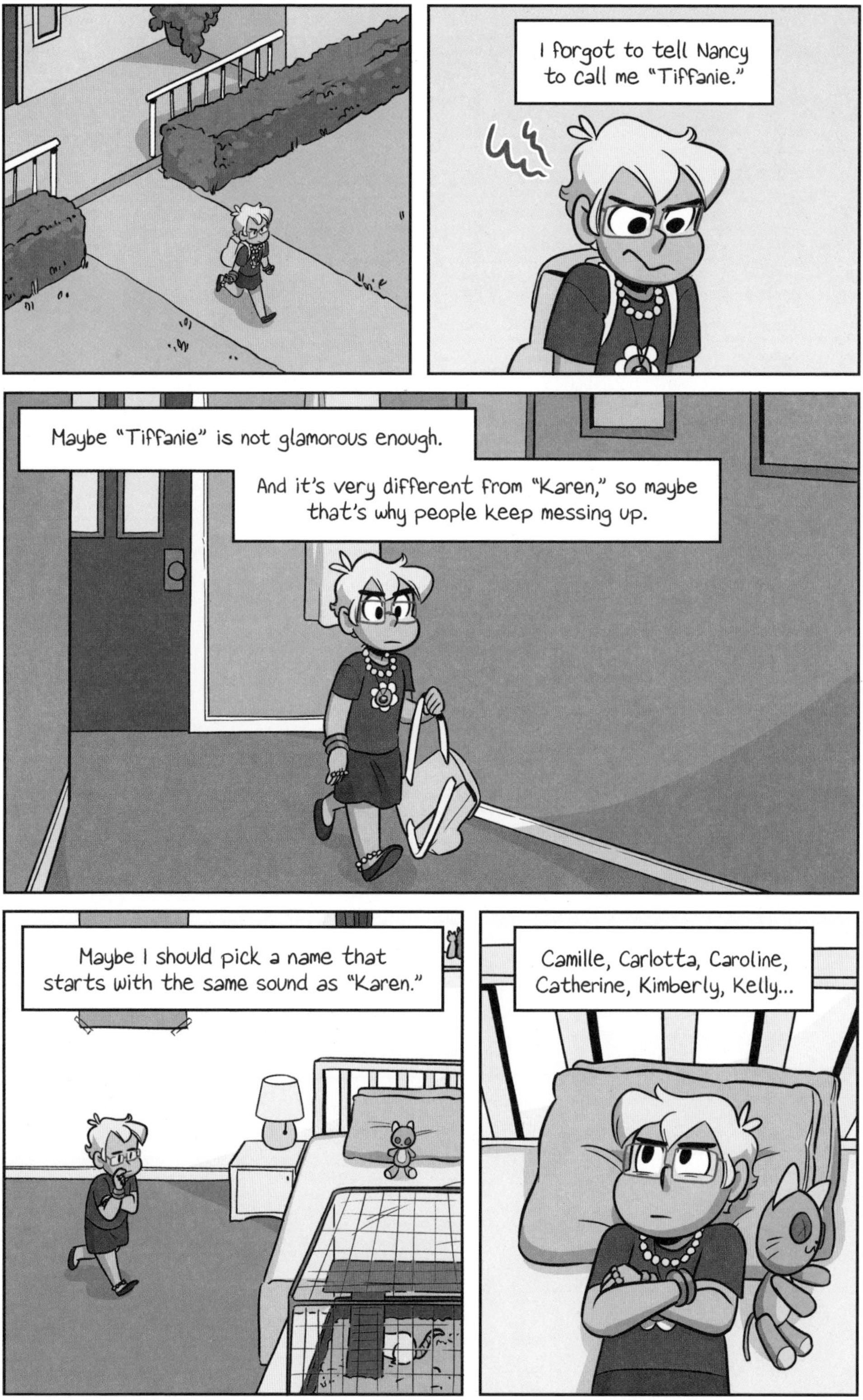
I forgot to tell Nancy to call me "Tiffanie."
Maybe "Tiffanie" is not glamorous enough.
And it's very different from "Karen," so maybe that's why people keep messing up.
Maybe I should pick a name that starts with the same sound as "Karen."
Camille, Carlotta, Caroline, Catherine, Kimberly, Kelly...

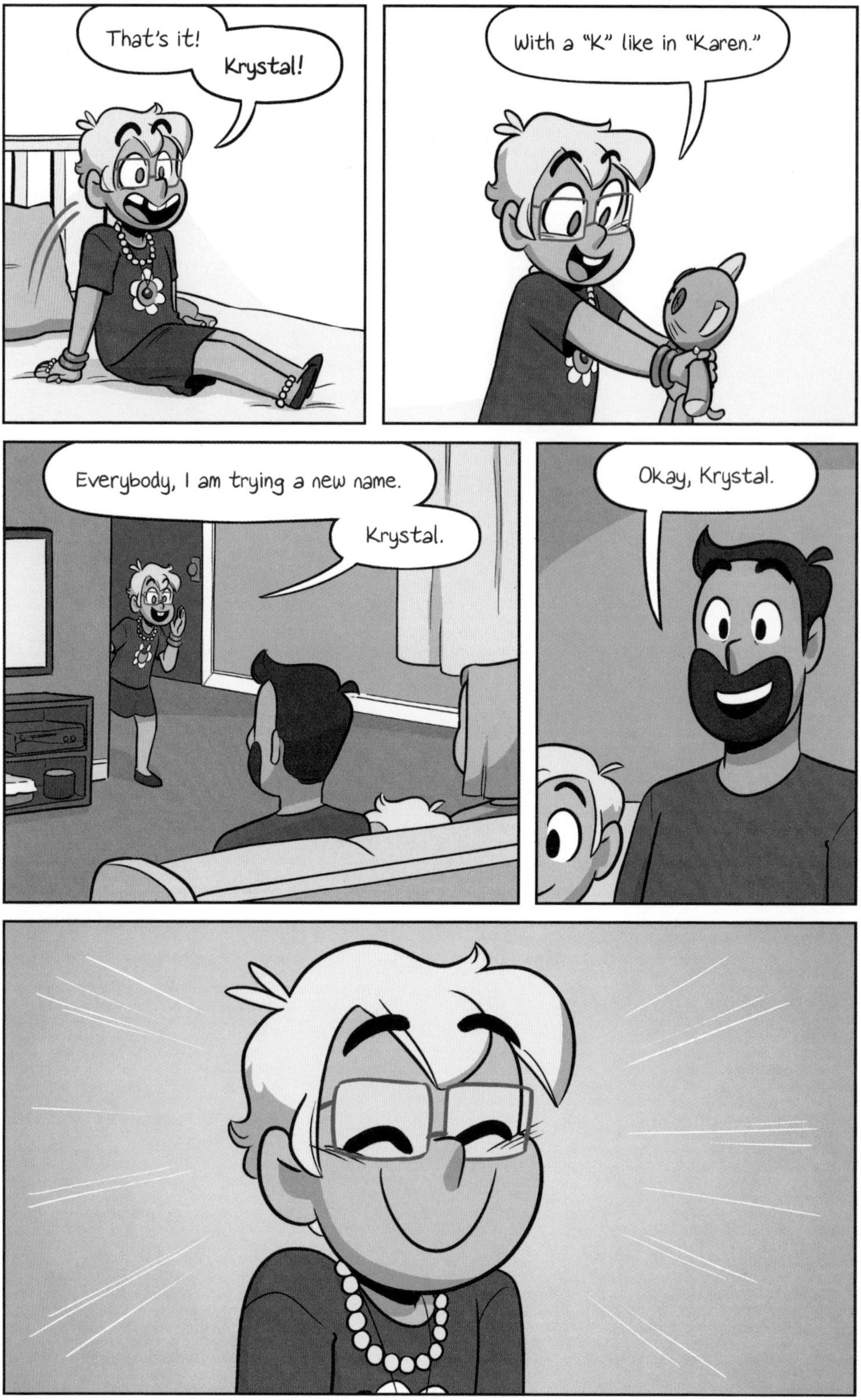
That's it!
Krystal!
With a "K" like in "Karen."
Everybody, I am trying a new name.
Krystal.
Okay, Krystal.

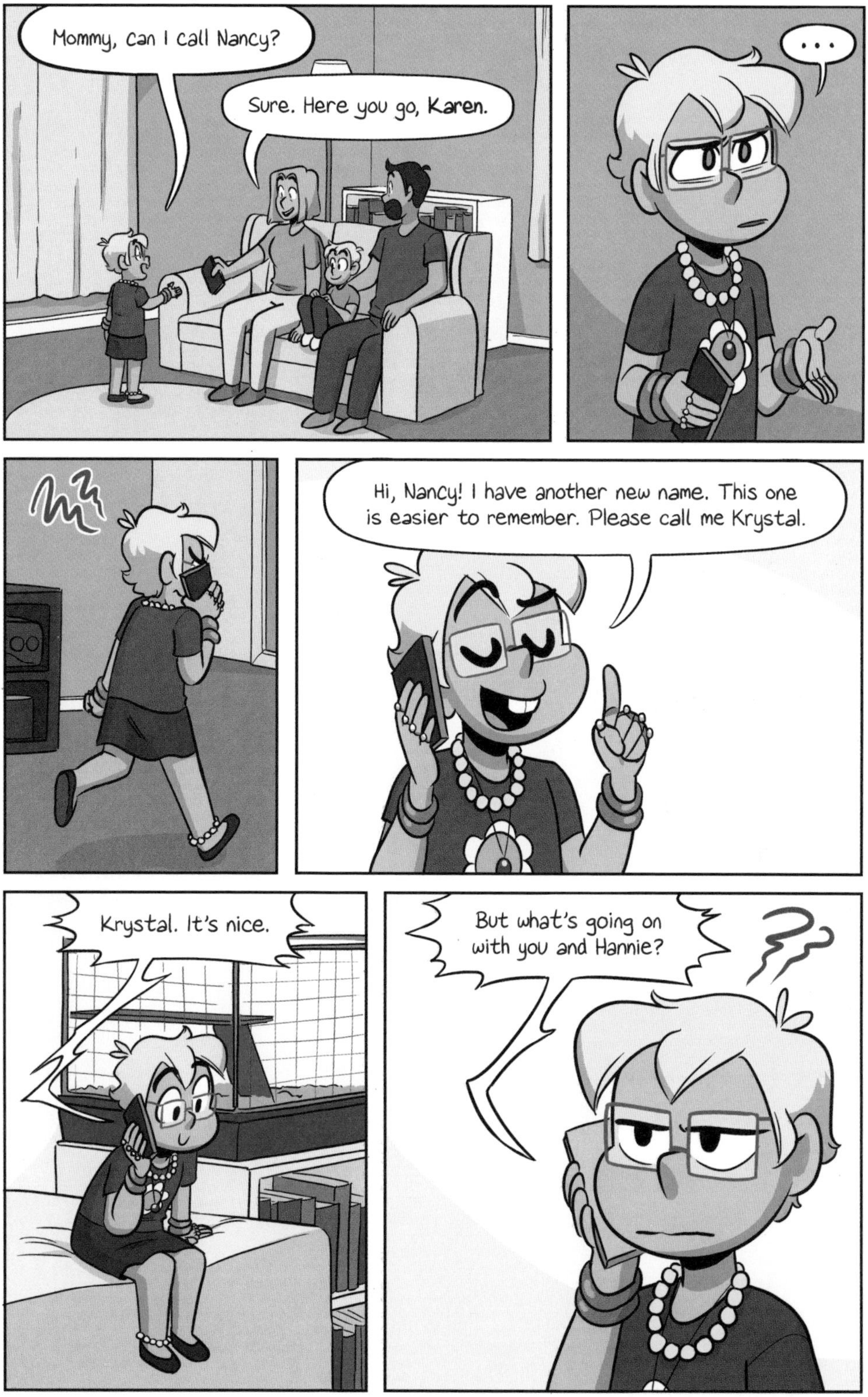

Mommy, can I call Nancy?
Sure. Here you go, **Karen.**
...
Hi, Nancy! I have another new name. This one is easier to remember. Please call me Krystal.
Krystal. It's nice.
But what's going on with you and Hannie?

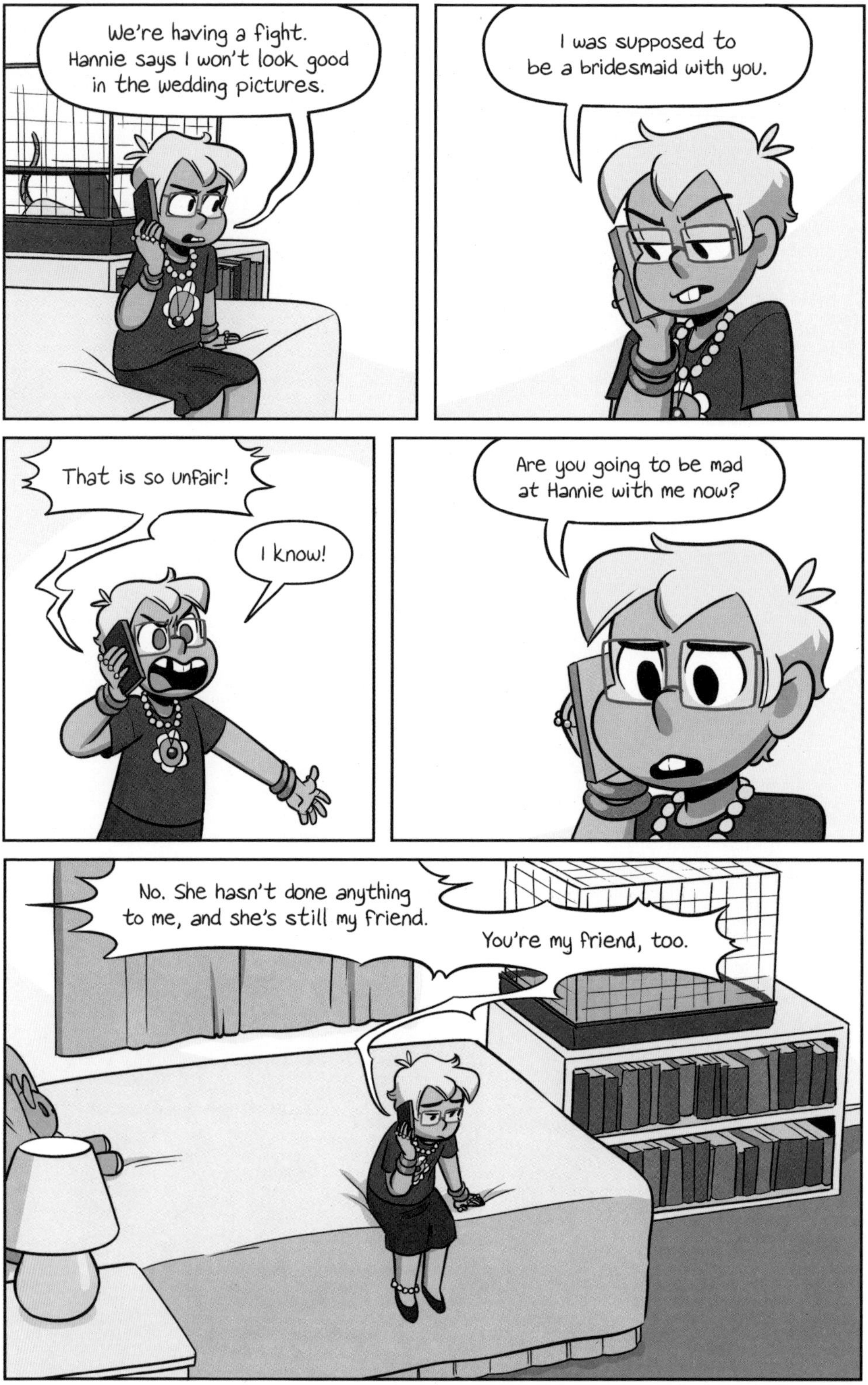
We're having a fight. Hannie says I won't look good in the wedding pictures.
I was supposed to be a bridesmaid with you.
That is so unfair!
I know!
Are you going to be mad at Hannie with me now?
No. She hasn't done anything to me, and she's still my friend.
You're my friend, too.

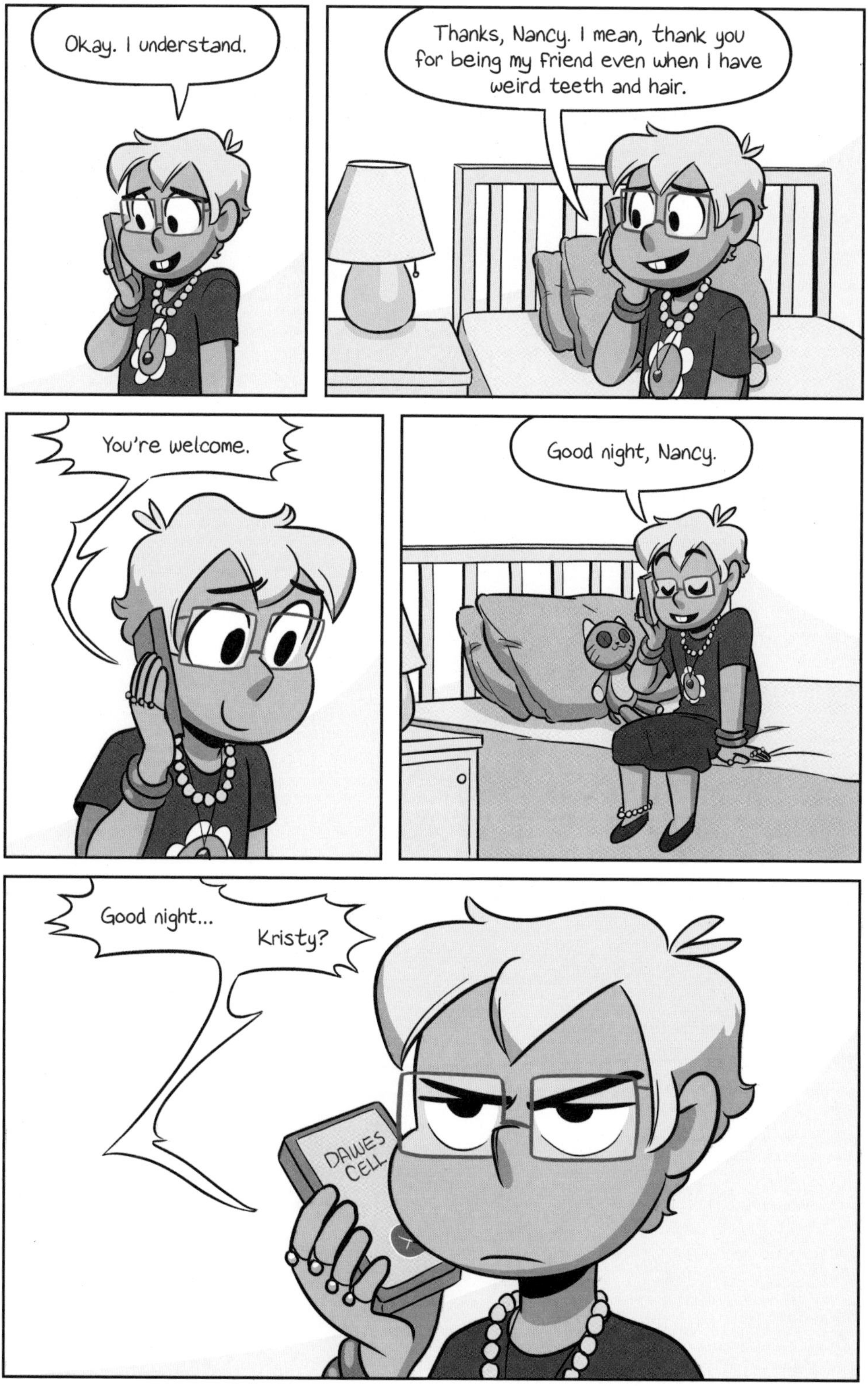
Okay. I understand.
Thanks, Nancy. I mean, thank you for being my friend even when I have weird teeth and hair.
You're welcome.
Good night, Nancy.
Good night...
Kristy?
DAWES CELL

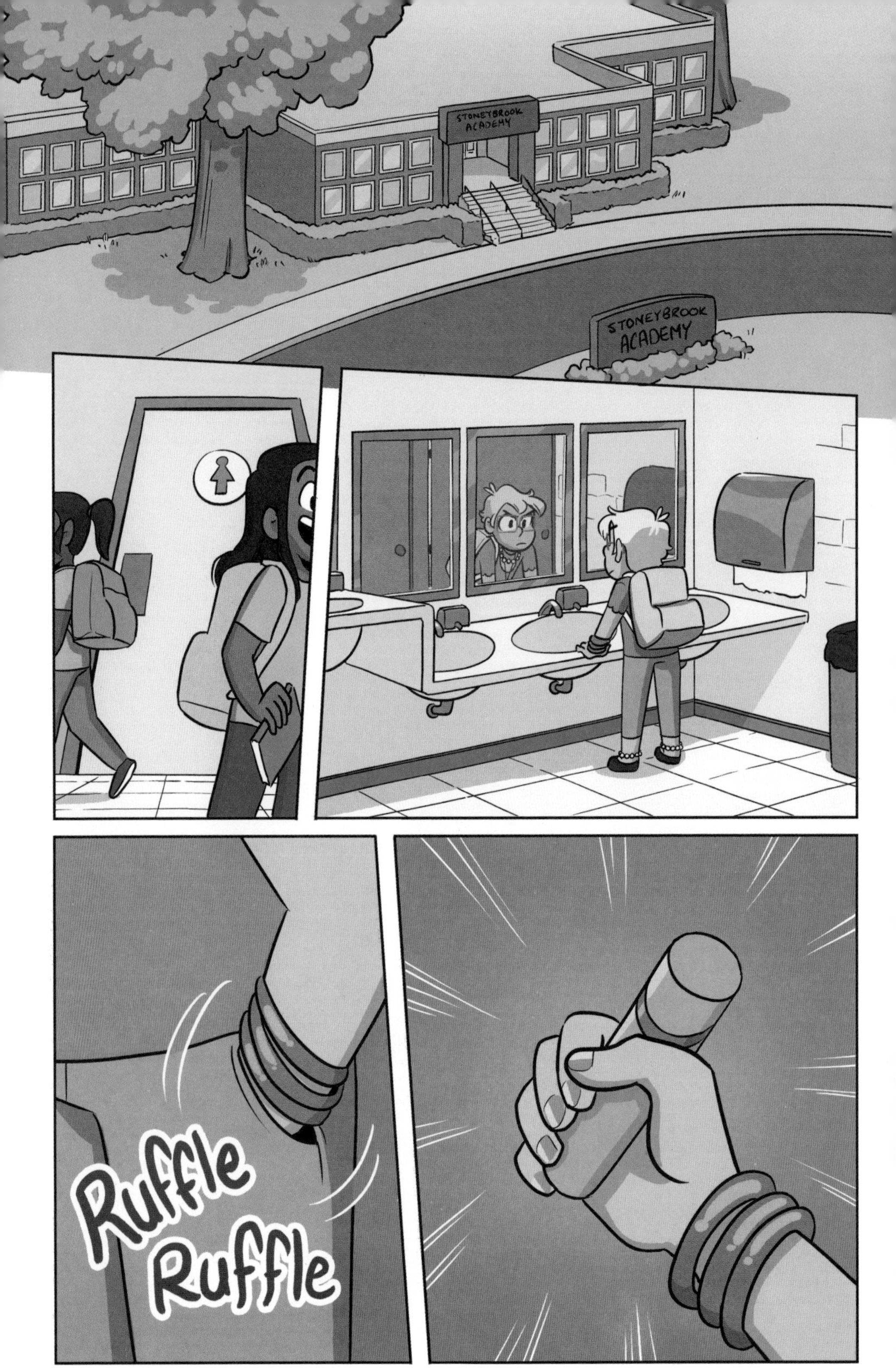
STONEYBROOK ACADEMY
STONEYBROOK ACADEMY
Ruffle Ruffle

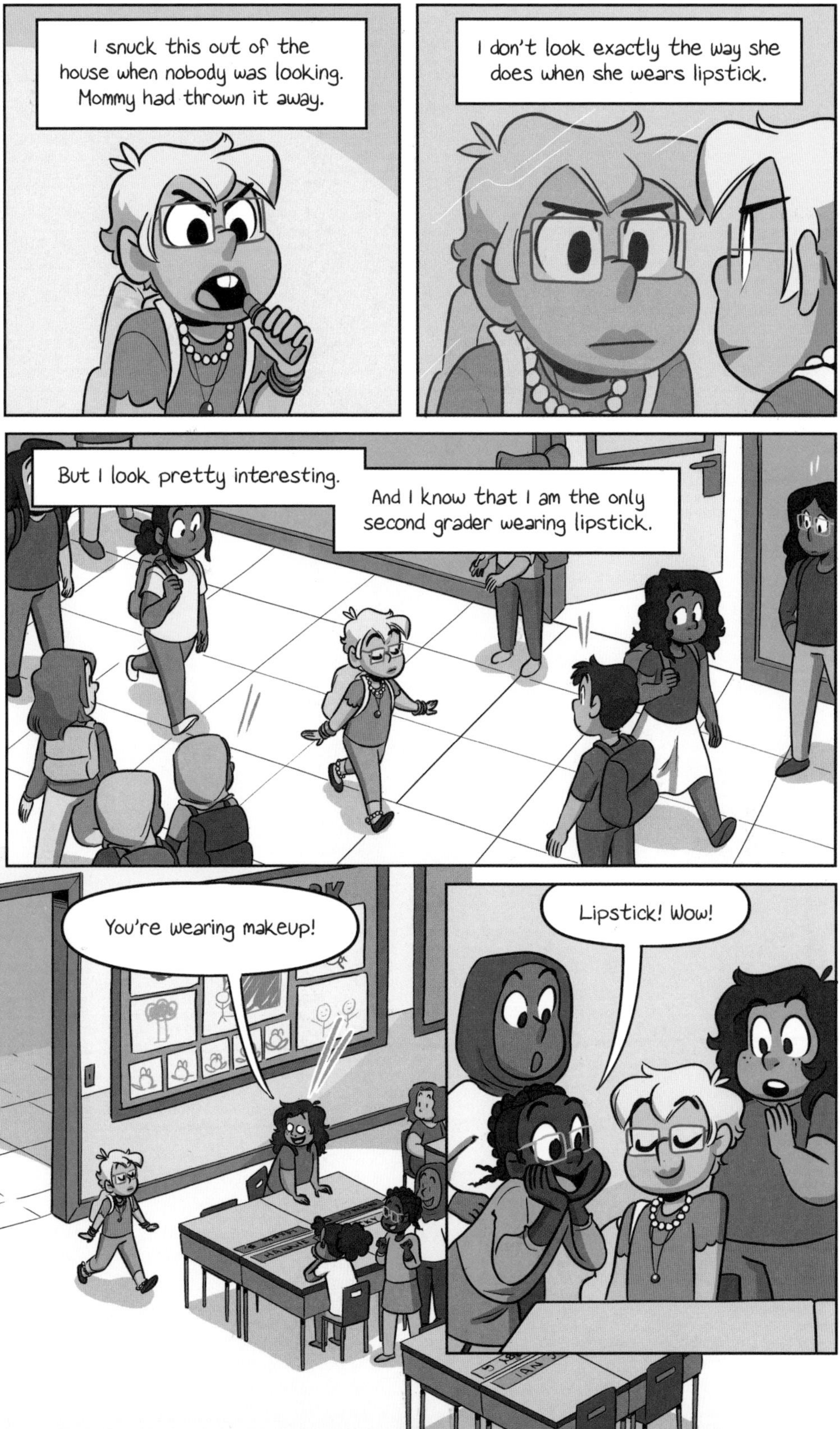
I snuck this out of the house when nobody was looking. Mommy had thrown it away.
I don't look exactly the way she does when she wears lipstick.
But I look pretty interesting.
And I know that I am the only second grader wearing lipstick.
You're wearing makeup!
Lipstick! Wow!

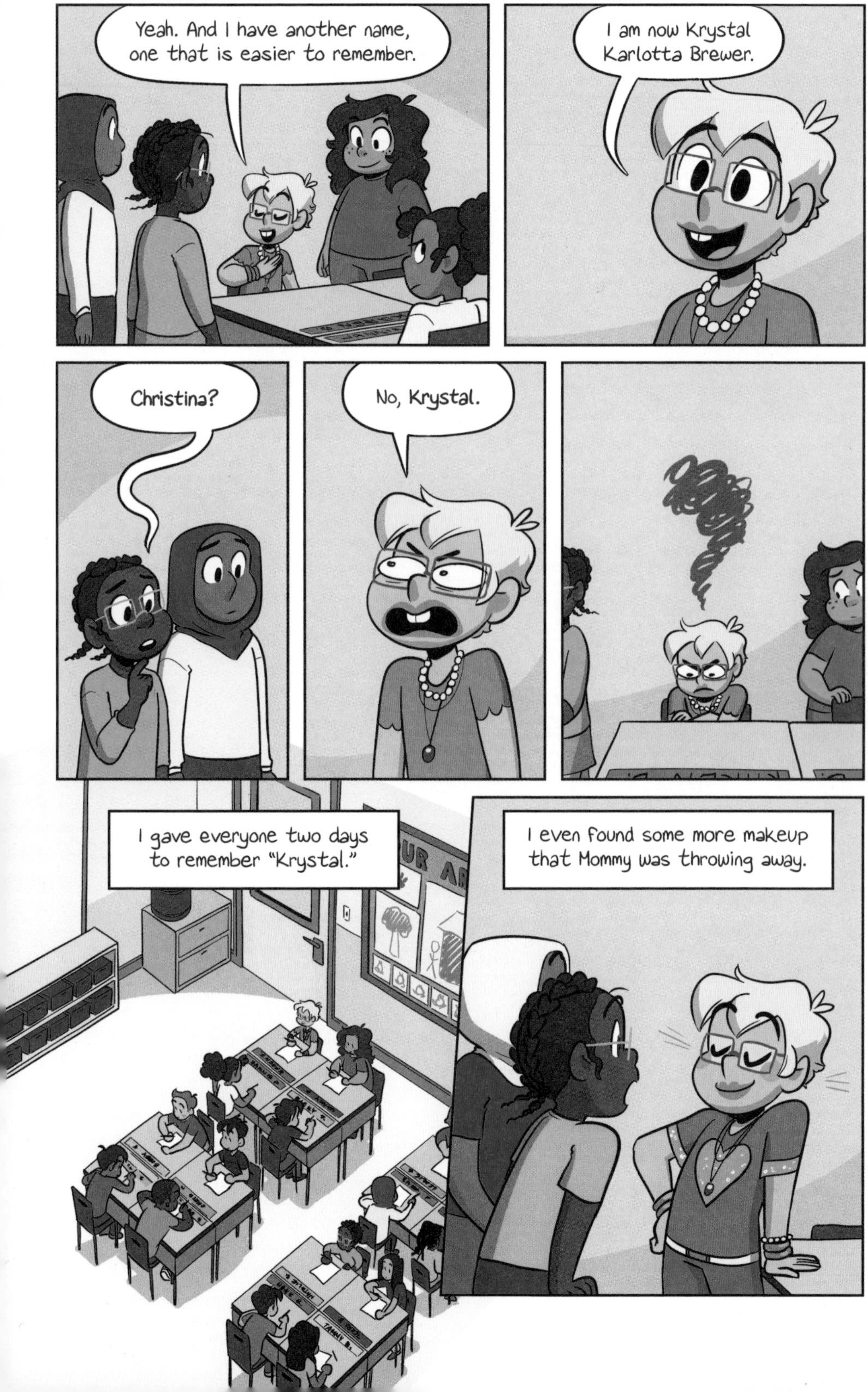
Yeah. And I have another name, one that is easier to remember.
I am now Krystal Karlotta Brewer.
Christina?
No, Krystal.
I gave everyone two days to remember "Krystal."
I even found some more makeup that Mommy was throwing away.

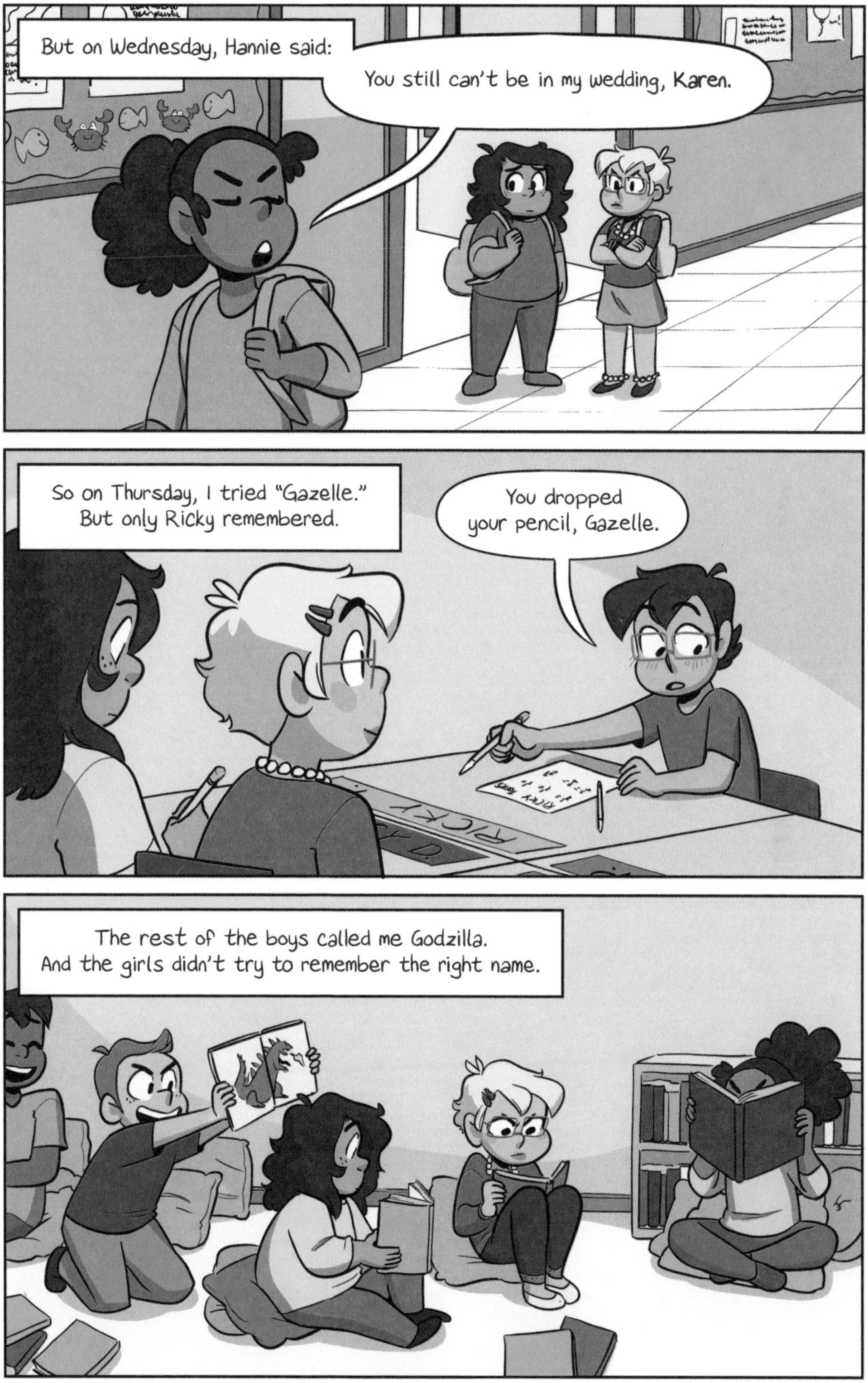
But on Wednesday, Hannie said:
You still can't be in my wedding, Karen.
So on Thursday, I tried "Gazelle." But only Ricky remembered.
You dropped your pencil, Gazelle.
RICKY
The rest of the boys called me Godzilla. And the girls didn't try to remember the right name.

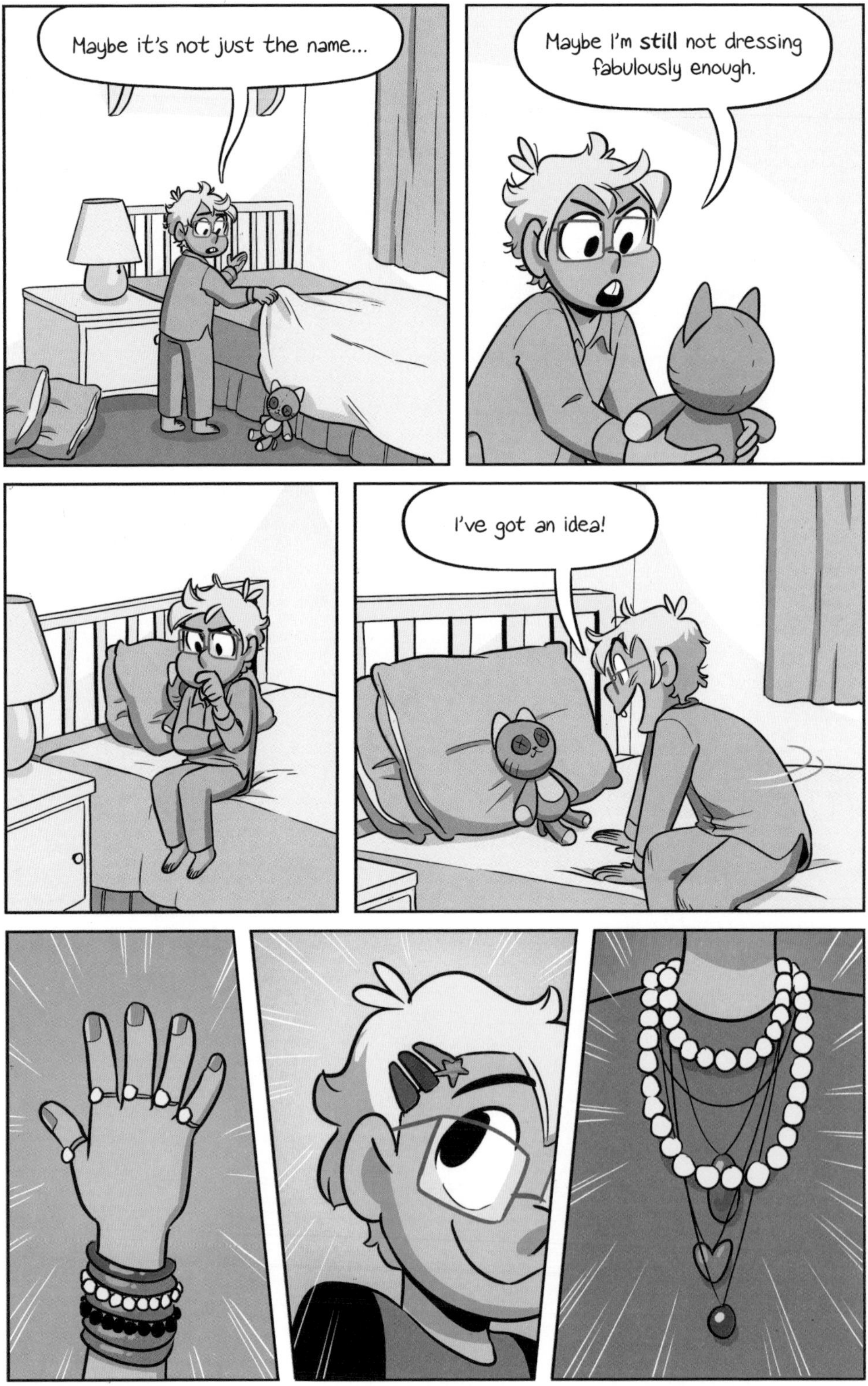
Maybe it's not just the name...
Maybe I'm **still** not dressing fabulously enough.
I've got an idea!

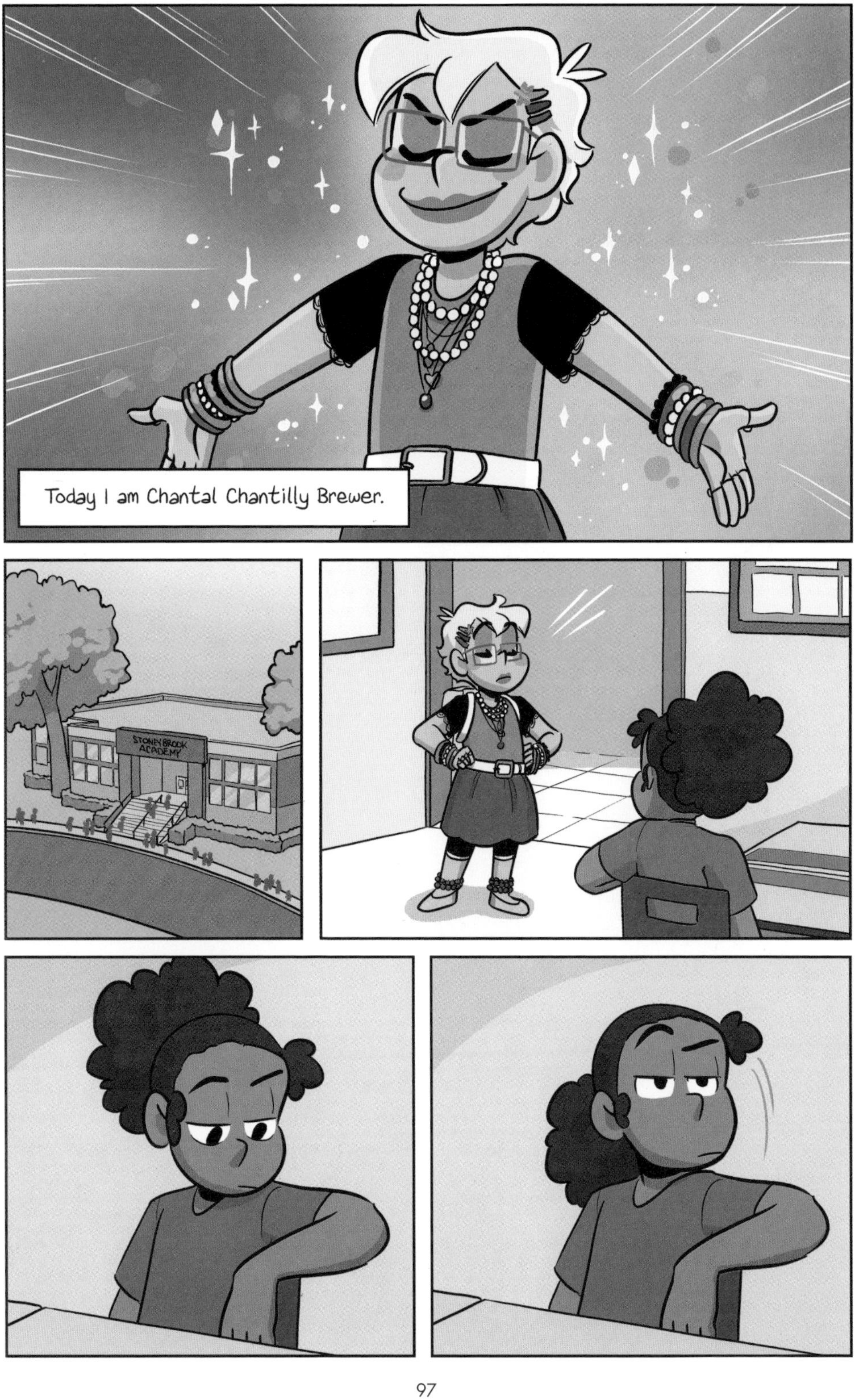
Today I am Chantal Chantilly Brewer.
STONEY BROOK ACADEMY

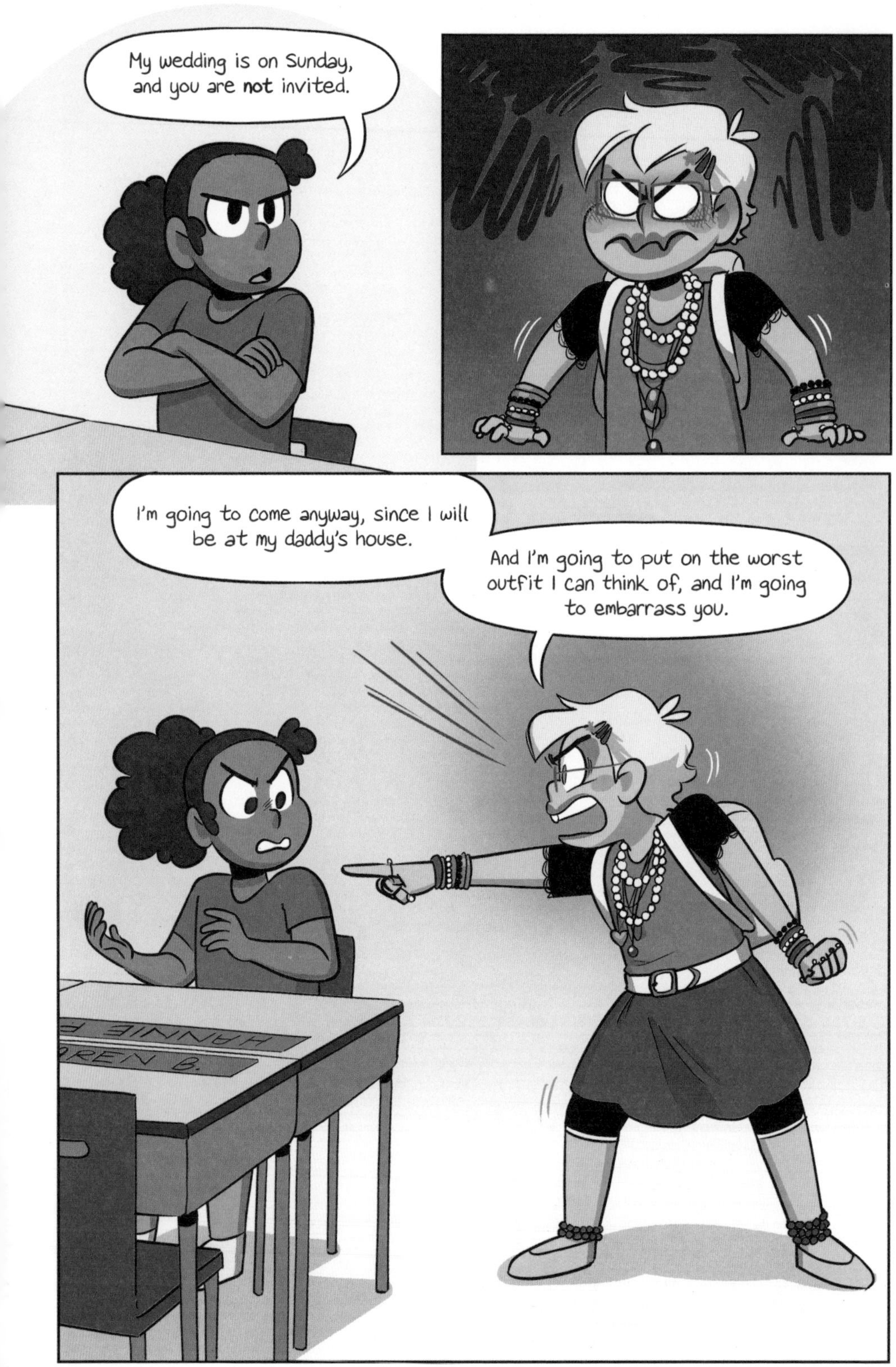

My wedding is on Sunday, and you are **not** invited.
I'm going to come anyway, since I will be at my daddy's house.
And I'm going to put on the worst outfit I can think of, and I'm going to embarrass you.

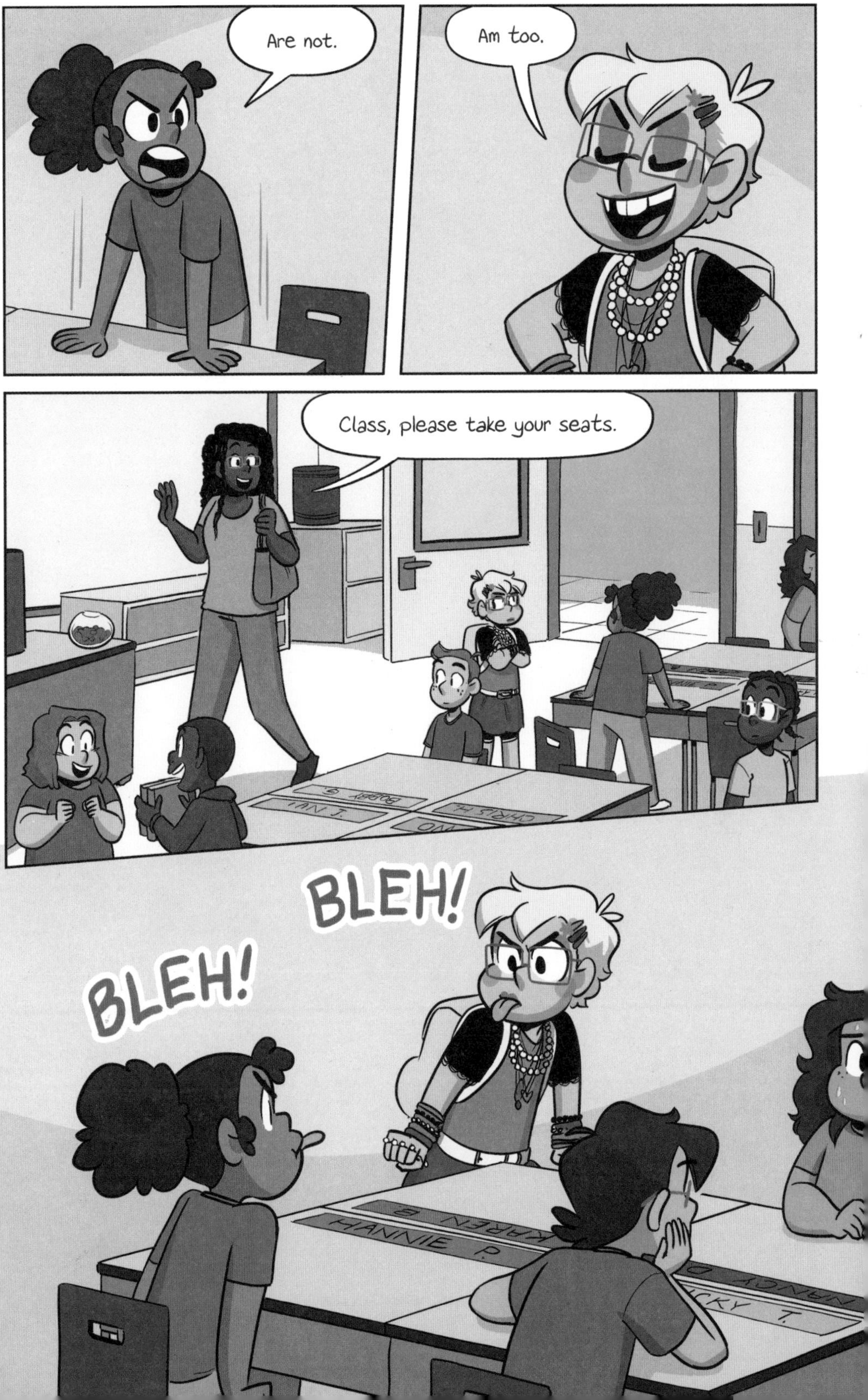
Are not.
Am too.
Class, please take your seats.
BLEH!
BLEH!
HANNIE P.
KAREN B

CHAPTER 8

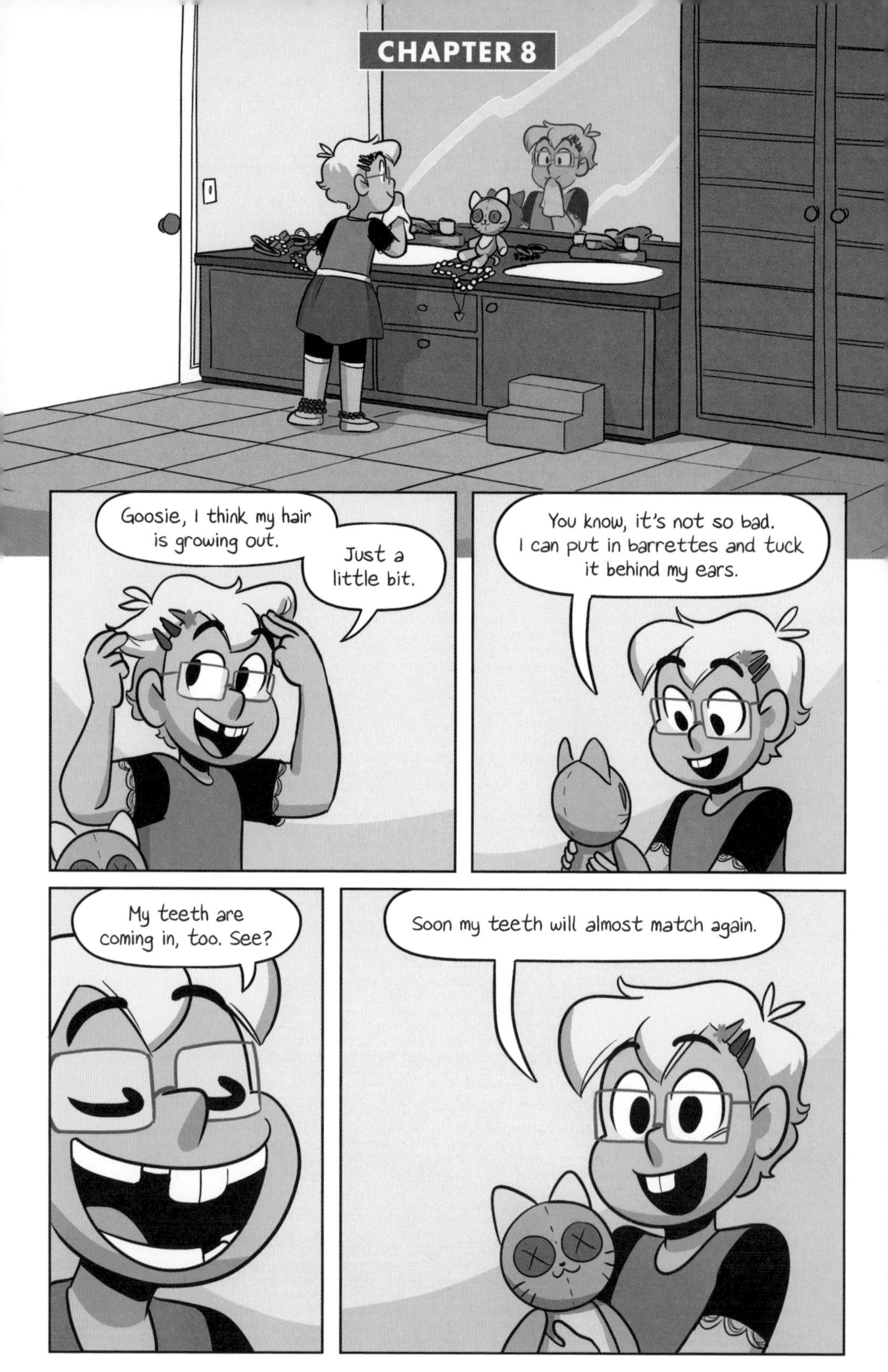

Goosie, I think my hair is growing out.
Just a little bit.
You know, it's not so bad. I can put in barrettes and tuck it behind my ears.
My teeth are coming in, too. See?
Soon my teeth will almost match again.

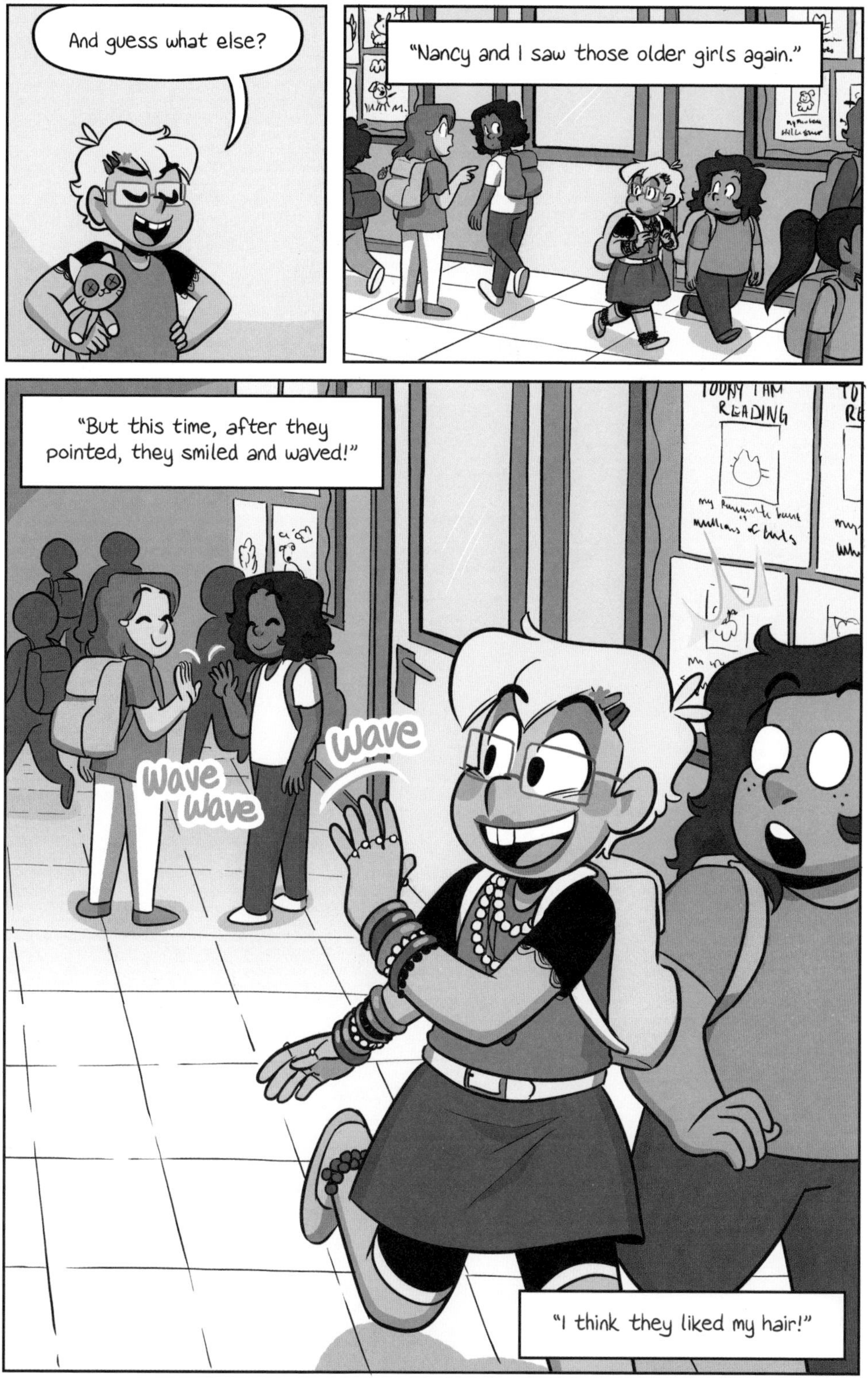
And guess what else?
"Nancy and I saw those older girls again."
"But this time, after they pointed, they smiled and waved!"
Wave
Wave
Wave
"I think they liked my hair!"

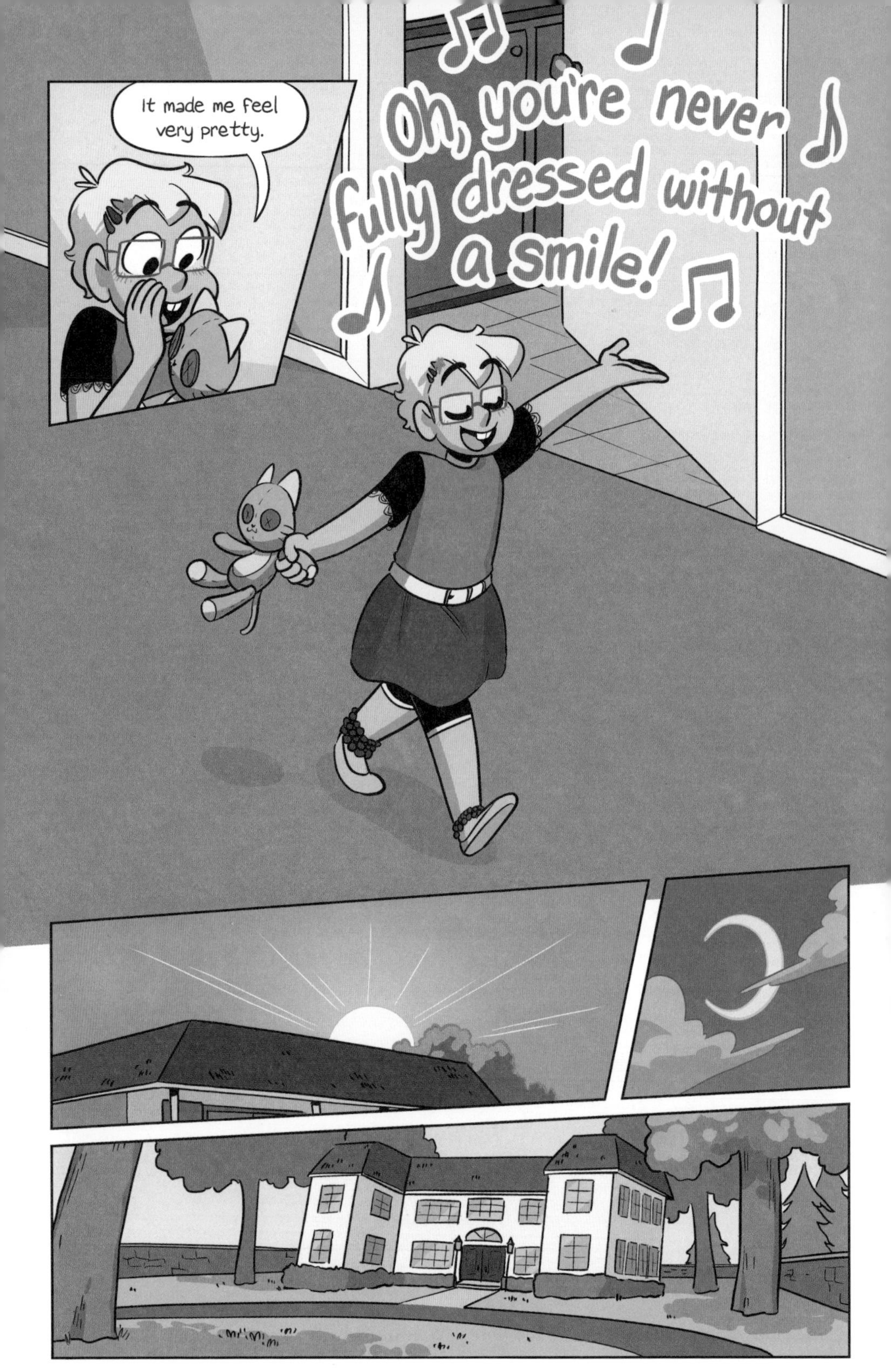
It made me feel very pretty.
Oh, you're never fully dressed without a smile!

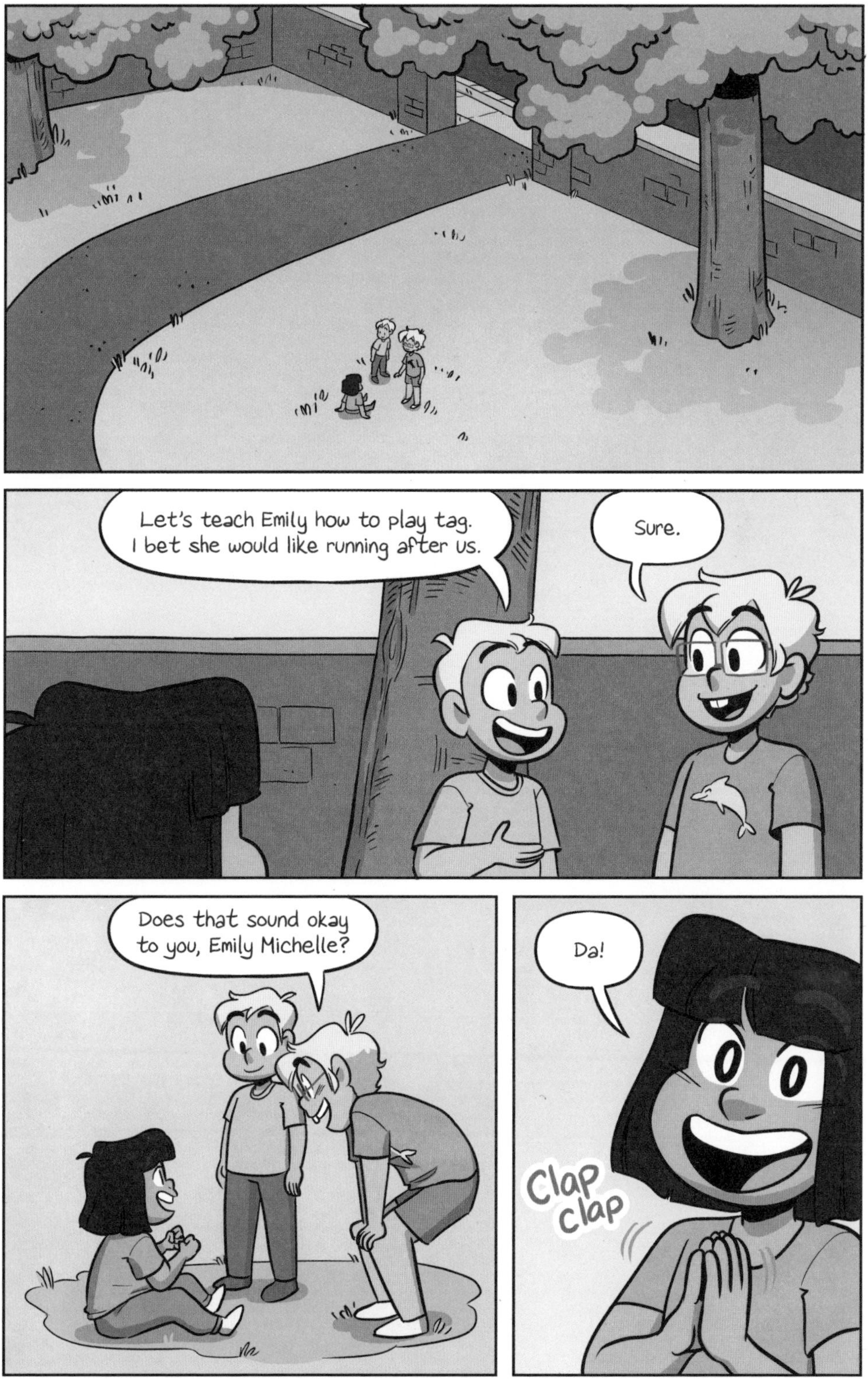
Let's teach Emily how to play tag.
I bet she would like running after us.
Sure.
Does that sound okay to you, Emily Michelle?
Da!
Clap clap

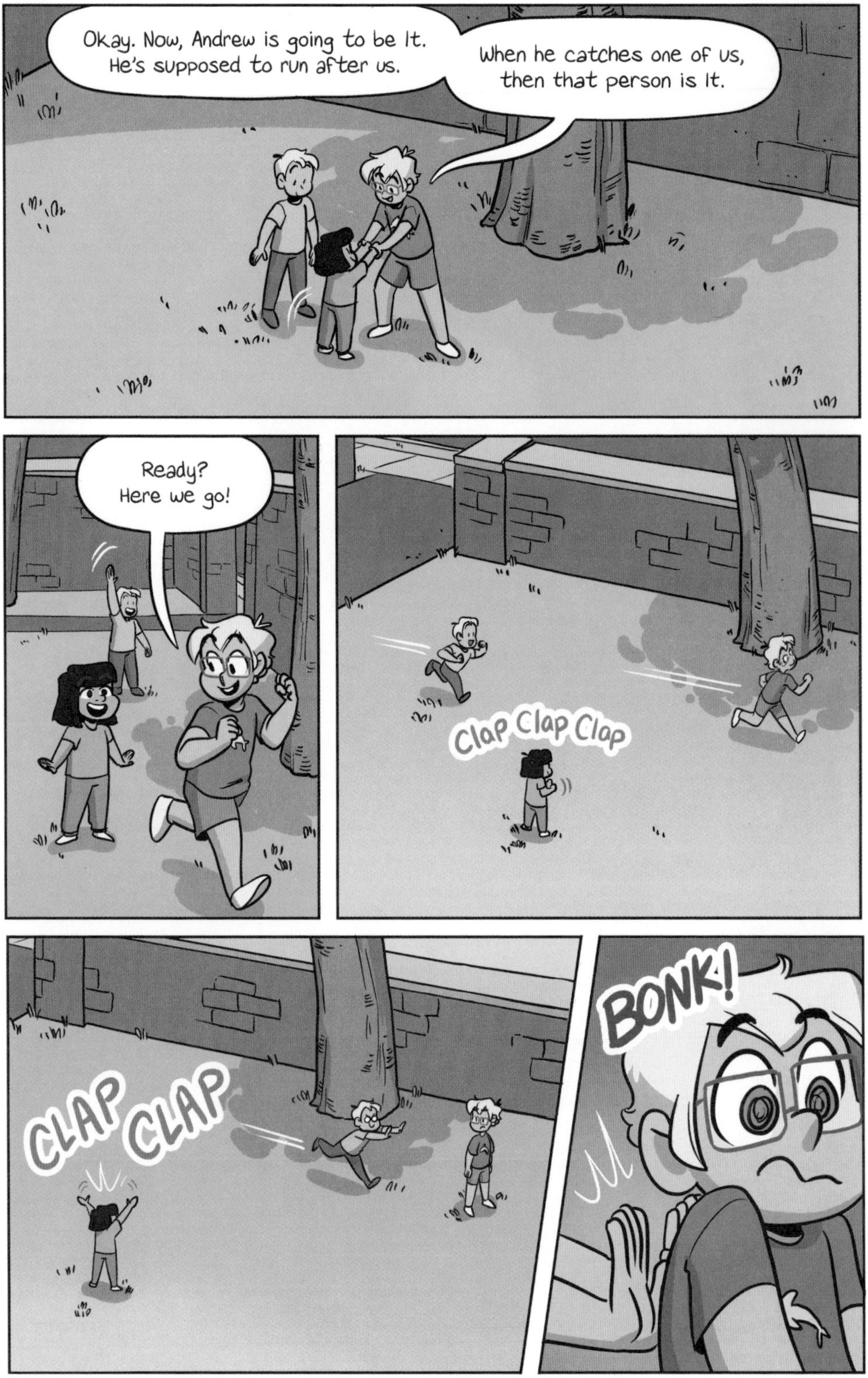
Okay. Now, Andrew is going to be It. He's supposed to run after us.
When he catches one of us, then that person is It.
Ready? Here we go!
Clap Clap Clap
CLAP CLAP
BONK!

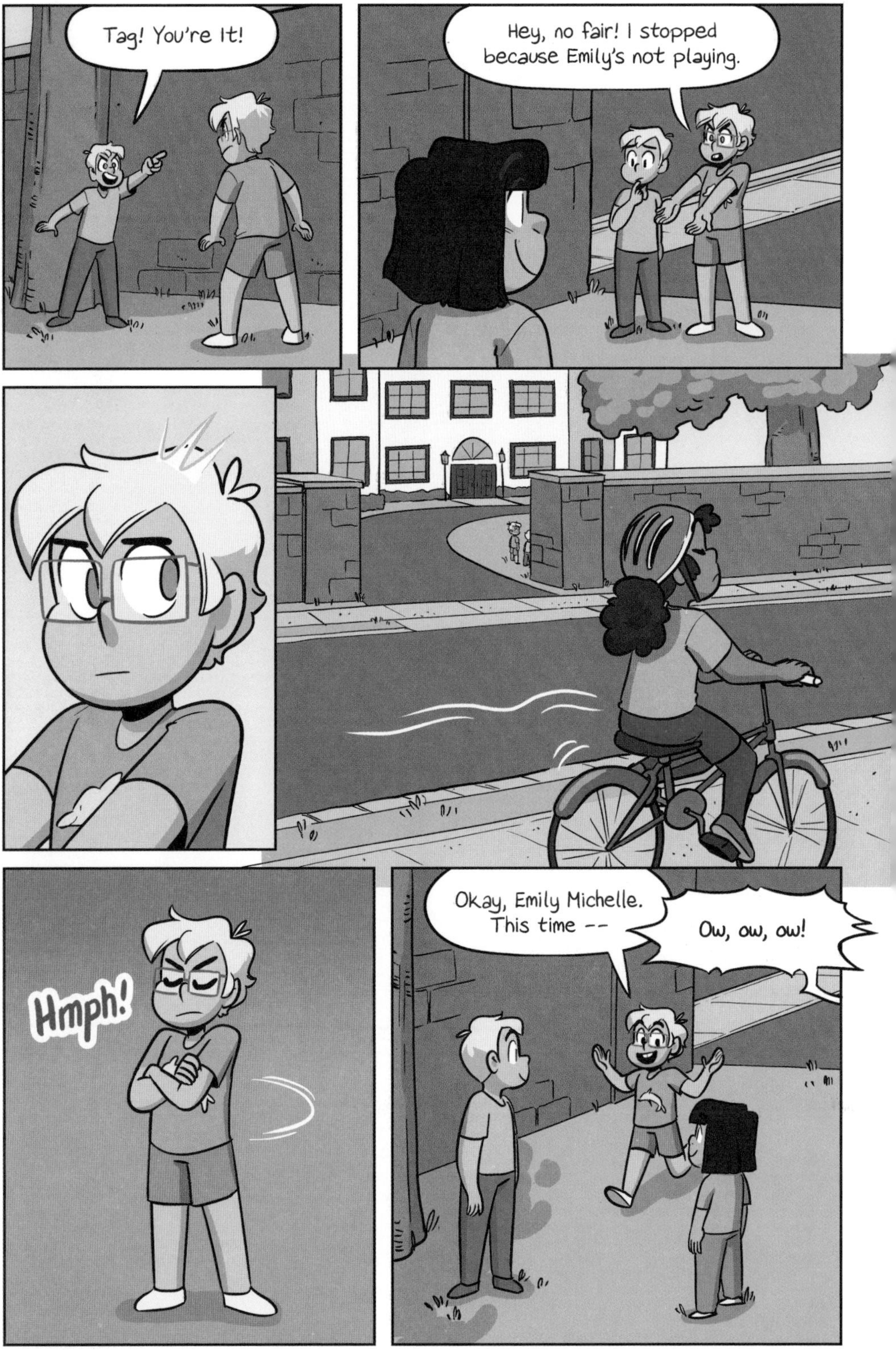
Tag! You're It!
Hey, no fair! I stopped because Emily's not playing.
Hmph!
Okay, Emily Michelle. This time --
Ow, ow, ow!

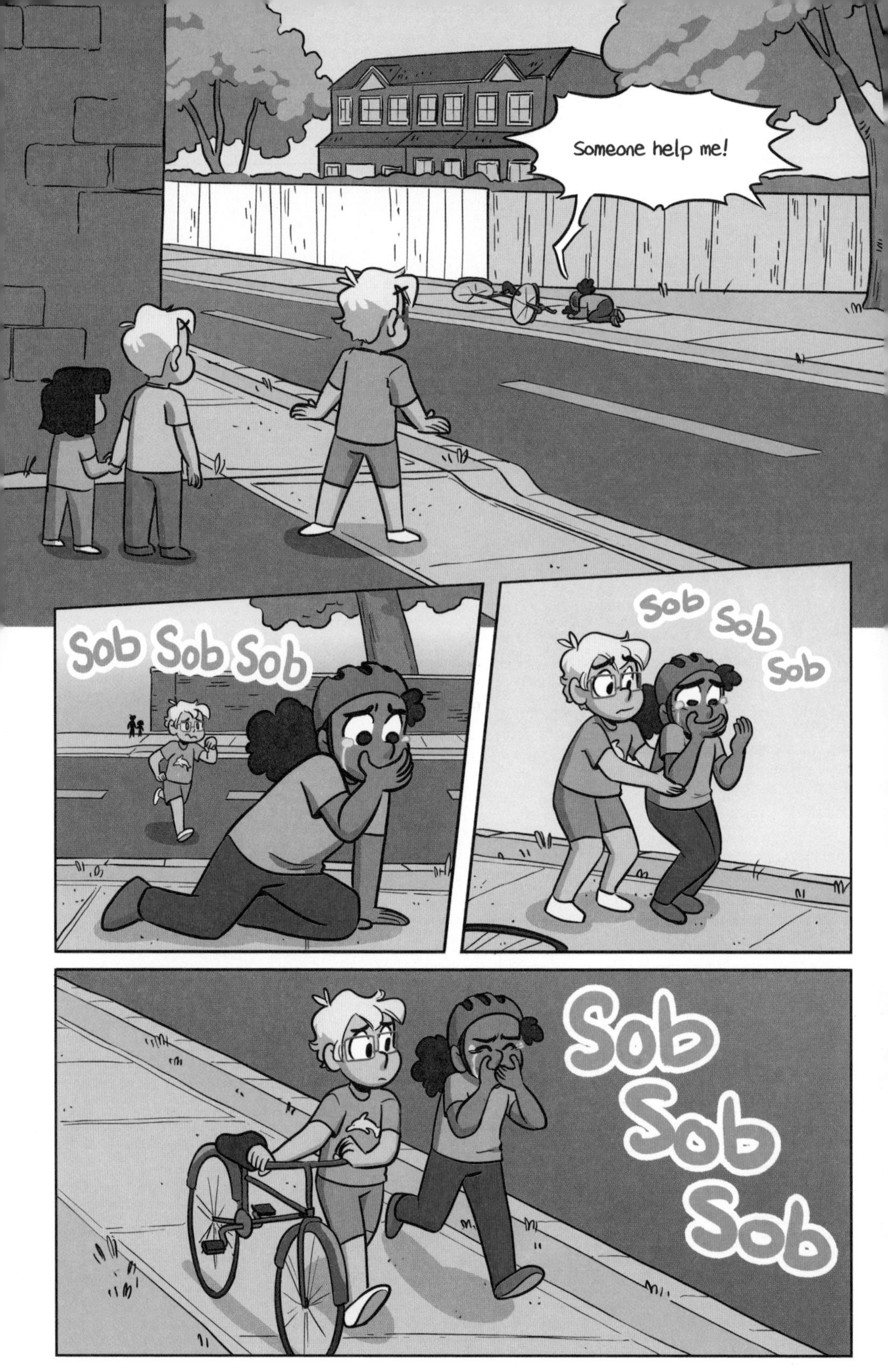

Someone help me!
Sob Sob Sob
Sob Sob Sob
Sob Sob Sob

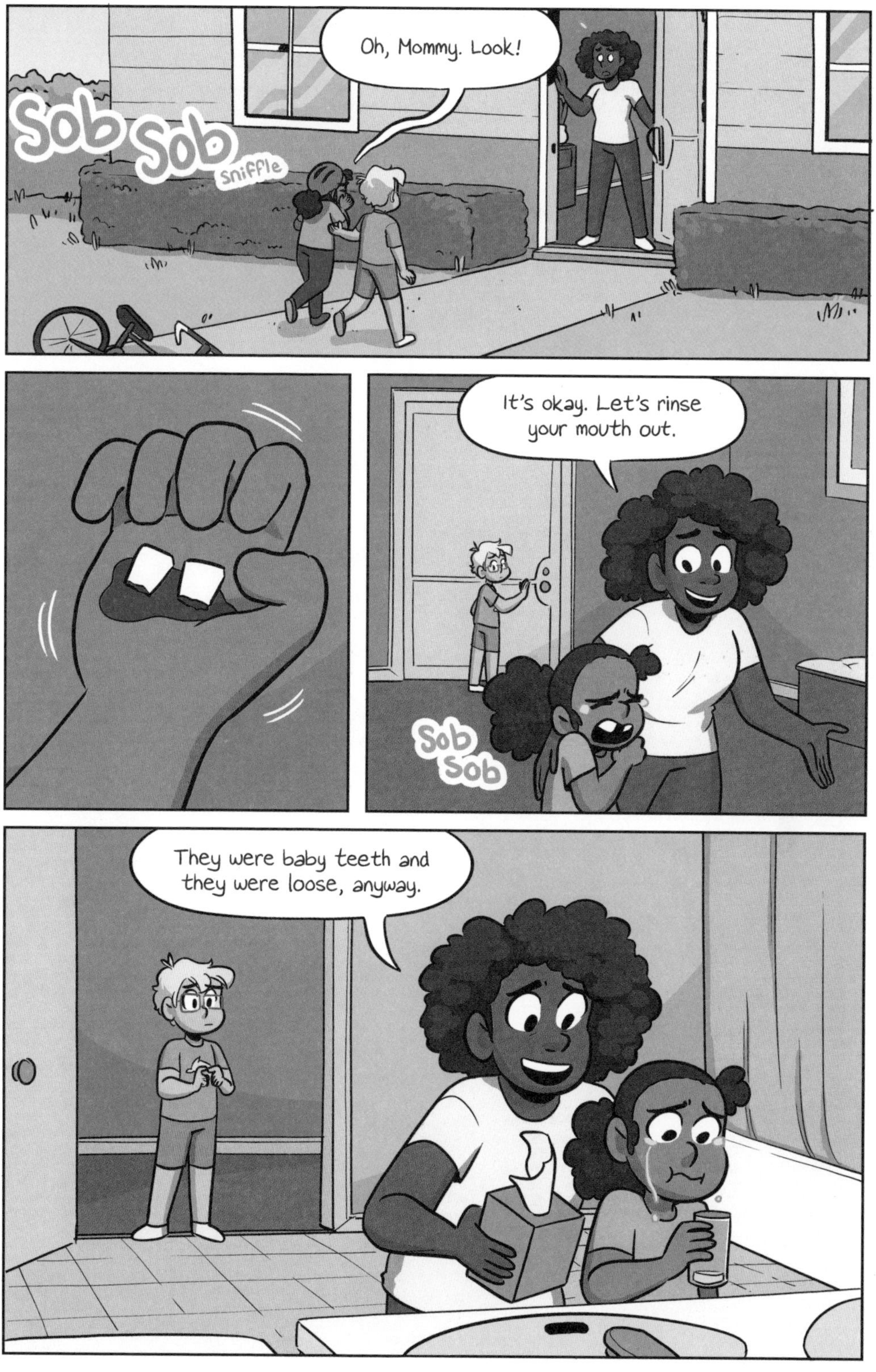
Oh, Mommy. Look!
Sob Sob
sniffle
It's okay. Let's rinse your mouth out.
Sob Sob
They were baby teeth and they were loose, anyway.

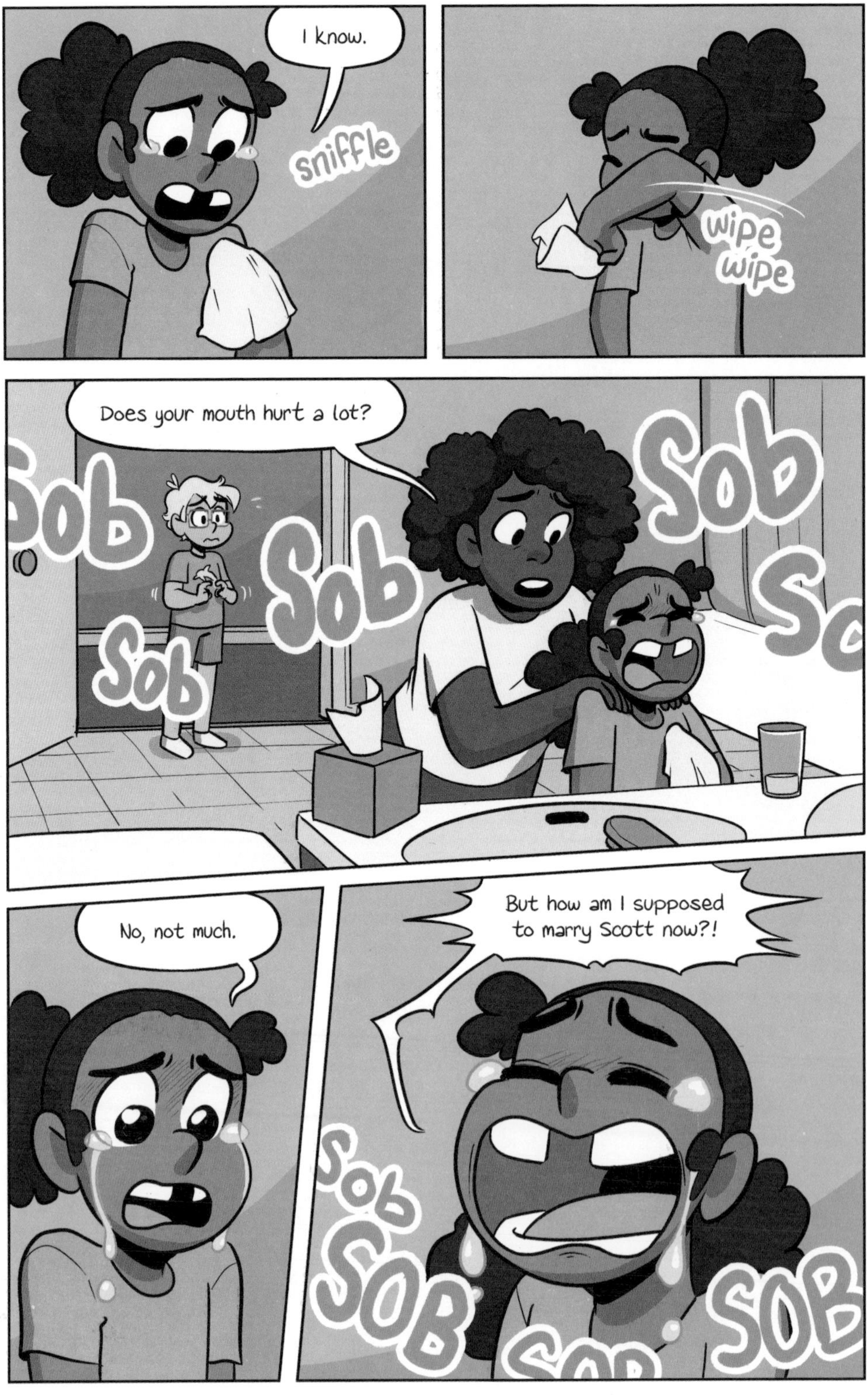
I know.
sniffle
wipe wipe
Does your mouth hurt a lot?
Sob
Sob
Sob
Sob
So
No, not much.
But how am I supposed to marry Scott now?!
Sob
SOB
SOB

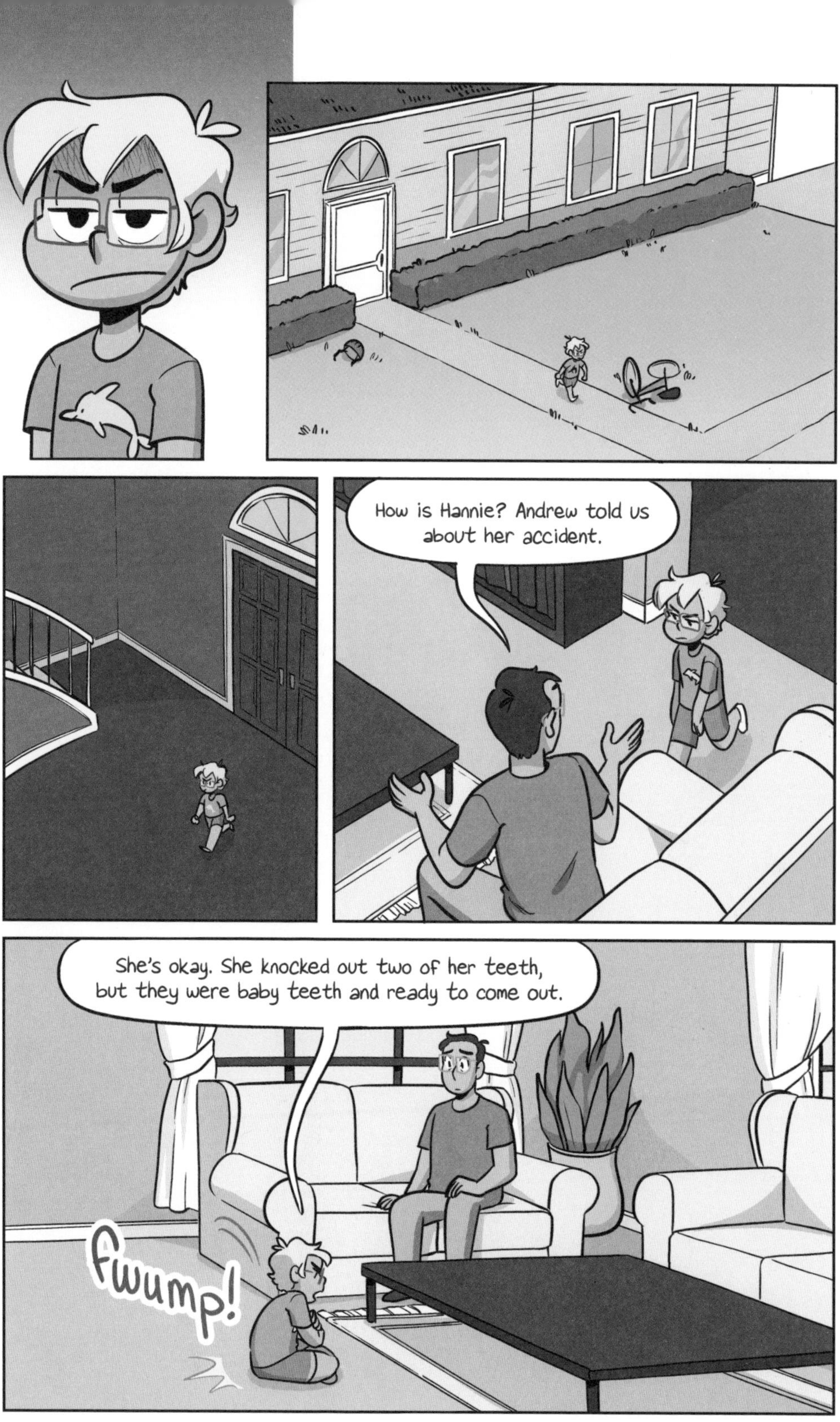
How is Hannie? Andrew told us about her accident.
She's okay. She knocked out two of her teeth, but they were baby teeth and ready to come out.
fwump!

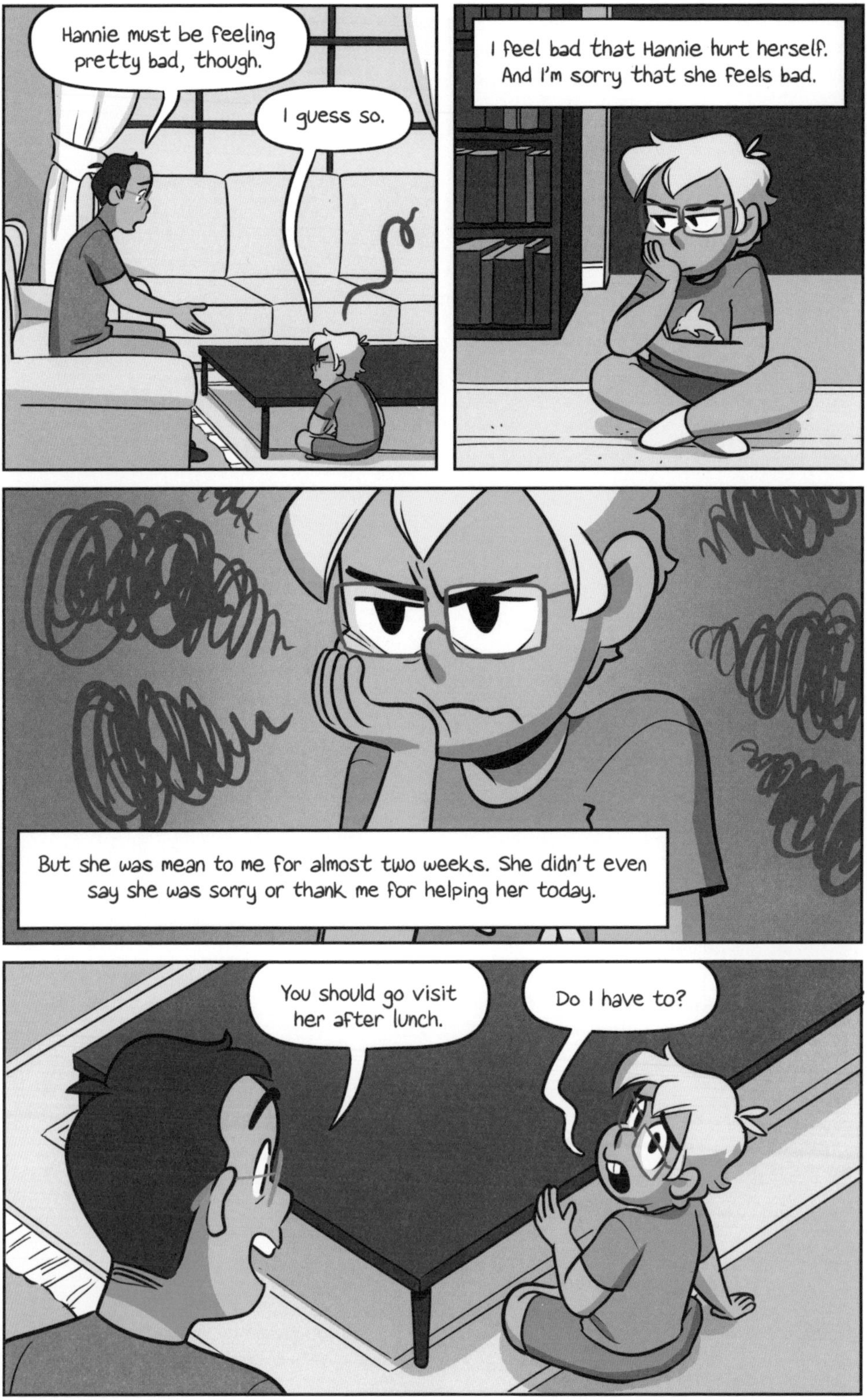
Hannie must be feeling pretty bad, though.
I guess so.
I feel bad that Hannie hurt herself. And I'm sorry that she feels bad.
But she was mean to me for almost two weeks. She didn't even say she was sorry or thank me for helping her today.
You should go visit her after lunch.
Do I have to?

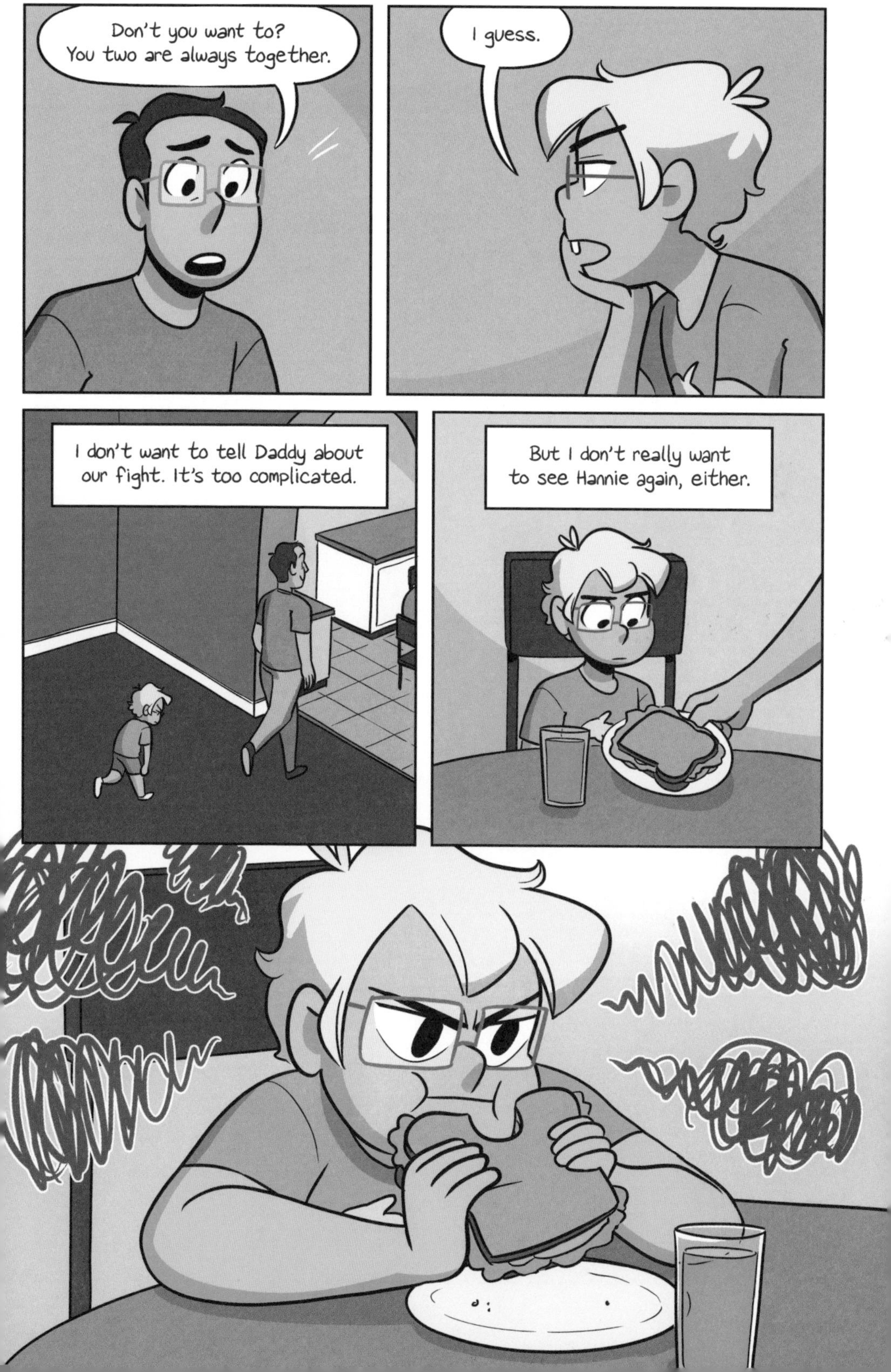
Don't you want to? You two are always together.
I guess.
I don't want to tell Daddy about our fight. It's too complicated.
But I don't really want to see Hannie again, either.

CHAPTER 9

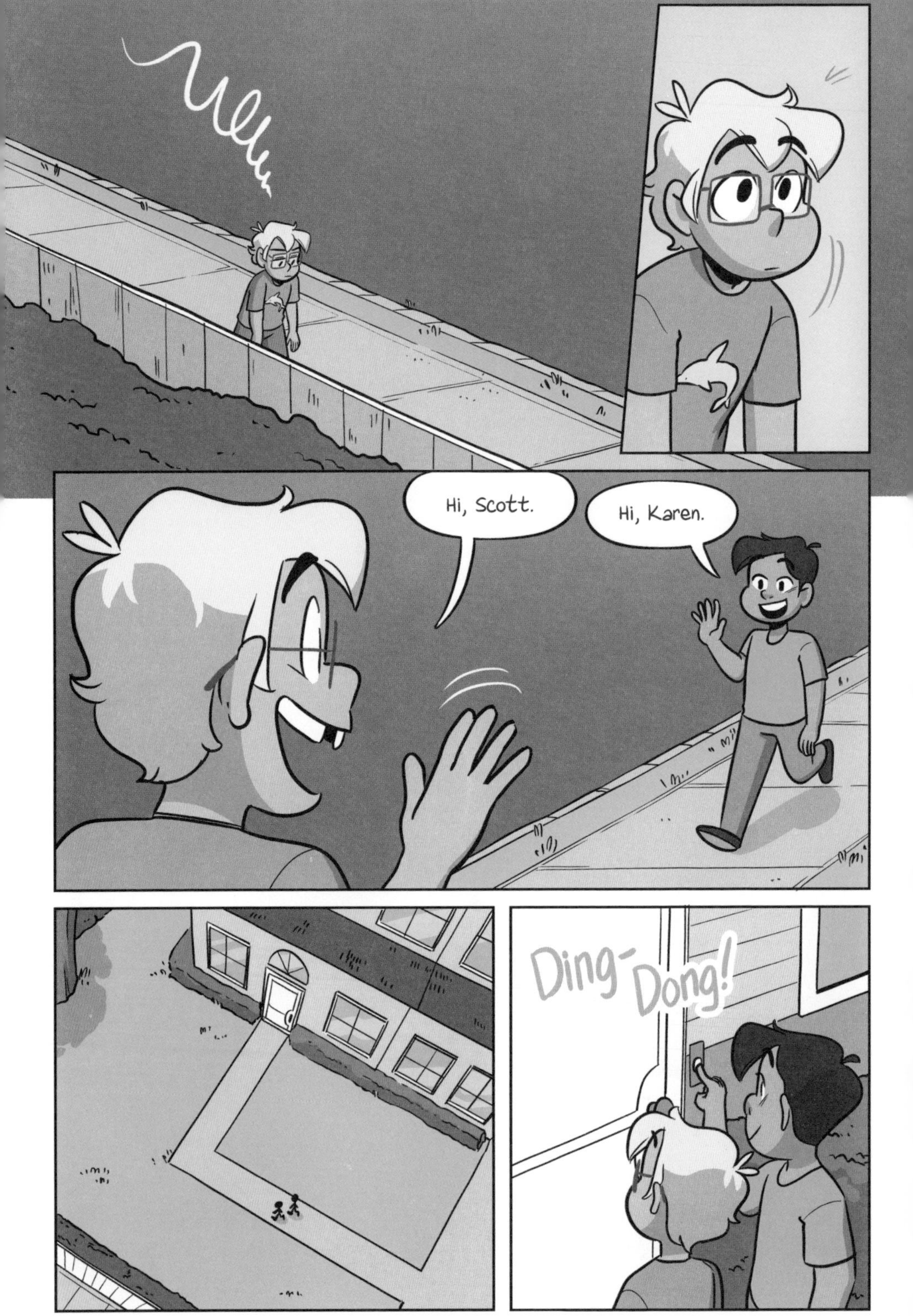
Hi, Scott.
Hi, Karen.
Ding-Dong!

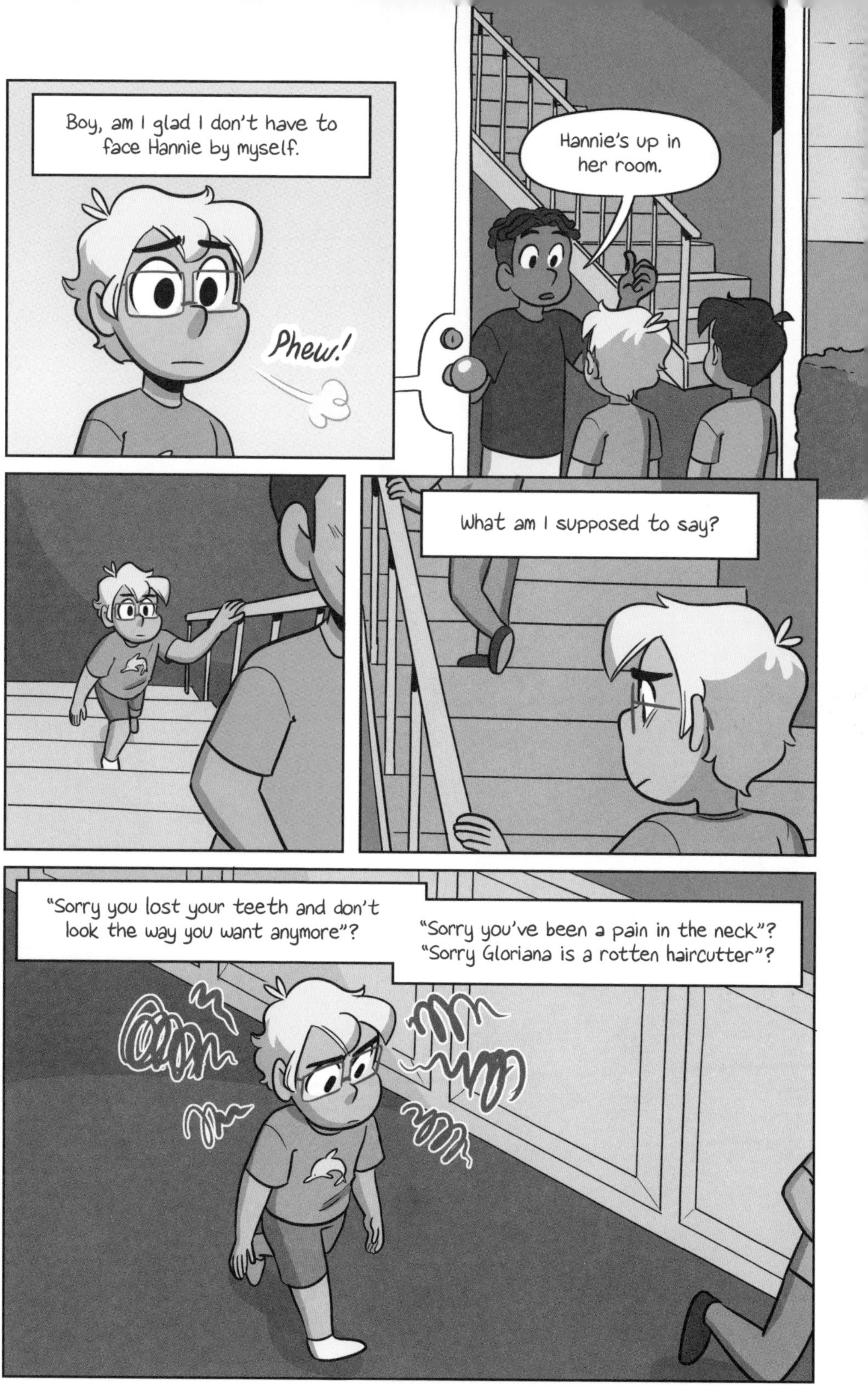
Boy, am I glad I don't have to face Hannie by myself.
Phew!
Hannie's up in her room.
What am I supposed to say?
"Sorry you lost your teeth and don't look the way you want anymore"?
"Sorry you've been a pain in the neck"? "Sorry Gloriana is a rotten haircutter"?

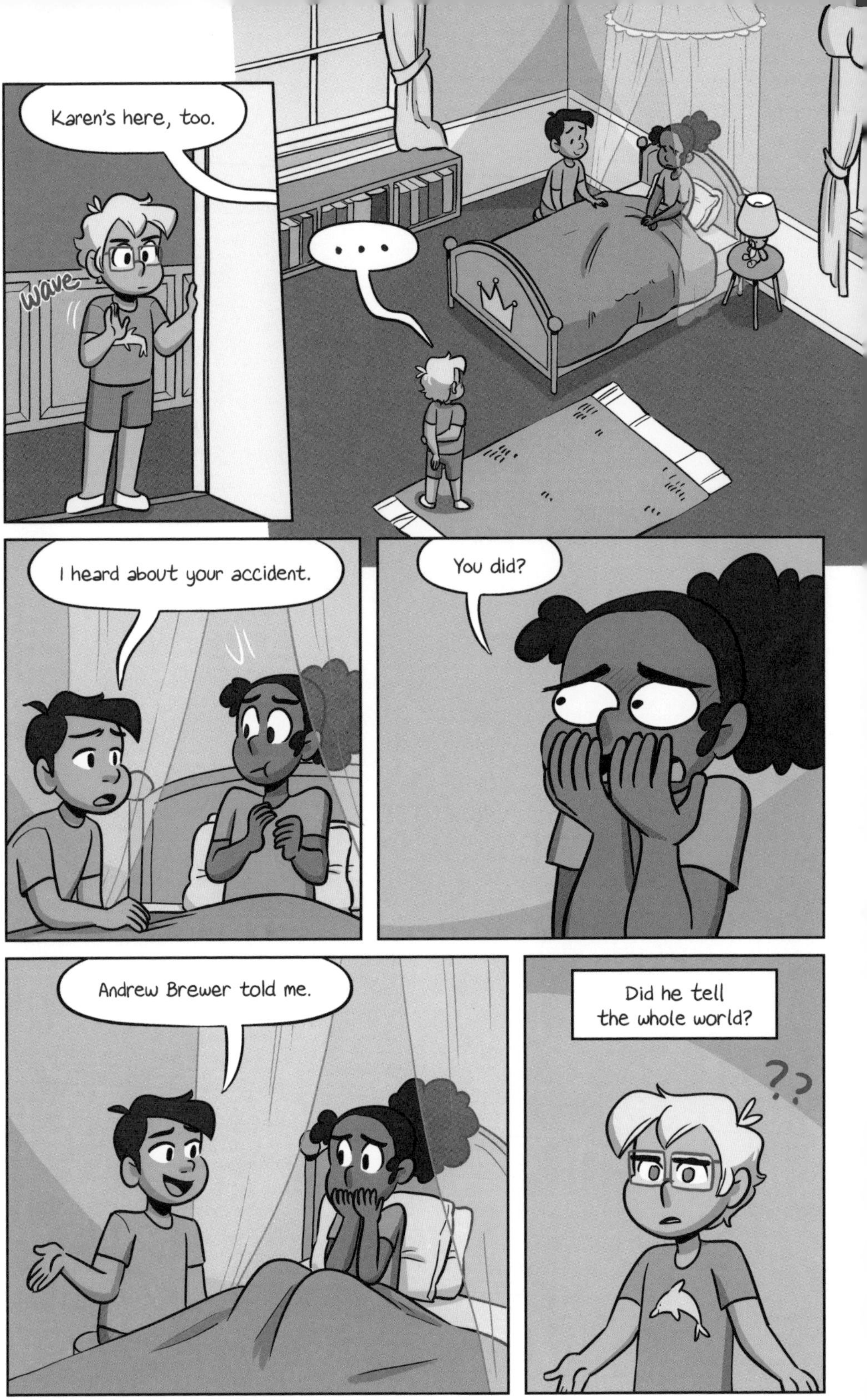
Karen's here, too.
WAVE
. . .
I heard about your accident.
You did?
Andrew Brewer told me.
Did he tell the whole world?
??

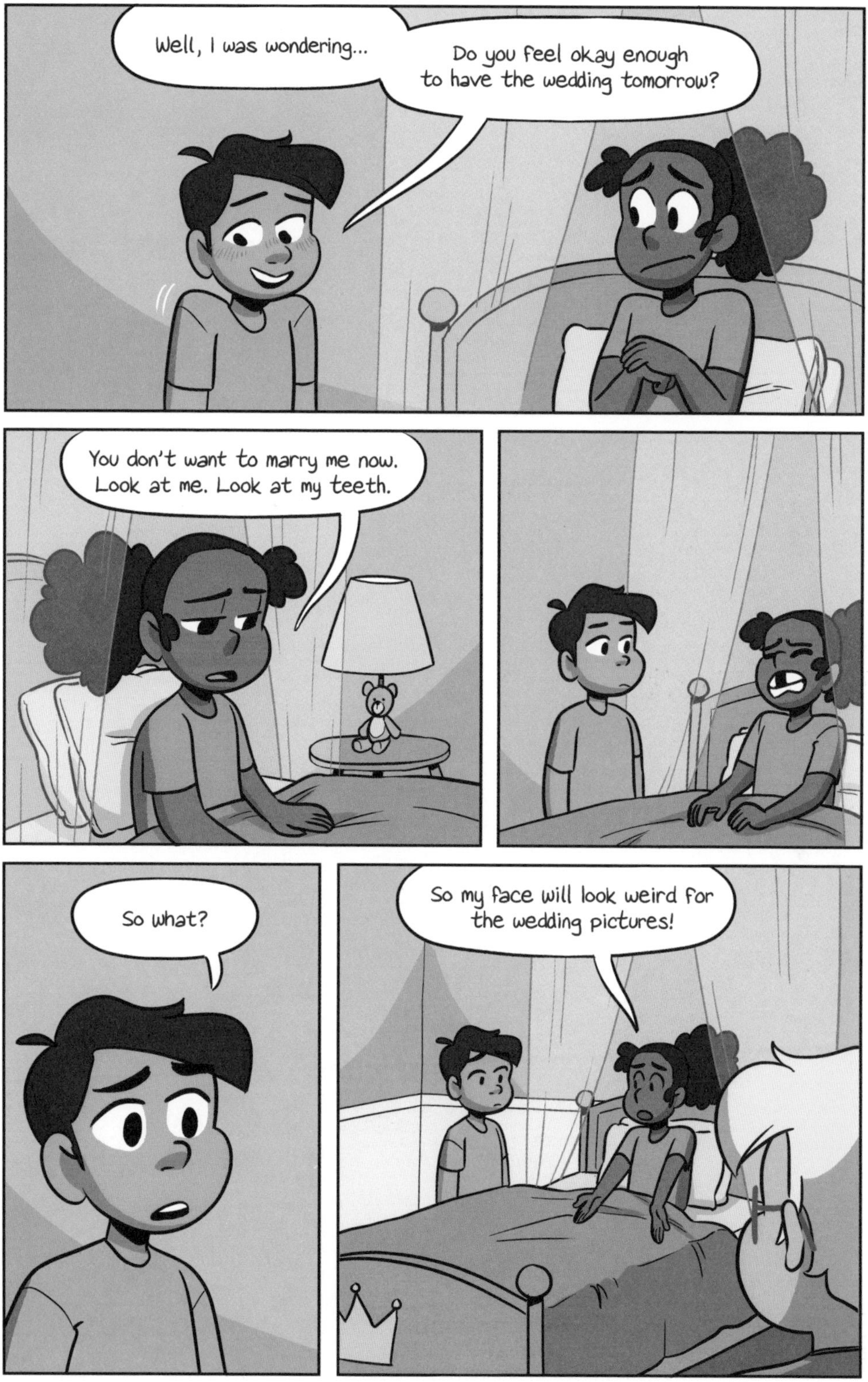
Well, I was wondering...
Do you feel okay enough to have the wedding tomorrow?
You don't want to marry me now. Look at me. Look at my teeth.
So what?
So my face will look weird for the wedding pictures!

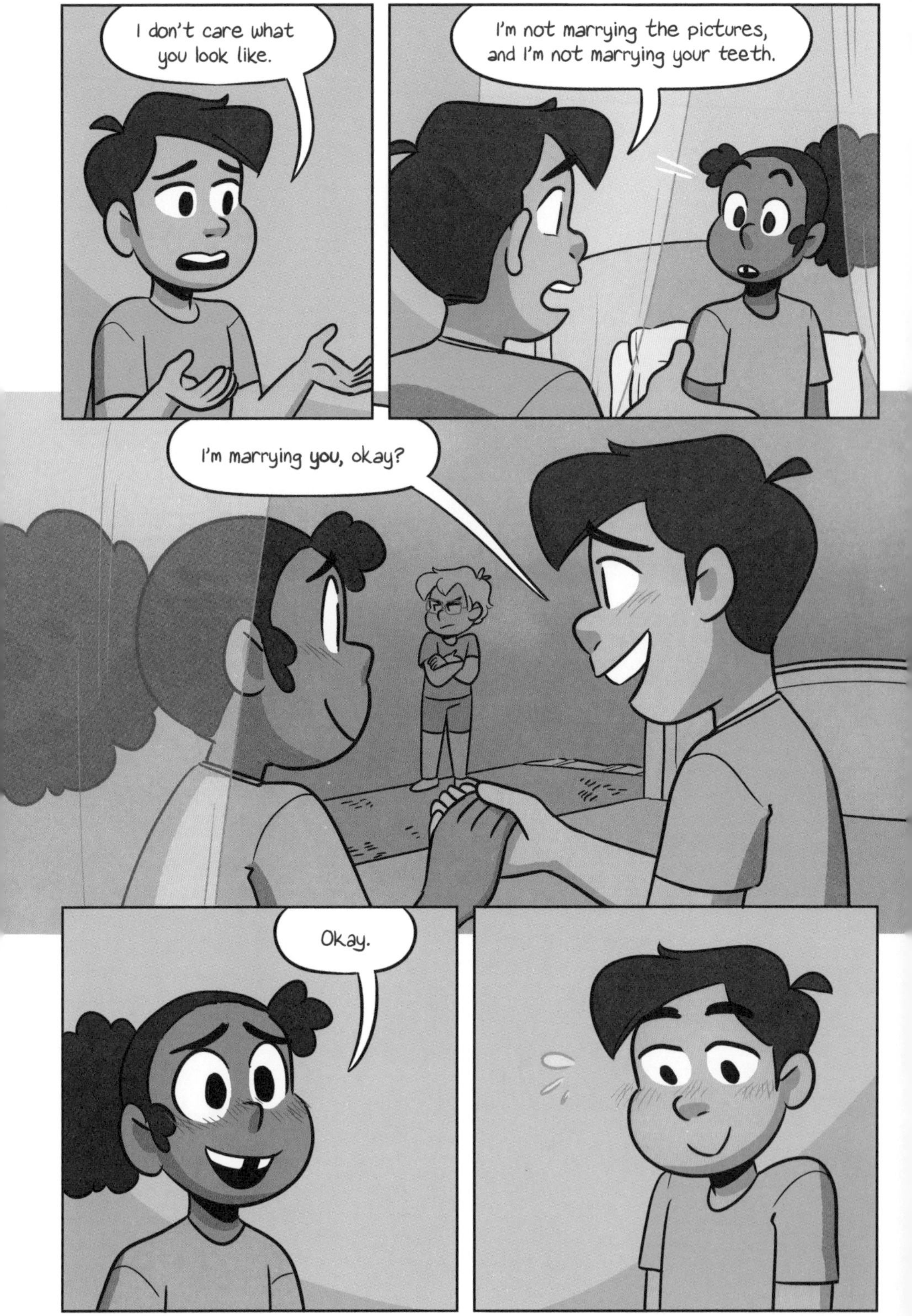
I don't care what you look like.
I'm not marrying the pictures, and I'm not marrying your teeth.
I'm marrying you, okay?
Okay.

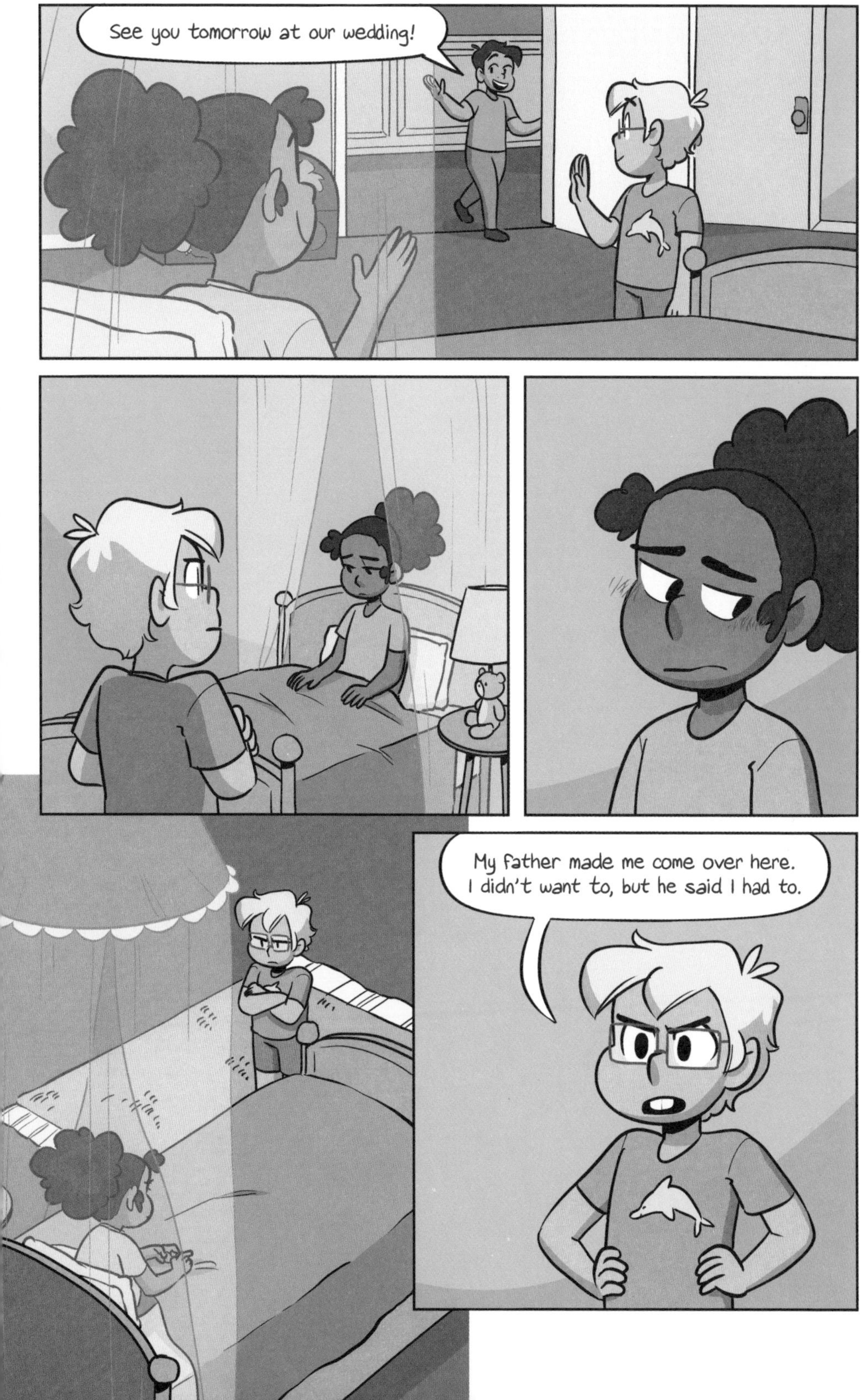
See you tomorrow at our wedding!
My father made me come over here. I didn't want to, but he said I had to.

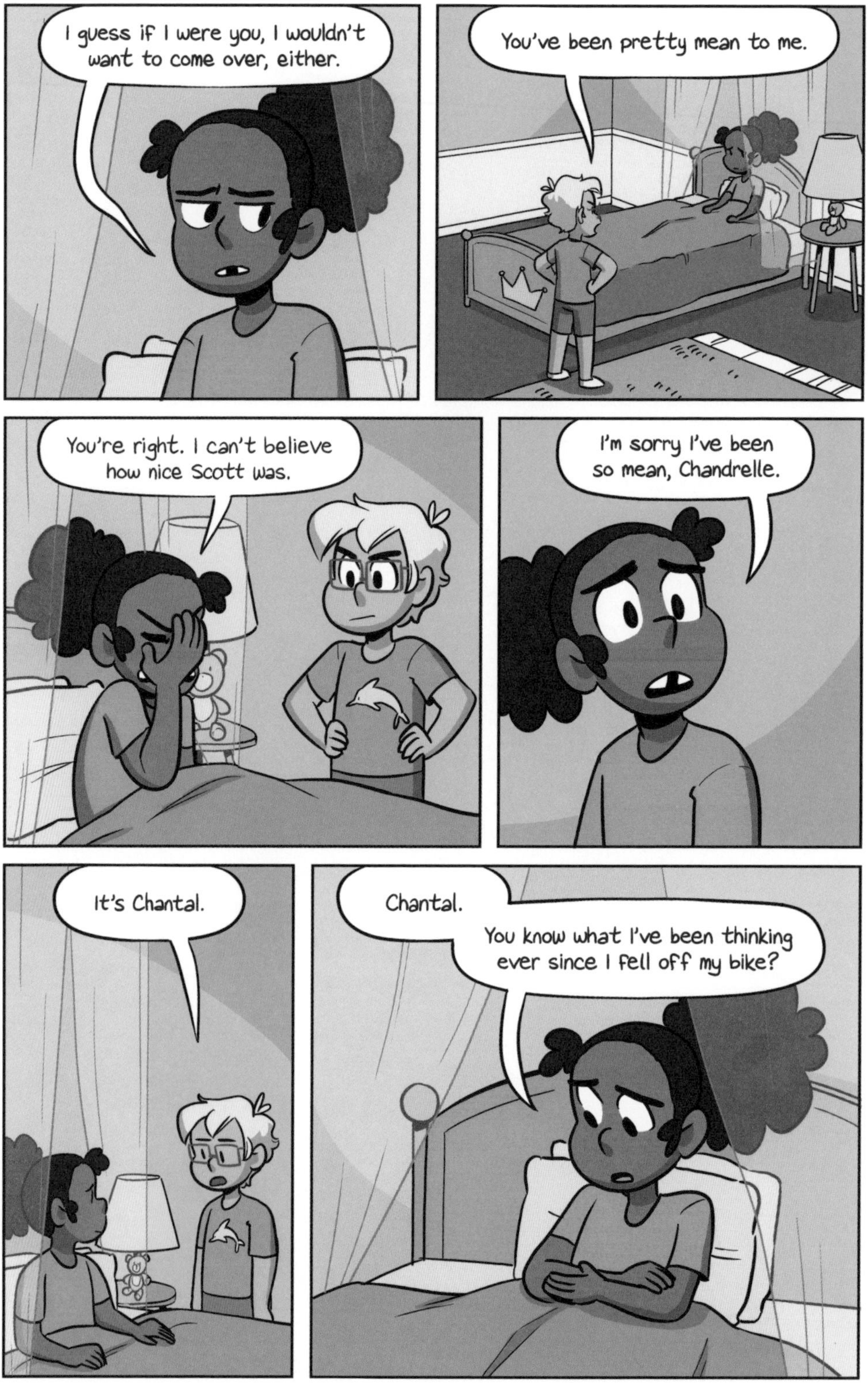
I guess if I were you, I wouldn't want to come over, either.
You've been pretty mean to me.
You're right. I can't believe how nice Scott was.
I'm sorry I've been so mean, Chandrelle.
It's Chantal.
Chantal.
You know what I've been thinking ever since I fell off my bike?

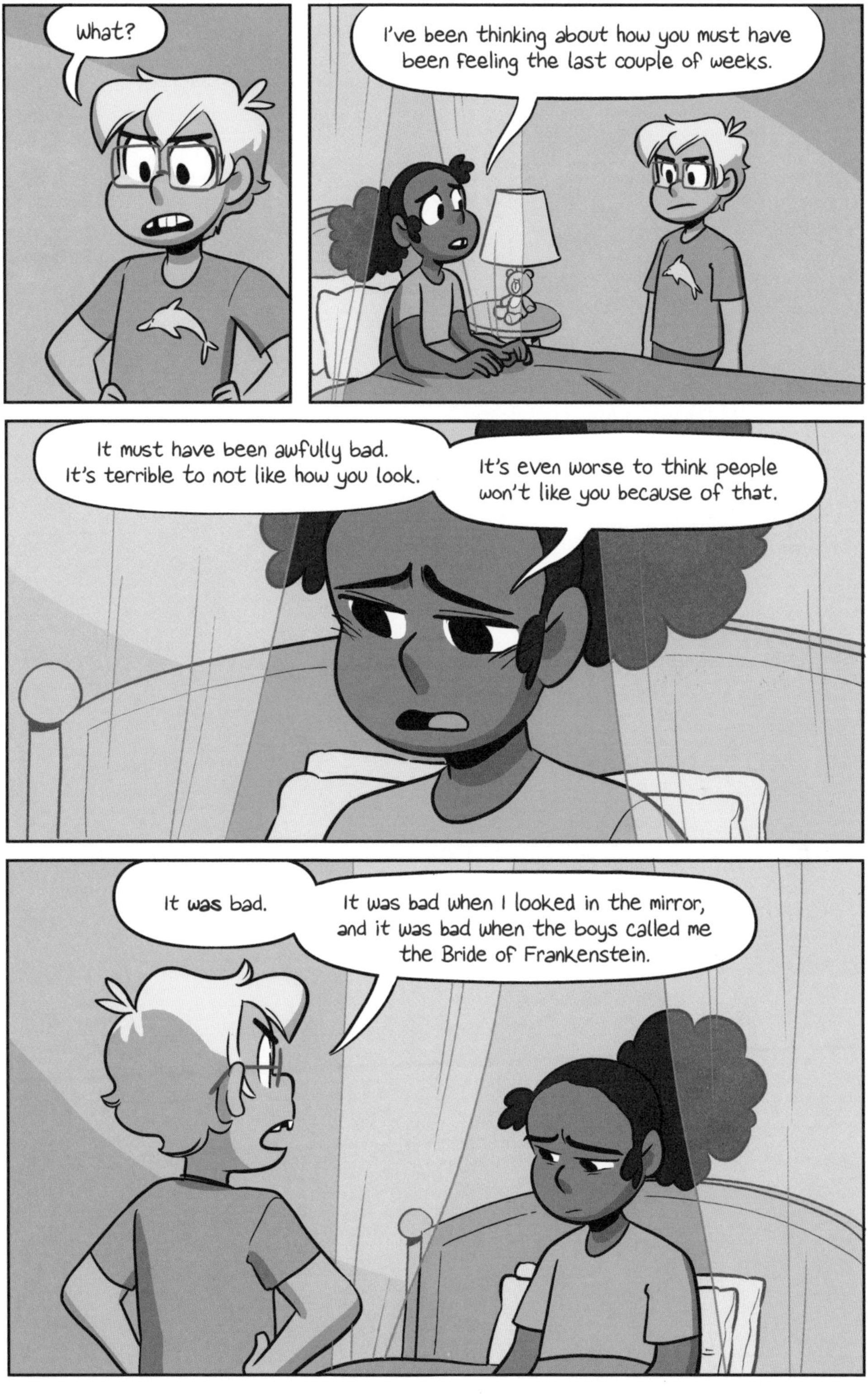
What?
I've been thinking about how you must have been feeling the last couple of weeks.
It must have been awfully bad. It's terrible to not like how you look.
It's even worse to think people won't like you because of that.
It was bad.
It was bad when I looked in the mirror, and it was bad when the boys called me the Bride of Frankenstein.

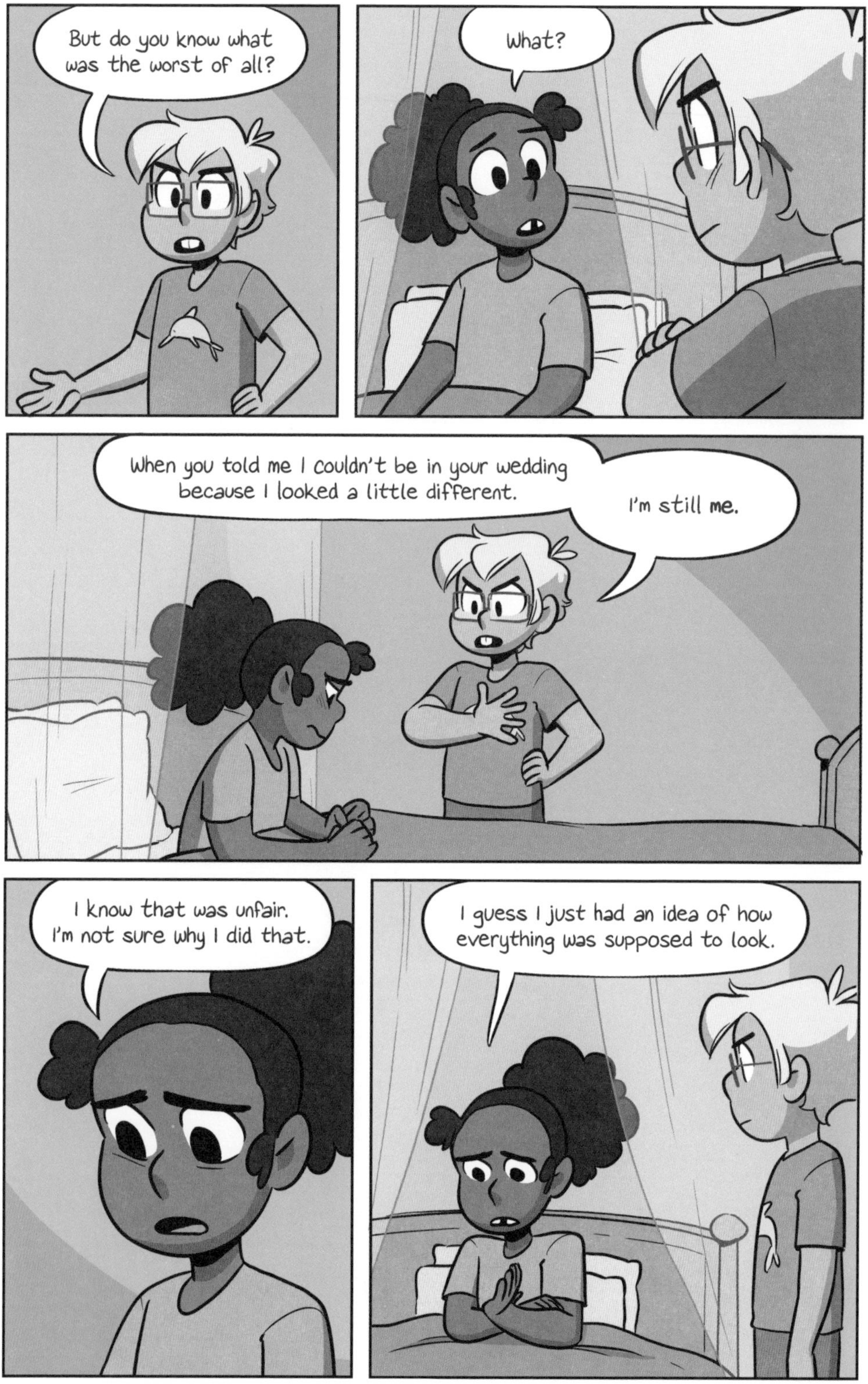
But do you know what was the worst of all?
What?
When you told me I couldn't be in your wedding because I looked a little different.
I'm still me.
I know that was unfair. I'm not sure why I did that.
I guess I just had an idea of how everything was supposed to look.

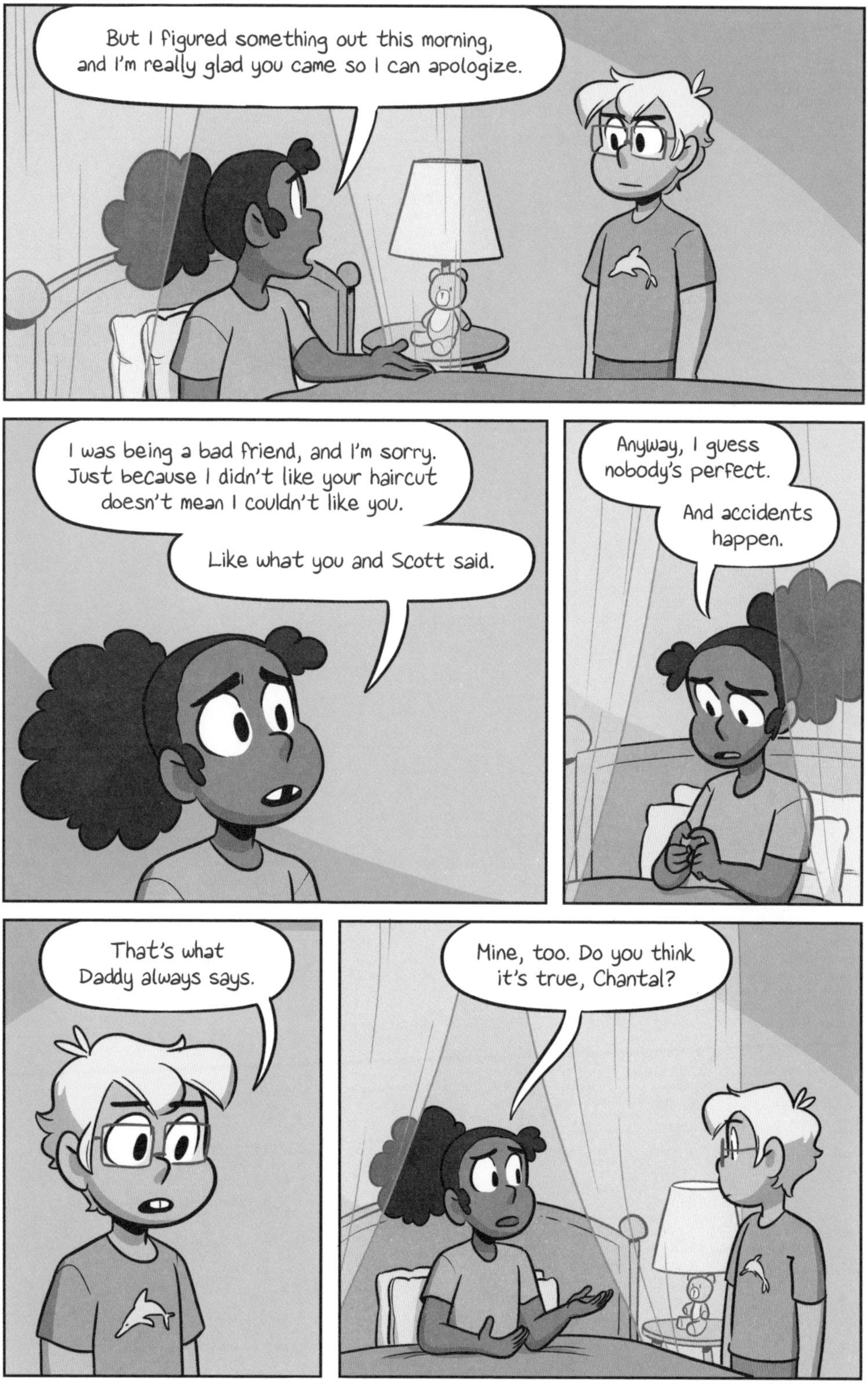
But I figured something out this morning, and I'm really glad you came so I can apologize.
I was being a bad friend, and I'm sorry. Just because I didn't like your haircut doesn't mean I couldn't like you.
Like what you and Scott said.
Anyway, I guess nobody's perfect.
And accidents happen.
That's what Daddy always says.
Mine, too. Do you think it's true, Chantal?

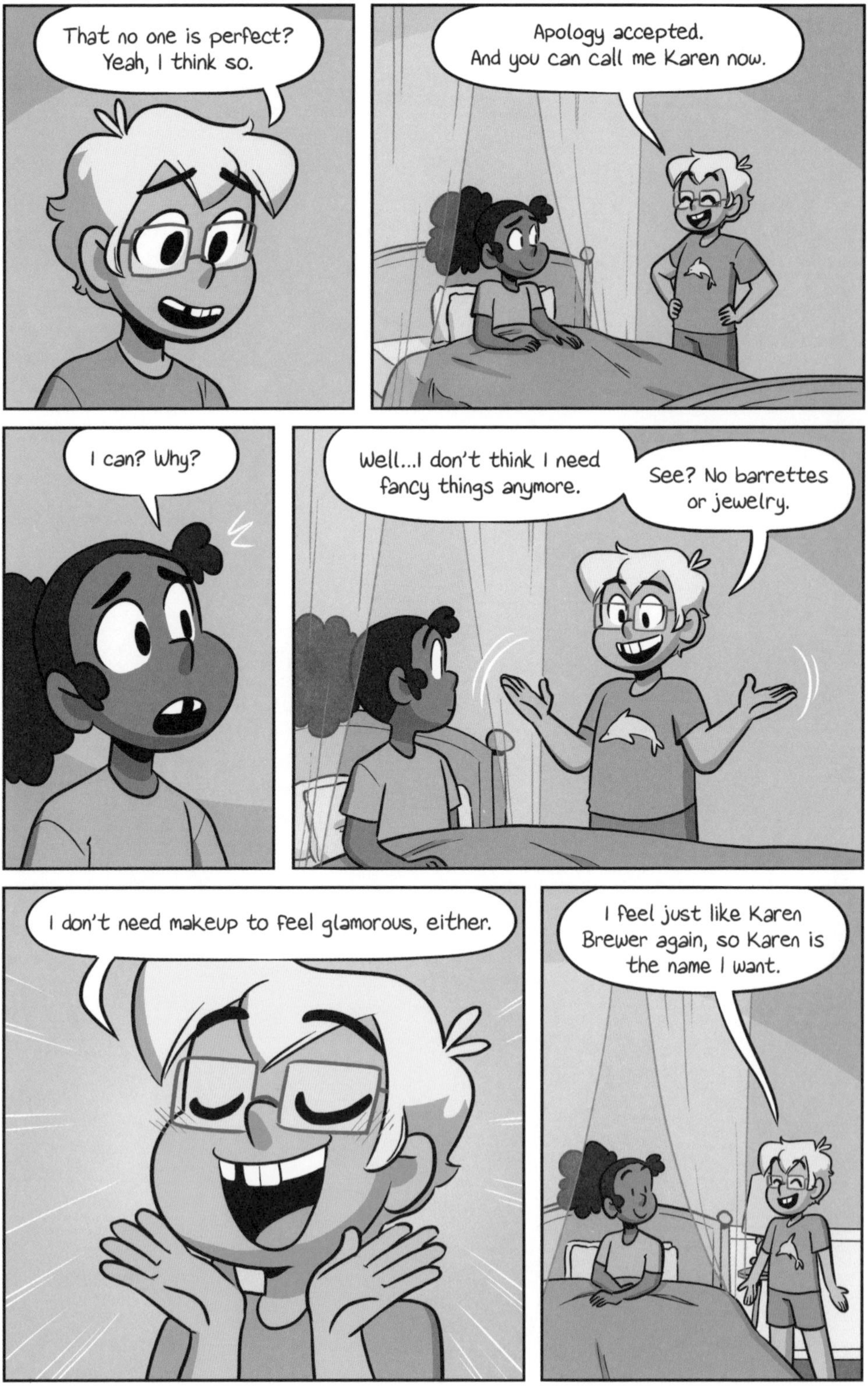

That no one is perfect? Yeah, I think so.
Apology accepted. And you can call me Karen now.
I can? Why?
Well...I don't think I need fancy things anymore.
See? No barrettes or jewelry.
I don't need makeup to feel glamorous, either.
I feel just like Karen Brewer again, so Karen is the name I want.

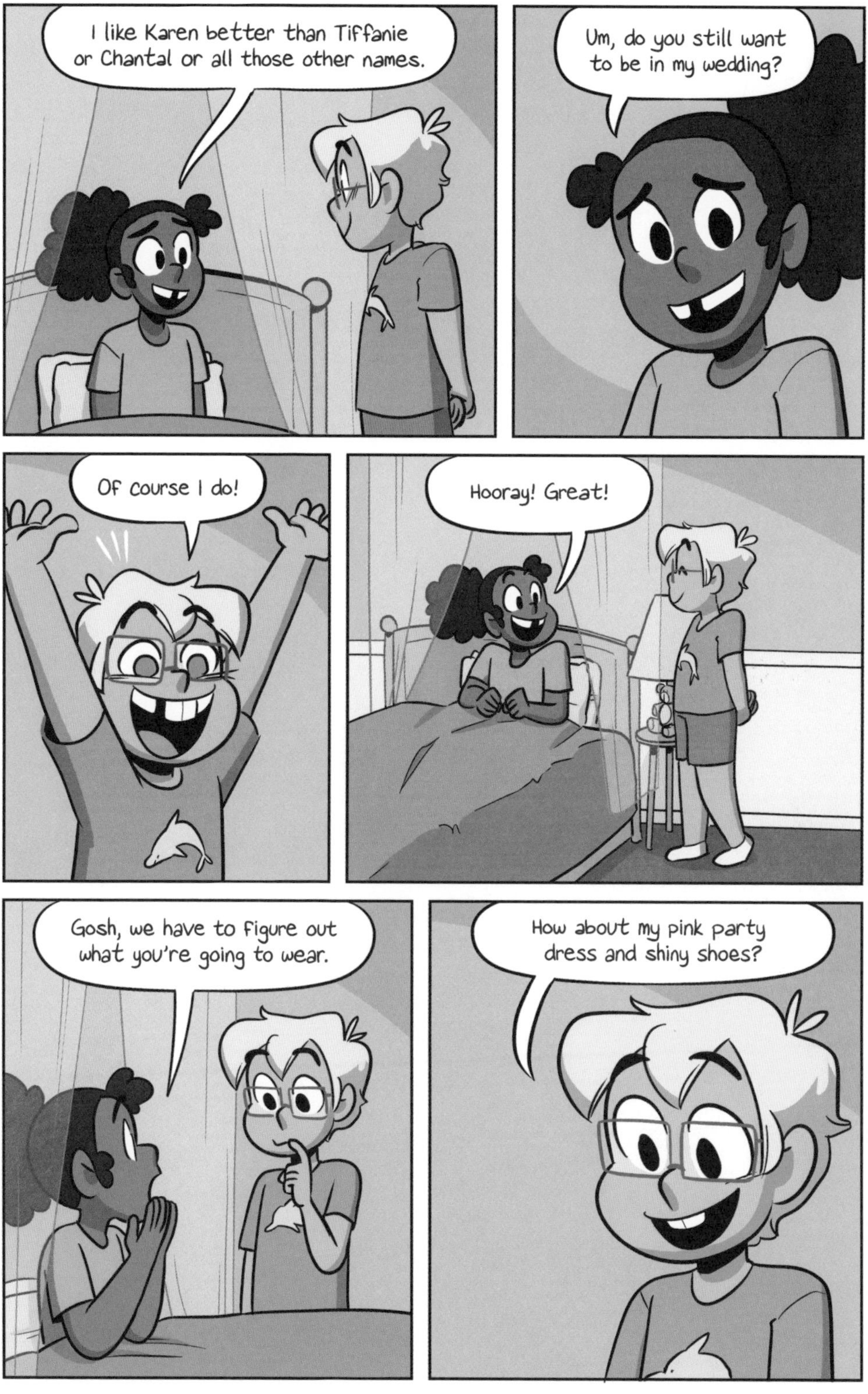
I like Karen better than Tiffanie or Chantal or all those other names.
Um, do you still want to be in my wedding?
Of course I do!
Hooray! Great!
Gosh, we have to figure out what you're going to wear.
How about my pink party dress and shiny shoes?

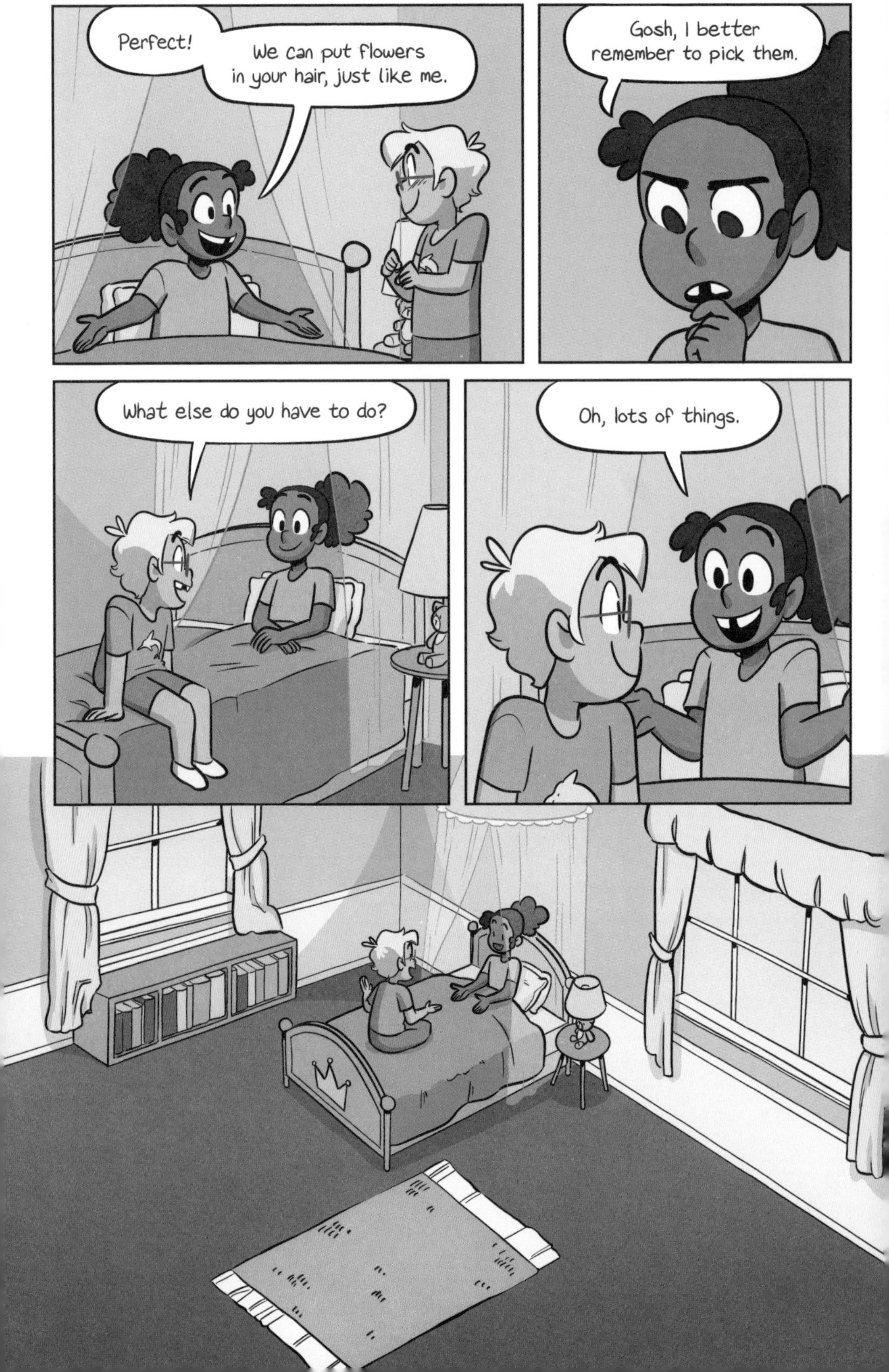
Perfect!
We can put flowers in your hair, just like me.
Gosh, I better remember to pick them.
What else do you have to do?
Oh, lots of things.

CHAPTER 10

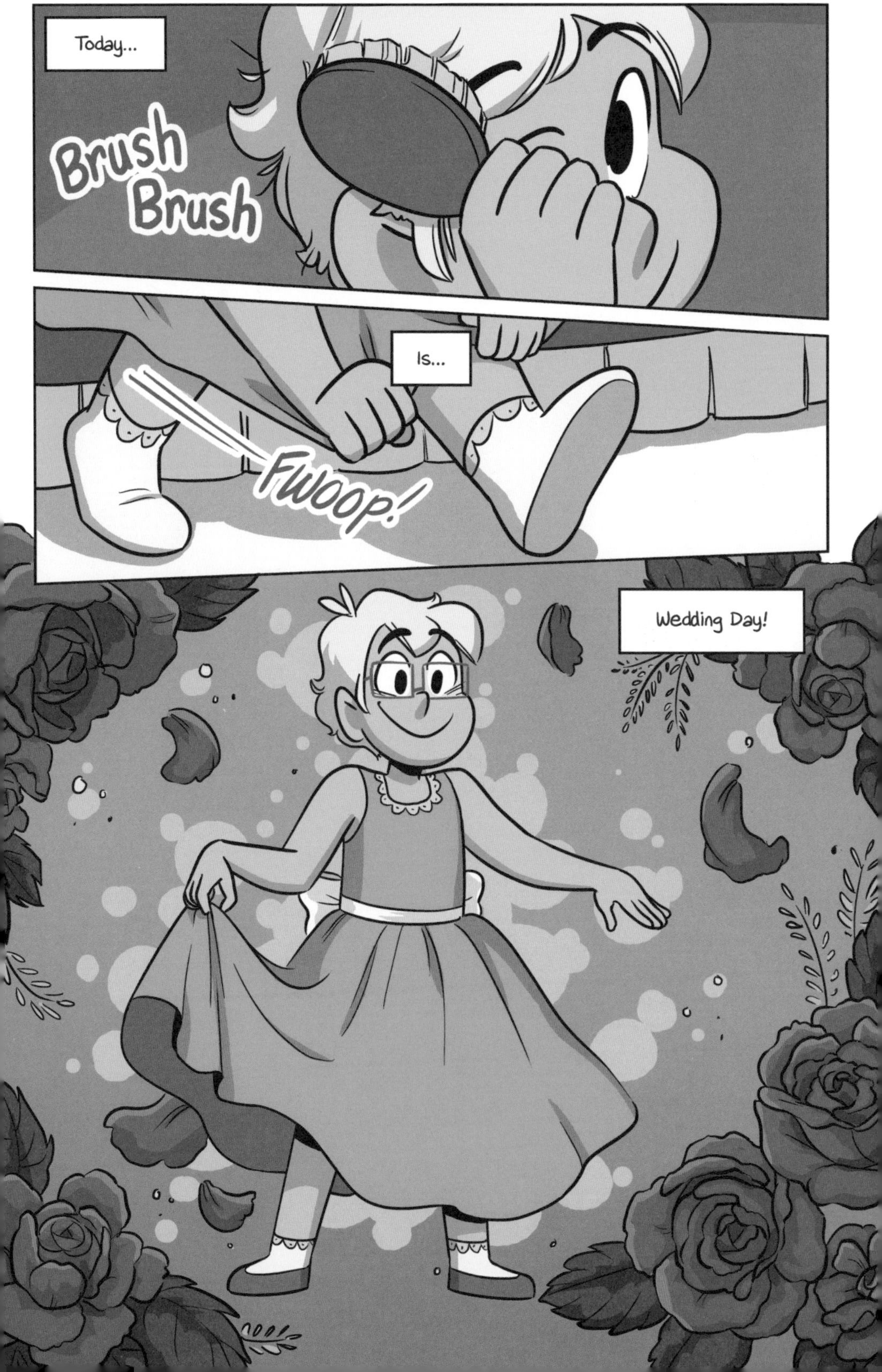
Today...
Brush
Brush
Is...
Fwoop!
Wedding Day!

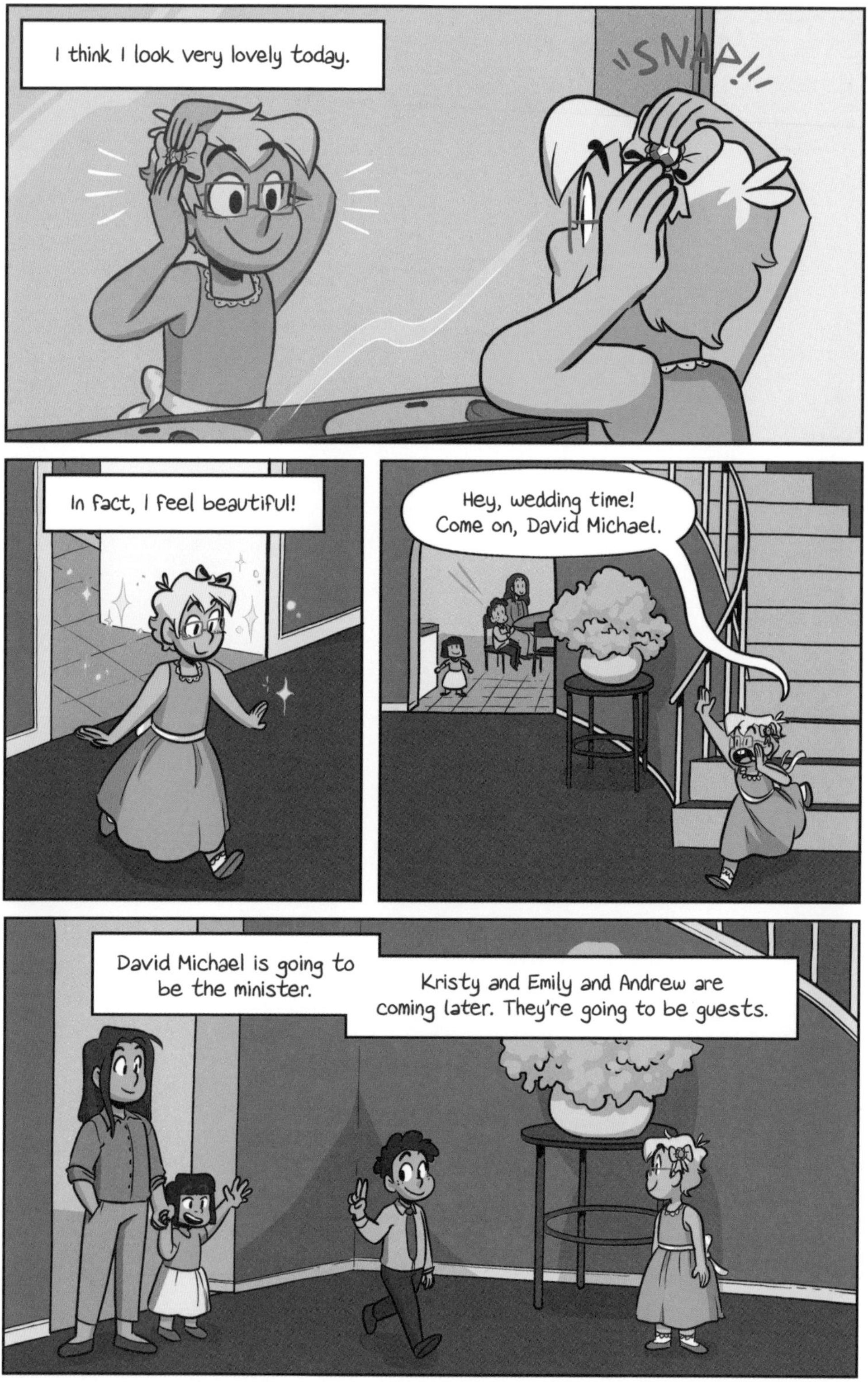
I think I look very lovely today.
SNAP!
In fact, I feel beautiful!
Hey, wedding time! Come on, David Michael.
David Michael is going to be the minister.
Kristy and Emily and Andrew are coming later. They're going to be guests.

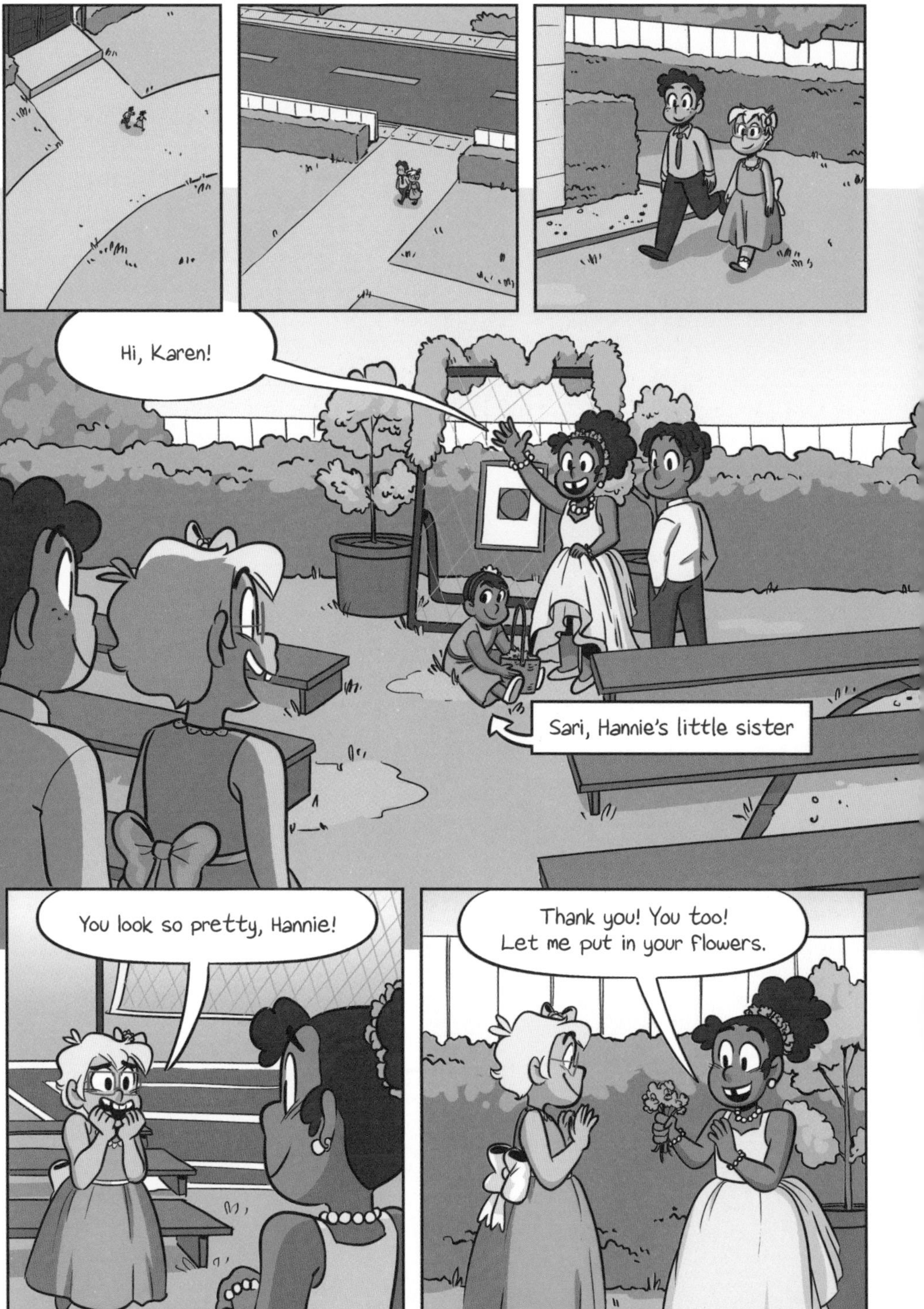
Hi, Karen!
Sari, Hannie's little sister
You look so pretty, Hannie!
Thank you! You too!
Let me put in your flowers.

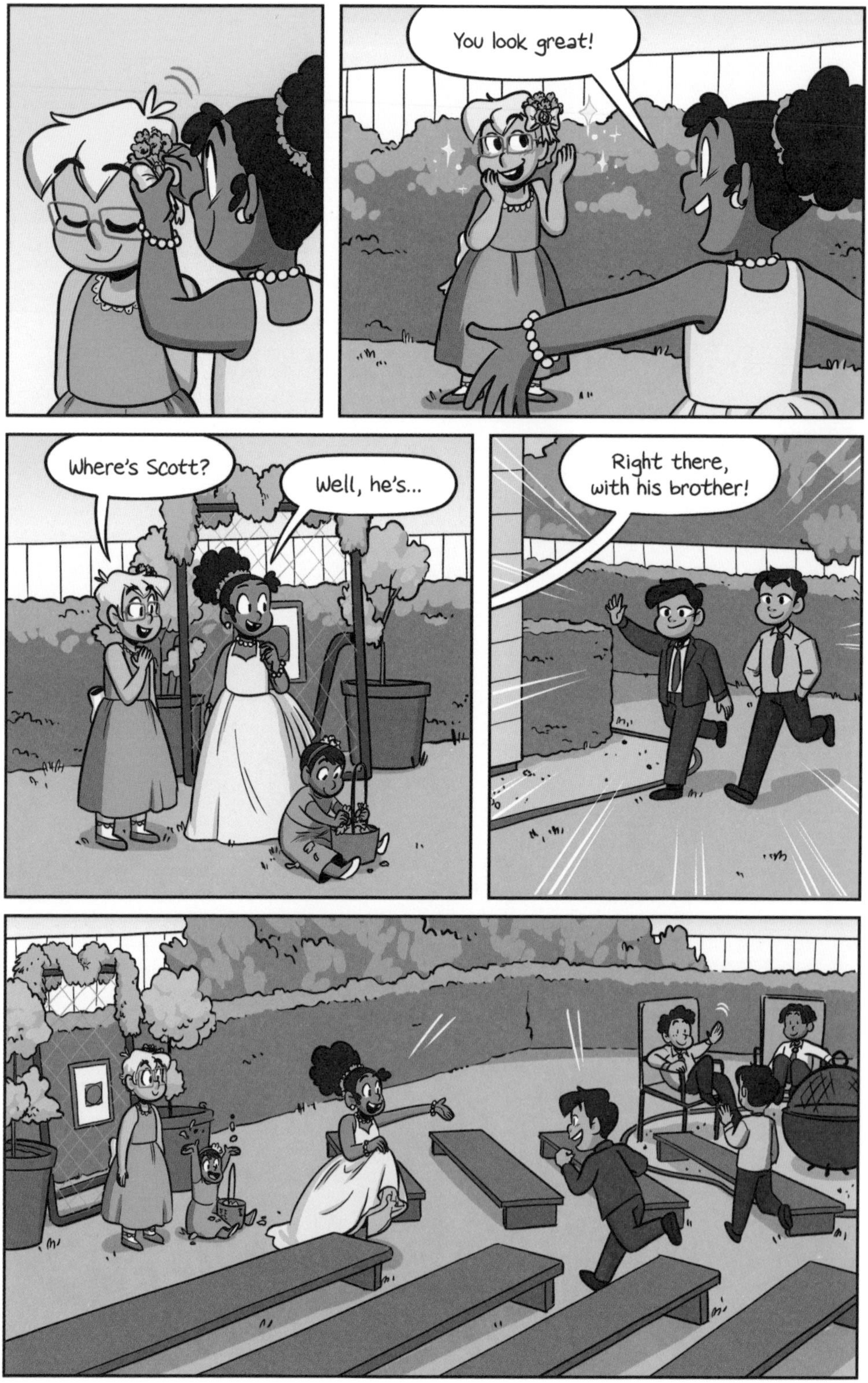
You look great!
Where's Scott?
Well, he's...
Right there, with his brother!

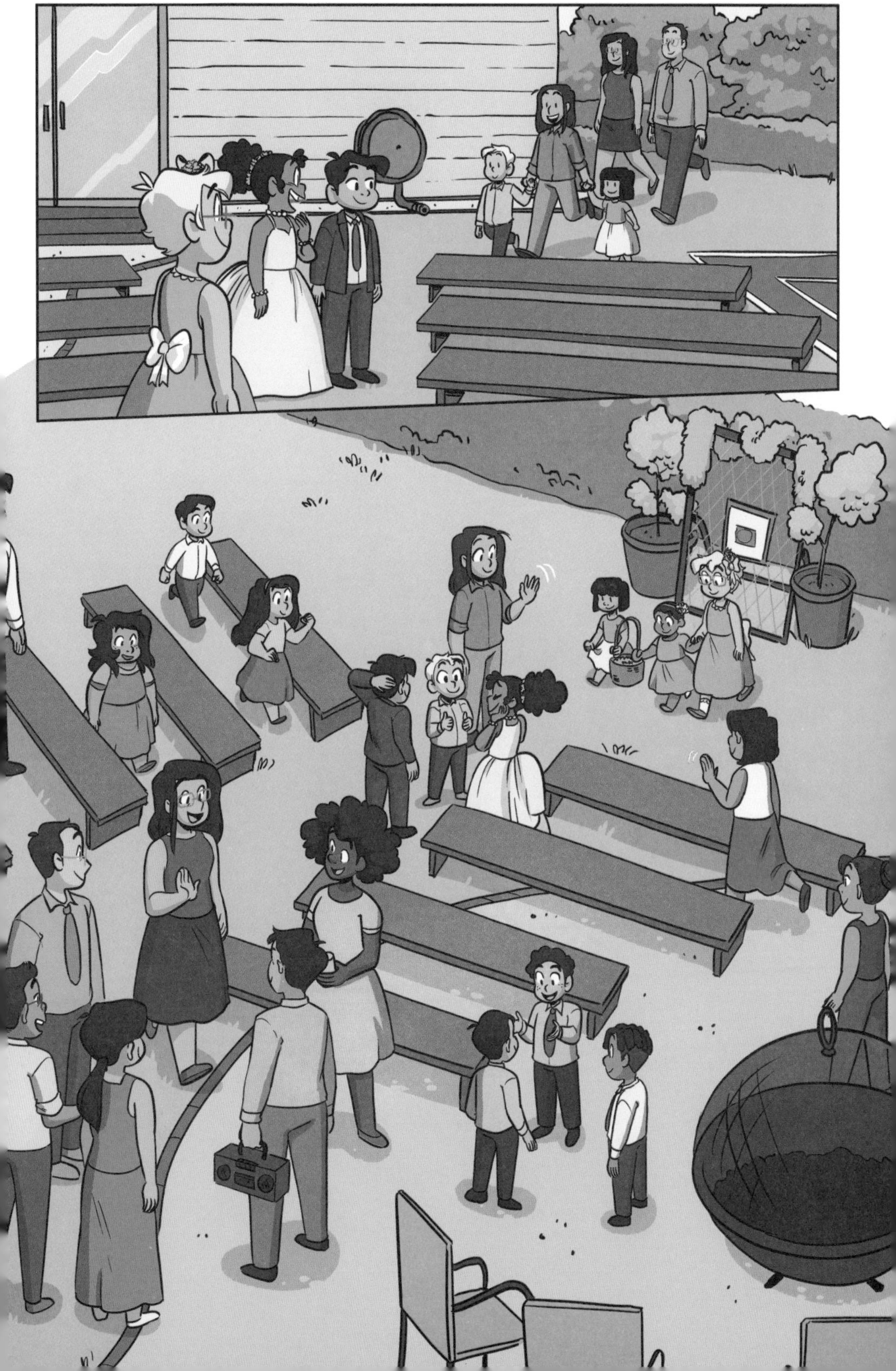

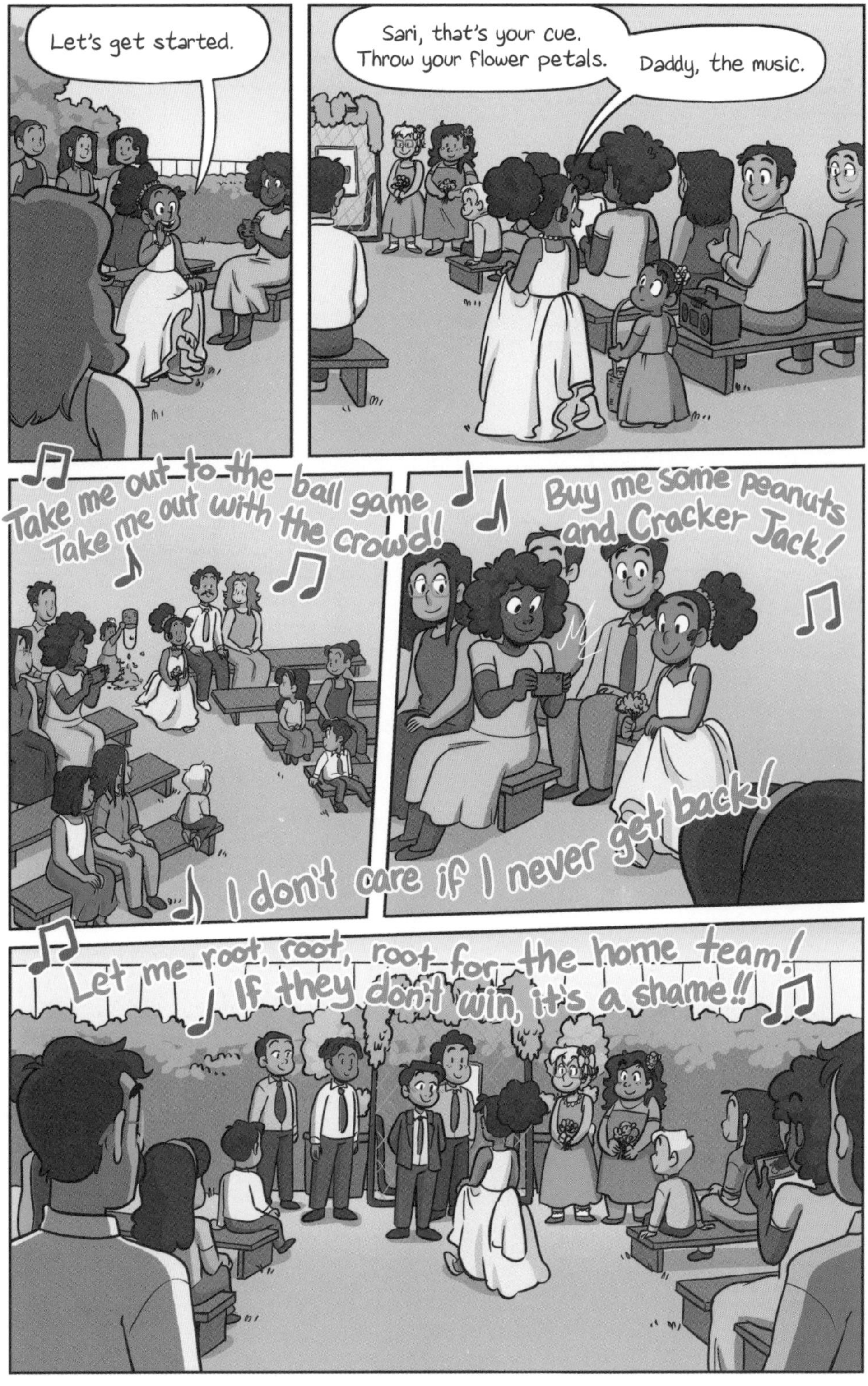
Let's get started.
Sari, that's your cue. Throw your flower petals.
Daddy, the music.
Take me out to the ball game
Take me out with the crowd!
Buy me some peanuts and Cracker Jack!
I don't care if I never get back!
Let me root, root, root for the home team!
If they don't win, it's a shame!!

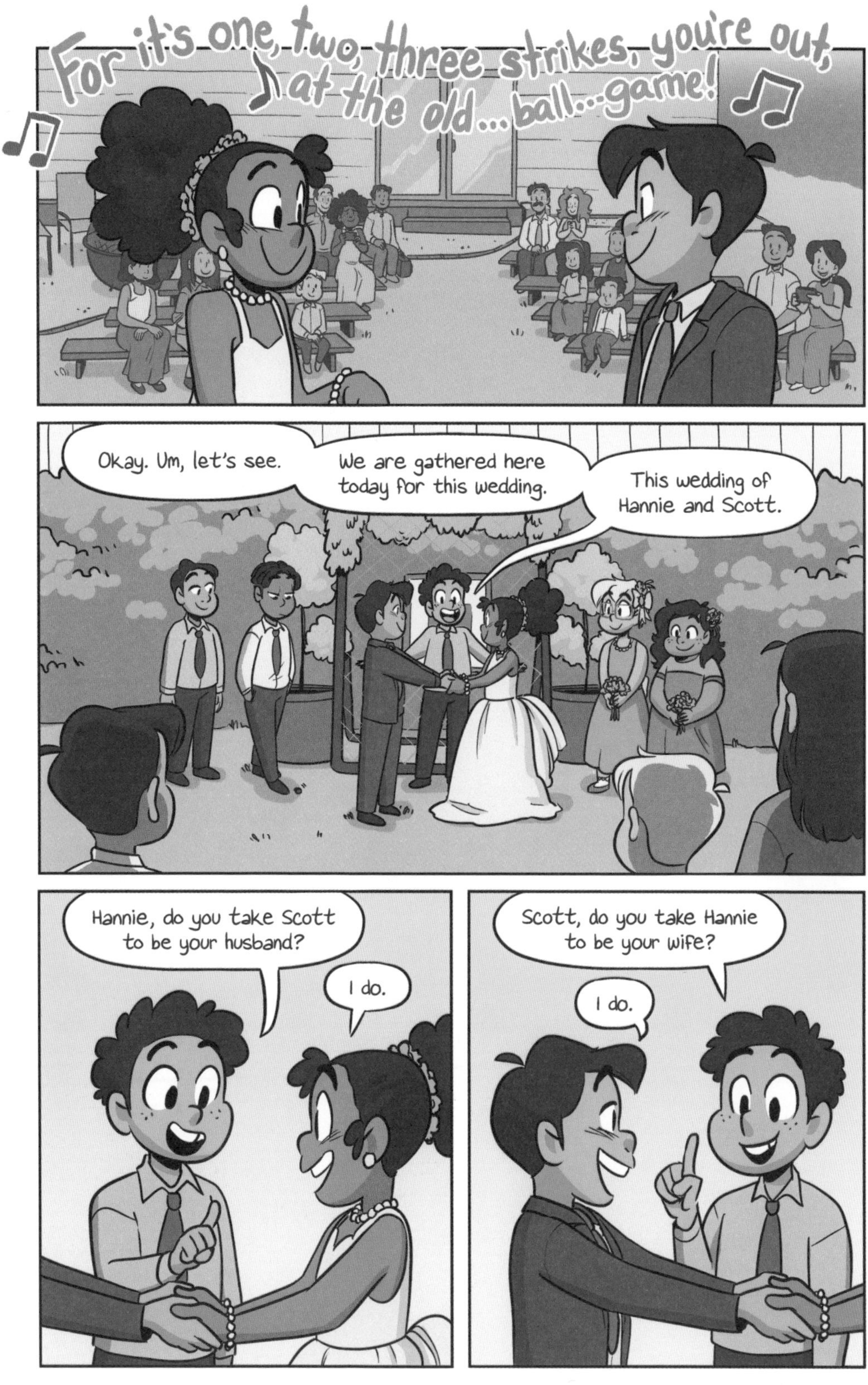
For it's one, two, three strikes, you're out,
at the old... ball...game!
Okay. Um, let's see.
We are gathered here today for this wedding.
This wedding of Hannie and Scott.
Hannie, do you take Scott to be your husband?
I do.
Scott, do you take Hannie to be your wife?
I do.

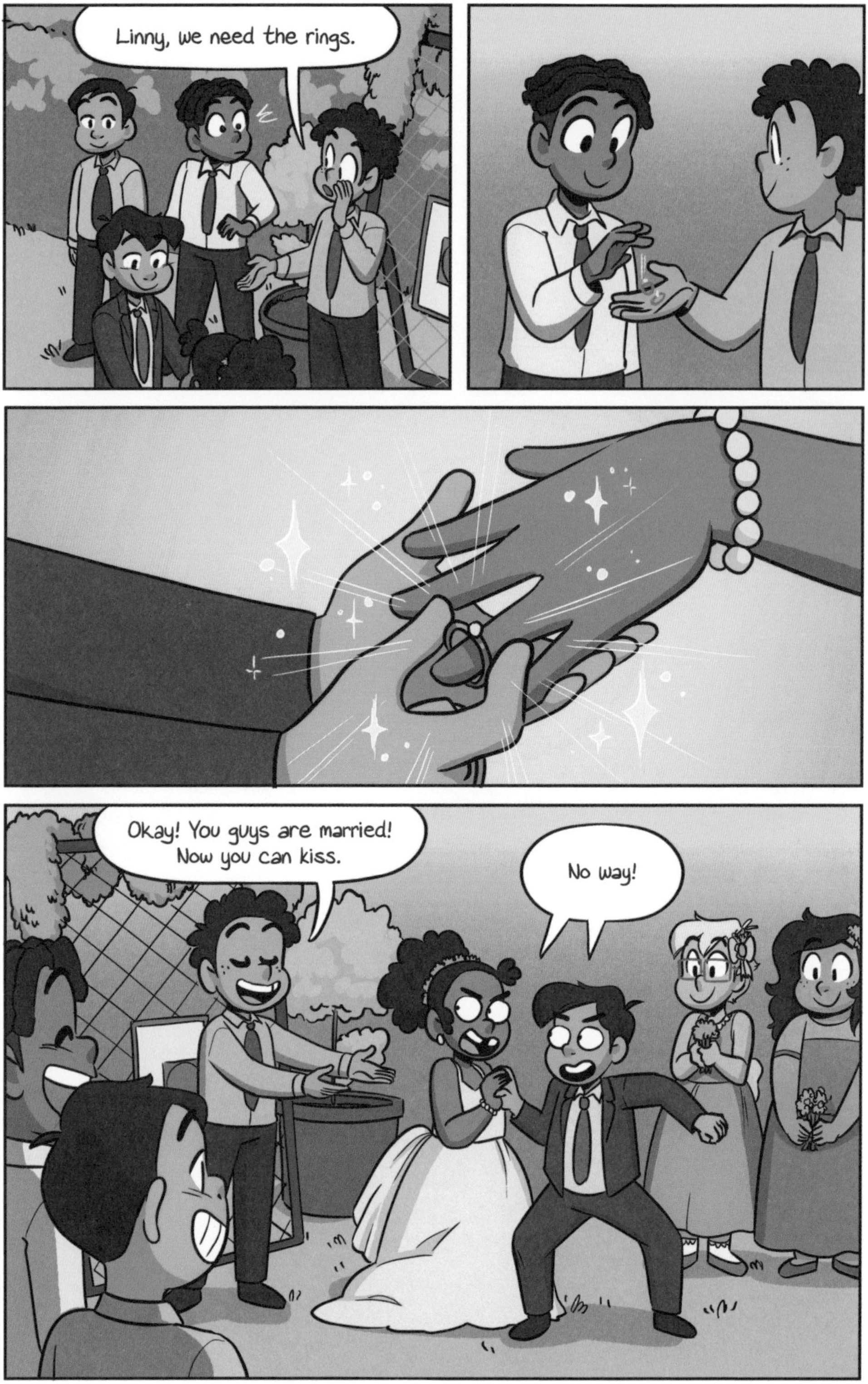
Linny, we need the rings.
Okay! You guys are married! Now you can kiss.
No way!

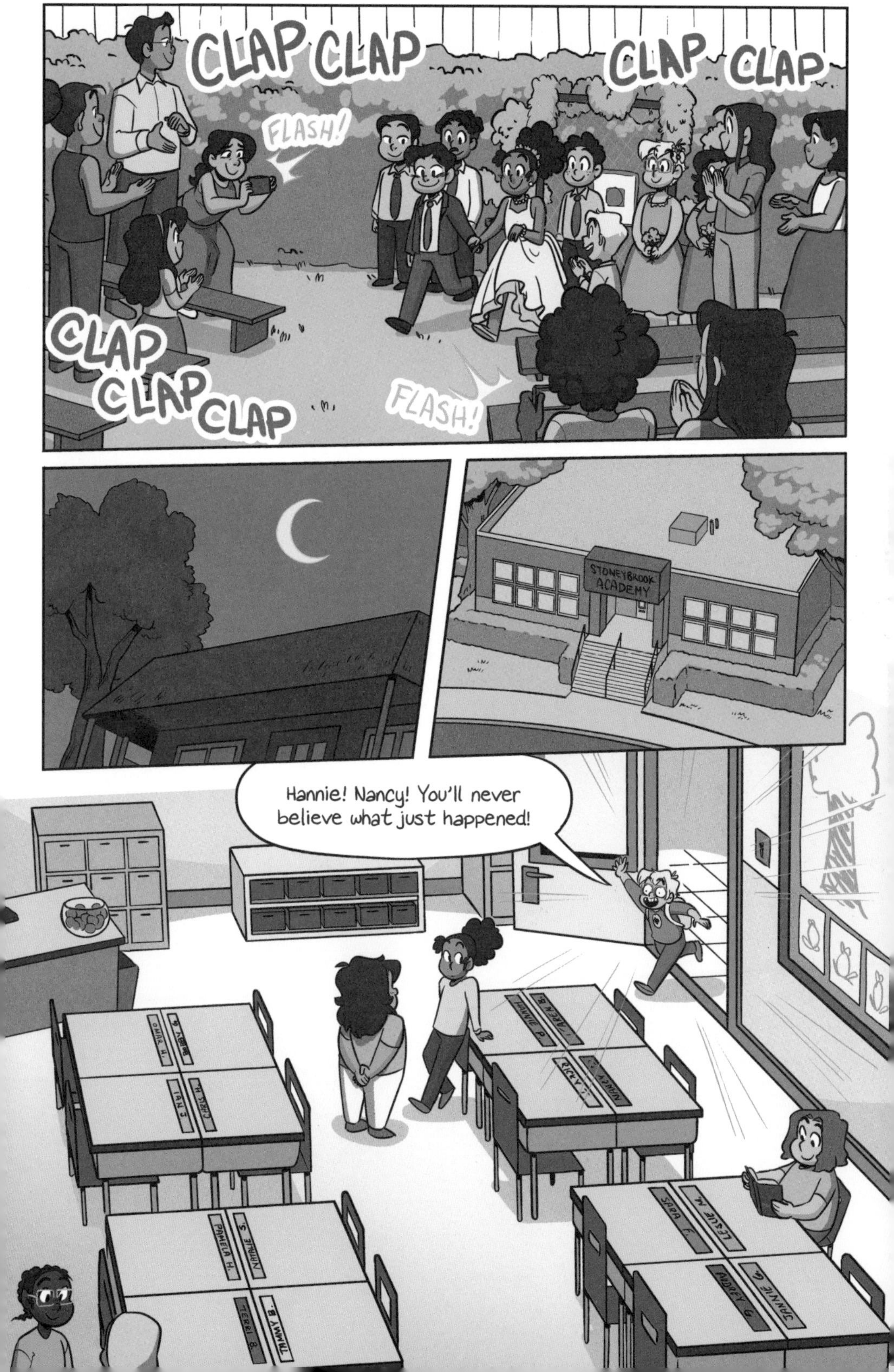
CLAP CLAP
CLAP CLAP
FLASH!
CLAP
CLAP CLAP
FLASH!
STONEYBROOK ACADEMY
Hannie! Nancy! You'll never believe what just happened!

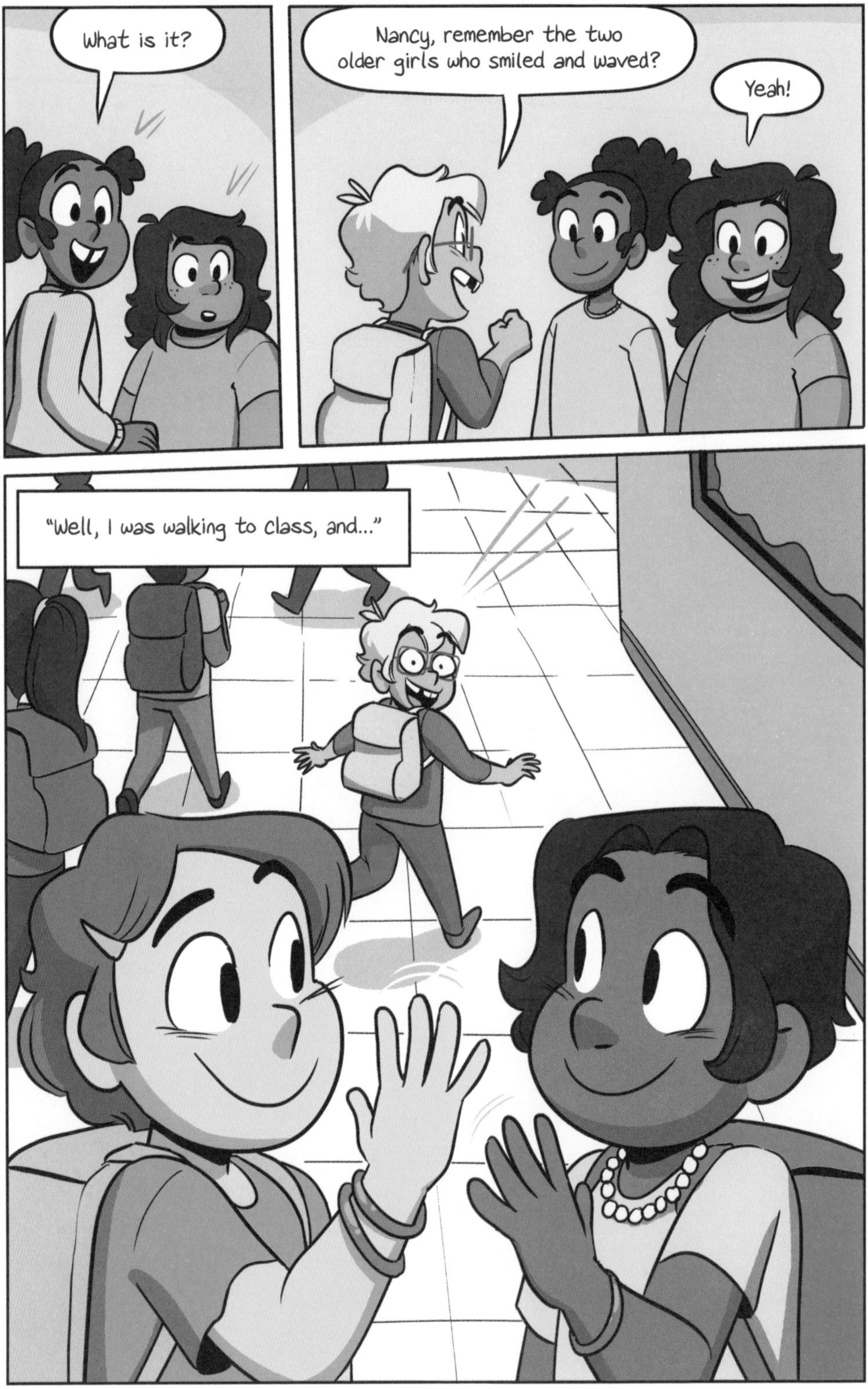
What is it?
Nancy, remember the two older girls who smiled and waved?
Yeah!
"Well, I was walking to class, and..."

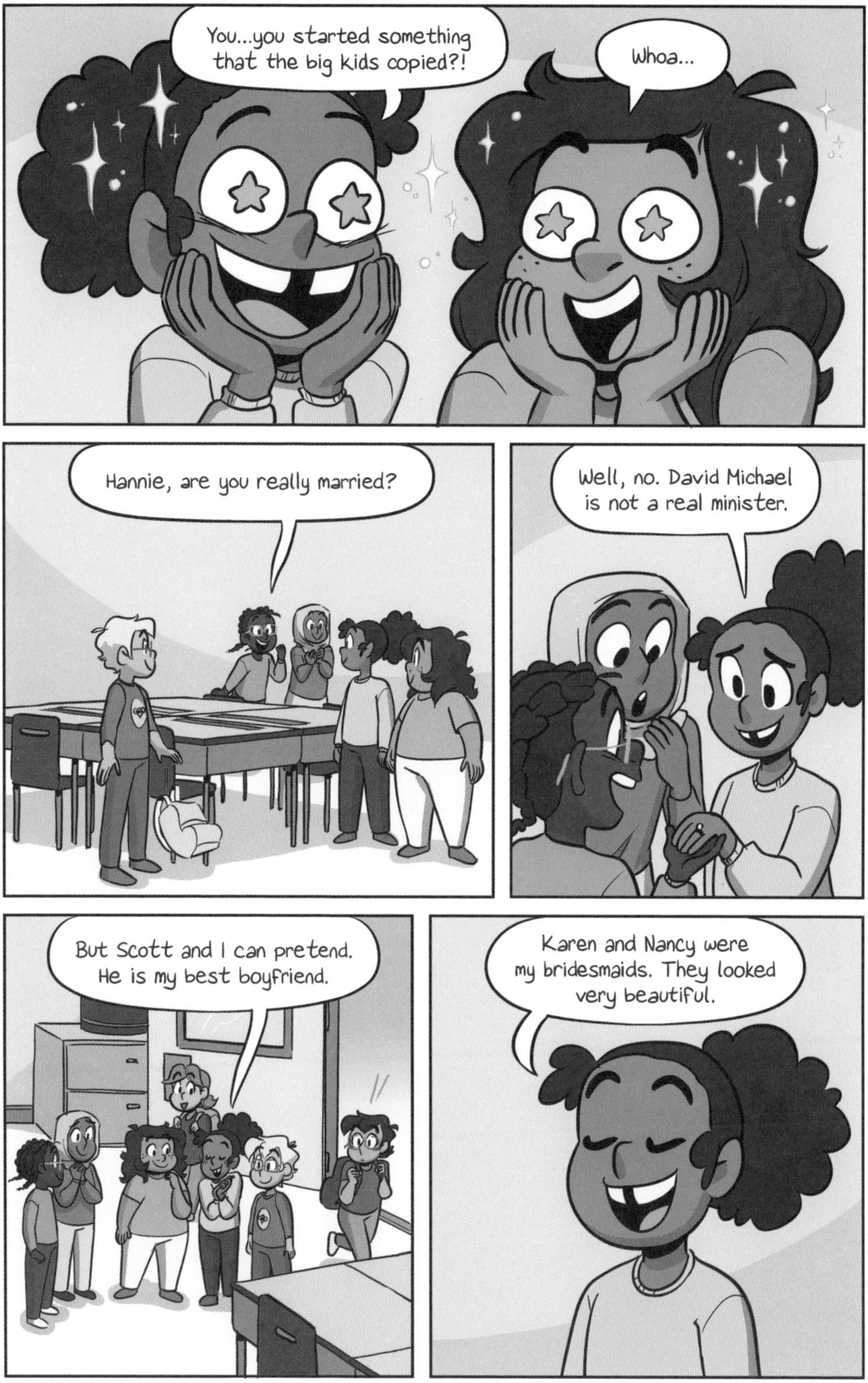
You...you started something that the big kids copied?!
Whoa...
Hannie, are you really married?
Well, no. David Michael is not a real minister.
But Scott and I can pretend. He is my best boyfriend.
Karen and Nancy were my bridesmaids. They looked very beautiful.

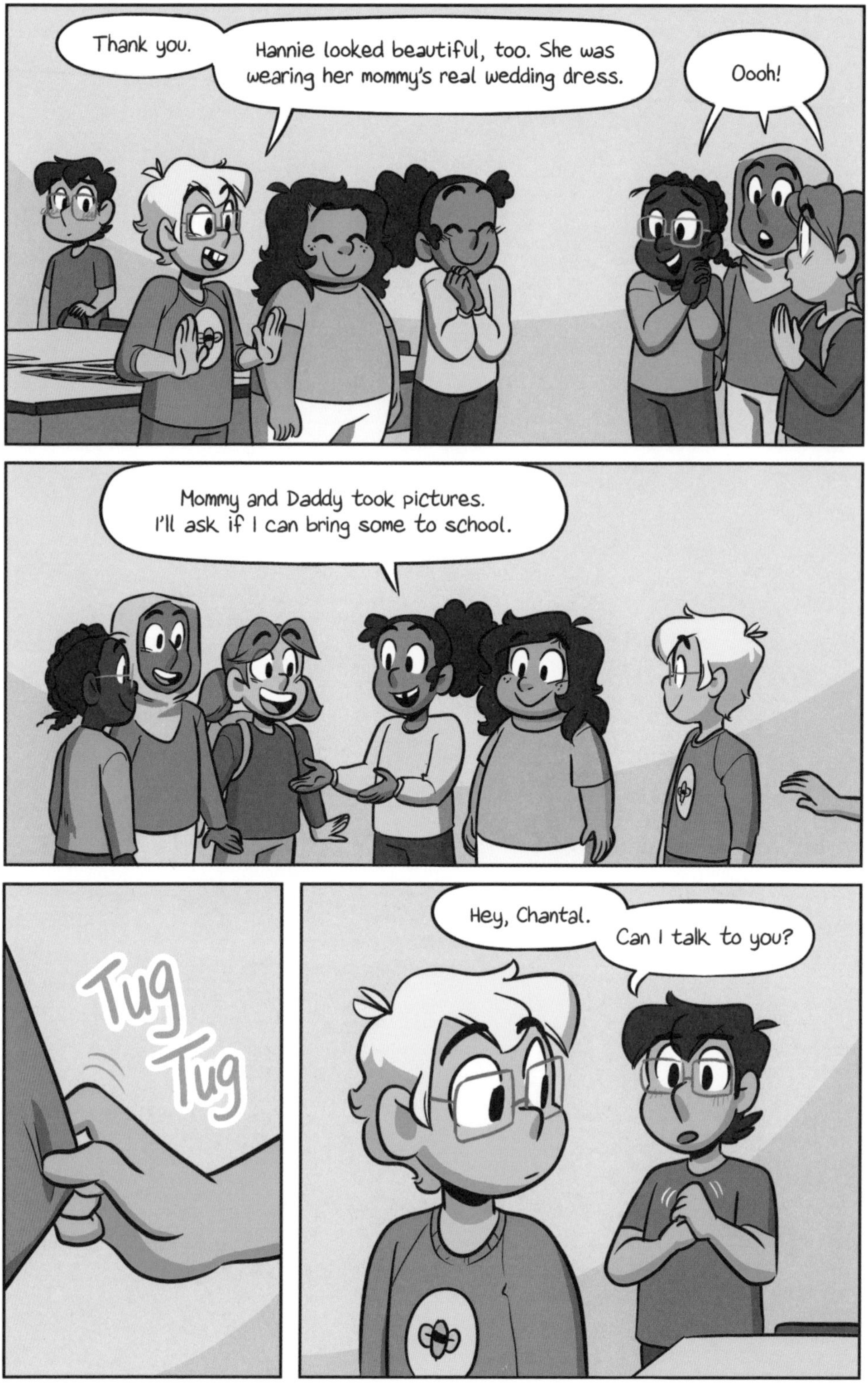
Thank you.
Hannie looked beautiful, too. She was wearing her mommy's real wedding dress.
Oooh!
Mommy and Daddy took pictures. I'll ask if I can bring some to school.
Tug Tug
Hey, Chantal.
Can I talk to you?

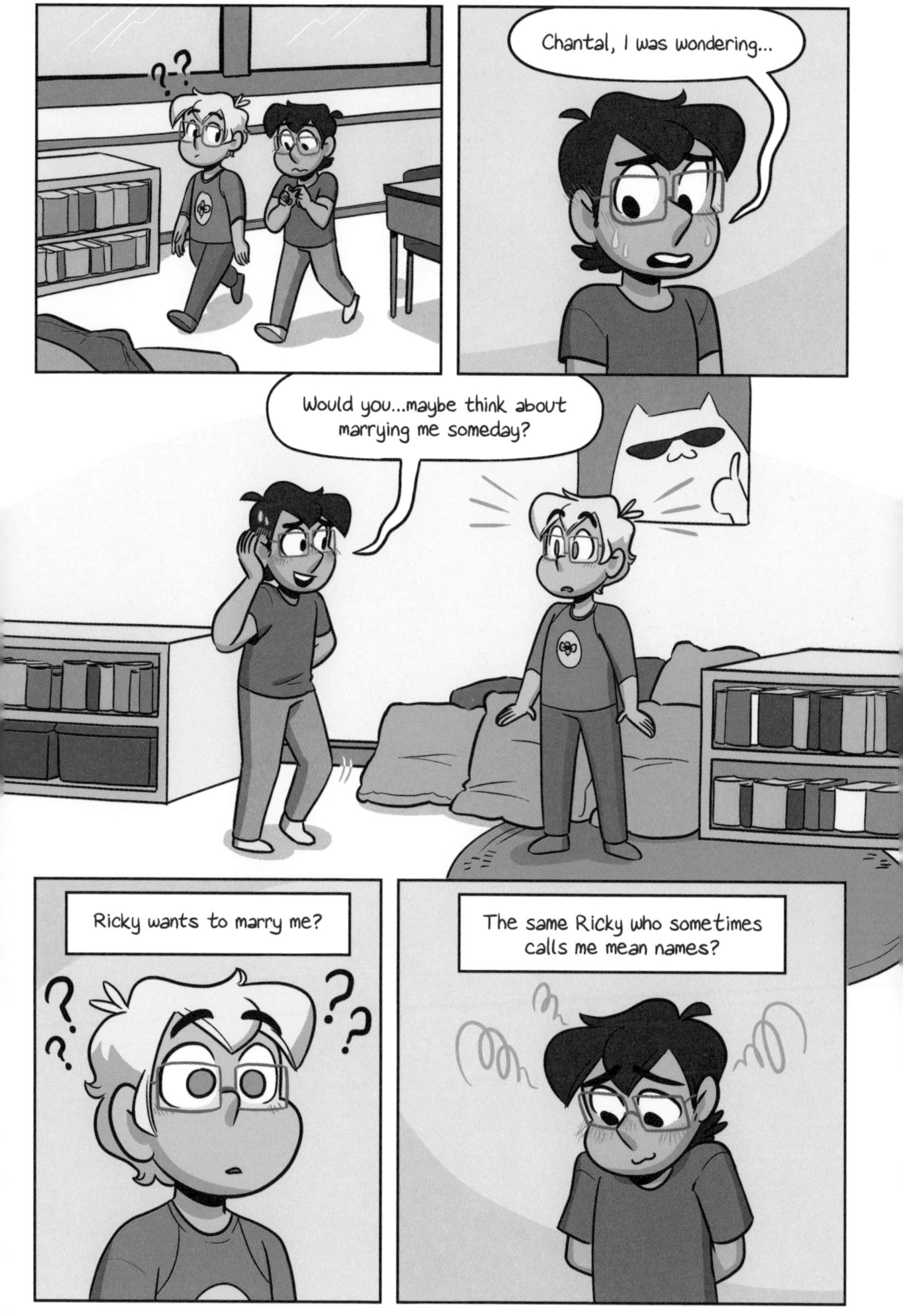
?
?
Chantal, I was wondering...
Would you...maybe think about marrying me someday?
Ricky wants to marry me?
?
?
?
The same Ricky who sometimes calls me mean names?

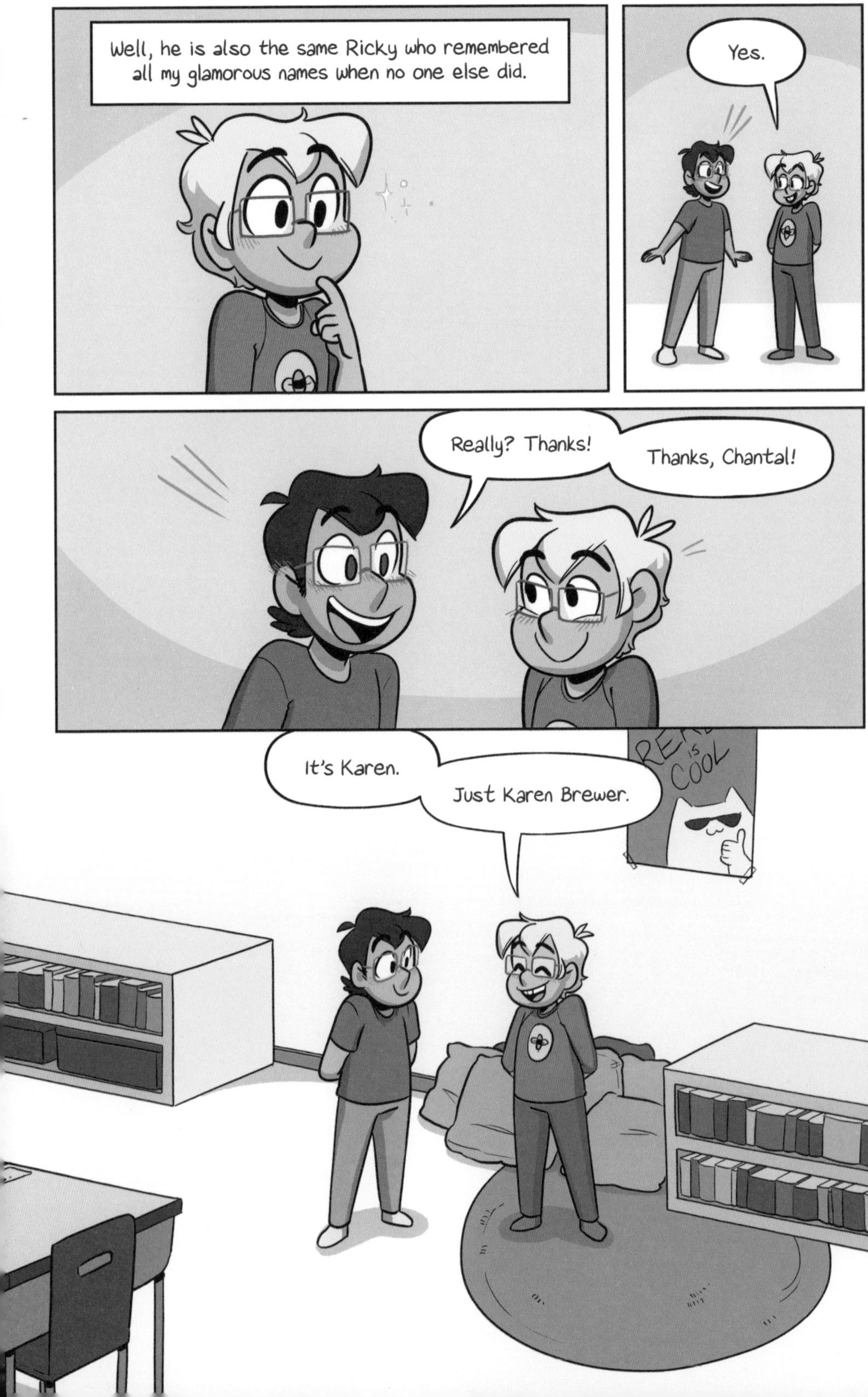
Well, he is also the same Ricky who remembered all my glamorous names when no one else did.
Yes.
Really? Thanks!
Thanks, Chantal!
It's Karen.
Just Karen Brewer.
READ IS COOL